Agony
Hill

Also by Sarah Stewart Taylor

Agony
Hill

A MYSTERY

Sarah
Stewart
Taylor

MINOTAUR BOOKS
NEW YORK

First published in the United States by Minotaur Books, an imprint of St. Martin's Publishing Group

AGONY HILL. Copyright © 2024 by Sarah Stewart Taylor. All rights reserved. Printed in the United States of America. For information, address St. Martin's Publishing Group, 120 Broadway, New York, NY 10271.

www.minotaurbooks.com

Designed by Meryl Sussman Levavi

Map © Maggie Vicknair

Library of Congress Cataloging-in-Publication Data

Name: Taylor, Sarah Stewart, author.
Title: Agony Hill : a mystery / Sarah Stewart Taylor.
Description: First edition. | New York : Minotaur Books, 2024.
Identifiers: LCCN 2024003612 | ISBN 9781250826626 (hardcover) | ISBN 9781250826633 (ebook)
Subjects: LCGFT: Detective and mystery fiction. | Novels.
Classification: LCC PS3620.A97 A74 2024 | DDC 813/.6—dc23/eng/20240129
LC record available at https://lccn.loc.gov/2024003612

Our books may be purchased in bulk for promotional, educational, or business use. Please contact your local bookseller or the Macmillan Corporate and Premium Sales Department at 1-800-221-7945, extension 5442, or by email at MacmillanSpecialMarkets@macmillan.com.

First Edition: 2024

1   3   5   7   9   10   8   6   4   2

For my parents, with so much love.

Author's Note

Students of Vermont geography will know that you will not find the town of Bethany on any map of the Upper Connecticut River Valley of Vermont and New Hampshire. It exists, fictionally, between and among actual towns and villages, in the words of Tasha Tudor, "West of New Hampshire and East of Vermont."

A note about the spelling of "Vietnam": In 1965, some Vermont newspapers, including ones my characters would have read, were still using "Viet Nam," while *The New York Times,* other Vermont papers, and many national news sources had adopted "Vietnam" as accepted usage. I have chosen to use "Vietnam" to avoid reader confusion.

Agony Hill

Prologue

The day was hot and clear, the sky overhead a thick blue traced here and there with ragged wisps of stringy clouds that reminded Sylvie of the bloody scratches she got when pruning brambles. They'd cut the hay two days ago, raked it, and nervously watched the skies all day yesterday; it had threatened rain but never delivered, and when the morning dawned bright and dry, Hugh and the boys ate quickly and went out into the fields to bale. Sylvie made sandwiches for lunch—ham from last year's pig, and fresh butter—and took them out to the fields, Daniel, who was two, trailing behind, crying about the feel of the stalks on his bare legs. She couldn't lift him because she was carrying the lunch basket.

"Beer?" Hugh asked when she dropped the basket on the ground in the shade on the other side of the baler. He liked a beer in the field, once the day was more than half over, but there'd been no extra money the last time they went to the market.

"Wasn't one," she said, trying to skate over it so he wouldn't dwell. She laid the sandwiches out and called the older boys over. Scott was sweaty and sunburned. Now that he was fourteen and past a growth spurt that had swelled his biceps and stretched him to nearly six feet, he could throw bales as well as a man. Andy, twelve, was driving the truck and he pulled it up when he saw her and came over gladly, smiling, touching her skirt, his heavily lashed eyes darting up to hers. He didn't like the work, maybe never would, but he tried not to let Hugh see it.

Louis came up next to her. At six, he was old enough to be pressed into service, young enough that he didn't like being away from her for the day. She gave him a little squeeze and told him to eat.

"I was thinking," she said, when they'd finished and the basket was empty, "that we could go down to the swimming hole later. Cool off."

"Can we, *Maman*, can we?" Louis asked. The older boys had started calling her Ma or even Sylvie, but Louis still used the name she'd used for her own mother when she was growing up with French Canadian parents on the Quebec border. Louis loved swimming, loved water, and he splashed in it like a seal. She brushed a piece of chaff off his cheek. They all waited for Hugh to answer. He took a long sip of water from the thermos and looked out across the nearly empty field. They'd made good time.

"When we're finished getting in the hay," he said, standing up, dusting crumbs off his pants. Lunchtime was over.

It was four before the boys came rushing into the kitchen. "We can go, we can go!" they shouted, gathering around her, laughing and shedding bits of hay onto the kitchen floor. She took off her apron, dropped it right in the middle of the floor, and laughed out loud. "All right then."

Scott and Andy ran ahead, streaking through the field, tiny dots in the distance hopping over the gate and disappearing into the tall grass and trees that led down to the brook.

By the time she and the smaller boys had made their way through the thick trees and down the bank, Scott was standing on the diving rock, ready to jump.

Green greeny water ripples soft as milk-top cream.

"Yahooooooooo!" His yelp broke the silence and then the other boys were in, leaping, splashing, filling the swimming hole.

It was almost supernaturally lovely, the little green pool formed where the brook dropped beneath the road. The first time she had seen it, Hugh leading her down by the hand for skinny-dipping at dusk after their wedding, she'd decided it was an enchanted fairy glade. The birches all around the brook were covered with green moss, beyond the basin were little waterfalls and hidden lands among tree roots. Higher up the banks, ferns waved.

Fern fronds filling.

She sat on the huge rock, a seat worn into the surface by decades of sitters, and then she stripped Daniel naked and let him sit in the shallow edges. He dug his fingers into the wet sandy soil, pulled up roots, shouted at the small fish that darted in and out of the little pools.

The other boys splashed and jumped and she trailed her feet in the water, a hand on her belly.

Curled minnow hiding, a beginning in my middle. The baby was moving now. She had felt the little bubbling feeling a few times. It would be born just before Christmas, Dr. Falconer had told her when she went to see him.

"Stop splashing me!" Andy yelled. He didn't like to be splashed before he'd gotten wet. Sylvie met Scott's eyes and shook her head. Reluctantly, he turned to Louis, who loved to be tackled and splashed and thrown into the water. She smiled, feeling satisfied and happy. For this moment, she was giving them exactly what they wanted and needed. For this moment, they were all where they wanted to be.

They must have been there for an hour when she looked up and saw the man. He was standing up on the bank on the other side of the brook, staring down at them, a dark hat pulled down low over his face so that she knew he was male only from his body. He had a straggly dark beard and he was smoking a cigarette; that was what made the boys look up, the smell of smoke on the wind.

Despite the fact that she couldn't see his face, she knew she had never seen him before. He was completely unknown to her. And he had come out of the dark acreage of the forest.

Scott froze where he was standing in the cold water and looked at her. Something in the downward cast of his gaze made her drop her eyes to the man's hand.

He had a knife, a dark, small thing he held out in front of him.

She thought about saying something, about screaming, but she was as incapable of it as she was of flying.

He spoke for her.

"Come on up here," he told her. "I want you to do something for me." He shifted the knife to the other hand, then back to where it had been. The blade was pointing down toward the boys in the swimming hole.

They were almost a mile from the house. Hugh wouldn't hear her over the rushing water. If she told the boys to run, they'd have to pass the man with the knife.

Scott started to speak, but she shook her head and said, "Stay with them. Keep them safe." Then to the man, "I'm coming up." Her voice carried out and up and over the glade.

Green innocent moss. Pillowy planks of rock.

She stood up and started walking.

One

The wicker basket sat in the very center of the porch, a yellow cloth tucked over the contents. Franklin Warren opened the screen door and stepped outside, the fresh air welcome after the close, dusty inside of the house. The basket was clearly meant for him; there was something precise about the way it had been placed in front of the door so he couldn't miss it, a clear communication of intent.

It was heavy and when he got it inside onto the kitchen table and folded back the cloth, he found it full of riches: a pint of milk, the glass cold to the touch; a parcel, wrapped in wax paper, that proved to be a slab of yellow butter, flakes of salt glistening on the surface; cheese, also in wax paper; a loaf of bread, still warm, the crust a deep brown; six brown eggs, wrapped in individual scraps of cloth and nestled in a small box; a jar of red jam—raspberry, according to the precisely lettered label, which also said, "From the kitchen of A. Bellows."

Bellows. The large house to one side belonged to a family called Farnham. "That's the Farnham place," his new landlord had said off-handedly, as though even a recent arrival from Boston would know of the Farnhams. To the other side of Warren's rented house was a law office—DAVID WILLIAMSON, ESQ., read the sign.

So who were the Bellowses?

To whoever had left the basket, Warren said a silent thank-you. He found a knife, tore a piece of bread from the loaf, and slathered it with butter and jam. The milk and eggs and remaining butter and cheese went into the giant white Kelvinator pushed against the back wall of the kitchen. He folded the yellow cloth into the bottom of the basket. He'd return it on his way out later, if he could discover the identity of the gift-giver. It was a well-made basket and the cloth looked like some sort of antique, with intricate embroidery around the edges.

He had awakened that morning, sore from the effort of carrying boxes, the sun slicing in through the bedroom window and onto his bed, making it uncomfortably hot. His hand, reaching out to the other side of the bed, found only the rough sheet he'd bought before leaving Boston. He'd dreamt of Maria; that was nothing new. But his certainty that she would be there when he reached across to her side of the bed had startled him awake.

It took three hours to unpack the rest of the boxes. The movers had brought the bed and bureau up the stairs the night before and now he muscled the bookcases into the parlor and unpacked the books into them. He was organizing utensils and pots and pans when there was a knock on the door.

A teenaged boy now stood exactly where the basket had been. He had light hair shorn close to his scalp and he was wearing dungarees and a dirty collared shirt that had seen better days. He had a malnourished, haunted look about him, as though he'd stepped out of *Life*, a ghost from one misery or another, a flooded river, dust bowl migrant camps.

"Missus Bellows says there's a phone call for ya. Fire up on Agony Hill. She's holding it since there's no phone at the vicarage," the boy muttered. Warren had to lean forward and listen closely to catch the words. These Vermonters had a funny way of talking, their mouths rolling over the ends of their sentences. Agony Hill? Vicarage? None of it made any sense to him.

"Thank you. I'll follow you?" The boy didn't answer but turned and walked briskly down Warren's steps and around the side of the house. The house next door—the Farnham house or the Bellows house?—was a large white Greek Revival, elegantly maintained, with a broad snowy porch and black shutters on the windows that looked out over the large almond-shaped green that comprised the center of the town of Bethany, Vermont, Warren's new home. The boy unlatched a high side gate and let Warren through; it wasn't until he had closed the gate behind him and started hustling up the stone path toward the back of the house that Warren looked around him.

He had entered paradise.

The house was backed by a huge garden, the tall, trimmed hedges forming an impenetrable border around the outside perimeter and rows of flowers and vegetables and fruit trees forming intricate spirals inside it. Running water could be heard from somewhere inside the plot. A floral scent wafted on the air: Rose, perhaps. Or violet.

"Do you live here?" Warren called up to him.

The boy turned around, shocked. "I help Missus Bellows with the garden," he said, as though Warren had greatly offended him.

Warren said no more and followed him past the beds and paths, onto a stone patio and through wide glass doors into a hallway, a pantry, and then a large kitchen. A thin elderly woman was standing at the new electric range and stirring a large pot of steaming stock. A strong smell of chicken and onion rose on the steam. She was sweating profusely and looked unhappy. Was this Mrs. Bellows? But she didn't speak to him, and the boy pointed to a black telephone on the wall, the shiny black cord curling across the floor. Warren walked past the woman and took the receiver from the small table it rested on.

"Hello?"

Tommy Johnson's voice came down the line. "Warren? Tommy here. Sorry to throw you into the soup before you've even unpacked. There was a fire at a farm there in Bethany last night. It's out, but they're sifting through what's left and they've got a body. I thought it'd be a good way for you to meet some of the local folks, and it'll be your jurisdiction anyway."

"All right," Warren said. The smell of the stock wafted up from the rangetop again. The woman had barely moved. One hand slowly stirred the pot. "Where do I—?"

"I drove down from Montpelier this morning. I'm at the barracks now, but I'll meet you at the field with the bull. The one looking at the mountain. You'll see. The boy will tell you. Bye-bye." The connection ended and Warren replaced the receiver on the wall.

"Thank you very much," he said to the boy and the woman, though neither of them acknowledged him. He stood there for a moment, looking through the doorway at one end of the kitchen into a graceful sitting room or living room. The walls were hung with paintings or drawings of green forms arranged in geometric designs. The green silk chairs and settee were grouped around a low wooden table piled with neatly arranged books. There was an air of cool gentility that confused him. Who lived here? Were they Farnhams or Bellowses? Who was the woman? Who was responsible for the garden? But the boy had already started heading out the back door and into the garden again and Warren had no choice but to follow him, asking, "Could you tell me how to get there? He said there's a bull . . ."

At the side gate, the boy wordlessly stepped aside to let him pass, and said, "Go out that way," pointing to the way Warren had come into town on Route 5. "Take a left on County Road, go two miles, and you'll see the Churches' bull standing in the field, looking at the mountain. Turn up there. That's Agony Hill." He shut the gate behind him, disappearing from view without another word.

Warren headed back toward what he supposed he ought to start thinking of as his own house, feeling very much in exile, as though after being ushered into Eden, he'd now been turned out.

Two

The directions brought him to the bottom of a steeply climbing dirt road and, just as the boy had promised, a bull stood in the field, staring at the mountain that arose from the landscape across the road in the near distance and slowly moving his jaws. He was the picture of perfect contentment, reddish brown, with a huge set of horns, and his back rippled and shone in the bright August sunlight.

Warren pulled the Galaxie over to the side of the road and was rolling up the windows when a sedan with the words STATE POLICE and a seal with a pine tree in the center turned up the road behind him and pulled over.

Detective Lieutenant Tommy Johnson of the Vermont State Police's Bureau of Criminal Investigation called to him, "Don't bother with the windows. How are you, Frankie? How's the moving going?" It had been Warren's father's nickname for him when he was a boy so of course Tommy would use it. But it felt strange, a relic of his childhood. Everyone but his parents just called him Warren now. Carefully locking the driver's side door and then feeling silly about it since his windows were wide open, Warren got into the sedan and grinned at Tommy, who grinned back and winked before pulling out and speeding along the road. Tommy, an army buddy of Warren's father who had been a regular if infrequent presence in Warren's life, had always reminded Warren of an elf. Though he was nearly six feet tall, his thin face, small nose, and slightly protruding ears gave him the mischievous air of a character in a children's book. A radio crackled on the car's dashboard stand.

"Almost done," Warren said. "I was unpacking the dishes when the boy came over."

"How are you finding the place?" Tommy had put Warren in touch with the real estate agent who had arranged the rental, sight unseen. "Nice town, Bethany, isn't it?" His voice held a little uncertainty. Warren had never been to Bethany, Vermont, before Tommy had convinced him to move here.

"Yeah, it's a pretty little place all right."

"Well, sorry to call you out before you've settled in, but it's a good chance for you to get the lay of the land."

They started up the hill. Both sides of the narrow, hard-packed dirt road were lined with low stone walls tumbling over in places, brownish-green fields stretching beyond. As they climbed, a herd of black-and-white cows came into view and they passed a white farmhouse and a big red barn.

"Fire was at a farm owned by a man name of Weber," Tommy said. "His wife smelled smoke and sent one of her kids down to call it in. They've got a volunteer fire department here in Bethany and they rang the alarm and the boys went up and put it out. Took a little time, but they kept it contained. The farmer—Hugh Weber's his name—they couldn't find him last night so it wasn't a surprise when they found a body. The regional medical examiner has been here to look at the remains but they're not much more than bones at this point."

The scent of smoke was getting stronger through the open window.

"Tell me about the farmer. Weber."

A little smug grin flashed across Tommy's mouth for a moment. "According to the chief of police here in Bethany, he's a bit of an odd duck. He pronounced his name *Vay-ber*."

"Was he German?"

"Not for a long time. Grandparents, maybe. Grew up in New York City."

"Really? How'd he end up running a farm here?"

"Chief says he was one of these back-to-the-land types, came up for the simple life and so forth. We'll find out more once we get up there, I'm sure."

"Wife?"

"Yeah. Although . . . I guess she's an odd duck too. Chief Longwell said she might be slow, not right in the head. Not much more than a girl herself but she's got a bunch of kids around the place, all boys. Ah, here we are." They'd reached the top of the hill. Warren could feel the land fall away on either side, the fields open, sloping down from around a small homestead, with a gray house, stone walls, outbuildings, and a big wooden barn, one side of it a black dent where it had burned. Across the road, twenty or thirty sheep grazed, white-and-black dots in a sea of green. A couple of cows stood by a tree in a small paddock next to a smaller barn.

Out of Tommy's car, the air was thick with the smell of burnt wood. Agony Hill. He wondered how it had gotten that name.

A large pickup truck with a pile of hay in the bed, a Bethany Police Department cruiser, and a fire truck sat in the barnyard. There were a couple of firefighters still hosing down the side of the barn, but the fire was mostly out. "They think they saved about half of the hay," one of the men said and Tommy nodded seriously. Warren wasn't sure how valuable hay was. Obviously it meant something for the man to mention it, though.

The barn was standard New England fare, from what Warren

could tell, tall, with a steeply pitched roof and a simple rectangular shape, except for a few small extensions, one of which had clearly been the source of the fire; it had burned down to its headers, beams, and a few sections of roof. The front of the barn was blackened by the fire and a large set of double sliding doors lay on the ground, splintered by what looked to Warren like a hatchet blade.

A young officer, gangly, red-headed, dressed in the green uniform of the Vermont State Police, was guarding the entrance to the barn. He stepped forward and Tommy introduced him as Trooper Goodrich. "Trooper Goodrich here is interested in criminal investigation," Tommy said with a wink. "He can be your assistant, help you get up to speed. It's going to be great to have you helping out down here."

Warren smiled at the young trooper. He couldn't have been more than nineteen or twenty and he looked extremely nervous. "Franklin Warren. Nice to meet you." The kid blushed deeply and shook Warren's hand.

"Who called it in?" Warren asked Goodrich.

"One of her boys," Goodrich said. "They don't have a telephone here so he drove down to one of the neighbors' places."

Warren pointed to the splintered wood on the ground. "Tell me about these doors here."

"Well, the fire chief said it was bolted on the inside when they got here so they broke it down," Goodrich said, his voice squeaking a little. Warren knelt and inspected the pieces of door that had been splintered and destroyed by the firemen.

"This was the only way in?" Tommy asked.

Trooper Goodrich nodded and Tommy said quickly, "Get a cordon up. This is evidence." Goodrich nodded and went off to do it.

Warren studied the pieces of wood and the hardware for a few more seconds and then said, "Let's go in."

The barn was cavernous inside, the ceiling soaring high above them. Sunlight shone in through holes and gaps in the boards high on the walls, sending strange beams of light here and there that reminded Warren of a spiderweb. To one side, bales of golden hay were stacked high like a staircase. That hay seemed not to have caught fire, but across a narrow channel to the right, more stacks were blackened and soaked with water.

"By God, they're lucky they didn't lose it all," Tommy said. "Those boys did well to put it out before it all went up." Warren took that in. Tommy was right. The barn was essentially a tinderbox. That the firefighters had managed to save so much of it was a small miracle.

The body had been found in what was left of the scorched extension to the side of the barn by the ruined hay, about twenty feet by twenty feet. There had been a door separating it from the central space of the barn, but it was gone now, burned and on the ground. A small group of men, some in uniforms, were standing around, looking at something, and Warren, knowing it was probably the body, slowed his pace, trying to steel himself. Tommy looked back and waited for him.

"You okay, Frank?" he asked.

"Yeah, fine."

They entered what was left of the extension.

The object of their interest lay on a metal cot. Warren took a handkerchief from his back pocket and covered his mouth and nose with it as he approached. He felt dizzy all of a sudden; the room smelled horribly of cooked meat. The remains were heavily damaged by fire, the familiar stick-figure shape of the skeleton barely recognizable.

It was hard to tell what else the small room had contained; everything had been burned almost beyond recognition. But as Warren looked at the collapsed forms in the early light filtering through the gaps in the roof, he thought he could make out a desk and chair and a bookcase, some blackened and waterlogged piles that must have been books.

"Tommy," said a tall, burly man in a uniform. *Not green, so not state police,* Warren thought. He must be local, an assumption that was confirmed when Tommy introduced him as the chief of the Bethany Police Department, Roy Longwell.

"Good to meet you," Longwell said to Warren. "Tommy told me he was bringing a hotshot new guy up from the city." There was a bit of an edge to the words and Warren found himself glancing over at Tommy, who looked slightly uncomfortable and said, "We know anything about this yet?"

"Just what you've got in front of you," Longwell said slowly. "You heard they had to break down the door?"

"Yeah," Tommy said. "I heard. What do you think, Detective Warren?"

Warren looked up quickly, letting the handkerchief drop and feeling suddenly on display. "He was lying on the cot," he said to Tommy. "I don't think he tried to get up. So sleeping, maybe. This room is definitely where the fire started, so the question is, why didn't he wake up?"

"That might have something to do with it," Longwell said, pointing to a gin bottle against the wall, the label scorched.

Warren patted his trouser pocket, looking for his notebook. But of course it wasn't there. He hadn't planned on working this morning.

"Is there a crime scene photographer?" he asked. "I'd like to get some snaps of the floor." He strode across the room to the doorway to the little office. "And the doors out there." He pointed back to the main barn entrance.

Tommy, looking sheepish, said, "No, but there might be a camera in the car. I'll check when we're finished here."

Warren caught Chief Longwell studying him. He was an imposing figure, broad-shouldered and packed into his uniform, his thick head of salt-and-pepper hair like a helmet. He offered a small smile when he met Warren's eyes, and his were pale blue, intent, a little predatory. Warren could feel Tommy's nervousness at being under his watch.

Warren tried to fix in his head the location of the body, the bottle, and a few other features of the space. It would have to do. He thought for a moment about what he wanted to know. "Why was he sleeping out here?" he asked Goodrich.

"The neighbor referred to this as the 'pig house,'" the trooper said. "I guess he had a typewriter out here, books and so forth. He loved to write letters to the editor of our local paper here. Long letters. Practically every week. He was always mad about something."

Warren tried to imagine what kind of a person would come out to a pig house in the back of a cow barn to write angry letters to the editor of the local newspaper.

"You're the chief here," he said to Longwell, wanting to cut through as much bullshit as he possibly could. "What was the first thing you thought when you heard there'd been a fire up here?"

Longwell glanced at Tommy and then said, "I thought of Forrest Germond."

Nobody explained, so Warren said, "Who?"

Longwell sighed. "Farmer from a town twenty miles to the south whose land was taken for the interstate. You know they're building the interstate through Bethany? He locked himself in his barn, let the animals out, set the barn on fire, and then shot himself, the day before they came to bulldoze the farm. He loved it, didn't want to give it up."

Tommy said, "We investigated it, but it was pretty clear it was suicide."

Warren turned to stare at him. "When was this?"

"Last summer."

"You think there's any connection?"

When Tommy didn't say anything, Longwell offered, "Well, interstate's not coming up here on Agony Hill. Nobody wants this farm. But . . ."

Warren had to resist asking Tommy why he hadn't mentioned it until now. "But it could have put the idea in his head," he said.

Tommy rubbed a thumb and index finger over the bridge of his nose. "Seems odd he didn't get out of the barn otherwise. Even if he'd been drinking, I'd say. And there's the bolted door." Warren now understood Tommy's demeanor. He'd assumed this was suicide from the moment he heard about it. He was using the scene to show Warren around, get a sense of him as an investigator. He didn't think this was a real case. Longwell nodded in agreement. Apparently he'd decided too.

Warren got out his handkerchief again and wiped the sweat off his face. "I'd like to talk to the family."

"They're not there," Longwell said. "Dr. Falconer came up. Mrs. Weber, she wasn't feeling well." He averted his gaze for a second, then continued, "He took her and the boys down to Uptons'. Said he'd give her something to make her sleep."

Warren glanced at Tommy to see if he objected. It was standard practice to try to speak with witnesses as soon as possible after any unnatural death.

"I'd say it can wait until tomorrow," Tommy said, with a finality that Warren didn't like. "You and Trooper Goodrich can come back then. Now, Frankie, you want to come with me and we'll see if I've got that camera." Longwell and his men went to confer with the firemen, and Warren followed Tommy back to the cruiser. "There you go," he said, rummaging around in the trunk and coming up with a simple Canon. "There should be film in there. Trooper Goodrich can help you get up to speed on what they've got at the barracks. You'll find that our equipment's not the most up-to-date right now, but we're, uh, creative. I've been able to utilize some real up-to-the-minute techniques in some of my investigations and I know you'll introduce us to some even better methods now you're here. You'll get the barracks set up just the way you want it, I'm sure." Tommy seemed distracted, eager to hand this off to Warren and be on his way.

Warren watched the scene unfolding in front of the barn. "How does jurisdiction work in a situation like this?" he asked Tommy, trying to keep his voice gentle, merely curious. "With the local men, the chief there, and then with us here too?"

"Oh, well, I guess it depends on what it turns out to be. But this one's ours for now. Chief may be poking around too, but I want you to investigate it the way you're used to. If it's suicide, then we want to know that. Everyone will be a little jumpy because of the connection with that other farmer. The interstate's caused a lot of hoopla around here."

Warren nodded, feeling not at all reassured.

They found Trooper Goodrich back at the barn and Warren told him he wanted to take some photos of the remains. They were walking back inside when he thought of something. "Any animals dead?"

Goodrich pointed to what must have been a row of stalls. "Nah, they're out in the barnyard or on pasture in the summer. That's what she said anyway. Mrs. Weber." There was something about the way he said *Mrs. Weber*. He and Tommy and Trooper Goodrich went back to the remains of the pig house and Warren showed the younger man how to take crime scene photographs. "I like more rather than less," he said. "Take them like this if you can, so you can put the prints together and get a sense of the whole scene." He showed Goodrich how he used his finger to mark the edge of each section so they could put them all together once they were printed and they wouldn't miss anything. Goodrich seemed interested and told Warren he liked photography and was looking forward to learning more about it.

"Hey, Pink, give us a hand, will you?" one of the firefighters called out once they were done.

Warren's face must have shown curiosity about the nickname because Goodrich said, "Everyone around here calls me Pinky." Warren had just thought to wonder where the kid had gotten the nickname when Goodrich blushed again, more furiously this time, the color spreading alarmingly along his face, from his chin up to his forehead, and the question was answered for him.

Tommy followed him back out of the barn and Warren understood that he was on display. Tommy was the reason he had this job and Warren needed to show him that he had made a good choice in pulling whatever strings he'd pulled to go around the usual custom of promoting from within to bring Warren up here from Boston.

Tommy, who'd been the top detective for the Bureau of Criminal Investigation for five years now, had pitched the job to Warren over drinks at a bar in Cambridge last winter. Tommy had been at the hospital at Harvard for a training and he'd called up Warren's father and asked if he could meet Warren to talk about something. He'd taken their drinks to a back booth and after a little chitchat, he'd told Warren that he'd been handling investigations all over the state, but that it was becoming untenable as more and more crime seemed to be making its way to Vermont. He wanted Warren in Bethany to take on investigations in the southern part of the state.

Before 1947, Tommy had explained, Vermont hadn't needed a statewide police force. Any petty crimes that came up were investigated by local sheriffs or police departments. "Wasn't much to investigate," Tommy had said. But then, after World War II, there had been a Bennington College student who disappeared, and they'd created the State Police. By 1957, they'd put together a team with some expertise in crime detection and investigation.

Warren remembered stirring the ice in his whiskey sour as the door to the bar had opened and a cruel gust of frigid air came barreling through. The offer of the job had seemed like another kind of door, an escape route. He had agreed before he'd really thought it through. "We're doing our best, but we could use a crack detective like you," Tommy had said. "Up on all the latest stuff."

Warren was not too modest to admit that he *was* a talented investigator, but he was pretty sure the job offer had also been inspired by that faraway Italian battlefield where Warren's father had saved Tommy Johnson's life by hauling him out of the mud and tying his belt around Tommy's leg to prevent him from bleeding out from a shrapnel wound. Tommy and his leg had gone on to marry a woman named Judith, have five daughters, and become Detective Lieutenant Tommy Johnson of the Vermont State Police. He had never forgotten Allen Warren's act of heroism. How could he? He must look at those scars every morning when getting dressed.

Outside the barn, the cows had gathered at the fence line—*if only they could speak*—and Warren went over to watch them for a minute and get his bearings. The house faced the road, the barn to the south side. Behind that were fields sloping down to a tree line. He had the sense that somewhere, far in the distance, there was water running. A river probably. He didn't think there were any lakes around here.

The farmhouse was low-slung, with what looked like an old addition out in the back. Up close he could see the paint was peeling and dirty, that it wasn't so much gray as dirty white. The windows were dusty but when he looked through one on the porch, he could see what looked like a kitchen table, piled with dishes and papers. He walked around the back of the house, nearly tripping over a child's wagon on its side in the grass. There was a picnic table, scabbed together from scrap wood and painted green. The yard had been neatly trimmed, but beyond was a field of tall grass, a rusting tractor abandoned picturesquely at the edge.

The other windows yielded partial views of more rooms of the house, a cluttered corner of a living room, lined with bookshelves, what looked like a bathroom, an old-fashioned metal tub in the center of the room but no toilet or sink. The absence of the first was explained by the small wooden structure in the corner of the yard: the outhouse. He came back around to the front of the house just as three men came out of the barn with a wooden stretcher, the body zipped into a bag. They placed the zipped bag in the hearse to go to the state pathologist in Burlington. It looked very light; Hugh Weber's remains barely filled it.

Warren imagined the family sleeping inside the house. They must have heard the cows bellowing in the barnyard, awakened to the smell of smoke and the sight of flames engulfing the barn. But if it wasn't suicide, why hadn't their bellowing awakened Hugh Weber and why hadn't he gotten out of the barn? Why had he been sleeping in the barn anyway? Had he bolted the door so no one could get in to save him? And what had started the fire?

He'd get answers to all these questions soon enough. For now, he would have to learn what he could from the place. Once the hearse had driven away, he walked back around the house again.

That was when he saw the paper taped to a windowpane in the kitchen. Someone had pressed flowers and leaves between two pieces of wax paper and then written below, in black ink, words that he had to read backward through the window.

Summer end full leafing
Flowers filling ground space open
Petals blue and yellow on
Autumns open leaf pull

Warren stood there for a moment, trying to understand the message, then gave up and headed for Tommy and the car.

Three

Alice Farnham Bellows sat up on her knees and surveyed her gardens. She had begun to plan them, to sketch their outlines and turns, many years ago, in a very faraway place, and it still amazed her sometimes, to see them here in Bethany, in the flesh, so to speak.

In the flower.

It was high summer; the pools of water were still and wan-looking, the fountain running anemically. She would have to remind Billy to top them up when he got a chance. Or perhaps she would just do it herself. The lavender stood tall, a hazy purple, and the ornamental grass was the perfect foil to the lower, more colorful annuals, marigolds and cosmos and zinnias and dahlias, which she'd planted in whites and pinks this year. The bulbs had come and gone, but she knew exactly where they lay beneath the soil. The fruit trees provided shade in all four quadrants, the *gulistan*, or rose garden, in the center.

It made her very happy, her garden.

She pulled a few more weeds and took them around to the com-

post heap at the far end of her property, where the brook passed by slowly this time of year. Something had been at the pile and had dragged grass clippings out onto the path. She picked them up and replaced them on the heap of dead vegetation. One side of the back garden bordered a field along the small tributary that ran through the town and animals came through the fence sometimes, raccoons, foxes, wild turkeys, once a bear, to forage among her grass clippings and food scraps and drink from the pools. She saw their tracks. There were men in town who claimed to have shot catamounts in the hills in their youth. The mountain lions would come down for the sheep and had to be killed. But catamounts hadn't been sighted in Vermont in years and there was no logical reason for the fingers of awareness drawing themselves across the back of her neck.

But then she saw the stones. Six of them, carefully balanced on the fencepost, in a little cairn, undeniably human-made.

Someone had been in her garden and had left her a message. Or was it a threat?

Who?

The only person she could think of was the new neighbor next door. Mildred had told her about him. A policeman, a detective, quite a good one apparently, from Boston. He'd had some sort of misfortune and Tommy Johnson, with the state police, had brought him up to serve as the dedicated detective in the Bethany barracks. She had seen it coming, what with the larger numbers of tourists and vacationers coming from New York and Boston. It wasn't that city people were trouble, though Vermonters liked to say that; it was that human beings were trouble. The more of them there were, the more trouble you had. The local police could keep up with the speeders and the lost purses and bar disputes, but state police detectives were needed for more serious crimes. Drugs. Murder.

Tommy Johnson was a good judge of character. He would not have hired someone who was dangerous.

So, what could it be? The possibilities were numerous. None of them were reassuring.

She had learned, over her fifty-five years on earth, that she didn't have this feeling for nothing. Indeed, when she had experienced this sense of unease, of . . . being watched, she realized now, of being *tracked*, there had usually been good reason to be on her guard.

So, someone was watching her.

The revelation was a relief in a way. There was something. She would have to be vigilant.

She reached out and knocked the stones off the post. They tumbled to the ground, where they scattered innocently on the grass. She spent the next hour walking along the rows and deadheading lilies, noting places where perennials had failed, where she could fill in with divisions in the fall.

When she was finished, she went inside to pray.

Though she was a regular churchgoer and actively involved in the life of the Unitarian Universalist church in town, Alice Farnham Bellows was not devout in any particular religion. But while living for a time in Cairo during World War II, she had come to the habit of a late-afternoon prayer, a sort of ersatz Islamic ritual in which she kneeled upon her prayer rug or sat in the chair in Ernest's old study and spoke silently to the universe.

She remembered the sounds of the call to prayer in Cairo, the regular rhythms that had become so familiar and dear to her. Those had been good years, despite it all. Despite war. Despite her husband's being constantly in danger for his wartime work, his long disappearances and lack of communication. They had been happy, or a kind of happy anyway. She had been happy. It was natural that whatever sights and sounds she associated with that time in her life would become cherished. The prayer was part of that.

And yet, it somehow felt more urgent than that lately. It was as though she found herself newly . . . searching. The prayers, or medi-

tation, or whatever it was, made her feel centered, ready for whatever came next.

Mildred was mopping the floor in the kitchen and Alice tiptoed carefully around her, murmuring, "Mildred, put the kettle on when you're finished, will you? I'll make the tea myself. I just don't want to hover."

"Yes, ma'am," Mildred said. She was a spindly farmwife whose husband had sold his cows last year because they couldn't afford to install a milk tank. Mildred had come to work for Alice for some extra money and, Alice suspected, because she was tired of her husband and sons lounging around the house. She was satisfactory in most ways, though her cooking left something to be desired. But she had a quality that was even more important to Alice—she was a discreet busybody and she kept up with the news.

"Have you heard anything about the fire up on Agony Hill, Mildred?" Alice asked before leaving her.

"No, Mrs. Bellows. Just that Hugh Weber's dead, but I guess you know that. I wonder what will happen to the rest of them. Do you think she'll stay on at the farm?"

"Yes, I heard that at the store this morning. I don't know what Sylvie Weber will do. I think she has family up near Newport, but the boys have always lived here, haven't they? Perhaps she'll stay."

"How will she manage? Keeping that place going." Mildred looked horrified at the idea. Alice wanted to point out that the two of them, two women in their fifties, kept Alice's own "place" going, with a little help from Billy in the garden, but not much else. Just yesterday, they had carried heavy boxes of linens and silver down from the attic for the Ladies Aid Society's raspberry social booth at Old Home Day, which would be held on the weekend. They had worked for hours, rearranging things and moving furniture around, even carrying a bed frame down to the driveway to be donated to the rummage sale. Women were capable of so much more than people thought they were.

She settled on, "We'll see. I'm sure we'll hear more in the next few days."

Alice went through to the study, shut the door, and sat down in the recliner, closing her eyes and resting her hands on her knees.

She allowed her mind to drift a bit, trying to focus on the image of a candle's flame. She breathed in and then out, slowly, methodically. Everything blurred and swam and she felt her thoughts come into focus as she observed them passing by, small, distinct.

At the end of ten minutes, she opened her eyes and stood, coming back to herself.

And as she returned to the kitchen for the tea, a clear, crystal-line thought lingered in her mind, a fragment of something half-remembered:

There is someone here. Beware. Beware.

Four

Warren got to the Bethany state police barracks by eight the next morning, wanting to make a good start of things and then get back to the scene of the fire as soon as possible. Last night, lying in bed in his too-hot room, he'd found that something was bothering him about it. As an act of self-destruction, it seemed so . . . complete. The man could have shot himself, or slit his wrists. Why fire? Why risk destroying his family's means of livelihood, all that hay, shelter for their animals? It didn't make sense to him. He needed to know more about the man, to know if this was characteristic of Weber or not. And of course, he needed to speak to the family. Probably the answers would all be there. Weber may have told his wife what he was going to do. The son who drove to the neighbor's house to alert the fire department may have seen or heard something definitive.

The Bethany state police barracks were located in the back of a now-abandoned gas station on Route 5, out of town about a mile. They had tried to hide the building's origin, but a faded Citgo sign on a pole at the end of the parking lot gave it away and the long, low building had the unmistakable look of its former purpose.

Tommy had warned him about the repurposed barracks already, so Warren wasn't surprised, but the collection of vehicles clustered next to the building did give him pause. One cruiser was relatively new, freshly painted and clean-looking. The other three cruisers were older models, at least 1958 or so, the paint faded and, in one case, scratched up at the rear fender. Two other unmarked cars sat next to them and Warren's Galaxie looked positively shiny in juxtaposition. Tommy had told him that he'd have to use his own vehicle to start, that there wasn't money in the budget for a cruiser for the newly created detective position, but that he'd see what he could do once Warren had a few successes under his belt.

Warren forced himself to put it out of his mind. He was lucky to have a job, after what had happened to him in Boston. He wasn't going to waste time with regrets. He needed a new start, to make a go of it. The trappings didn't matter.

Trooper Goodrich met him at the door.

"Good morning, Detective Warren," he said cheerfully. "I can show you around if you want."

Warren smiled up at him. There was something about Goodrich's friendly face that lifted his mood. "That would be great, Trooper Goodrich. I thought I'd look through the files on some of the open cases, just to familiarize myself with the job, and then we can go back up to the scene."

"You can call me Pinky. Everyone does."

"All right, Pinky. And you can call me Warren. Everyone does. Everyone but Tommy anyways."

Pinky flushed.

There was a reception/dispatch desk right up front and as they came through the door, the woman sitting behind it looked up, was apparently uninterested in what she saw, and went back to typing extremely rapidly.

"Tricia, this is Franklin Warren," Pinky said. "Detective Warren, this is Tricia Green. She's one of our dispatchers here." Warren told her that he was pleased to meet her and she peered at him from behind a pair of dark-rimmed spectacles and murmured something in return he couldn't make out. The radio setup looked modern, at least, and he liked what he could see of Tricia Green's charts and note-taking systems.

Two middle-aged troopers, whose names Warren missed, checked in with Tricia and then went out on patrol. Before they left, Pinky gave them some information about an accident reported down in Springfield and then resumed the tour.

Beyond Tricia's desk was a large room with more radio equipment and four battered wooden desks with squat black phones and typewriters on them. Against one wall was a bank of wooden file cabinets. Two doors opened off the other wall and Pinky led the way into the first one, which was a large storage area. "Lieutenant Johnson and I have been working on this," he said. "They used to just shove evidence in boxes—what didn't go to Burlington anyway—and keep it anywhere on those shelves, but I've been trying to make a dedicated shelf for each case and to have plastic bags for everything. It's been working out pretty good so far."

"This is well done," Warren said, looking around at the shelves, neatly labeled with case numbers, cardboard dividers keeping everything separate. The key thing with an evidence room was that it kept items of evidence clearly labeled and safe and that there was a process for booking them in that could be presented during a criminal trial. The process they would have to work on, but Warren liked the neat rows, waiting for bags or boxes of evidence.

Pinky showed him a rudimentary darkroom they'd constructed in a supply closet at the rear and got a new Canon camera with a long lens out of a drawer stocked with film. Warren packed it into the black leather bag it had come in and handed it back to Pinky. "We'll take that with us. Can you develop the film we took yesterday with the body in situ?" Pinky nodded and said he'd get started while Warren read case files.

He pointed to one of the desks. "You can use that one," he said. "I'll go get the files and then you can let me know when you want to go back to Agony Hill."

The files turned out to be a manageable stack of about twenty cases, most of them resolved burglaries and other petty crimes. There was one case of embezzlement from a few months ago and two open unnatural death cases. One of them was the killing of a father by his son and the other was a woman poisoned by insecticide that could be homicide but was probably suicide. There had been six "forcible rapes" and eighteen robberies. Mostly there were burglaries and auto thefts.

And now a death and suspicious barn fire that were likely an act of suicide by arson.

He would need to spend much longer with the files, but for now, he felt like he had a good handle on the criminal activity of southeast Vermont.

"I'd like to drive myself so I start learning the roads," Warren said when he was done. "I'll meet you up on Agony Hill, Pinky. We'll see what Mrs. Hugh Weber has to tell us about her husband's frame of mind."

Five

The sun was up, all the way up already. Sylvie could hear sounds from downstairs, the boys moving around in the kitchen, Daniel's still-babyish voice protesting about something.

It was good to be home. She had hated staying at the Uptons' the night of the fire. Beulah Upton had tried to be kind, but her pity was so apparent Sylvie had felt like she was choking on it. She had felt so aware of the way Beulah watched the boys, taking in their clothes and hair. Sylvie cut it herself, but it had been a while and Louis's grazed his shoulders. Next to the Upton boys and their barbershop cuts, he looked ragged and moth-eaten. She hadn't felt she could refuse to go, though, and she'd had to pretend to take the doctor's sleeping pills and then pretend to sleep since she didn't like taking medicine, a skepticism she'd learned from Hugh. She had counted the minutes until they could go home.

Sylvie lay there for a minute, sun streaming in the windows, her hand on her belly. She felt the baby move. She'd been afraid to tell

Hugh when she'd realized she was expecting, but he'd been pleased. "Maybe a girl this time," he'd said with a smile. She had had a sudden image of a small girl running through a field, her black hair streaming behind her, the sun making a halo around her head.

The sob surprised her, rising from somewhere deep within, from something beyond her mind or heart. *From deep in body's dredge. Drudge. Dredging up.*

She cried a little, took a deep breath, and then pulled on an old skirt and settled it just under the swell of her belly. She put on one of Hugh's shirts and left the bottom three buttons unbuttoned. The shirt smelled of him, sweat and the faint yellow tang of the barn. She recognized that it didn't make her sad or wistful. Nor did it really remind her of him. It was the smell of them all, anyone who worked with animals. Sweat and shit. It wasn't particular to Hugh or anybody else. Her own father had always smelled that way, all her brothers, most of the men she knew.

Scott was in the kitchen, frying eggs for the little boys. The full basket of eggs sat on the counter and she touched his shoulder to say thank you. The little clock over the door said eight. Daniel called out, "*Maman*, Scott say I have one egg. I want two egg."

"Have one, love. We'll make a cake with the others later."

"Cake?" He grinned, his little fist clenched around a spoon. Scott slid one of the eggs onto the plate and put it in front of him.

"I can do that," she said, but he waved her away and put another plate with an egg on it on the table.

"I'll need to make bread today," she said.

"Do you know how?" Louis asked, his brown eyes wide. "Papa always made the bread." She swallowed, hard, looked down at the plate.

"Of course, silly," she said. "I know how to make bread."

Louis smiled at her, reassured.

"Now," she said, trying to keep her voice high and cheery, "I know it's hard to think of it, but work might . . . work might help. What do we need to do today?"

"Sheep need to be moved," Scott said. "And we'll be ready to hay again soon, if the weather holds." He looked worried. Of course he would be. How would they manage? She felt panic rise in her stomach. She would need to bury Hugh. He wouldn't have wanted a church funeral, but they'd need to put him somewhere. How would she pay for it?

"It's okay. Let's do one thing at a time," she said. "Let's move the sheep. The garden needs to be weeded too. Tomatoes harvested. And there are raspberries to pick, lots of them. I'm going to need to make jam. We can do that today. Tomorrow we'll start again." She felt a little bit of peace settle over her. A farm demanded work of you. When things were ready, you had to pick them, preserve them, put them up. If you didn't, you'd lose them forever. Sometimes, she was overwhelmed by the farm's demands, but today, she was glad of them. They gave her a map for the day.

Scott, his blunt face inscrutable, nodded and came over with his own plate.

It was the right thing to say. One thing at a time. It would be okay.

They finished eating and she tipped the plates into the sink while the boys dressed.

Then she stood at the back door for a minute looking out across the back fields, listening to the boys clatter down the stairs, arguing about a baseball Louis had found.

The sun had cleared the trees at the bottom of the field; the birds were in full chorus already. The smell of smoke was almost gone. Instead, the air smelled of fresh grass, of goldenrod, of green, growing things.

Warming roots. Sun-addled leaf.

She and Scott decided to get some manure for the garden first. Then they'd weed and spread it around.

The day grew hot as they worked, the sun rising steadily in the solid blue sky. She told Scott to go and get them some water and got down on her hands and knees to pull weeds around the beets and potatoes. Her back hurt. The baby rolled, faintly, delicately, as if in protest.

"*Maman?*" Louis was there, behind her suddenly. How long had he been standing there?

"Yes?"

"There's two men here. One of 'em's a policeman."

Six

It was a hot, hazy late-summer day. Warren kept the windows open so the breeze could stream across his face, and it was okay while he was driving, but as soon as they'd pulled in by the Webers' farm and he'd shut off the ignition, he could feel the day's heat come down on him like a blanket. He rolled up his shirtsleeves and used his handkerchief to wipe the sweat from his forehead and neck. His shirt was soaked through. When Pinky got out of the cruiser he'd been following in, he flapped his uniform jacket a few times and then used his own handkerchief to mop his forehead. When he was done, he hoisted the camera over one shoulder.

Now they knocked at the front door and waited a few minutes before Pinky pushed the door in. The cool of the house seeped out at them. A clock ticked off the seconds somewhere beyond.

"Hello? Anybody there?" Pinky called out.

Silence but for the clock.

They let the screen door slam shut and went over to the outbuildings.

The cows stared and then followed them along the fence line. A couple of white chickens pecked at the dirt.

"Hello?" Pinky called out again. "Anybody around?"

A metallic clank sounded inside a long building next to the barn where Hugh Weber had died and they followed it through a doorway and found themselves in a low-ceilinged space with a concrete floor, sloping down on both sides. It smelled strongly of cow manure. Indeed, a small boy was shoveling it off the floor and into a large cart. Another slightly bigger boy was replacing it with sawdust. They both looked up and froze.

"Is your mother here?" Warren asked them. The older one nodded and ran very fast out of the barn. The remaining boy stayed frozen, staring, as Warren and Pinky waited. After what seemed like too much time, Warren said, "We'll just go find her," and they went out again, trying not to step in the piles of manure all along the walkway. The sun was blinding outside and it took Warren's eyes a few minutes to adjust and make out two figures coming toward them, a woman and the boy. She was pushing an empty wheelbarrow and the boy was dwarfed by the collection of gardening utensils he held over his shoulder.

Warren studied them for a few seconds. When the woman put the barrow down, he saw with a shock that she was pregnant. Her belly curved tellingly under a men's work shirt, tucked into the swelling waistband of a gingham skirt. He had to ignore his urge to jump in and stop her when she took the shovels and pitchforks from the boy and hefted them into the wheelbarrow.

"Mrs. Weber?" Pinky called.

She came closer and Warren's first impression was of a small girl playing at adulthood. She had pink cheeks and dark blue eyes that curved in a vaguely feline way, reminding Warren, improbably, of Elizabeth Taylor. Her black hair was bobbed and cut in ragged bangs that curved toward high cheekbones. She did not smile at them.

The boy stared, his eyes wary. His mother stared too. Warren's second impression was of a feral cat and her kitten, both of them fearful and alert.

They walked toward the woman and the boy, hands up to shield their eyes from the sun. Pinky said, "Can we talk to you for a moment, Mrs. Weber? This is Detective Franklin Warren. He's just arrived. He lives here in Bethany and will be investigating the fire." She clearly knew Pinky. She gave him a little nod and stared at Warren.

Warren put a hand out and then took it back when she refused, showing him that her hand was smeared with dirt or manure.

"Is it okay to ask you some questions? We're so sorry for your loss."

She nodded, rubbed her hands on the gingham skirt, and said to the boy, "You go in for some water." Her voice was deeper than he'd expected, with a slight accent he couldn't place. There was something off about the way she looked at them, her gaze direct and curious, as though she didn't know why they were there. But Warren knew all too well that grief was not uniformly expressed.

Once the boy was gone she waited, and Warren jumped in to fill the void. "Could we sit somewhere, Mrs. Weber?"

She led them to the rotting picnic table. As Warren folded himself onto the bench, he felt a splinter catch his good trousers. He watched her face as she lowered herself onto the end of the seat, one hand going to her belly, instinctively protecting it from the edge of the table. He dispensed with small talk and asked her directly, "When did you realize that the barn was on fire?"

She hooked a piece of dark hair behind her ear and looked over in the direction of the barn. "I smelled it," she said, a bit stiffly. "Something woke me up. I heard the cows and then, when I went to the window, I smelled . . . smoke. I called to the boys and we went out. I called for Hugh, but I couldn't get into the barn. It was already burning. He didn't come out."

It was a concise recitation, so concise he couldn't glean anything from it. It offered very little for him to judge.

"And you called down to the fire department?"

"We don't have a telephone," she said.

They waited. Surely she would explain. But she just stared back at them.

"So, how was the fire department alerted?" Warren asked finally.

"Scott drove the truck down to the Uptons' and they called up Chief Williamson."

"Scott is your son?"

She nodded.

"How old is he?"

Her eyes widened and moved from Warren to Pinky and back again. "Fourteen. But . . . he had to drive. Even though he doesn't have a license. He knows how."

"Don't worry about that, Mrs. Weber. It was an emergency," Pinky said kindly.

Warren forced himself to make his voice quieter. "When did you realize your husband was . . . forgive me for having to ask . . . inside the barn?"

She thought for a moment, remembering. "I don't know," she said finally, not looking at him. "I . . ." She hesitated. "He went out there and then there was the fire, so like I said, I went to open the big door. But it was bolted on the inside. I couldn't open it. And then there were flames coming out of the pig house. It was very hot."

"There were no doors on the pig house?"

"No, we went through the main barn to get to it."

"The barn door was bolted from the inside?" he asked.

She nodded.

"And there are no back doors to the barn? There wasn't another way you could have gotten to him or that he could have escaped?"

She shook her head. "There is a door, but the hay is piled up in front of it. The hanging doors are the only way in. When the hay is in there, we can't . . . There's no other door."

Warren thought of the towering stacks of hay and nodded to show he understood that they blocked the whole back wall, where there otherwise would have been an exit. "And is there any other way that could have happened? For example, could he have bolted it and then planned to go out the back way, but been prevented by the hay?"

Her eyebrows dropped in confusion. "Why would he do that? He knows, knew, about the hay being there."

"I don't know, Mrs. Weber. I'm just asking if you ever did that, if your husband ever did that."

"No," she said simply.

There it was. They would have to confirm that, but if so, and if the fire seemed deliberately set, then this was fairly clear-cut. Hugh Weber had committed suicide in that barn.

Suicide while the balance of his mind was disturbed. "Mrs. Weber, how had your husband seemed earlier that evening? Was he upset about anything?"

"Not really, no more than he usually was." She reached up to scratch her nose and looked at them. Her dark blue eyes were still curious, appraising suddenly.

Warren had to resist the urge to laugh. What was wrong with her? She seemed so childlike. It was hard to believe she had given birth to and raised all those boys they'd seen. It seemed more likely to him she was their tomboy sister.

"He didn't say anything to you?"

She hesitated. "You mean, such as that he was going to burn himself up in the barn? No."

Warren didn't dare look over at Pinky. The situation suddenly seemed absurd. She was simple, that's what it was. She wasn't all there.

"Did your husband talk to you about this man who died last year, who was upset about the interstate?"

He could see it immediately, that there was something there. She sat up a bit straighter and tucked an escaped piece of hair behind one ear again, then met his gaze with her own direct one. "He hated it. He said it would ruin Vermont, bring evil things here. He wrote letters about it all the time. When he was . . . when he had gin he was especially upset about it all."

"But did he ever talk about the man?" He looked to Pinky for the name and Pinky obliged by saying, "Forrest Germond, Mrs. Weber."

"Oh yes, he talked about him a lot. He said he understood why he had done it, that the interstate was the government stealing people's land. He said . . ." She swallowed nervously and looked away. "He said he would do the same thing."

Warren watched her. Most grieving widows would be sobbing at this point but she barely seemed bothered by the fact that her husband had just incinerated himself. "I'd like to read some of the things he wrote," Warren told her. "Could I take some of them from the house?"

She glanced back toward the barn. "He made an office in the barn, in the pig house," she said. "He said he couldn't concentrate on his writing with the sound of the boys in the house. So he had a typewriter and books and cabinets in there. All his writing was in there. In the winter he had a little electric heater he brought out there." They all looked back toward the ruins of the office. Any paper that had been there was long gone.

Warren wanted to know about their financial arrangements but he wasn't sure how to get around to it. "I assume he's left the farm to you and your sons," he said finally. "Would there be any other beneficiaries?"

The quizzical look she gave him was sincere, he thought.

"Did your husband have a will?" he tried again.

She shrugged and scratched her nose again, as though the fine spray of freckles across its bridge was irritating her. "I don't know. We didn't talk about those things. He got checks from New York some-times."

Warren wrote that down on his pad of paper. *New York/checks?* She watched him do it. "I'm sorry, do you know who they were from?"

"His family. I think."

"Tell me about his family. They lived in New York?"

She nodded. "I never met them. His parents died when we were first married. He had a brother but they didn't get along."

"And his name is?"

"I think Victor," she said. He waited for more but it didn't come.

"Was there a lawyer whose name you might have heard?"

She shrugged and said, "He sometimes went to see Mr. William-son in town. He's a lawyer." Warren didn't know what else to ask her. He wanted to think a bit, figure out what to look for next. So he said, "Thank you, Mrs. Weber, we'll leave you now. We're going to go and do some more investigation of the crime scene. Please do look around for any papers you might have."

She got up from the picnic table with some difficulty and headed back toward the garden without saying goodbye. Warren stood there stupidly for a moment and then he and Pinky went to the barn.

"Now that the body's been removed, I want to document other as-pects of the scene beyond what we got yesterday," Warren said. "Have you photographed evidence in situ before?"

"A few times. Burglaries, I've taken snaps of broken windows. Once I responded to a car wreck and Lieutenant Johnson told me to get a picture of a whiskey bottle on the driver's side floor. So I did that."

Warren nodded. "Good. Assuming you've got enough film, the object is to get as many pictures as you can. In this case, I really want the doors and the position the hardware was in. I also want pictures of the place where Mr. Weber was found. And as much of the burned timbers and beams as we can get. Sometimes patterns of burns on the floor and what's left of the walls can tell us where a fire was set and how fast it burned. That helps to establish the fact that he set the fire himself. I'll show you."

They went to the ruins of the pig house. Warren tried to imagine the man sitting there, typing away at his typewriter, lifting the bottle to his lips every twenty minutes or so. Warren imagined him swearing as he typed, rising to his feet, perhaps taking a can of gasoline from the front of the barn and dousing the hay on the barn floor with it. He smoked. Surely there had been a book of matches in the barn. And then . . . had he just lain down on the narrow bed frame and waited for the smoke and flames to get him?

He pointed to the pattern of black on what was left of the walls. "The fire investigator will be interested in this too. I'm going to try to take a panorama of photos, so we can recreate it if we have questions later." He spun around, clicking pictures of the scene, then went out and took five photos each of the main barn doors and the hardware on them, and the back door, which he confirmed was blocked by the stacked hay.

He explained to Pinky what he was doing and then said, "You going back to the barracks?"

"Yeah."

"Take the camera. But be very careful with it. And let's get these developed as soon as we can so we'll have them by the time the autopsy's back."

The smell of charred wood from the barn was still strong, like sour milk you couldn't get off your tongue. The sun was high in the sky now and Warren could feel a thin rivulet of sweat make its way down his back toward his beltline. He examined the backside of the main barn door one more time; the metal bolt, blackened by the fire, was still in its engaged position, as it had been yesterday. From what he could tell, it was as Sylvie Weber had said, it had to have been bolted from the inside.

"What are the facts that favor suicide?" Warren said out loud. He meant it as a question for himself. It was part of his process to ask questions out loud and answer them.

But Pinky obviously thought the question was intended for him because he said, "Detective?" When Warren looked over, the blush had gotten him.

"Sorry. What aspects of this case make you think this was suicide, as opposed to homicide?"

"The bolt."

"Very good. But if it was a homicide, the perpetrator might have done that too," Warren said.

"Yes, but how did the perpetrator get out?" Pinky asked.

Warren scanned the front of the barn. The boards were flat and smooth. "There's a window way up there," he said, pointing to an opening high on the burned face of the barn. "Even if you could climb up the boards on the inside—and I don't think you could—you'd need a ladder, and a tall one too, to get down the exterior without killing yourself or breaking a few bones. I don't see any ladders around. I suppose he could have taken it with him, but that means he came in a vehicle and she would have heard that."

"That's right," Pinky said. "She would have heard it." Neither of them said what they were both thinking: *Unless she knows who did it and she's lying to us.*

"Right." Warren thought for a moment. "If it was suicide, I want to know his frame of mind, so I need to get those letters to the editor. If it was homicide, well, then we've got to figure out who had it in for him. He have any enemies in town?"

Pinky looked contemplative and then he said, "That'd be a lot of people, now. He was from away, but . . . it was more than that." He scrunched his eyebrows together, thinking. "It would be faster to maybe make a list of who didn't have a bone to pick with him, if you see what I mean."

Warren smiled. "I guess I need to get out and pound the pavement then, get to know my new hometown. I'll go see Williamson first," Warren said. "And, I'd like to talk to the doctor, see if he has any evidence of his state of mind. What was the doctor's name again?"

"Falconer," Pinky said.

"Would he be Hugh Weber's doctor, as well as hers?"

Pinky looked confused, then said, "He's everyone's doctor."

Warren smiled. "Ah, well, that makes it easy. I'll go down there right now."

"He'll be having his lunch, I'd say," Pinky said. "Best to wait until this afternoon."

"I'll start with Williamson in that case," Warren said cheerily, but Pinky's face clouded over. "Will he be on his lunch hour as well?" he asked. Pinky nodded. "Perhaps I'll stop at home for some lunch myself and then walk down to see them all when I'm through." Pinky seemed to like that.

Sylvie Weber was standing on the porch now. There was some kind of vine climbing the posts of the porch, and standing there, thoughtful-looking and framed by the green leaves, she could have been out of a painting. Warren hadn't thought of her as attractive, and she wasn't exactly, but there was a beauty to her, surrounded by the greenery and looking wistful, that surprised him.

Warren called out to Mrs. Weber, "Thank you, Mrs. Weber. I'm sorry for your loss. I'll be in touch."

She waved hesitantly. After he had reversed and was heading back down Agony Hill, he turned to look out the window. She was watching him go. The cows were too. The fields blazed green and gold in the midday sun.

Seven

Alice smiled at the girl behind the counter. "And how are you today, Lizzie? Isn't it hot this morning?"

"Yes, Mrs. Bellows." Lizzie Coller placed the newspaper on top of the bag and pushed it across the counter, Alice's change on top. She was a small girl of eighteen, Lizzie, with a thin, pinched face like a mouse and frizzy hair she never seemed to know what to do with. She had looked exactly the same since the day she was born. Alice had seen her not long after, a scrawny, unhappy-looking baby with a few tiny pieces of hair stuck to her pale scalp. Bea Coller had dressed her in a ridiculous dress, bedecked with ribbons, to show her off at church. Poor baby Lizzie had seemed to be drowning in a flood of fabric.

Lizzie tried to smile, but her brow remained furrowed, her mouth set in worry. Alice watched the girl for a moment. She had been stepping out with the oldest Gerhart boy lately, since they'd graduated from high school, Mildred had told her. He worked at the store too, had done since he was a boy, and when she had heard about it, Alice remembered hoping that Richie Gerhart wasn't just looking to his future employment by courting the daughter of the store's owner. Alice studied Lizzie for another second. Perhaps there was trouble between the two.

She was almost out the door when Lizzie called out, "Oh, Mrs. Bellows? Did the gentleman find you?"

Alice turned back. The shelves behind the counter were crammed with items, boxes of sugar and nails and jars filled with penny candy. The bulletin board in the center of it all was covered in layers of paper, but the poster advertising the upcoming Old Home Day celebrations on the Bethany Green was front and center. The counter area was visually chaotic, Lizzie barely visible against the clutter, but in fact the Collers knew where everything was. "Which gentleman would that be, dear?"

"The one who was in yesterday, asking about you? Older, uh, gentleman. He said he had been a friend of yours and your husband's and he happened to be in town and was hoping to look you up. I showed him where your house was and he said he'd say hello. I hope that was all right."

"Of course, dear. Perhaps he left a message with Mildred. Thank you, Lizzie."

"See you soon, Mrs. Bellows," Lizzie said morosely.

Well.

Alice forced herself to maintain the calm, placid look of a woman of a certain age out doing her shopping. She paused once outside the general store and walked across to the library, where she pretended to read the sign on the door, despite the fact that she knew the library wasn't open, this being a Tuesday.

But the library had a plate glass window and she was able to stand there for a moment and survey the quiet street in its reflection. Of course, no one was here now. But someone had been. Yesterday. In her yard.

Who was it? Mildred hadn't said anything about a visitor. She was careless in some respects, but Alice had been able to convey to her the importance of passing on messages and, as far as she knew, Mildred hadn't missed any.

Until now.

Perhaps.

Alice thought for a moment, remembering her feeling of unease. She'd been feeling it for days. But it wasn't fear exactly. Rather it was . . . anticipation, the anticipation of a certain kind of danger. It was familiar to her and it was scary but exciting to recognize it again.

She made a show of looking disappointed and walked back down Main Street to the green. Everything seemed to be in order at her house and she went around to the side gate, hesitating, not afraid exactly, but wishing she knew if Mildred was inside before she entered the house.

The breeze stirred the gardens as she started to open the side gate. She stood there for a moment, trying to read the atmosphere. Someone had been in here again, she thought. The air in the garden, which she knew better than the air of her bedroom or kitchen, had been disturbed in the last couple of hours. She waited, listened. A radio was playing in the yard of the vicarage, the new tenant likely.

An idea occurred to her. She'd been meaning to invite him for tea. Well, there was no time like the present. She'd put off whoever it was who'd followed her, let him know she had a policeman living next door. Alice put her basket down by the gate and wandered over to the yard. The past tenants of the vicarage hadn't had very green thumbs and the beds in the back were overgrown with mint and weeds. The transmission from the radio—a baseball game, she thought, from the sounds—grew louder. A man was on his knees on the ground, his head nearly buried in the Shasta daisies.

He hadn't heard her approach and she was able to observe him for a moment. He was still young, perhaps only thirty or so, with broad shoulders and arms that seemed too thin for his size. He'd lost weight and muscle recently, she decided. Oblivious to being watched, he worked diligently, quickly, as though he had something to prove.

"No, don't pull that up," she said after a moment. "It doesn't look like much now, but it will be a lovely sedum soon enough. Good fall color. Here, let me show you."

The man started, then sat up on his knees and watched as she pointed to the clump of sedum. "Leave those and pull these. That's pigweed," she said. He did as she instructed and then stood up and smiled at her.

"Hello, I'm Franklin Warren. I'd shake your hand, but I'm filthy, as you can see. You must be from next door. The gardener."

He was nice-looking, though not excessively so, with fair hair cut neatly—his sideburns were longish, however, as was now the fashion—and dark eyes and a thin, intelligent face. He was a few inches taller than she—five foot ten or so. She liked his face; it hid things.

"Yes, I'm Alice Bellows, from next door," she said. "I'd like to invite you for tea."

"Now?" He glanced down at his clothes.

"Yes. Please don't feel you have to change your clothes. We'll sit in the garden. Very informal."

"All right. I'll just wash my hands in the kitchen. Shall I . . ?"

"I'll wait," she said briskly. "I don't mind at all."

"All right."

He disappeared for a few moments and when he returned, he had changed into a clean shirt and he was holding the empty basket, the cloth folded neatly in the bottom. There was a piece of paper on top, a thank-you note, she thought approvingly. "I've been meaning to thank you for that," he said, handing it over. "It hit the spot while I was unpacking. I'm very grateful, Mrs. Bellows."

She nodded and took the basket. He followed her across the little expanse of lawn and driveway and through her gate.

"It's so beautiful back here," he said. "Did you do this all yourself?"

"My late husband helped me and I have a young man in to help out as well," Alice said. "Thank you. It is my pride and joy. Now, you just make yourself comfortable there in the pavilion and I'll have Mildred bring the tea out."

He sat down on the bench in the covered structure in the center of her garden, the roof twined with roses, and she went to the back door. She felt a wash of relief when she saw Mildred at the stove, making preserves. The steam rose around her in a cloud. The room smelled of raspberries and sugar.

"Mildred," Alice said, "I have Mr. Warren from next door for tea. Would you bring the tray when the water's boiled? We're under the pavilion."

"Yes, ma'am." Mildred didn't ask questions. She never did. That was another reason Alice liked having her around.

"Oh, and Mildred, I meant to ask, did a gentleman call for me yesterday? Lizzie mentioned something about it."

Mildred stopped stirring. "A gentleman? No, Mrs. Bellows. I try to be very careful about passing on messages to you." She looked indignant at the implied accusation. Alice would be dealing with that for some time to come, she knew. There would be repeated reminders of messages given, pointed comments about how Mildred wouldn't want Mrs. Bellows to think she *forgot now*.

"I know you do. Lizzie must have made a mistake. She seemed to think that a man was looking for me yesterday."

Mildred raised her eyebrows and lit the burner under the kettle. Alice resisted the urge to giggle. Mildred must think she had a suitor.

When she returned to the garden, Franklin Warren was leaning back against the bench and looking out across the beds appreciatively.

"Now, what do you think of our little town so far?" she asked him, sitting opposite on a wicker settee. "A bit of a change of pace from Boston, I imagine."

He met her eyes. They were intelligent eyes, a reddish brown in the light, gentle eyes, haunted ones too, she thought. Her first impression, that he was hiding something, was only confirmed by seeing them up close. "It's very nice," he said. "I love the silence. I'd hoped to have a bit more time to move in but I was called out to the fire up on Agony Hill practically as soon as I got here."

"Mmmm. Terrible thing," Alice said. She was curious now about his purpose in bringing it up and his next question told her what she needed to know.

"Hugh Weber seems to have been an odd man," he offered, after a heavy pause. "Did you know him?"

"I did." She made sure to control her facial expression. "He used the library quite frequently." He looked confused so she explained, "I'm the chairwoman of the board of trustees, you see. He could be difficult. Didn't have many real friends in town."

He nodded. She'd confirmed something he'd been told, she thought. "The wife seems odd as well. What do you know of her?"

Alice tried to read his face. "Sylvie Weber? She's quite unusual-looking, isn't she? Lovely in her way."

He looked annoyed at that. "Did she grow up around here? Does she have family around?"

Alice heard the screen door swing. Mildred was coming with the tea. "No. I believe she grew up on a farm way up in Orleans County somewhere, almost on the Canadian border. Her parents had lots of children and not enough money. You know, I don't know how she and Weber met. No doubt you noticed the substantial age difference. I think it's been a difficult life, very hard work, all those children. Hugh Weber believed in doing things the old way, even if they could have afforded some conveniences. It was an idea he had, you see, about returning to the way things used to be. Do you know who Helen and Scott Nearing are?"

Warren shook his head, so she said, "Back-to-the-landers, I think they're called. They wrote a book called *Living the Good Life*, about, well, homesteading, living off the land and so forth. Anyway, I believe Hugh Weber read the book and wanted to be like the Nearings. Back to the land. Hard work. Raise your own food. But Sylvie bore the burden, I think. If she'd been older, she might have been able to see what things would be like. But I suppose she came from a situation that made it imperative to *get out*. Hugh had books. I think she likes books. Very much. I've let her borrow some from me from time to time and she's written some quite accomplished poems. I showed them to a friend at the college and . . . well, he thought they were quite good." She wasn't sure why she'd told him that, about the poems, but it seemed suddenly important for him to know.

Warren looked surprised at that. The dark eyes widened. He was momentarily silent. Then he nodded and said, "I almost wondered if she was . . . well, not quite right in the head. Slow, you know."

Alice tried not to show her disappointment plainly, but she could hear it in her own voice when she replied, "Is that what you thought? Personally, I think she's quite brilliant in her way, with an unusually perceptive mind. But yes, atypical, I suppose. Oh, here's Mildred with the tea. Mildred, this is Mr. Warren, the new tenant at the vicarage."

He seemed flustered now, but he stood and greeted Mildred and took the tea tray from her to put on the table in the pavilion. Mildred didn't acknowledge his presence in any way, which didn't seem to throw him. *He's used to having help around*, Alice thought to herself.

"Do you mind hot tea on a hot day?" Alice asked him once she'd poured and he'd added a bit of milk to his cup.

"I don't," he said, sipping the steaming liquid and then sighing, as though he already felt refreshed. "I always find it cools me down. Isn't it the way they do it in tropical places? India and so forth?"

Alice sipped her own tea and said, "I lived in Cairo for a time, Morocco too. Other hot places. You're right, it does cool you down.

Something about the relative temperature and the evaporation of perspiration."

"That must have been interesting," he said, testing the waters. "Egypt."

"Oh, it was. It was during the war. My husband was stationed in Cairo and I went along. It was a very interesting time, as you might imagine."

"Your husband was . . ." he ventured.

"Oh, at the embassy, you know," she said quickly.

"How long have you lived here?" he asked.

"I was raised right here, in this house," she told him. "My husband and I mostly lived abroad, and then in Washington, DC. We spent summers here in Bethany, but I moved back when he died ten years ago."

Something crossed his face and she knew suddenly that *he* knew that Ernie had likely been something more than a mere diplomat. Many of the Americans in Cairo at that point were, one way or another, intelligence officers with the OSS, men like Ernie, who wore many hats but were there to gather intelligence in the shadows of the war. Warren didn't say anything, though a tiny smile played at the edges of his mouth. He was satisfied he knew something about her, she thought. This was interesting to Alice because it meant he had some connection to the military or intelligence worlds himself. She wanted to know what it was. He sipped his tea and looked out across the garden.

"Have there been any breakthroughs on the Weber fire?" she asked innocently, steering him back to Agony Hill and Sylvie Weber. She wanted to know what he was thinking about the case. She wanted to know what he knew.

He set his cup down and said, "Nothing definite. It seems Hugh was quite upset about the coming of the interstate. I'm hoping to find out more about the letters to the editor he wrote. I understand that the newspaper office is on the green?"

"Yes. Fred Fielder is the editor. He'll help you out. There's an archive at the library as well, but Fred can probably find you the letters quickly. Hugh Weber was indeed a prolific correspondent." She smiled in a way that was meant to convey the obsessive nature of Weber's letter writing. Hardly a month had gone by that didn't include one of his acidic letters about some aspect of life in Bethany, or about state or national politics.

Warren thought for a moment and then he said, "You understand, we have just begun our investigation. But I wonder, would you be surprised if it was determined that Hugh Weber had set the fire himself? Knowing him as you did?"

A bird called from the back of the garden. Another one answered. Alice had to give him credit. He was trying to flatter her, to make her feel that her opinion was valued. Of course, she needed to be careful here, but she could be honest. "He had a particularly unpleasant character," she said. "There are probably many people in town who would have liked to kill him, but I would be surprised to find that one actually did. He had a large ego. Large egos rarely destroy themselves on purpose, but I will say that he had a vengeful personality. If he somehow felt that he didn't have long to live anyway, I can see him taking his own life as a sort of punishment, for all the poor souls who didn't understand him. I might ask at Dr. Falconer's, to be sure." She waited, to be sure he'd taken in her meaning. "On the balance, I would say no, but there are circumstances where it might be possible."

He seemed impressed. And interested now. "Thank you," he said. "I was planning on speaking with Dr. Falconer today, in fact. That's helpful. Mrs. Weber said he had a brother in New York. I assume she will inherit the farm?"

"I don't know. You wonder what the financial arrangement was, don't you? Well, I suppose you'll have to find out from David Williamson."

"The lawyer?"

"Mmmm." Alice thought about revealing that David was her attorney too and that she'd heard from Gabriel, who did the books, that there was some significant money in that family, that in fact Hugh Weber's father had been a rather wealthy man, on paper at least, though there was clearly some sort of difficulty with the family. But, no. This Franklin Warren would have to find that out for himself.

"I'm going to see him this afternoon too." He checked his watch. "In fact, I hate to say it, but I should probably be going. I need to stop at the newspaper office and then at the lawyer's, and then at the doctor's. It's like a joke, isn't it? But it will be a good way to get to know my new home. I've hardly had time to get my bearings."

"Of course," she said. "I enjoyed chatting with you. Welcome to Bethany. Let me know if there's anything you need. We have a small but vibrant social and cultural life here, and if you're interested in music, there are concerts at the Universalist church. Are you a reader, Mr. Warren? If so, we have a reading group at the library that is very popular."

"I am a reader. I've been reading Lawrence Durrell lately. I keep seeing posters for Old Home Day. Should I put it on my social calendar?"

Alice wanted to ask what he thought of Durrell, but that was for a time when he didn't have to go. "Oh, yes. It's a big event here in town. It's this weekend, you know. Make sure to stop by the Ladies Aid Society's booth. I'll be doing the flowers. Our raspberry cake is quite famous, if I do say so myself."

He put his cup back onto the tray and stood up. "I'll be there. Thank you for the tea. And for the time in your garden," he said. And then, "It was good for me, for my soul."

She smiled at his apparent sincerity. The words had not been uttered lightly. He meant it, she thought. "Good day, Mr. Warren."

Alice watched him as he returned to his side of the hedge. It was one o'clock now. Time for a rest and a bit of prayer. The mystery man, whoever he was, wasn't going to come back now. She could feel it. She closed her eyes and breathed in the scent of jasmine.

Eight

The Bethany Green was the shape of an almond, a large grassy expanse that must once have been used for public grazing. Now, it held some benches and some trees Warren thought must be cherry or apple, lovingly pruned, and a large covered gazebo like the ones he'd seen in many a small New England town. Warren's house, and Mrs. Bellows's, sat at the northern end of the almond, on the west side. As you traveled south, you passed a few more houses, and then the imposing structure of the library, a white marble building with graceful white columns and large windows. On the other side was a string of lovely houses, one white, one yellow, one blue, another white, that reminded Warren of laundry hanging on a line. All had colorful and well-tended gardens out front. At the very center of the almond was the wide façade of Collers' Store. Warren had been in once for staples and had found the experience overwhelming. Everywhere he'd looked there had been things for sale. A huge wheel of cheddar cheese sat under a glass dome on the counter. Glass canisters in the large display case held a dizzying array of candy: lemon drops, chocolate

babies, licorice, gumballs. The shelves were laden with many different kinds of canned and dry goods and as you went deeper into the
deceptively simple-looking building, you walked through sections
containing clothing, footwear, ammunition, tools, and children's toys
and games.

Past Collers' was the drugstore, the Universalist church, and then
at the southern end of the green, the Bethany Inn. The inn occupied
nearly an acre of land and its columns and large green sign gave it an
air of permanency and elegance. Past the inn were more houses and
offices, including Dr. Falconer's office and an insurance agency, and
finally, the huge, white-columned Congregational church, almost directly across the green from Warren's house.

Surveying the center of his new hometown, Warren once again
had the thought he'd had when he first drove into town: that he had
stepped back in time.

The offices of the *Bethany Register*, he'd been told, were on the
second floor of the drugstore, up a narrow flight of stairs reached from
behind the long lunch counter. It took Warren some time to ascertain
this and by the time he understood that the white-hatted middle-aged
man frying burgers who was waving vaguely at a door behind him really did mean for Warren to come behind the counter and go through
the door, he feared that he might no longer be welcome at the counter
the next time he entered. The man's face was suffused with frustration
as he yelled, "Through there! Up the stairs!"

There were stenciled letters on the door at the top of the stairs,
at the end of a short hallway. Warren knocked and when no one answered, he turned the doorknob and went in.

He had the immediate sense of having stepped into an alternate
dimension. It didn't make architectural sense that there would be this
cavernous space on top of the small drugstore building, but here it
was, filled with people and stacks of papers and two rows of huge
slanted boards at which three men stood arranging slips of paper

covered with typing. The young woman sitting at the desk closest to the door looked up at him and said, "Ads are back there." She was perhaps twenty, with bright red hair that made him think of Pinky; she was wearing a clashing orange blouse and skirt and she had a pencil behind one ear.

"No, I . . . I don't want to buy an ad. My name is Franklin Warren. I'm the new detective at the state police barracks and I'm looking into the fire up on Agony Hill. I'd like to see some old copies of the paper, if I can."

That had her attention. She stood up and called out, "Fred!" and a guy about Warren's age, fair, balding, and bespectacled, wearing a dress shirt with the sleeves rolled all the way up to his biceps, emerged from the din and walked over. Warren described what he wanted while the red-haired girl listened intently.

"Detective Warren," the man said. "It's nice to meet you. Welcome to Bethany. I heard you were living at the vicarage. Tragic case, isn't it, the fire? First thing I thought of was whether he was aping that farmer. That the direction you're thinking too?" The man's blue eyes were too alert behind the spectacles, too probing. Warren told himself to watch his words around this newspaperman.

"Sorry," he said. "What was your name?"

"Fred Fielder," the man said. "I run the paper here."

"Well, Mr. Fielder, I can't tell you what we're thinking and to be fair, we don't know much at this point. That's why I'd like to see his letters. From what I hear he was a particularly active correspondent?"

"You can say that again!" Fielder laughed. "Hugh Weber was an obsessive. I'm going to make your job easy for you. I had a file of the letters, because there were so many of them and because I fully expected that one day someone like you was going to come and knock on my door. Though to be honest, I thought it would be him burning someone *else's* barn down. Follow me."

He led the way to a tiny office and pointed to a wooden swivel chair set opposite a desk completely covered in piles of papers and magazines and books. "Sit there. I'll be right back." Warren did a quick scan of the framed newspapers on the walls. All seemed to be the front pages of the *Register* from historically significant dates. The one over Fred Fielder's desk had a headline reading "Ground Broken on Vermont Portion of Interstate 91."

"Here it is," Fielder said, dropping a thick cardboard folder on the desk in front of Warren. "Have a look through. It won't take you long to get a feel for it. I've got to get back to layout—we go to press tomorrow—but you're welcome to have a read."

Warren hesitated over the folder, trying to shake off the feeling he ought to put on a pair of cloth gloves to handle what could be evidence before remembering how many hands had touched these letters since they'd left Hugh Weber's hands. It was *what* he'd written that mattered.

The earliest letter was from 1959, a short screed decrying "Progress at any cost" and went on to conclude that "those who say the coming of the interstate will bring new life to Vermont may be dismayed to find in the end that the 'old life' is worth preserving."

They continued on like that for a few years as ground was broken and as Warren imagined that the construction was creeping ever closer to Bethany. Weber seemed to have written a letter every week—sometimes about the interstate, sometimes about other issues, including calling for the redistribution of all property taxes in town according to need. His argument was convoluted, though; Warren couldn't figure out if he was a communist or was speaking against the communists. Maybe it was both.

Then, a year ago, he started writing more frequently, clearly in response to the farmer's act of suicidal protest. "This brave man has spoken," one letter read. "He has spoken for a way of life that is fading. He has spoken for his God-given right to his land and home. He has spoken for the men and women of this great state, who remember a time when it was not for the federal government to control our destinies, but for ourselves."

And then, two months ago, the final letter in the file.

"Yesterday, as I made hay on my farm, I heard the sounds of the beastly machines chewing at the earth over the hills, destroying it, gouging it, killing it, all in the name of progress. I thought of that brave neighbor of ours, of his last thoughts that fateful night, of his hope that he could stop the rampaging machines. I understand his action, gentleman, and I revere it for it is but one strike against that monster called 'Progress.'"

Warren read it again. There was something unhinged about the letter. It was nearly a suicide note. He closed the file with an air of finality. It seemed pretty clear what had happened here.

"That helping you at all?" Fielder asked from behind him, sticking his head in the door.

Warren stood up. "Very much so," he said.

Fielder smiled. "Glad I could be of assistance. Now maybe you can help me. Is there anything on that Armstrong fellow, the one from Washington, DC, who bought a cottage out on Downers Road and got shot during a burglary?"

His tone had shifted so quickly that Warren wasn't prepared. "I'm sorry . . . I don't . . ."

Fielder watched him carefully. "Thought Tommy Johnson might have put you onto it. Seems like a case that could use a dose of real professionalism."

Warren recovered himself. He was going to have to watch out for this newspaperman. "We have no comment at this time, Mr. Fielder." He picked up the file folder. "Okay if I take these with me? I'll need to get copies made and we'll have them back to you as soon as possible."

Fielder nodded. "Sure thing. He's not going to complain anyway. The fire's put an end to that, at least." Warren was momentarily shocked, but Fielder didn't seem inclined to apologize.

¤ ¤ ¤

The lawyer's office was around the other side of the green, almost back to Warren's house, and he had to pass the doctor's office to get there. He decided to eschew efficiency, though, and do the lawyer first. Mrs. Bellows's comments about the Weber family possibly having money had been interesting to Warren. He wanted to know more.

David Williamson practiced law out of a neatly kept beige Victorian with a sign out front reading DAVID WILLIAMSON, ESQ. Warren pushed open the door on the porch and went into a small lobby with a few chairs placed around a coffee table. When he introduced himself to the receptionist, a woman of forty or fifty with precisely curled black hair, she told him that Mr. Williamson was with a client, but that he could sit down and wait. He settled into one of the hard chairs and leafed through the copies of *Vermont Life* magazine stacked on the table. He was halfway through an article about maple sugaring when the door opened and a man in a three-piece suit came aggressively through the door and let it slam behind him. "I want to see David Williamson," he announced to the secretary.

He was not from Bethany. Warren knew that as soon as he opened his mouth.

He was not from Boston. Warren knew that too.

He was from New York. Warren perked up in his chair.

"He's busy, sir. I'm sorry," the receptionist said.

"I don't care if he's busy! I want to talk to him!"

"Sir, may I ask your name and—"

"Victor *Weber*." He pronounced it in the American style. "My brother burned himself alive day before yesterday and I want to know what his will says. I have that right as his executor and as a beneficiary. Where's Mr. Williamson?" Warren watched his face for a few moments before he stood up and put a hand out. The man was furious, right on the edge of violence, but even more than that, he was terrified, Warren thought, his face pale, his eyes lined and anxious.

"Mr. Weber," Warren said. "If you could calm down, please."

"Who the hell are you? How do you know my name?"

"You've just announced it to everyone within a two-mile radius," Warren said with a small smile, trying the defuse the situation.

"I won't calm down. I want Mr. Williamson to give me my brother's will!"

"I'm a police officer. I'd like you to calm down." Warren took a step toward him and Victor Weber dropped his shoulders and retreated.

"I just need to talk to Mr. Williamson," he said in a smaller voice.

The secretary must have had some secret way of alerting Mr. Williamson because a few seconds later a man came out into the lobby, looking flustered. "What's this all about?" he asked. He was trim, middle-aged, with a precise moustache and a snowy-white dress shirt and green tie. Warren recognized him as the chief of the volunteer fire department who had been spraying down the barn when Warren and Tommy had arrived at the scene of the fire.

"My brother was Hugh Weber and I want to know about the will," Victor Weber said, glancing at Warren and staying where he was. "Last I knew I am the executor, so it's my right."

The moustache twitched and David Williamson hesitated before saying, "Now, Mr. Weber, there is a process to be followed and I need to speak with your brother's widow. We'll have to—"

"Are you denying that I am the named executor?" He was agitated again, throwing his hands into the air and striding toward Williamson, whose eyes widened. "I demand you produce the will right now, Mr. Williamson!" His face was very red and he seemed not to be in control of himself.

Warren knew the signs of someone in great psychological distress. Whether it was grief or something else that was causing it, he couldn't say. But people were dangerous when they were overcome like this. He let the man see the weapon in his belt holster and said again, "Mr. Weber. I'm an armed law officer and I will bring you in if you don't calm down and act like an adult. I'm very sorry for your loss, but you can't come in here and cause a disturbance."

Weber's eyes flashed and he forced himself to step back.

"When will you be reading my brother's will?" he asked in a tight and constrained voice that barely disguised his raw fury. "I will be staying at the inn until this is sorted out."

Williamson, understanding that there was no immediate danger now, seemed to relax and said, "I don't think we'll have a public reading, Mr. Weber. That's only for detective novels. But as the executor, you will have access, of course, and will be responsible for handling your brother's affairs. I would be happy to go over the probate process with you and to be helpful in any way I can."

"When?" Weber threw the words out. "I have business to get back to in the city. I can't lose any more time than I already have."

"I will contact you once I've examined the will and consulted with Mrs. Weber but I would imagine we could do it tomorrow," Williamson said.

"Yes, you can leave a message for me at the inn." He started to say something else then, but apparently thought better of it and nodded to Warren before stalking out of the lobby.

There was a long silence and then the secretary said, "Well," in a deadpan tone before going back to her work.

"I'd like to thank you, uh, Officer . . ." Williamson's shoulders slumped and he removed a neatly folded handkerchief from his pocket and ran it over his forehead, which was now glistening with perspiration.

"Franklin Warren," Warren said, putting out a hand for him to shake. "I'm the new detective out of the state police barracks. I saw you up at the fire yesterday. You must be Mr. Williamson."

"Yes, I'm awful glad you were here to talk him down. I'd heard he and his brother were alike in temperament. I had no idea quite how much. You here to see me?"

"I am, if you have a minute to talk."

"Sure, come on in."

Williamson's office was neat and unremarkable, though Warren found little touches here and there that told him he wasn't in Boston. One wall was decorated with a stuffed deer head. A bright orange wool jacket hung on a coatrack in one corner, and in front of the small woodstove on one wall, a pair of high leather gum boots sat, as if waiting for their time to come.

"Chief Longwell told me the state police had a new detective coming to work out of the barracks. Tommy Johnson threw you right into it, didn't he?"

Warren smiled. "I suppose. I gather this sort of thing isn't a regular occurrence?"

Williamson snorted. "No, thankfully. I assume you want to know about his will?"

"Well, yes. I also wanted to get a sense of Hugh Weber from you. Had you been his lawyer long?"

Williamson considered that. "Ever since he bought the Hickson place fifteen years ago. He needed someone to do the transfer of the deed. He didn't like me much—he didn't like anyone much—but he came back a few times for some different . . . legal matters."

"Like his will?" Warren said it quickly but the lawyer was too sharp.

"That's right. I imagine I'll have to tell you all about that at some point, but I need to speak to someone in New York first and out of respect to Mrs. Weber, I'd like to tell her about it before I tell you. And of course, Mr. Weber—the other Mr. Weber—has access as the executor."

Warren hesitated, then said, "Yes, but Mr. Williamson, I wonder if I could ask you a favor. I'd like to see both Mrs. Weber's and Mr.

Weber's reactions to whatever is in the will. For the investigation, you understand. Would you consent to telling them about it while I'm present tomorrow?" He winked. "Just like in the detective stories?"

Williamson looked up, a little gleam of mischief in his eyes. "Aha, I see. I suppose that would be okay, if it's okay with her, that is. It might be good to have you on hand to manage Mr. Weber and I could use the investigation as the excuse for why you're here."

Warren inclined his head in thanks. "Exactly. So, what was he like? Hugh Weber?"

"You just got a good taste of him. Imagine that man out there, only with longer hair and dressed in dungarees and boots so old they have holes in them. Back-to-the-land type, always going on about the evils of capitalism and the modern world. He moved up here from New York to 'live simply,' he told me when he bought the place. He paid cash for it and said he wanted to feed his family with the fruits of his labor. From the look of that crew, he wasn't feeding 'em much."

"Do they make any money from the farm?"

"Not much," Williamson said. "They sold lambs, I gather, and bits and pieces here and there. Vegetables in the summer. Milk to the neighbors. They sugared and sold syrup at Collers' Store. I think she may have sold cakes and some yarn and things sometimes, but they weren't making much. You know, I'm glad we were able to save some of that barn for her. It's down to that boy, I'd say. He must have driven like a bat out of hell to get to a phone."

"If Mr. Weber's brother's temperament is any indication, it seems like he must have had a lot of enemies in town." Warren kept his voice neutral. "Lots of people in town who might have had reason to do him harm?"

Williamson shrugged. "*Enemies* is a strong word, Mr. Warren. He wasn't much liked, but that's different from someone having a reason to kill him. I thought he set himself on fire?"

"He probably did," Warren said. "But I need to do my due diligence.

You know how it is. I know you can't tell me the details of the will yet, but is there anything about it that is out of the ordinary?"

Williamson's eyes widened. "You mean, did it give anyone incentive to kill him?"

Warren tried to convey that this was just between them. "I suppose that is what I mean."

Williamson thought about that for a moment. "I'd rather wait until tomorrow," he said finally. "There are a few things I need to understand first about the legal situation. But I would be very surprised if this was anything other than Hugh Weber making a gesture while three sheets to the wind." He raised his eyebrows. "I'm sure you've heard this from others, but he liked to drink."

"I've gotten that sense," Warren said. "Did he fight or cause problems when he was drinking? Maybe he made someone mad."

"He wasn't a violent man," Williamson said. "It was more that he was annoying, if you see what I mean. Always spouting off about politics or how everyone but him was ignorant or backward. That sort of thing."

"So he fought with words rather than fists?" Warren asked, thinking of the file of letters.

"That's it exactly. He wasn't a regular at the tavern over there at the inn, but about once a month he'd go in and get good and sloshed."

Warren wrote that down. He'd need more information about these monthly benders.

He thanked Williamson and said he'd see him the next day. He was almost out the door when he thought of one more question.

"Mr. Williamson, what do you know about the marriage? Do you think he was ever violent there?"

Williamson considered that. "I wouldn't say so, but, well, who really knows? They lived up there and they came down sometimes, but I don't think there's a person in Bethany who really knew what went on up there on Agony Hill."

Nine

Dr. Norman Falconer had a house and surgery on the other side of the Bethany Inn, a sprawling white Victorian with a porch and an extension to the side for the surgery with a sign and separate entrance. Next to the door was a small pile of tennis balls.

Warren opened the screen door and immediately encountered the owner of the tennis balls, a husky tan-colored Labrador retriever, lolling in the entryway and blocking Warren's path. Even when he used his foot to carefully push the dog's tail out of the way, it continued snoozing, its breathing rough and snuffly.

"Oh, just step around him," a woman's voice called out and Warren awkwardly stepped over the dog. The owner of the voice was sitting behind the desk at the other end of the doctor's otherwise empty waiting room. "Hello," she said, a bit of a question in her voice, but with a smile. It was clear she didn't recognize Warren and equally clear that she usually did recognize the patients who came through the door. Warren felt immediately at ease with her. She was fifty or so, his mother's age, with blond hair streaked with silver cut short in a style that somehow reminded him of a nurse's cap, and an open, friendly face. He imagined that she was good at calming people down when they needed calming, when they were afraid or in pain.

"Hello," Warren said, smiling back at her. "My name is Franklin Warren. I'm the new detective stationed at the barracks here in town and I'm looking into the fire up at the Webers' farm, on Agony Hill. I was hoping I could talk to Dr. Falconer."

"Oh, it's so awful," she said. "Poor Sylvie . . . Well, Norm is in there struggling with his paperwork so he'll be glad of an interruption. Here, I'll show you in. Don't worry, he won't make you take off your shirt!" She laughed at that and led the way along a corridor that, like the waiting room, smelled of dog.

"Dear," she called out as she pushed open the door. "Don't bother pretending you're doing your paperwork, I have a policeman here to see you about the fire up at Webers'." The doctor, in shirtsleeves and khaki trousers rather than a white coat, did indeed snap his head up guiltily, rubbing at his eyes. He'd been napping in his chair.

"There he is, Mr. Warren. I'll leave you to it. Norm, dear, don't forget you have Mrs. Leary to go see at three."

"Ah, yes, of course." Dr. Falconer stood up and reached across the desk to shake Warren's hand. "Sorry, you're a policeman? You must be the new detective Pinky was talking about."

"That's right. Franklin Warren, but everyone calls me Warren. I just got here and I'm already looking into this fire. Do you mind if I ask you some questions about Hugh Weber and his, well, his state of mind?"

"Sure, happy to help. I was up there the next morning to have a look at Sylvie, his wife. She's pregnant, you know, but she's been through it before, four times to be precise, and I think she'll be all right. Terrible thing for him to do to her." He shook his head. "Can't say it surprised me. I suppose that's what you want to know."

"It is. Why didn't it surprise you?"

Dr. Falconer thought for a moment, then gestured at the chair. "Here, sit down. Well, he was an angry person, always upset about some perceived slight or insult. He was one of those people who woke up every morning thinking of himself as a victim of a great conspiracy by everyone around him to thwart his desires. Do you know what I mean?"

"I do. How was his health, mental and physical?" Warren asked, his pen poised over his notebook.

"Well, he was in the process of pickling his liver with gin and he'd started to have some normal, age-related arthritis. His knees bothered him, especially after hard work. I encouraged him to let the boys do the really taxing chores around the farm and I think he did, to some extent, but these farmers can't exactly put their feet up, can they? I could tell you some stories about some of these old-timers working themselves right into the grave."

"But nothing like cancer or a terminal diagnosis." Warren was thinking of what Mrs. Bellows had said. "Was the drinking going to kill him anytime soon?"

"Depends what you mean by *soon*, but no, nothing like that."

"What was your first thought when you heard he'd died in a fire up there?"

Falconer looked surprised at that. "Well, I thought of Forrest Germond. You know about him?" Warren nodded. "I suppose I said to myself, 'Well, Hugh's gone and done it.' Do you know about his letters to the editor?" Warren nodded. "Well, he'd practically told us he was going to do it, hadn't he?"

Having read the letters, Warren had to admit that in fact he had. "Were you concerned about his mental health? Did you ever think he was a suicide risk? Did he ever mention suicide to you?" He tried to ask it neutrally, not accusing the doctor of negligence.

"I thought he was an angry bastard, but no . . . I suppose I never thought he was in immediate danger of doing himself in, if that's what you mean. I would have been compelled to intervene if I had. He liked to say, 'When I'm gone, they'll all be sorry.' That sort of thing." He looked up quickly. "I think he was referring to people in town, not his family. It was a bit like he saw himself as some sort of prophet and he felt we weren't heeding his call." Warren wrote that down. That certainly sounded like someone who might do himself in to make a point.

Warren watched the doctor's face. "Did you ever imagine he was a danger to anyone else?"

"Like his wife, you mean?" Falconer gave a small smile. "I always wondered. But I never saw any marks on her and her pregnancies were healthy, her boys well-cared for, even if their parenting was . . . unorthodox. They all tiptoed around him a bit, I think, because of his temper, still I never saw anything that made me think he was physically abusive. But . . . they kept to themselves up there. They weren't much for modern medicine; he liked to treat things with natural remedies. Honestly, I'm not sure there's anyone who really knows what went on in that house. Does that answer your question?"

"Yes, it does." Warren shifted in his chair. "The boys, were they in school?" It had just occurred to him that because it was the summer, he hadn't wondered about how they got to school. But they must go, mustn't they? And where was the school? Warren hadn't noticed one in his limited wanderings around town.

As if he knew what Warren was thinking, Falconer said, "We're down to three primary schools in Bethany now. At one time we had twenty. If some of us get our way, that will be only one in a couple of years. It's easier to deliver a high-quality, modern education if you bring all the pupils to one building, but there are some who say it would be the end of the world. Hugh Weber was one of them. He wrote letters about that too. His boys walk down to the Goodrich Hill School. There are twenty-five students in that building, all from the western districts of town, and two teachers. My daughter Barbara is one of them."

"Could I talk to her, do you think?" Warren asked. "I'd like to get a perspective on the boys and what she might have seen of their home life."

Falconer studied him for a moment. "You don't think there's something wrong about that fire, do you? I get called out to look at suicides from time to time and I know you have to ascertain state of mind before making a determination, but you seem to have some questions about this one."

Warren smiled. "Just trying to make a good impression in my new job, Doctor."

"Ah, I can see that. Well, Barbara's in there." He pointed vaguely toward the house. "Our Labrador bitch had puppies a few weeks back by that magnificent fellow in the waiting room and she's in with them. Rose can show you."

Warren stood up. "Thank you, Dr. Falconer. It was nice to meet you. And I appreciate the help."

"Welcome to Bethany, Mr. Warren. I hear you're living at the vicarage. I'm sure I'll be seeing you around." He opened the door and called out to Rose, who Warren now understood to be both his wife and the practice's nurse, to show Warren into the house so he could talk to Barbara.

☖ ☖ ☖

"Barbara, dear, are you with the puppies?" Rose Falconer called out, leading Warren through a connecting door behind the desk in the waiting room and into a neat mudroom, coats and skis and winter boots organized against one wall, and then a kitchen, quiet but for the ticking of a clock and, from somewhere in the house, a radio. "Go on through to the porch, Mr. Warren, she'll be out there," Rose Falconer said. "Just tell her I said to go through. I have to get back and make sure Norm doesn't sleep through his next appointment."

Warren thanked her and went hesitantly into the room she'd pointed to, a formal living room, newly carpeted in pale blue, with shining furniture in a combination of good antiques and newer pieces, including one from Warren's father's latest living room collection, New Classics by Winchester. On the fireplace mantel was a row of family photographs, a wedding portrait of the Falconers in black and white, a portrait of a young man in an army officer's uniform—a son, perhaps—and a studio portrait of a beautiful young woman with a blond bouffant and a strong resemblance to Rose Falconer. Another formal portrait showed her standing next to a different man, also in a dress uniform, her left hand prominently displaying a diamond engagement ring.

He thought he was lost, until he heard laughter coming from the next room and he followed it out onto a screened-in porch at the back of the house that looked out onto the same brook or small river that passed behind his own house. A large yellow Labrador, the feminine counterpart to the one in the office, lay on her side in a shallow box, a wriggling mass of small tan puppies contained in the curve of her body. A woman who must be Barbara Falconer was sitting cross-legged on the floor, picking up puppies trying to escape and putting them back. When Warren said, "Hello, your mother told me to come through," she turned and looked up and smiled widely.

"Come in. Are you interested in one of the puppies?" she asked. "They won't be ready for weeks yet, but you're welcome to have a look. Aren't they just the loveliest?" The puppies varied in shades from pale beige to a darker gold. Their bellies were fat and rounded, full of milk.

"No, I . . . I'm not here about the puppies. I'm the new detective with the Vermont State Police. My name's Franklin Warren. I wanted to ask you about the Weber children, who I understand are students of yours at Goodrich Hill School."

"Oh, good Lord, I've got things the wrong way around, haven't I?" She laughed and stood up, putting out a hand for him to shake. She was tall, nearly his height, wearing a yellow oxford shirt, the sleeves rolled up and the shirttails tied at the waist of her yellow ankle-length trousers. Maria had had a pair of pants like that, blue, Warren remembered. "Sit down and we can keep an eye on these little devils while we talk. I'm Barbara, by the way." He shook her hand.

"What a nice view you have," he said, gazing out at the river. It was a small tributary of the Connecticut, he assumed, slim and shallow and lazy today as it meandered through Bethany. "You'd never know you were right in town."

"You must be able to see the brook from the vicarage," she said, then looked embarrassed for a moment. "I know you're living in the vicarage because Pinky was telling my mother in Collers' Store. Pinky seems to think he's going to be your assistant. He said you're going to teach him to investigate crimes and everything. He was quite proud, I think." She smiled. "I've known Pinky forever. He was the same class as my brother Greg."

"So, you had all of the Weber boys? I don't know how it works at these small schools."

"Well, there are two teachers at Goodrich Hill School. I teach the little ones and Jean Webster teaches the older ones up to fourteen, when they finish."

"Don't they have to go to high school?"

"Some of them do go on to the high school here in town, but some of them, farm kids and anyone who's going to the machine shops, the ones who have jobs to go into, well, they finish up after eighth grade. That's changing, though."

"So you had the Weber boys—sorry, I don't have the names right here. What are they like?"

She smiled. "Scott, Andy, Louis, and, well, Daniel won't come to school for a few years yet. They're nice boys, they really are. Quiet, you know. Scott was a solid student. We, Jean and I, encouraged him to go on to the high school, even though he wants to work on the farm. Hugh and Sylvie thought he should too. I hope this . . . the fire, won't change things. He'll feel a lot of responsibility now and with Sylvie pregnant, I don't know how they'll manage."

"What about the other boys?"

"Oh, Andy is quite intelligent. He's a wonderful student. Louis can be a little devil. He reminds me of the puppies, always wriggling and pushing. He's sweet. They're all quite sweet. But the other kids could be cruel and I think it's made them wary."

"What do you mean, the other kids were cruel?"

"Well, they're different. The rest of the kids come from farms too, but they would be more . . . traditional, I guess you'd say. Even if they were poor, their clothes are neat and they have haircuts and they know how to behave and they go to church on Sunday. The Weber boys are . . . different. On the one hand, they came to school already knowing how to read, how to write. They had been read to and they had memorized poems; they were quite far ahead. But the other kids make fun of their strange clothes. Sylvie lets their . . . she lets their hair grow long, like girls' hair. They have funny manners. I had to teach them to say *please* and *thank you* when they came to school. Scott told me once that their father had told them not to say thank you unless they really meant it. He didn't want them to adopt insincerity or something like that. He was . . . he was a strange man. But I expect you've already heard that from others?"

He nodded. "What about her? I gather she wasn't from Bethany?"

Her face did something complicated. "No, neither of them were. She might be Canadian, I think I heard that somewhere. And I heard he came from New York City, that his family had money, and yet he chose to . . . well, to live as though he didn't. He had unconventional ideas about things."

"Do you think he was ever abusive to her or to the boys?"

Barbara Falconer took a deep breath. Her hands twisted in her lap and when Warren glanced down at them, he saw the engagement ring catch the light. No wedding band. Engaged then. Not married. "It's hard to know, Mr. Warren. I didn't see bruises, if that's what you mean, but he could be stern while at the same time being quite . . . well, laissez-faire, I suppose. He really was a strange man. When my mother told me about the fire, I thought to myself, *She's made him mad in some way and this was his way of punishing her for it.* Do you see what I mean, he was the kind of man who instead of hitting her, would kill himself and burn their barn down? I'm sorry, I know that doesn't make much sense, but it's what I thought."

He studied her for a moment. "No, that's very interesting," he said. "Thank you."

"I don't know if you know, but his brother has come to town. I was at Collers' this morning and he came in, demanding to know where David Williamson's office was. He was so angry, and rude, and I knew before he said it that he must be Hugh Weber's brother. I wonder what their mother was like. She must have been a real witch." Barbara winked at him and stooped to return a wayward puppy to the box. "Wouldn't you like one of these puppies, Mr. Warren? They're from a champion bloodline. My father will sing the praises of them as retrievers if duck hunting is your thing."

Warren stood up too. There was something about her that lifted his mood. He couldn't help smiling at her. "They're beautiful, Miss Falconer. My job keeps me pretty busy, but I'll think about it. And thank you for your help."

⊠ ⊠ ⊠

Home again by seven, he decided to have his supper at the inn. Warren entered the tavern through a side door and told the waiter that he would eat up at the bar if that was okay. The man, who appeared to be the bartender as well, said that suited him just fine.

No one else came in.

He had half expected that Victor Weber might eat his supper here as well. After all, where else had he to go? But Weber didn't show up in the tavern.

Warren ordered clam chowder and tried to make small talk with the waiter, but he seemed totally uninterested, so Warren finished his clam chowder and asked for the check.

"Room number," the waiter, a dour older man, asked.

"No, I'm not staying here. I've recently moved to town." The waiter nodded and silently handed over the check. Warren found some cash in his pocket and paid, waving away the change. As he left, he wondered where Victor Weber was having his dinner. There weren't many options and he lingered in the lobby for a few minutes, looking through the tourist maps and information displayed against one wall, on the off chance, unrealized in the end, that they might meet.

The walk home through the quiet evening didn't take long. Though the green was empty of pedestrians, he had the sense of being watched from behind the windows that lined it. When he passed the Falconers' across the green, he found himself wondering if they were eating their dinner, if Barbara ate with her parents or with her fiancé, wherever he lived.

His own house—even he had started to think of it as the vicarage—was dark and silent. Next door, at the Bellowses, there was one light on downstairs. He poured himself a bourbon neat and sat in what was now his living room. He needed to call his parents and tell them he was settled and he thought about calling Tommy to discuss the case, then remembered he didn't have a phone yet. Anyway, there wasn't anything they could do about anything tonight. Tomorrow, he'd find out how much money Hugh Weber had had and whom he'd left it to.

Warren tried to read the Lawrence Durrell, which he'd picked up at a bookstore in Boston, but he kept losing his place and he finally walked around the rooms of his new house, shutting off lights, and then climbed the stairs to the bedroom.

His grief was strongest when paired with loneliness. It wasn't just Maria he missed, but himself when he was with Maria. He missed the feeling of being partnered, of having a place to go, someone to be accountable to. Now, he merely . . . floated. The bedroom was stuffy, the night air from outside only a few degrees cooler than the air inside. The moon was full or nearly so and the light muscled into the bedroom. He finished the bourbon, lay there staring at the dark ceiling, finally slept.

He was awakened by a loud knocking on the door. It was deep into the middle of the night, heading toward morning, he thought when he spied the olive-green sky outside his window. His watch, fumbled from the bedside table, read three A.M. Warren pulled on a shirt and trousers and took the stairs two at a time.

This time it was Alice Bellows herself, wearing a flamboyant yellow-and-pink floral silk dressing gown, her dark-and-gray hair let down and in a thick braid over one shoulder. "There's another fire up on Agony Hill," she said a bit breathlessly. "Tommy Johnson called. Chief Longwell and Pinky Goodrich are up there now with the volunteer fire department and he said you're to go up and meet them."

Ten

Once again, he could smell the fire as soon as he turned onto Agony Hill. Alice Bellows had said to go past the Webers' farm and keep going until he saw a tree shaped like a fork. The Weber house was dark, everything quiet as he passed, long moon shadows falling on the side of the house closest to the road. He imagined Sylvie Weber and the boys sleeping inside. He couldn't envision the inside of the house beyond the small glimpse he'd had through the windows, couldn't imagine what it contained. Were the furnishings simple or elaborate? Was the house tidy or messy?

The road became narrower and more desolate as he drove, the headlights of the Ford making bouncing pools of light on the dark road. There was one small house past the Weber farm and past that was only forest, crowding in on either side as the dirt road narrowed to a track. At what felt like must be close to the end of the road, the smell became stronger and he saw the tree, exactly like a fork, along with ten or so cars parked alongside it, including Pinky's battered cruiser and Roy Longwell's shiny Bethany Police one. He left the

Galaxie on the side of the road, grabbed an old flashlight from the glove compartment, and ran down the short driveway. There was a truck with a tanker on the back and the men were spraying water at the blaze, but Warren could see that it was futile. It wasn't much of a house, more like a cabin, built from logs like the ones in Western films, and it was almost completely engulfed in flames. At this point, they were mostly trying to prevent the fire from spreading to the trees, he thought.

"Detective." Chief Longwell, standing by the trucks, acknowledged Warren with a raised hand. He was wearing civilian clothes but he stood there with an air of authority you couldn't miss.

"What do we know? Who called it in?"

Longwell sighed. "Kids. They'd come up here to drink and saw the flames. They drove back down to one of the farms on the flat and used the phone there."

Warren surveyed the chaotic scene. He recognized David Williamson, in fire gear, sitting on the rear bumper of a pickup truck and drinking steaming liquid from a thermos top. A few other men stood around, looking grim. "Any idea about how it started?"

"Not yet. It'll be hard to find anything in that. But it's a hunting cabin," Longwell said. "Owners are from Boston. Name of Fredericks. Only built it last year. David Williamson said there wasn't any car here when he arrived but we won't know if anyone was inside until they put that out."

Warren stood around for a bit, watching as the flames died down under the stream of water and the men began to go in and check what was left. Pinky had thought to bring the camera and Warren asked him to coordinate with the firefighters and to get some photos of the scene.

"More than I think we'll need, right?" Pinky asked, winking at Warren.

"That's right. You got it."

Someone had brought coffee and they drank it while they watched some of the firefighters pack up their equipment, leaving a few men behind to keep hosing water on the smoking timbers. David William-son waved to Warren. The sun was beginning to rise and suddenly the woods around the cabin were glowing with a strange, moony light. It took Warren a moment to realize they were birch trees, bright white, a huge stand of them, and in the early sunlight, the trees looked like ghostly figures, standing on the hill.

Warren was looking up at the blur of pearly white when he saw movement in the trees. A person, not an animal. Slowly, he turned away so the lurker wouldn't know he'd been spotted. Warren pre-tended to tie his shoe, looking up at the hillside out of the corner of his eye. Sure enough, someone was standing behind a tree toward the top of the hill, watching the scene unfolding below. Warren walked slowly over to Pinky and whispered, "There's someone up in the trees. I'm going to circle around and see if I can get him there. Can you keep an eye on us, but without letting him know he's been seen?"

Pinky raised his eyebrows. "Sure thing. I'm gonna sit down on that stump over there and pretend I'm just taking a load off."

Warren pretended to wave goodbye to him and walked down the driveway before cutting back along the road and into the woods, then circling up and around behind the property. It was slow going, step-ping carefully so he wouldn't make a sound, and it took him twenty minutes to reach the top of the hill. The guy was still there, a couple hundred yards below him now, the rising sun revealing the outline of his body against the white trees and the hat pulled low over his face, and he was still hiding behind the tree and watching the men fight-ing the fire below. Warren counted to twenty and then he shouted, "Freeze. Police. Put your hands on the tree and stand still!"

The guy ran. He didn't seem to think about it, just took off toward the crest of the hill and disappeared in the other direction. He was fast.

Warren had been fast once too. He'd been St. Paul's track-and-field champion three years in a row and he used to keep in shape by sprinting at the Tufts track, running laps and then short distances. Once he'd graduated, he would drive to Medford; he'd used running as a valve for the stress from his job. But it had been ruined for him and it had been a long time since he'd visited a track.

Now, he crashed through the underbrush. There was no path and so he had to maneuver around small trees and scattered sticks as branches and brambles pulled at his clothes. The man had to dodge them too and Warren might have caught up to him, but for a sapling growing across the path; he tried to leap over it, but his right foot caught and he went down on his knees, his face hitting a protruding branch. He felt pain race through his body and when he put his hand up to his cheek, he felt blood.

Warren rolled over and lay back on the leaf-strewn ground. Above him, the trees reached toward the pale sky. He was beat. All that running had been a long time ago now. He felt drained of life, utterly spent and suddenly vulnerable, lying there on the ground like a wounded animal.

Longwell and Pinky came up the hill, stopping when they saw Warren.

"He get away?" Longwell called. "Should we keep chasing him?"

"Nah, he's gone," Warren said, carefully standing up and flexing his muscles to make sure everything was in place. "And I didn't see enough of him for it to be useful. But you could get some of your men to search. What's on the other side of the hill there? We probably ought to get someone down on the other side in case he comes out."

"Yeah," Longwell said. "We'll do that. It's fairly dense forest all over the hillside and then it comes down on River Road, down at the bottom of the hill, and borders Weber's farm."

Warren considered. "If he set this fire, maybe he set that fire too. Arsonists like to watch their handiwork, don't they?"

Longwell shrugged. "It's an idea. We'll get out there and look for him."

They walked back down to the staging area. The fire was under control now, a stream of dark smoke pouring from what was left. The camp would likely be a total loss.

"Anything inside?" Warren called out to the remaining firefighters. "Was our guy in the house before setting the fire?"

"Can't tell yet," someone called out. "It'll be a few hours before we can get in safely."

Warren did a quick search of the cleared land around the camp. There was a lovely view from up here, of the distant hills and fields, and in the near distance, a slope of the mountain. He found a couple of beer cans that looked new and had Pinky bag them to go back to the evidence room at the barracks. He was betting they had been dropped by teenagers like the ones who had reported the fire, but he could show Pinky how to lift fingerprints from them.

A cruiser pulled up and Tommy Johnson got out, joining Warren, who got him up to speed on the man in the woods. "Chief Longwell's going to organize a search," Warren said. "I'm going to go home and make something to eat and then head back to the barracks. You want to join me when you're done here?"

Tommy grinned. "You cooking?"

"Sure am. I have some fresh eggs and good bread in."

"The cooking detective," Tommy said, grinning. "I knew I'd get my money's worth out of you."

¤ ¤ ¤

Back in the house on the green, Warren, now with a bandage on his forehead where he'd scraped himself in the woods, carefully broke six eggs into the bubbling fat in his cast-iron pan, shaking salt across the glossy surface and watching as the white quickly clouded over in the heat. He cut two thick slices of bread and dropped them into the hot fat sizzling in the other skillet, turning them quickly and getting both sides golden brown before flipping them out onto plates and sliding the barely set eggs on top.

The coffee was done percolating and he poured two cups, pushing Tommy's over with a little pitcher of milk.

"Ahhh, that's good," Tommy said. "Judith's coffee is too damn weak, no matter how many times I tell her."

"Benefit of marrying into an Italian family," Warren said lightly. Tommy's eyes snapped up and he nodded without smiling, then sliced the toast and eggs into squares and popped one of them into his mouth, sighing.

"What do you think about this new fire?" Tommy asked, changing the subject.

"Feels like arson," Warren said. "That man watching? That's what they do, arsonists. They get a charge out of it, don't they?"

"You mean a lunatic?" Tommy asked.

Warren nodded. "There was a case like that in Charlestown couple years back, a man who went around setting fires in the middle of the night. He only did it when the occupants were asleep, so he'd kill as many people as possible. One family died when they couldn't get out, but the others escaped. He was disturbed, couldn't help himself."

Tommy chewed thoughtfully. "So you think we've got one on the loose here in Bethany?"

Warren shrugged. "Otherwise, it was an accident. The man we saw running away was, what? A vagrant of some kind? Do you get much of that sort of thing around here?"

Tommy, a bright yellow speck of yolk on his chin, considered that for a moment. "Not down this way so much. But you know, times are changing, Frankie."

Warren handed him a napkin. "Let me ask you something. Roy Longwell. What's he like to work with? He resent us being here?"

Tommy looked up from his food. "Roy? Why? He say anything to you?"

"Not exactly. Just a feeling I get. A lot of these local guys, they don't appreciate the detectives coming in and taking over when something's really interesting."

"Roy will be fine," Tommy said vaguely. "He's been around a long time, I guess. He knows everybody and everything that's ever happened in this part of the state. He'll be a good resource for you." He pushed the eggy bread around on his plate.

"Tommy." Warren leveled a skeptical look at him. "The least you can do is tell me what I'm walking into here."

Tommy bowed his head "Okay, okay, yeah, Roy Longwell's pretty protective of his turf. Guess he got used to doing his investigations the way he likes, but like I said, times are changing and we need to change with them, right? He's old school. Doesn't think we need all this fancy stuff. Those techniques I learned when I was down there at Harvard Medical School, when we met up to talk about this job? That's the stuff we need here and Longwell's skeptical."

"You have any recommendations for how to handle him?" Warren asked.

"Just do your job well and stay out of his way."

"You tell him why I left my job in Boston?"

"Nah. That's your business. He doesn't know a thing."

Warren nodded, to indicate that all was forgiven, though he retained a small sliver of resentment, and he didn't think Tommy was right about Longwell's ignorance of why Warren was in Vermont. He might not have the whole story, but he knew something. Warren was sure of it.

Tommy took a deep breath and finished his eggs, then looked around the kitchen. "Nice place here. You settling in okay?"

Warren stood up and took their plates over to the sink. "Yeah, I like it. I'm getting a feel for it. There's something about the landscape that kind of . . . calms you, you know?"

Tommy smiled. "I do. Did I ever tell you about when I took a job in Philadelphia? When Judith and I were first married? I couldn't take it. I walked out of my house and I was already dialed up to ten, the traffic, the noise, and the concrete and so forth. Here, I walk outside and I'm at zero. The events of the day may take me up to ten, but I can handle it because I started at zero. That's how I think of it anyway."

Warren watched him for a second. It was a vulnerable, human side of Tommy he hadn't seen much. "How long did you last?"

"Two years. It was Judith who decided for me. She said she wouldn't raise her children in the city. Soon as a position opened up here, we came back. Good decision. I liked the investigative work best and eventually moved over to the bureau."

"Well, I'm grateful for everything you've done for me," Warren told him. "It's good to be here." He nodded in what he hoped was a meaningful way that would let Tommy know that he intended the words to say that the peace of Bethany had allowed him not to think so much about Maria, which was true, though perhaps it was just the different scenery that had jogged his brain.

He wasn't sure if Tommy took his meaning because the older man jumped up and said, "Is that the time? I've got to hit the road. What are you doing today?"

Warren slugged the rest of his cup of coffee. He told Tommy about his visit to the lawyer's office and about Hugh Weber's brother. "Williamson's going to tell them about the will today. I want to get a sense of what she knew, Sylvie Weber. If she stands to inherit everything, well, we need to know that, right? And if the brother has a stake, then we ought to be looking into his movements the last couple of days."

Tommy nodded. "Get Pinky to start asking at the hotels and so forth. He working out okay for you so far?"

"He's a good kid," Warren said. "Has he always had his . . . problem?"

Tommy laughed. "Poor bastard. Yeah, I guess he has. Someone

told me he could never tell a lie when he was a kid, 'cause his face would give him away. Tough for a detective, but he seems to make up for it in other ways. Hope he works out for you."

"I like him. Hey, I have a good excuse to go poking around some more at Webers', don't I?" Warren added, "With this fire. I can start out asking if they saw anything, see if there's been any sign of our fire setter around."

Tommy studied him. "What are you thinking about Hugh Weber? This change things for a hotshot detective like you?"

Warren laughed. "I don't know about the hotshot part, but if there's one arsonist loose on Agony Hill, I have to wonder if it's the first time he's done his thing."

"Yeah, well, I gotta go," Tommy said, draining his coffee cup and making an appreciative sound. "Seems like you're on top of things, Frankie. I'll leave you to it."

It was only once he was gone that Warren remembered he'd wanted to ask about the burglary Fred Fielder had referenced. He'd have to call Tommy later. He rinsed their dishes and left them in the sink. Then he found the box containing his envelopes and writing paper and penned a quick note to his parents, letting them know he'd arrived and moved in and that he would call them once his phone was installed. Once he'd signed his name, he saw that he had only used half of the sheet of paper. The expanse of white mocked him—all the things left unsaid between Warren and his parents.

He stamped the envelope, addressed it, and dropped it in the mailbox at the end of the green. The duty completed, he felt a small wave of relief, tinged with something else, guilt maybe, about how quick he'd been to write rather than find a way to call. He shrugged it off and walked back to get the Galaxie for the drive up to Agony Hill.

Eleven

Alice slept until nine and woke up agitated, an unremembered worry lodged in her mind, tugging at her consciousness as she dressed and readied herself for the day.

After the phone had rung at three and she had gone next door to awaken Warren, she had lain awake for some time, confused thoughts ricocheting around in her brain. Finally, around five, she had drifted into a deep sleep that ended with the sound of Mildred banging on the door at nine.

Alice never slept until nine.

What was wrong with her? Her watcher, whoever they were, was on her mind, of course, and there were the fires—she would have to get more information in town today—but it was something else that was worrying her.

She dressed and drank the tea Mildred made for her, and it was while she was deadheading lilies that she realized. Lizzie Coller. That's what it was. When Alice had been in the store yesterday, she had felt that Lizzie was out of sorts. Now, she was sure of it. Clearly there was something wrong with Lizzie, and Alice's subconscious wanted to know what it was.

Perhaps her mysterious watcher would make himself known today as well. Alice didn't like the way the possibility of him just sat out there, unresolved. She wanted to know who it was, but it was entirely beyond her control and she didn't like it one bit.

She prepared herself for her day, taking a shopping basket and covering her hair with the large cherry-red silk scarf she'd bought in Paris in 1947. It was bright enough to be seen from anywhere on the green and she had with her a number of items to prolong her shopping trip.

First she stopped at the library, where she returned the Irving Wallace novel she'd borrowed. She hadn't read it yet and would have to take it out again, but it gave her the opportunity to be seen going in and out and to stop on the walkway outside to chat with some ladies she'd known for years through the church. She found them especially tiresome and boring to talk to, but this morning she made a special point of asking one about her daughter in Connecticut and inquiring after the other's husband's always-precarious health. They stood on the sidewalk for nearly twenty minutes. Certainly long enough, she decided.

Next she stopped at the store to purchase a can of cooking oil and some dry beans. Lizzie wasn't there, but her sister Dorothy was and Alice asked Dorothy for a wedge of cheddar from the big wheel behind the counter, both because she wanted some and because it took a bit of time.

"Where's Lizzie today?" Alice asked casually. Dorothy was wiping her father's huge cheese knife with a clean cloth.

Dorothy's face clouded over. "She's not feeling well," she said in a grim voice.

"Oh, I'm so sorry. Nothing serious, I hope." Alice watched Dorothy lean on the knife. Dorothy was five years older than Lizzie, already married and, Alice suspected from the way her apron strained over her middle, expecting sometime in the winter. The Collers were private about such things, though. Always had been. They wouldn't say anything until it was unmistakable.

"She'll be all right," Dorothy said. She wrapped the cheese in wax paper and taped it closed. Alice loved a wedge of cheese wrapped like that. It reminded her of going to buy it when she was a girl. She could almost taste the slight salty, tangy bite of it on her tongue, the way the cheese crumbled when you took a piece.

"I haven't seen Richie in a few days. Has he been ill too?" Alice asked, tucking the proffered cheese into her basket and handing over the money after Dorothy rang it up on the huge brass-and-chrome register that sat on the counter like a king on a throne.

Dorothy grunted something about not knowing but Alice wasn't fooled. *Something* was going on with Lizzie and her beau. Perhaps he had wronged her, stepped out with another girl, and the Collers had fired him for his disloyalty.

Dorothy's face didn't invite any more questions.

"Has my paper come yet, Dorothy?" Alice asked, though she knew very well it hadn't or Dorothy would have handed it over. Dorothy always seemed put out by the special order of Alice's *New York Times*. Alice knew she thought Alice ought to make do with the local papers.

"No. It should be here after lunch. Do you want the other papers?"

"No, thank you, Dorothy. I'll come back this afternoon and get them all at once."

Dorothy shrugged dispiritedly.

Outside the store Alice saw Jean Fielder and asked about *her* daughter, who was now ten and had begun to study the piano, and then, as though it were an afterthought, about whether Fred had any information about the fire last night up on Agony Hill. If Fred did, Jean did not yet know of it. But she did nod toward a tall man in a well-cut jacket walking quickly along the sidewalk in front of the inn. "That's Hugh

Weber's brother," she said. "I guess he's here for the funeral, maybe. I heard from Ginny that he stormed into David's office demanding his inheritance. Apparently, the new state trooper living in town had to arrest him."

Alice thought perhaps Jean was inflating the drama—Jean tended to do that—but it was clear that something had happened and that Hugh Weber's brother was angry about the will. That was very interesting to Alice.

Of course, no one would be getting anything while they were investigating the fire at the Webers'. Had there been insurance? If it was determined to be suicide, then Sylvie Weber wouldn't get anything. Alice wondered how the family would manage in the meantime. The oldest boy could do a lot of what needed to be done, she thought. But could he handle other things around the farm? Did Sylvie even know how to go to the bank and ask to withdraw money for groceries? Was there any money to withdraw? Alice would have to see if there was something she could do for them.

She made a note on the ongoing to-do list she kept in her head. It had taken years of discipline to hone this skill, the visualization of the list, the constant adding and subtracting. She'd gotten so good at it that she rarely needed to write things down at all.

Take a basket of food up to the Webers, she added. Really, she should have done it before now. It was this man, this stranger, who had distracted her, whoever he was.

All in all, Alice was on the green for an hour and by the time she ducked into the Universalist church and took a seat in the rear pew, she was a bit sweaty and ready for a rest.

She waited for nearly twenty minutes but no one arrived to talk to her, so she walked slowly back to her house and stood outside for a long moment, examining the blooms on her Asiatic lilies in the front beds. They were small for the date but then it had been dry for at least three weeks. *Tell Billy to water twice as often the next week or so.* Finally she went around to the side gate and entered the garden.

Mildred had returned home to make lunch for her husband and the gardens were peaceful, lying in wait, all the flowers and plants waiting for . . . something. Alice closed her eyes and inhaled. A breeze stirred.

She waited. This was where the stranger would speak to her. It would be simple for him to get over the back fence or even to just walk through the gate, with Mildred and Billy both gone. Oddly, she was no longer afraid. She sat on the bench at the back and waited and after a few moments, she heard a twig break in the hydrangeas.

"Hello," she said, turning around just as he stepped out from behind the willow tree at the back of the garden. "Oh, Arthur. What a relief! I should have known it was you. We're quite alone. My woman has gone home for lunch. Oh, how long has it been?" She had the urge to giggle, to cheer. She had been so afraid and after all it was just Arthur Crannock.

Arthur was older certainly, his hair mostly white now and a lot less of it too, but he retained the boyishness she remembered and he was still fit. He was Ernie's age, or the age Ernie would have been, so that made him sixty-one now. His blue eyes twinkled at her from an unremarkable face. He had the quality that so many of his kind had— the ability to disappear utterly, to take on the characteristics of their surroundings, to look unremarkable. In her blooming garden, he was a deceptively commonplace thing, a simple coreopsis, a retiring ornamental grass.

"Hello, Alice. It's lovely to see you again. You're looking fine." He was holding a small white box and he handed it to her and sat down, close enough that she could smell his spicy shaving lotion. Bay rum, she thought. With a hint of lime.

She opened the box. Inside was a small piece of blue pottery with a silver loop so it could be worn as a necklace. "Arthur!" Alice said, taking it out and turning it over in her hand. "It's lovely." It was Egyptian faience, a wedjat eye amulet, meant to protect the wearer.

"I happened to find it the other day and I thought you would really appreciate it." She couldn't tell from his voice if he meant anything more than that by the gift. It was a possibility with Arthur, of course, ruled as he was by his old handler's obsession with transactions. He might be reminding her of Cairo, might be hinting that he knew something he could hold over her.

On the other hand, it might just be a thoughtful gesture.

"Thank you, Arthur," Alice said, leaning back on the bench and choosing to accept the simpler explanation, for the moment anyway. "Ahhhhh, I love this time of year. The summer is past the halfway point, you know. Things are in motion. The air can be so sweet, so very sweet, in August."

"Nothing like the air in Cairo, though," Arthur said.

"No," she said, watching him closely again. "Why are you here, Arthur?"

He smiled. "I wanted to give you a heads-up, before any awkward meetings on the sidewalk. You're a good actress, old girl, but it would be asking a lot. Wanda and I have bought a place down the road in Woodstock. We'll be spending summers and weekends here and I wanted to let you know. You'll see us around of course, since we're so close. Didn't want it to be a shock."

Alice let out a breath. She had been expecting something else, something more . . . concerning. "How wonderful," she said. "What made you choose this area?"

"Wanda has always wanted a place in the country and now that I'm based in Boston, well, it made sense. We've always remembered yours and Ernie's wonderful stories about Vermont."

"Well, I will look forward to seeing you and Wanda soon," Alice said. It was a bit surreal, sitting there having a pleasant conversation with a man who had hopped her fence and hidden in her garden to avoid being seen. "Tell me about the house."

He told her all about it, the Victorian on the Woodstock green. The sale had gone through last month. It had a lovely back garden. They would have to repair the roof and there was some updating to be done, but all in all it was a lovely house. A friend from Wanda's girlhood also had a place in town and she was delighted to be able to walk to see her in the mornings. They were finding the social life very diverting.

Finally he stood up and glanced around the garden.

Alice knew there was something else coming but she wondered whether he would pass it on this visit. He gave her a quick kiss on the cheek, whispering, "I'll be in touch, old girl. Something else afoot you ought to know about but it will have to wait."

It was to be another visit then. She found she was pleased, to know that he would be back. The anticipation, not knowing when or how he would make contact—she had forgotten how much she craved it.

"You and Wanda must come for supper," she said. "Shall I arrange a chance meeting?"

"That would be lovely. She may suggest calling you as well. She knows you're up here."

"What's your work these days? Still the institute?" During the years that she and Ernie had lived in Washington, Arthur's cover had been a foreign policy institute that often sent him abroad on research trips.

"Yes, same as always. It's served me well over the years." He was ready to go. She could feel his energy. But she wanted something from him. She hadn't even realized she did want it until she spoke the words.

"Arthur, I wonder, would you do me a favor? The man who's moved in next door, Franklin Warren. He's from Boston, was a police detective down there. Now he's been hired by the Vermont State Police. He'll be a detective out of the Bethany barracks here. It doesn't quite add up. I'd love a bit of background."

"Franklin Warren. You'll have it as soon as I do." Arthur smiled. "Goodbye, old friend."

Alice turned away discreetly, as though she were allowing him to adjust a piece of clothing. She slipped the faience amulet into her skirt pocket, feeling its weight against her hip. It called up a memory she couldn't quite access. She had felt so relieved when it had turned out to be Arthur, but the weight of the amulet in her pocket had her on edge again. Arthur knew things about her and of course she knew things about Arthur too. She thought Arthur knew she could be trusted, but she knew better than anyone that if it were a matter of information that could be damaging to the interests of the agency, of the country, and if there was a question of trust or lack of it, well, then things like history and friendship didn't matter at all.

Arthur, in Vermont. It had her off-kilter now. She had always thought of Vermont as her haven from the world, the place where no matter what, she would be safe. But Arthur and Wanda were here now and she found that she now had more questions than answers.

"Arthur?" she started to say. When she turned back, he was gone.

Twelve

The skies over Agony Hill were gray and thick with clouds, the air hot and close. Warren got out of the car and stood there for a moment as a weak breeze pushed the humid day around, then died away. The smell of smoke was still strong alongside the tang of animals and manure that rose from the barnyard. Somewhere in the distance, a cow bellowed and a dog barked. No one came out so he went up onto the porch and knocked at the door. He could hear voices inside but no one came so he knocked again, louder, and called out, "Hello? Mrs. Weber?"

Suddenly the door opened and she was standing there, wiping her hands on a dishcloth. He heard the laughter of children from inside the house. Her hair was messy and there were smudges of dirt on her face and long streaks of wetness down the front of her apron. She had been washing dishes, he thought.

"I'm so sorry to bother you," he said. "You must have heard about the fire last night at the camp at the end of the road. Is it okay if I come in and ask and your children some questions?"

She looked scared, but nodded, and stood aside so he could come into the house. It was cooler in here, and he followed her through a messy room littered with stacks of books and papers, tools, old bottles, and cardboard boxes filled with strange assortments of dishes and knickknacks. A contraption Warren took to be a spinning wheel sat at one end of the room, a basket filled with fluffy wool next to it. Warren remembered that David Williamson had said she sold yarn.

The kitchen was at the rear of the house, a large room with a table and chairs against the back wall and a huge stone sink. A wood cookstove took up one corner of the room and was the source of the hot, close air and the reason for the open windows. There was no electric stove. The boys seemed to fill the room; the oldest one, a teenager who was whittling a piece of wood into something that looked like a doll, was sitting at the table and he looked up, his eyes worried and suspicious. He was old enough to feel a sense of responsibility to protect the family. It would be a hard life for him from here on out, Warren thought.

Sylvie Weber stopped to tousle his hair, reassuring him before she went back to the stove where she had two large pots steaming. With a pair of long-handled tongs, she retrieved a glass jar from one of them. The air smelled of sugar and berries. The other boys were playing with some marbles on the floor. Warren saw what Barbara Falconer meant about them looking different. There was something feral about these boys; they seemed of a different time in their patched and too-large clothes, their strange, ragged haircuts. The second-youngest boy had what looked like bloodstains all over his dingy white T-shirt. Berry stains, Warren realized, seeing a bowl on the counter.

"We're making jam," Sylvie Weber said, explaining the mess of production. "There were so many berries and they don't . . . well, they don't wait for you, do they?"

Warren nodded and sat down at the table. "I'm sorry, can you tell me the names of all of the boys, just so I make sure I have it right?"

He winked at the boy sitting closest to him on the floor and said, "I wouldn't want to mix you up with one of your brothers, would I?"

The boy, not realizing it was a joke, shook his head solemnly. "What's your name?" Warren asked him.

He whispered, "Andrew Charles Weber, sir." Warren wrote it down. The kid at least pronounced it the American way.

"And how old are you?"

"Twelve." He was a startlingly good-looking kid, with his mother's blue eyes and exactingly regular features, high cheekbones, and thick dark hair that came down below his ears.

"Tell me your brothers' names and their ages, if you would."

Andrew looked to his mother and she nodded. He said, "Scott is fourteen." He pointed to the boy at the table. "Louis is six, Daniel is two." Warren glanced at Sylvie Weber. She couldn't be more than his age—thirty this year. She must have had the oldest one when she was a teenager herself.

"Thank you, Andrew. Or is it Andy?" He smiled down at the boy, trying to convey that he was a friend, but the boy still looked terrified. "Andy's all right?" The boy nodded.

"Did you all hear there was a fire last night at a hunting camp down at the end of your road here?" he asked all of them.

"I heard the trucks going by," Sylvie Weber said. "In the morning, we could smell the smoke and Scott drove the truck down to see."

Scott looked up from his whittling. He had a prominent chin and broad face that wasn't as classically handsome as his brother's, but Warren thought he saw kindness and humility in it. His darker blue eyes were guileless when he said, "Tried to go see. They wouldn't let me through. Do they know what happened?"

"We don't know exactly. The fire may have been an accident, but . . . You haven't seen anyone around, have you, anyone strange in the woods, anyone who seemed out of place?"

He happened to be looking at Andy's face and surprise flashed across the boy's eyes. Warren was sure he was about to say something when his mother cut in quickly, "No, we haven't seen anyone."

Warren studied her face before she turned back to the stove. Had she been too quick to cut in, as if she wanted to prevent the boy from saying something? He wasn't sure. "What about you boys? Have you seen anyone around your farm, or in the woods?" He met Andy's eyes, but the boy looked away and stayed silent. His brothers were quiet too, the little one clutching his mother's leg now and hiding his face behind her apron.

Sylvie Weber went back to the jars on the counter, plunging them into the huge pot of hot soapy water and swishing them around before taking them out and lining them up on the counter. "I'm sorry, Mr. Warren. I don't think we saw anything at all."

He watched her, sure she was lying to him now. But what to do about it?

"Mrs. Weber, I have a few questions I'd like to ask you and Andy. Just you two. Would it be possible for the other boys to . . ." He raised his eyebrows meaningfully but she just stared at him, not understanding. So he went on, awkwardly, "Could they leave us alone for a moment?"

The eldest boy, Scott, was the one who caught his meaning. "I'll take them out to check for the kittens again, Ma," he said. The younger boys followed Scott out the side door. He closed the door quietly behind them.

Andy looked up at him, then down at his hands. Sylvie Weber stood in front of the stove, wary, her eyes fearful.

"Andy, are you sure you haven't seen anything strange around lately, perhaps someone who shouldn't be on Agony Hill, someone you didn't recognize? I know that everything must be so confusing right now, with the fire here and with . . . your father's death. Maybe you forgot when I first asked you."

The boy didn't look up. "No," he said. "Nothing like that."

"Are you certain? You know how important it is that you are always honest with a person like me, a police officer, don't you?"

Andy nodded, still not looking up. Warren waited a long moment and then he said, "Okay, why don't you join your brothers. I'll talk to your mother now." The boy, shoulders hunched, stood and glanced back at Sylvie before scuttling out of the house.

Once they heard the door close, Sylvie went back to her work at the stove.

Warren considered how to approach her. If he said right up front that he thought the boy was lying, she was likely to close up and not give him anything. So he decided to start with the brother. "Mrs. Weber, I need to ask you about your husband's brother, Victor Weber. My understanding from when I was here yesterday was that you had never met him. Is that correct?"

"Yes," she said after a long moment. "Hugh didn't talk to his family. I think they . . . didn't like him marrying me and they didn't like him living here. Living the way we live, I guess you'd say. I don't know. When his father died, we didn't go to the funeral. I would have." She turned around and smiled shyly. "I would have liked to go to New York, to see it. But Hugh didn't want to. He said he was always a disappointment to them and he might as well keep on disappointing them."

"Do you know that he is in town?" he asked her.

She had focused on the steaming pot again when she said, "Well, Mr. Williamson called at the Uptons' to say I should come down to his office at two today. That Hugh's brother was here and that he wanted to talk to us about Hugh's will." She had a thermometer clipped to the side of the pot and she unclipped it and turned it toward the light to read it. "The message was that I should call Mr. Williamson if I minded Hugh's brother being there."

Warren waited. "And do you?"

"Do I what?" She licked a finger and then wiped jam from the glass-covered thermometer.

"Mind him being there?"

She turned, perplexed. "I don't think so. Mr. Williamson said that it would be helpful to have us both there."

Warren watched her scoop some jam from the pot with a spoon and let it run off back into the pot. "Do you have a ride down to town? I'd be happy to drive you. Mr. Williamson has asked me to be available, since your brother-in-law seemed quite upset when he stopped by the office yesterday."

"About Hugh?" She turned, holding an empty jar in a pair of metal tongs and looking confused. "They weren't very close. Hugh hated Victor. He complained about him all the time, about how he was a tool of the forces of capitalism." There was a small edge of sarcasm to the words that made him think she had not been completely blind to her husband's flaws.

"I think he was curious about the will. Did your husband ever explain it all to you? What would happen to his property and, uh, assets, if he should die?"

She shook her head, then turned to look at him. "Will we have to move? I never even thought of that. I didn't . . . Oh." She lifted the thermometer again and whatever she saw on it made her forget what she'd been saying. With the tongs, she took three more steaming jars from the pot and put them on the towel spread out on the table. Then she used a ladle to take the sweet-smelling ruby jam from the other pot and pour it through a funnel into the jars. Quickly, she took lids out of the large pot and put them on the jars, then flipped the jars upside down next to a long row of them on a towel. "*Do* you think we'll have to move?" she asked when she was done. "How does it work when someone . . . dies?"

He didn't sugarcoat it. He didn't think he would be doing her any favors by lying to her. "Mrs. Weber, even if the farm is left to you in your husband's will, you would need money for its upkeep, for things like the electricity and for groceries and property taxes."

She nodded, worried now, and he felt a flash of guilt at introducing the idea of them being turned out. Better she faced up to it, though.

He didn't know what else to say, so he just stood up and told her he wanted to see if there was any evidence related to the investigation into the fire at the camp. "I'm going to go for a little walk in your woods, if that's okay. I'll check in with you when I get back and then I can take you down to Mr. Williamson's office. At about a quarter to two."

She nodded, focused on her task again but newly preoccupied. It was very hot in the kitchen now, the steam from the pots on the big stove doing its work. They were both sweating and Warren rolled up his sleeves, embarrassed by the large circles beneath his arms.

He let himself out and walked around the side of the farmhouse toward the cleared pastureland and the woods beyond. Now that he'd seen the map of Agony Hill, he saw how the wedge of land behind the hunting camp doubled back, abutting the Webers' farm back in the dense woods behind their fields. He skirted the fence line, keeping an eye on the cows who were standing quietly and watching him. He didn't think any of them were bulls, but he wanted to be sure. When he got to the end of the field, he was able to hop over a low stone wall and then he was in the woods.

It was immediately cool beneath the trees and he walked due south, toward what he imagined was the back of the camp parcel. Once he found it, he'd retrace the supposed arsonist's path and then walk back toward the Webers' along the most logical route.

The woods were thicker than he'd thought they would be and though he'd left his suit jacket behind in the car, he could feel his shirt and tie and trousers getting snagged by twigs and brambles. He should have worn dungarees for this job. Next time he'd know.

It took him twenty minutes of careful walking between the trees before he saw the remains of the camp. One car—the fire marshal's, he assumed—sat in the drive. Warren walked up the hillside, following the path he'd taken last night and stopping at the spot where he'd tripped. The hill crested here and he could see a path through the low brambles and weeds growing along the hillside. He advanced carefully, walking to the side of the path so as to preserve any evidence and scanning the route the man had taken for cigarette butts or anything else he might have dropped. The path disappeared once it hit the tree line and Warren started jogging, looking for the easiest way through the trees. Their arsonist would have been scared, and he would have taken the route that would have meant the least ducking and jumping over stumps.

He kept going, unsure now of where he was and where the Webers' farm was, but he was seized with a desire to press on, as though he was suddenly in the man's head and knew exactly where he'd gone. A barely visible path drew him through the woods, toward the sound of water in the distance.

As he went, the rushing sound became louder and after a few minutes of almost jogging, he came out by a sort of pond. Except it wasn't a pond but a large, hollowed-out pool where a waterfall passed over a wall of rocks and fell dramatically, lingering long enough to form an area deep enough for bathing, before making its way into the brook where it disappeared down into the trees again.

It was a paradise, a fairyland, the sort of place where you might expect to see a water nymph sunning herself on a rock.

It looked so cool and inviting that Warren, who was now sweating from his run through the woods, couldn't help himself. He stepped carefully onto the rocks and bent down to fill his hands with the cold water, splashing it on his face and drinking as much as he could take.

When he stood up again, he'd somehow lost his bearings.

Had he come from this direction or that one? When he looked into the woods, everything looked the same, green and sun-dappled.

Something about the pool disoriented him; oddly, his watch had stopped and he had no idea how much time had passed, and instead of going carefully, he ran up into the woods, seeking high ground so he could see where he was, could look for the Webers' barns. But every time he thought he'd reached a high spot, there was another one beyond it that was even higher.

Within minutes, he was completely and hopelessly lost. He walked aimlessly, trying to mark the way he'd come with stones dropped on the forest floor, like Hansel and Gretel, but they disappeared on the ground when he tried to find them again. Low-hanging branches scratched his face and arms. The trees grew thickly and they all looked the same, the trunks sometimes wound around each other to form strange, embracing shapes.

He could feel panic starting to grow. Surely, if he didn't come out, someone would come looking for him. But who? Tommy might go to his house tomorrow if he didn't show up at the barracks, but by then he would have spent the whole day and night in the woods. Would Sylvie Weber come to look for him if he didn't come back to drive her to town? Somehow he thought not.

"Get ahold of yourself, Warren," he said out loud. This was Vermont, not Wyoming. A few miles' walk in any direction would bring him to a farm. Surely it would?

And then he heard it, the low whine of a tractor. He followed the sound for a few minutes and came out at the edge of a field. A tractor was slowly crossing it at the other end. One of the boys was driving it. He was right behind the Webers' house.

Relief poured through him and he burst out onto the field, wanting to shout to someone that he was okay, that he would survive, but of course that was ridiculous. No one even knew that a drama had played out in the woods in which he'd imagined himself lost forever. The boy didn't even see him.

He walked quickly back to the house and this time, he found Sylvie Weber alone on the porch, a large bowl of beans on the table in front of her. She was snapping the ends off and throwing them onto the grass, where a few chickens were quickly gobbling them.

She looked up in surprise. "Are you all right?" His face was scratched, his clothes wet in the front.

"I must look a bit terrifying," he said. "I'm fine. I got turned around. It sounds ridiculous, but I thought I was lost in the woods."

She smiled. She had changed her clothes—she was now wearing a sleeveless dress in golden yellow—and brushed her hair. "That happened to me when I first came here," she said. "You can always follow the brook, though. Just walk along and you'll either come out at the river or the road."

But he'd thought of something when he was in the woods, thinking about all of the intersecting brooks and fields and property lines.

He studied her as she watched the chickens. "How did your husband get along with the farmers down at the bottom of Agony Hill? I saw on the map that your fields abut the other farms. That must have made for conflict sometimes."

A small frown touched her lips. "It did," she said. "Hugh didn't know how to make friends very well. He didn't really understand how to get along with people. Mr. Spaulding was always complaining about our pigs running loose and instead of apologizing, Hugh went to war with him over it." She gestured vaguely. "Mr. Spaulding wanted to buy our back field and Hugh couldn't just say no. He took it personally. I don't . . . I tried to explain. It was because he was from New York, I think. From the city. He had different ways."

Something occurred to Warren then. People in town must have already understood what Warren had understood before in the kitchen: Hugh Weber may have left the farm to his young wife—Warren would know that soon enough—but surely she would put it up for sale within months. Her boys weren't old enough to keep it going on their own. As he'd told her, she would have to come up with tax payments and money for animal feed and insurance. Hugh Weber's death might benefit one of those farmers. You'd only have to wait for Sylvie Weber to sell the farm. Desperate, she might take a price that was far less than what it would be worth otherwise.

"What did he do?" he asked her.

"Oh, he just yelled at Mr. Spaulding, told him he was insulting us, that sort of thing. Threats." She shook her head as though it had all been a silly joke.

"What about the other farm down there?"

"Mr. Hatchett wanted to buy it too, but he knew how to handle Hugh. He just sent a letter and then stayed quiet." A tiny smile turned up the corners of her mouth.

Warren felt a passing buzz of curiosity. At some point he would find out about these relationships. But for now, they needed to get to the meeting.

He thought of something else then, though. "How did he find this place? Originally, I mean. If he was from New York City?"

She looked up. "It was before I met him, but he said he came to live on a farm with some other people. They were all connected to a man Hugh always referred to as the Prophet. His real name was Jeffrey." Warren's face must have shown his surprise because she smiled a little and said quickly, "It was just Hugh's joke, calling him the Prophet. This man had a farm and they were going to create a peaceful community there, but Hugh didn't get along with him. He said Jeffrey wanted to tell everyone what to do. And he took money from Hugh. He got angry if I asked about it. That's how he found out about this place, though, because the farm, Jeffrey's farm, was in Bethany. I don't know where exactly."

Warren checked his watch. He'd see if Pinky knew anything about this Jeffrey character. But now they had to get back down to town. "Shall we go?" he asked.

"Yes, I'm ready," she said, standing up. She was holding something behind her back. "I got lost once when I was a little girl. You know, I thought I'd never find my way home again. I was terrified.

When I found home again, I tried to explain that I'd been through . . . something. I tried to tell them, but I'd only been gone an hour or two. I felt like I'd gone away to the land of eternal youth, though, like I'd been gone years and years there, but back home it was only a short time. No one understood. Here, take this home with you. It's very good, raspberry. Keep it upside down for a little while, to make sure it seals, though." She had been holding a jar of jam and now she handed it to him. It was still warm, the quilted shape of the glass catching the sunlight and refracting it onto his hand. "When you eat it, you'll be going back in time to today."

Flustered by the kindness, unsure if he should take it, he stammered out a thank-you. She picked up a basket that had balls of yarn in it, and followed him to the car. When she settled into the seat next to him, the basket at her feet, he was surprised to find that she was wearing perfume, something delicate and expensive-smelling that reminded him of citrus groves.

He thought about trying to make conversation, but he wasn't sure what to say, and he felt oddly self-conscious about saying something banal, so they drove in silence all the way back to town.

Thirteen

Alice had the silver waiting when Mildred returned from lunch. The cutlery was spread out on a sheet on the table in the dining room and she had put the polish and three clean rags out for Mildred to use. A steaming pot of strong coffee was ready in the kitchen.

Mildred's delight was evident. She liked polishing silver. Alice knew she found it relaxing and satisfying, something Alice understood, and when she sensed Mildred was feeling down or needed a treat, she would have her polish the silver whether it needed it or not, or ask her to spend a day ironing table linens. Mildred would turn on the radio and let her mind drift as she completed the tasks. Alice wondered if it was the only time in her days when she could just think. At home, she had a husband and two grown sons who wanted meals and clean clothes and conversation and Alice thought that she must like letting her brain wander and think about what it wanted to think about, rather than reacting to the men in her life.

"I'll give a hand, Mildred," Alice said. "Would you like a coffee while we work?"

Mildred looked vaguely surprised, but not unhappy. She said she would love a coffee and started on the forks while Alice went to get it. Alice turned up the radio and they worked in peace for a bit before she said, "Remind me to go get my papers later. I was at Collers' this morning and my *Times* hadn't come yet. It was odd, you know, but Lizzie wasn't there. Dorothy said she was feeling ill. I hope it's nothing serious."

Mildred took her time, carefully wiping the fork in her hand and then saying, "I don't think it's a physical ailment, Mrs. Bellows. Helen Talbot told me that Lizzie's young man has been fired and she was so angry with Bob that she's refusing to work."

Alice looked up sharply. Well, this was interesting. What could poor, placid Richie have done to warrant his firing? Whatever it was, it must have been ambiguous enough that Lizzie herself was not convinced of the justification.

"Whatever could Richie have done?" Alice asked. "He's such a . . . respectable young man."

"That's what I always thought," Mildred answered. "But Dorothy told Helen that her father suspected Richie of stealing and fired him." She didn't look up at Alice or raise her eyebrows, but Alice could hear the surprise in her voice.

Alice stared at Mildred. "Stealing? Richie? He's the last person I'd ever suspect."

"I know. That's what Dorothy said. But her father is set on it."

"What is he supposed to have taken?"

"Cartridges," Mildred said.

"Cartridges? Oh, for a hunting rifle, you mean?" Alice's husband Ernie had not been a hunter, though of course he'd known how to shoot. He had taught Alice to shoot a pistol, and of course her father had been a deer hunter.

"Richie is a hunter and he was working alone when the cartridges disappeared. I guess Bob had just put them on the shelf so he knew exactly how many there were and when he went to check, eight boxes had gone!"

"But couldn't someone have come in and stolen them? Why does he think it was Richie?"

"I don't know. He must have known no one else was in the store. Dorothy was quite upset about it all. Mostly because she had to work extra hours to cover for Lizzie. And Bea is so upset. Lizzie won't speak to her father."

Well. Alice worked quietly for a bit and then at three she said, "Go home early if you want, Mildred. I appreciate your attention to the silver. I have things to do and Sylvie Weber may stop by later with some yarn. Feel free to take some of the fruitcake Frannie brought. You know me and fruitcake. I detest it; it's all for you and Herb and the boys."

Mildred looked delighted at her good fortune, sighing happily and attacking the polishing with new vigor. "Don't forget to go and get your papers, Mrs. Bellows," she sang out after she cleared the lunch things.

As if Alice could.

Alice found Dorothy at the counter, ringing up a pile of tea towels and a few cans of carrots for Sarah Bertram. Alice pretended to browse, wandering toward the back of the store where the hardware was displayed. She took a box of nails from the wall; Billy had mentioned that he needed some to fix a fencepost in the garden. She swept her eyes along the shelves, seeking out the boxes of ammunition that Bob Coller kept there for the hunters and farmers. She ducked down, as though she was picking up a small dropped item on the floor and found that she was entirely concealed from Dorothy and anyone else in the store. She didn't know enough to know which sort of ammunition it was that might have been stolen, but her investigation proved one thing: if someone had come in without Richie noticing, he would have been able to put the boxes of cartridges into a pocket or a bag without Richie seeing him.

Or her, Alice reminded herself.

Once Sarah was gone, the bell on the door ringing behind her, Alice approached the counter and said, "I'll have my papers now, thank you, Dorothy."

Dorothy pushed them over—the *Times* headline was about the Vietnam protesters in Washington—and rang up the papers and the nails. "It's gotten hot, hasn't it?" she grumbled.

"Yes, it has, Dorothy," Alice said. "I don't like it. And of course, I feel a bit unsettled with the fire and Hugh Weber and now a second fire. Doesn't it seem like there have been a great too many *events* lately?"

"That's right," Dorothy said. "Especially for summer. Did you hear that they almost caught the man responsible for the fire at the camp? He might be someone we know. Mrs. Fielder said that they saw someone watching from the woods and tried to catch him but he got away. Could be anyone. The new policeman living next to you chased him into the woods but he disappeared. They think maybe he was some sort of lunatic. Imagine it, a lunatic on the loose in Bethany! Maybe it was him that killed Mr. Weber!" It was the most animated Alice had ever seen Dorothy in all the years she'd known her. But this was interesting. Perhaps if some sort of vagrant was living in Bethany, he had been the one to steal the cartridges. She would have to get some more information out of her new neighbor.

"Thank you, Dorothy," she said. "I trust Lizzie will feel better soon so you can have a rest. You work so hard. I hope your parents appreciate all you do."

This was a calculated gambit. Dorothy did not feel her parents appreciated her. As expected, it unleashed her normally contained emotions.

"Well, my dad only has himself to blame." Dorothy looked around to make sure they were alone in the store. "He accused Richie of stealing. Richie said he didn't and they should have Chief Longwell come in and investigate. He said how could Dad even think that and then he quit and Lizzie got caught in the middle. She said she wouldn't work or get out of bed until Dad apologized to Richie, but Dad is stubborn and he says Richie is the only one who could have stolen the cartridges. Ma and I don't know what to do."

Alice studied Dorothy. "What do you think, Dorothy? Did Richie take them, do you think?"

"I don't know what to think, Mrs. Bellows. Richie is . . . funny sometimes. He keeps a lot to himself, but stealing, I wouldn't have thought. He's stubborn, though. Maybe he took the cartridges, thinking he'd pay out of his wages, and then when Dad found him out he got too hot under the collar to admit it. Lizzie won't say anything so I don't know what she thinks. It's got us all mixed up around here. I don't like it. There's bad air here now."

Alice looked around the store. She knew exactly what Dorothy meant. There was a noxious atmosphere in Collers', as though the air had absorbed all of the cross words and hurt feelings and was refusing to let it go. The store had always been a place of refuge and nostalgia for Alice. When she'd been away and returned home, she never felt she'd really *landed* until she'd been in to get the papers and hear the news. But now, it felt ruined.

Dorothy handed her change over and said, haltingly, "Do you think you could ask around, Mrs. Bellows? You're so good at finding out about things. Everyone in Bethany says so. Remember how you found out what happened to the money that went missing from the drugstore register last year?" Alice nodded. That had been a simple case of forgetfulness, easily solved, but she didn't say that to Dorothy, who went on breathlessly, "Well, I thought maybe you could see if, well, if there's any chance it wasn't Richie. If you think it was some-one else, well, then I would go to Dad and stand up for Lizzie. But if it was Richie, well, then Lizzie's better off, isn't she?"

Alice tucked the box of nails into her basket. She tried not to smile. She wanted Dorothy to think it had been her idea. "Of course, Doro-thy," she said. "You leave it to me."

Fourteen

They convened in David Williamson's office a few minutes after two. Warren had stopped in front of his house, leaving Sylvie Weber in the car while he ran inside to change his shirt. She'd been quiet on the drive, looking out the window and clutching her basket and a small notebook and pencil. She was very nervous, Warren thought, and he wanted to ask her why—if it was the anticipation of meeting Victor Weber for the first time or if she was still afraid of losing the house. He didn't know what to say to her if that was the case, though, so he stayed quiet and held the door for her as they went into the lobby.

Victor Weber had already arrived, and when Williamson showed them into his office, Sylvie Weber hesitated before stepping over the threshold.

"Sylvie," Victor said, offering her his hand, suddenly charming. "I'm sorry that we are only meeting for the first time under these sad circumstances." She shook his hand and nodded, but didn't answer, carefully placing her basket of yarn on the floor. She was still holding the small notebook and as she sat down in the seat Williamson offered her, she clutched it in her lap. Victor Weber was actually quite a handsome man, Warren saw now, though he was haughty and didn't seem capable of smiling. Warren made his way to a chair at the side of the room, so he would have a good view of both Sylvie's and Victor's faces.

"Now," Williamson said. "You all know each other. I offered to give Mrs. Weber a private accounting of the contents of the will, which is her right, but she said it was fine to do it once and to have Mr. Weber present since he is named as the executor. I've allowed Detective Warren to be here as the details of Mr. Weber's last will and testament may have some relevance to his investigation. It seems . . . efficient to deliver the information at one time. I assume there are no objections?" The look Williamson gave Victor Weber seemed to convey that they all knew why Warren was here, even if Williamson was too much a gentleman to mention it and that Victor had better not have any objections.

Victor nodded.

Williamson took a thick stack of paper out of a folder and placed it on the desk. "Because of the nature of Mr. Hugh Weber's death and the understandable interest that Mr. Victor Weber has in the contents of the will, I am going to give an overview of the history of Mr. Weber's estate planning. Hugh Weber signed the current and operative will ten years ago," he said. "I believe that was after your father died and your parents' estate was settled, Mr. Weber, and the two of you, as heirs to your parents' estate, received equal shares in the Weber Paper Company. Is that correct?"

Victor Weber had been sitting forward in his chair, his whole body poised in expectation. But instead of answering the question, he demanded, "Did you say ten years?"

Warren leaned forward so he could see Victor's expression. He was angry, but more than that, he was confused.

David Williamson pressed his lips together and went on. "That's correct. We'll get back to the shares. The remainder of Mr. Weber's estate is comprised of the house and farm where Mrs. Weber and the children are now living, the contents of the house, the land associated with the farm, and a bank account at the Bank of Vermont here in Bethany. The amount of available funds in the account as of close of business yesterday was $263." He paused, looking very grim, and said, "Mr. Weber did not hold a life insurance policy and unfortunately, there was no policy on the barn."

The room was silent. Warren glanced at Sylvie Weber. If the news of her poverty disheartened her, she did not show it. How would she manage?

"What about the shares?" Victor demanded. "Who did he leave the shares to?" He seemed suspended in a desperate state of anxiety.

Williamson ignored him and said to Sylvie Weber, "Mrs. Weber, your husband's estate in its entirety has been left to you, as his wife. Now, since the will mentioned the inherited shares in the paper company, which was bought by a larger company a few years ago, I called the administrator of the brokerage account in New York. It turns out that Mr. Weber sold the shares a few years ago." His voice changed, became gentler then. "Mrs. Weber, did you know anything about this?"

She looked genuinely surprised and shook her head.

Williamson said, "Well, ideally, I would be able to give you all of the information about the estate now, but I haven't been able to track down the proceeds of the share sales. I called a few banks this morning, but they have not been able to get back to me and sometimes these things take—"

"What did the will say?" Victor Weber asked in a tight voice. "Was there anything else in it?"

Williamson hesitated. "He did not leave any special instructions. Except for one bequeathment to his brother, Mr. Victor Weber."

Williamson pressed his lips together and held a typed piece of paper in front of him.

When he hesitated, Victor said, in an almost whisper, "Go on, what was it?"

"'To my brother, Victor, I leave my copy of *The Communist Manifesto* by Mr. Friedrich Engels and Mr. Karl Marx.'" Williamson's voice got very quiet. "'Perhaps it will do something to educate him as to his bloodthirsty capitalist impulses and how he might temper them.'"

Victor Weber roared. Warren thought later that he had sounded like a beast, thwarted. He jumped up, ready to stop the man from attacking Williamson, but it was Sylvie Weber he went for, leaning down and grabbing her by the arms so that he could shout right into her face.

"What did you do?" he demanded. "What did you do? He told me about you, you *low-class whore*! He said he wouldn't leave anything to you because women are all the same, too dumb to manage money. *What did you do?*"

"Mr. Weber!" Warren shouted, pushing him away from her and revealing his revolver in its holster on his belt. "I will place you under arrest right now if you continue threatening Mrs. Weber." Sylvie Weber looked terrified and so did David Williamson.

"This is a travesty," Victor shouted. "His money was meant to go to me. When Hugh told me about her, he said I wasn't to worry. She was just a child and too stupid to know what to do with money. She's committed some sort of fraud. I don't know how she's done it, but you've helped her!" He spat it out in David Williamson's direction. "I'm the executor. I have *rights* and I will get to the bottom of this. You are *warned*!" And he stalked out of the room, slamming the door behind him.

"Mrs. Weber, do you want me to arrest him for assault?" Warren asked Sylvie, who was still sitting stunned in the chair.

She shook her head. "Let him go. He just yelled at me. He didn't hurt me."

They were all silent for a moment. The stuffed deer head looked down passively at them. Warren was aware that he was breathing hard, his heart pounding.

"Well," David Williamson said. "Never had that happen before. Thank you for being here, Mr. Warren."

Sylvie Weber looked over at him and nodded. "Thank you," she said.

Williamson went on. "Mrs. Weber, the will has to go through probate and then the deed of the house and farm will be transferred to you. I'll let you know when I hear from New York. You're sure he never talked to you about his will or these accounts?"

"No." She shook her head, worried and preoccupied again, her shoulders rounded and her eyes on her lap. "I don't remember it anyway."

"Did you know that he hadn't paid up the insurance on the barn?"

She blinked. "Oh, he didn't believe in it. He said you just paid and paid and it didn't benefit anyone but the insurance company."

Williamson closed the folder that was sitting on the desk in front of him. "Do you have any further questions?"

She seemed in shock when she said quietly, "I . . . My head is all swimming. I need to think but then I can come back, perhaps. Maybe I can write down my questions. I . . . Thank you, Mr. Williamson, but I think I want to go."

"Okay, Mrs. Weber." Williamson stood up and showed them out. "I'm so sorry for your loss."

"Thank you, Mr. Williamson," she said quietly, picking up her basket.

Outside, they walked together toward where Warren had parked his car, but when they reached it and he started to go around to open the door, she shook her head at him and he had the sense she was on the verge of tears. "Thank you, but I'm going to stop at Mrs. Bellows's house. She'll run me home in her car."

"Oh, of course." He felt an odd layer of disappointment fall over him.

"Goodbye," she said. "Thank you for driving me."

He got into the car and, forcing himself not to watch her walk along the street, pulled out and passed her, the air through the windows smelling of roses. As he drove toward the barracks, he tried to put together what he'd learned. Victor Weber had thought he was the sole beneficiary of Hugh Weber's estate. It had seemed from the man's reaction that he had been expecting to inherit from his brother upon his death.

Interesting.

And then there was Sylvie Weber. Warren couldn't figure out her reaction at all. She had seemed not to know about the existence of a bank account or accounts containing the proceeds from the sale of the shares. Had she known but was lying to them for some reason? Because she knew how much money there was and that it gave her a motive for her husband's murder? Perhaps that was it.

Or . . . she didn't know and she just . . . didn't care. Warren remembered her casual assertion that she would manage just fine as long as they could stay in the farmhouse. Did she just not understand how difficult it would be? Was she even competent to manage the money, if there was money there? If Victor Weber challenged the will on that basis, how would a judge decide the issue?

And why was Warren thinking about all of this anyway? Despite the second fire, it was still most likely that Hugh Weber had set that first fire himself.

He had just pulled into the barracks when Tommy Johnson pulled in behind him. Warren got out and Tommy waved something at him from the open window of the car. "Frankie!" Tommy called out. "I got something for you!"

"What is it?" Warren called out, jogging the twenty yards to the cruiser.

Tommy jumped out. He was holding a manila envelope and he grinned at Warren, the news spilling out of him as Warren took it from him. "Autopsy report on Hugh Weber is in," he said. "State pathologist thinks it could have been murder."

Fifteen

Sylvie thanked Mrs. Bellows again, for the ride and for the meal and the basket of food she'd given her to bring home and for the conversation. Mrs. Bellows smiled and said she'd enjoyed it too. Then she hesitated and said, "Don't worry too much, Sylvie. It's all going to be okay. You're resourceful and creative. I've always known it. I'll help you if I can. Will you and the boys be at Old Home Day on Saturday?"

Sylvie spun her wedding ring and watched a chickadee dart from one tree to another in front of the house. *Chickadee quick, chickadee meet, chickadee be.*

"I don't think so. It's too soon and I don't want everyone staring at us," she said finally. "At the boys."

Mrs. Bellows sighed. "I can't promise they won't, Sylvie. Maybe you're right." She turned to meet Sylvie's gaze, her blue eyes bright against the graying tendrils of hair escaping from her neat bun in the humid air. Mrs. Bellows always wore her hair up, secured with expensive-looking tortoiseshell combs, but Sylvie liked when she

could see what the older woman must have looked like as a girl, a little bit messy, curls coming down around her forehead. "You're going
to be okay, you know."

You don't know that, Sylvie wanted to say.

Mrs. Bellows seemed to want to say something else, but in the
end she just patted Sylvie's hand meaningfully, told her to call if she
needed anything, anything at all, and Sylvie said goodbye and thanked
her again for the food, feeling lighter and a little better.

Hooking the large basket of food and the now-empty yarn basket
carefully over her arm, Sylvie shut the car door behind her, standing
in the road and waving until the car disappeared down the hill. It was
overcast now, an electric closeness in the air. She needed to get the
washing off the line and she needed to bring the sheep up too. The
baby kicked, as though it knew too that she needed to get going.

They came running as soon as they heard the door. "Mama,"
Louis called out. "A man came and took Papa's book and he said our
house was a didgraze and he wanted to know where you were and
why you left us alone."

"What?" She put the basket down in the hall. Andy was standing
in the doorway, biting his lip. "Tell me, Andy, what happened?"

She sat down on the couch and Daniel, who had been standing
there sucking his thumb, came over and crawled into her lap. He
smelled of raspberry jam. He had been at the jars again, popping off
the tops and wax seal and eating it with a spoon. Now wasn't the time
to scold him, though.

"It was Papa's brother," Andy said, his blue eyes darting between
her and the door in worry. "Hugh's brother. I knew as soon as I came
to the door. He looks like him." A tear squeezed out of one eye and he
furiously rubbed it away. She gestured for him to come and sit on the
other side of her and he did, leaning in and letting her take his hand.
"He came in demanding to see you and asking us our names and saying the house was a disgrace and what was wrong with you anyway,

were you simple? We didn't know what to say. Then he asked us if you often left us alone and he went over to the bookcases and looked around and took a book, saying it was his, that Papa wanted him to have it. He said we should tell you that he was just taking what was coming to him and that if you had anything to say about it, you could say it to Mr. Williamson."

"That awful man," she said.

Andy started crying. "I should have fought him, Ma, I know I should have. But he was so big. Scott's out on the tractor and we would have got him but we didn't know where he was. I'm sorry, I'm sorry."

"No, my darling. I'm sorry I stayed so long at Mrs. Bellows's," she said, pulling him closer to her. "It's my fault, not yours. Don't worry. He won't come back. Now, let me show you what Mrs. Bellows gave us. There are cookies and chocolates too. She said we should have some, even if it's before dinner." The boys looked up, wary and delighted. Hugh had never let them have sweets, before or after dinner. He said that sweet foods made people morally bankrupt and that they could get addicted to them.

This was something he had learned from Jeffrey. *The Prophet.* Hugh had talked about Jeffrey a lot, even though he said he hated him, and once Sylvie had asked why, if Jeffrey was so important to him, he didn't ever visit him? After all, the farm where Jeffrey lived was just at the other end of town, not far from Agony Hill. Hugh had gotten very quiet and said that she didn't understand at all, that Jeffrey wasn't *important* to him, he was just explaining what a hypocrite the man was, and she should understand why Hugh had left Jeffrey's farm. He'd gotten out the gin bottle then and gone out to the barn and he hadn't talked to any of them for a few days.

Sylvie had actually met Jeffrey once, at the Bethany Fair a few years back, not long after she'd had Daniel. Hugh was looking at the tractors and she had taken the boys to get lemonade since it was such a hot day. As they wandered, looking at animals while sipping the tart lemonade, and smiling at all the sights and sounds, a very tall man in a worn green army fatigues jacket had watched them for a few minutes before approaching her and saying, "You must be Hugh's wife, is that right?"

She'd been too afraid to do anything but nod at him.

"You have a beautiful family," he'd said. "I hope that your life is full of peace." Then he'd nodded and walked off, disappearing into the crowds. She had never told Hugh about it. It was just one more thing that would make him mad. Sylvie had learned that it was easier to be quiet. When you said something, the other person had to confront your thoughts about things. When you were quiet, they could keep thinking their own thoughts. Hugh had always described Jeffrey as an awful man, cruel and cheap and dominating, saying *the Prophet* with a mean little sneer in his voice. If Sylvie had said that he seemed kind to her, Hugh would have been furious, so she didn't say anything and neither did the boys. They had learned a long time ago not to say things to Hugh, so long ago that Sylvie couldn't remember teaching it to them.

"Come on, boys, come see what's in here," she said.

The boys fell upon the basket like wild dogs, tearing at the wrappers and the cloth around the cake, laughing and stuffing the sweetness into their mouths, and by the time Scott came back from the field, Louis's face was smeared with chocolate.

Sixteen

Warren called Pinky into the back room at the barracks once Tommy had gone home for supper and showed him the reports Tommy had brought from Burlington. In addition to the autopsy results, he had brought a report from the state fire investigator, who had concluded that the fire had been deliberately set. The point of origin had been next to the cot and gasoline had been used as an accelerant, just as Warren had suspected.

The state pathologist had completed the autopsy on what remained of Hugh Weber. He had likely died, the report concluded, from concurrent smoke inhalation and bleeding on his brain due to a head injury sustained at some point before death.

"The extent of thermal degradation makes it difficult to ascertain whether radiating fractures to the skull and the brain damage that would result caused subject's death or whether the injury occurred first and then Mr. Weber died of smoke inhalation."

Warren read the description of the injury to Pinky. There was a linear fracture at the back of the victim's skull that, if he had still been alive, would have caused massive bleeding in his brain. Indeed, what was left of his brain tissue did indicate catastrophic bleeding. But it was unclear if it had happened before or after the smoke inhalation. The upshot of the report was that Hugh Weber could have been killed by an attack with a blunt object and then, almost at the exact same moment, died in the fire. It was also possible that he could have died when the fire caused a timber from the barn to fall and hit him on the head. Warren remembered that the firemen had removed a charred timber from the burned cot where they'd found Hugh Weber's body.

"Unless he was so drunk he couldn't move, he would have to have been sitting up and turning toward the door to the office in order for the timber to hit him on the back of the head," Warren said.

Pinky's eyes widened and he said, "So you think . . ."

"I don't know what I think, but do something for me, will you?" he told Pinky, dragging two chairs together to make a small bed. "Lie down there on your back." Pinky gamely assumed the position, tucking his knees up to fit on the chairs. He folded his hands over his chest and closed his eyes in an expression of mock repose. Warren laughed and Pinky grinned, then blushed furiously, the pink spreading across his cheeks and temples.

"Okay," Warren said. "Now, sit up, like you're checking on something. You're lying on the cot and maybe you hear something. Yeah, just like that, not all the way. Now, turn your head to the right. Yeah." Pinky did as he said, holding the position. Warren let his hand drop from a few feet above Pinky's head to mimic a falling beam. The back of his skull did jut out a bit; it was the natural spot where the beam would have hit his head, but Warren thought the angle might be wrong. If the beam was falling from above, it would have to have rotated slightly as it fell in order to hit the back of Pinky's skull head-on. Was it plausible that it had? Yes. Likely? Warren wasn't sure, but he'd found in his line of work that, just as with medicine, the most obvious solution was usually the correct one in criminal investigation.

Yes, strange things happened. But they didn't happen as frequently as normal things happened.

So, possibly an accident, but more likely murder. Warren felt his heart speed up and touched the back of his skull. He would have been hit from behind. A picture jumped into his mind: Hugh Weber sitting at his desk in the barn, typing away at the typewriter, someone—the arsonist?—coming up behind him, hitting him in the back of the head with a blunt object, Weber falling to the ground, the assailant dragging him to the cot and then pouring gasoline on the floor and lighting the match. Or maybe he was already on the cot. So . . . a lover? That seemed unlikely. Wouldn't Sylvie Weber have seen someone arrive? The picture grew murky.

"If someone killed him," Warren said aloud to Pinky, who was looking curious about what was going on in Warren's head, "then we're back to the same question. How did the assailant get out of the barn? We know that the barn door was locked from the inside. Sylvie Weber said the only other way out was blocked by the piled bales of hay and when we checked it out, it looked like that was the case."

"Right." Pinky tapped his head, thinking. "And we don't think he could have climbed up the inside or down the outside without a ladder. There might be another way out of the barn, though. My grandparents' barn has tons of little doors and hatches and things. There were boards nailed to the walls that you could climb up to get into the haymow. My sisters and brothers and I used to play hide-and-seek in there and I liked to sneak out and go around to hide somewhere my brother had already looked. Used to drive him crazy."

Warren looked at him. "You're right. But if there was a door like that, why didn't she tell us?"

Pinky shrugged, then flushed as he realized what Warren was implying. "You think Sylvie Weber . . . ?"

"I don't know what I think," Warren said. "Anyway, if someone hit him on the head and then dragged his body over and set the fire, it must have been someone who was determined, who felt they had a good reason to murder him. And someone fairly strong."

"*If* he was murdered," Pinky pointed out. "That report only says he could have been."

"Dammit, you're right," Warren said. *If, if, if.* He felt a sudden flash of frustration. He needed something to go on. Something solid. And right now, the most solid thing he had was that man in the woods, the one who had been watching them after they responded to the second fire. He told Pinky about his realization that wanting to get hold of the Webers' farm could have been a motive for murder too.

Warren sighed. Outside the barracks, the dark had closed in, just a few streaks of yellow-and-gray sunset in the sky. "It's late, Pinky," he said. "It's been a long day and I need some supper and a night of real sleep. But tomorrow I want to go talk to those farmers who wanted Weber's land and I'd like you to come with me. Sylvie Weber said there was bad blood there. If someone did kill him, it's got to be someone with a motive like that."

Pinky looked delighted at the new angle. This was the stuff, *real investigation*. This was what he'd imagined when he'd thought about assisting the new detective, Warren thought, a real lead, a new thread to pull.

Just wait until he experienced the way the threads of an investigation could unravel before you, though, just like a sweater caught on a nail.

Seventeen

For breakfast the next morning, Warren toasted a slice of bread and spread a thick layer of Sylvie Weber's raspberry jam across its craggy surface. The jam tasted of the sun-drenched fields, its flavor round and red and acidic, and when he was finished he prepared another piece of toast, just to taste the berries again. Then he showered and drove to the barracks where he met Pinky and waved him into the Galaxie; Warren knew he'd learn the roads faster if he drove himself.

The sun rose in the sky as Warren followed the curve of the river along Route 5. He had copied out a map from the atlas on his desk at the barracks, creating a visual for himself of Agony Hill and the land stretching down the eastern slope of the hill to the river, and he handed it to Pinky so Pinky could study it too.

Neither of the two farms that abutted the Webers' land was on Agony Hill. Rather, both farms were down below, along something called River Road, tucked next to the Connecticut in the fertile valley formed when the ancient ocean had receded, leaving behind the dark rich soil in which corn and alfalfa and other feed crops grew as though they'd been touched by magic. The corn was up above Warren's chest, the hayfields tall. There was something about all that bounty that made him feel calm and satisfied, though he couldn't think exactly why.

As they drove, he told Pinky more about the scene in the lawyer's office.

Pinky wrinkled his nose, confused. "You think the brother had something to do with all this?"

"I don't know," Warren said. "It only makes sense if Victor Weber thought he was going to inherit something upon Hugh Weber's death. Williamson said he was going to get some more information from the bank in New York about the estate, but the way it looks now is that Victor Weber had some reason for believing that he stood to inherit. He was the executor, after all, so he must have seen an earlier version of the will, the one before Weber's marriage. We need to find out more. After we visit the farms, can you check to see if he's still staying at the inn? I'll have to go talk to him." Pinky nodded. "The other thing is, Sylvie Weber told me that her husband first came to Bethany to live on a farm owned by someone named Jeffrey; *the Prophet,* she called him. Do you know who she was talking about?"

Pinky nodded his head. "Jeffrey Sawyer, it must be. He has a farm out near Goodrich Hill. He had some other people living there at one point and I think I did hear that he and Hugh Weber had some sort of feud going. He's an odd old character. Now it's just him and his, uh, wife. They keep themselves to themselves, though. Sell vegetables in town sometimes."

Warren slowed the car at a stop sign, then turned onto a narrow dirt road. He could see the river now, beyond a few layers of fields planted with vigorously growing crops. He glanced over at Pinky. "A feud? Was that in the past or do you think there could still have been bad blood between him and Hugh Weber?"

"I don't know. He keeps himself to himself is what I've heard. I'll ask my dad, though. He'll remember what the argument was about."

"Thanks." Warren drove in silence for a bit and then he said, "You think she could have been mentioning this Jeffrey Sawyer character as some sort of red herring, to throw me off her trail?"

Pinky shrugged. "You said she didn't seem to know about the will and all."

"Maybe she's lying about that too," Warren said. "She could have seen a piece of mail, done some research."

Pinky made a little skeptical noise. Warren knew what he meant. Sylvie Weber didn't seem canny enough for something like that. Warren wasn't even sure how much she understood about her whole financial situation, even now.

"How did Hugh Weber get his farm?"

Pinky said that Weber had bought his twenty-acre parcel from a man named Horace Hickson fifteen years ago, right around the time he got married.

"Mr. Hickson's wife died and he moved in with his daughter," Pinky said. "I suppose Weber must have made an offer for the farm. Hickson always had a few cows and sheep and so forth, but the land is pretty poor up there. Not like the farms down here by the river."

"What can you tell me about these farmers, Spaulding and Hatchett?" Warren asked. "If there was animosity between Weber and these men, what was it likely to have been about? Sylvie Weber said they wanted the land, but you just said it's poor quality."

Pinky studied the map some more while Warren focused on the road. "Weber's parcel runs up against the two farms here and here," he said, pointing to a spot on the map. "They'd both probably like to get ahold of these pastures here and here. Give 'em a few more grazing options, or they could be additional hayfields. Some of the farmers around here are trying to expand. Need to produce more milk to make it all pay."

Warren must have looked confused because Pinky went on. "See, they're making the dairy farms get bulk milk tanks, to store the milk hygienically, and lots of 'em can't afford it. The interstate too. They bought up a lot of land from farmers for the construction, like that farmer who burned his place down. Farms closing down left and right. For the ones that are trying to survive, only answer is to make more milk."

They drove another half-mile down the road. "That's Terry Spauldings' place, up there," Pinky said.

"What's he like?" Warren asked, alert to a hint of disdain in Pinky's voice.

"Well . . . he looks out for himself."

Warren smelled the farm before he saw it, the ripe tang of cow manure rising in front of them as they turned into a wide driveway lined with a couple of Ford pickup trucks and a shiny, brand-new tractor of some sort parked in the large driveway. It wasn't the mellow animal smell of the Webers' farm, but rather the sharp, fresh smell of a working dairy farm. He took in the panoramic scene. The farmhouse was large and well-cared for, freshly painted and neatly landscaped. A long structure, with a shiny new metal roof, sat next to the older barn on the far side of the drive. Across the road were deep corn fields, the plants already tall and shiny green in the sun. Beyond was the river.

No one came to meet them.

"They'll be in the milking parlor," Pinky said, pointing to the long building. Warren could hear cows inside, but no human voices. When they pushed through the door, though, and Pinky called out, "Mr. Spaulding? Anyone here?" someone called back, "Through here," and they followed the voice into a large room with concrete walls. Beyond was an even larger space, a milking parlor with six stanchions and a gate at the far end. Three men were working with the cows, adjusting the machines attached to their udders and dropping scoops of grain into the feeding troughs.

A large man in a yellow coverall said, "Hiya, Pinky."

"Hello, Mr. Spaulding, this is Franklin Warren. He's the new detective at the barracks. Just moved to Bethany. He's looking into this thing with Hugh Weber."

"That right? How do you like it here?" Spaulding had a fleshy face, pink and smooth, his small eyes studying Warren shrewdly. Warren waited for Spaulding to introduce the other men but the pleasantry never came. The men, both in their twenties, looked up and nodded, then went back to their work. One was attaching the milking machines to the udders of the black-and-white cows on either side of the parlor, while the younger of the two was filling the troughs in front of each cow with grain. They were munching happily, oblivious to the machinations at their hindquarters. As Warren watched, milk began to whoosh through the clear plastic tubing and up into the ceiling. He'd thought that cows were still milked by hand, but Spaulding's setup seemed state-of-the-art and he could see what an advantage it would be. You could milk three or four times as many cows in the same amount of time with a system like this one.

"Uh, it's very nice, so far. Is there a quiet place we could talk for a moment?" he asked Spaulding.

Spaulding looked annoyed, but pointed to a door at one end of the milking parlor and then led them through into a small, neatly organized office. He sat down behind the large wooden desk, the top clear of clutter, and Warren and Pinky sat down in the two chairs opposite.

"How well did you know Hugh Weber?" Warren asked him, a bit abruptly, to throw him off in case he knew something. But Terry Spaulding didn't flinch.

"Not very well. I doubt anyone would say they knew him well. He was a strange bastard. I never understood what his interest in that place was. He didn't know how to keep it up. It was falling down around him and his stock was poor quality, animals he bought at auction for cheap. What's the point of doing something if you're not going to do it right?" He looked around at his gleaming, sterile office with an air of self-satisfaction.

"Let's go back fourteen years. Was he the only buyer interested in Horace Hickson's farm on Agony Hill?" Warren asked.

Spaulding scowled. "I make no secret of the fact that I would have liked it, but I didn't have the funds at the ready then. Weber came in with cash, told Horace he wanted to buy it, gave him the money the next day. He had an inheritance, I think I heard. I guess he liked the idea of farming, but he didn't know the first thing about it. Made a hash of it, all right. That woman of his knew a bit. He would have starved if not for her. I suppose she'll have to sell it now."

"The Weber property abuts another farm," Warren said offhandedly. "Uh . . ." He looked to Pinky for the name, as though he'd forgotten.

"Hatchett's," Terry Spaulding said. "No love lost between Jorah Hatchett and Weber, I can tell you that."

"Was he also interested in Hickson's property?"

"I suppose." Spaulding wasn't going to go any further than that.

"Mr. Spaulding, as you know, we're now investigating Mr. Weber's death as suspicious. Do you remember the night of his death and the fire?"

"Yes, of course. My boy there, T.J., and my son-in-law, Gordo, too, are on the fire department. They went up and put it out and told me he was in the barn. I could smell the smoke of course. And the news was all over town the next day."

Warren waited. "So you and your wife were here at home that whole evening?"

Spaulding looked up quickly. "Yes, well, I had a calving I came out to here. It was a bit complicated and I thought I might need the vet, so I stayed out in the barn most of the night. It was okay in the end, though. But yes, we were here all night."

"And the rest of the family?"

"My daughter, Joanie, and her husband—Gordo there—live in the house up the hill." He pointed vaguely to the outside. "Gordo was out at the fire, but otherwise, I think they were in." He glanced away. "I need to get back. Is there anything more?"

"Well, I'm curious if you can think of any reason why anyone would want Mr. Weber out of the way. When I told you that we think Mr. Weber's death might not be suicide, who was the first person you thought of, Mr. Spaulding?"

Spaulding leaned back in his chair and broke into hoarse, unpleasant laughter. "He was a miserable son of a bitch, Mr. Warren. I can't think of a person in this town who wasn't happy when they heard he was dead. But if I were you, I might look at that woman of his. Don't they say that malice starts close to home? Now, I need to get back to milking."

Out in the milking parlor, Warren hesitated for a minute, trying to see how he might ask the son and son-in-law—T.J. and Gordo—about where they were the night of the fire at the Webers'. But Terry Spaulding glared at them and they both put their heads down and focused on the milking. He'd just have to come back, preferably when the domineering paterfamilias wasn't around.

"Thank you for your time, Mr. Spaulding," he said.

Spaulding didn't answer. They had finished with the cows in the parlor and were moving them out through a different gate than the one they'd come in by. One of the cows stopped, sniffing at the ground, and Terry Spaulding whacked it hard on its hip bones with the wooden stick he carried. The cow jumped and hurried out the door.

⊠ ⊠ ⊠

The Hatchett farm was three miles down the road, set up a bit on the hillside, with what Warren assumed must be spectacular views of the river valley. There were no shiny new pieces of farm equipment here, just an older tractor and a few clean but worn-out-looking trucks in the driveway. The farmhouse was smaller and older than the Spauldings'; there was something austere about it, the dark gray clapboards weathered and the small garden around the front door pruned and trimmed to within an inch of its life.

Jorah Hatchett was also milking, but unlike Terry Spaulding, he was almost alone. Only a thin teenager helped with the task of bringing the cows in, attaching them to the milking machine, scooping grain into the feeding troughs, and then moving the cows out once they had finished.

"Mr. Hatchett?" Pinky called out. "We're sorry to bother you." He introduced Warren, which elicited nothing more than a curious glance.

When Jorah Hatchett looked up, Warren found himself intrigued by the man's timeless face, its sharp angles and noble nose and brow. He was thin but wiry and seemed taller than he actually was. There was a Lincolnesque quality to him; his last name seemed appropriate. Hatchett said nothing, just nodded and went back to what he was doing. Pinky waited a minute, seeming to absorb the atmosphere of the milking room, before he said, slowly, "Looking into this Hugh Weber thing, the fire."

Hatchett nodded, but didn't say anything. Warren waited before realizing the response was complete. Hatchett hadn't been asked a question so he wasn't going to offer one.

"Mr. Hatchett, what was your relationship with Mr. Weber like?" Warren asked.

Hatchett looked up. "Didn't have one."

"But you knew him? He was your neighbor."

"That's right."

Warren had to push down his annoyance. Did the farmer think this was a game?

"Mr. Hatchett, is there anything you can tell me about Hugh

Weber that might be of interest to us? I have heard that he bought a piece of land that both you and your neighbor Terry Spaulding were interested in. Is that right?"

A long silence and then, "Yuh, that's right. The farm up on Agony Hill isn't worth much, but with some clearing, the hillside would have made a good extension of my pasture." He took a deep breath as though the effort of speaking so many words had exhausted him.

"But Mr. Weber got it?"

He nodded. The answer didn't need words.

"And at some point you wrote a letter, asking to buy some of his fields?"

Hatchett said, "Never heard back though, so I left it."

The milking parlor returned to silence, except for the sounds of the cows and the machines.

"So there's nothing else you can tell us?" Warren asked. "What kind of man was he?"

Jorah Hatchett took his time considering. Finally he said, "Wasn't much of a stockman. Had money but no sense, and then he spent the money on land that was only valuable to myself or Terry Spaulding. Spent the rest of it on animals that were poor quality."

"What about that?" Warren asked. "Was he taken advantage of?"

Hatchett shrugged. "I wouldn't know about that. He had a few heifers that are sound now, but he didn't know much about breeding. Some nice sheep, I've heard. But he didn't know what he was doing. His woman, she knew more than he did. Any success they had was down to her."

"Really?" Warren asked. It was what Spaulding had said as well. "Did she grow up on a farm?"

"Wouldn't know. She's not from around here." The milking machine on the cow closest to Warren made a sucking sound.

"How did you hear about the fire up on Agony Hill?" Warren asked him, raising his voice to be heard over the machine.

"Smelled it." The milk stopped swishing through the tubes and Hatchett pulled it off the cow's udder and moved her out. He stood up and gave the cow a gentle push to move her along and out the door at the end of the room, murmuring something under his breath.

Warren caught Pinky's eye and asked the silent question, *Is that it?* Pinky shrugged.

Warren was about to thank Hatchett when the man walked past him and said, "Finish up, will you, Gene?" The teenager bent to his work and Hatchett gestured with a hand for Warren and Pinky to follow him. Warren, not knowing what else to do, went behind him out the door and around the back of the barn. The cows that had been milked and were outside again watched them placidly as they followed Hatchett up a low slope and toward a field bordered by a high fence. They seemed somehow more vigorous than the cows at Spauldings', their coats glossier, their eyes calmer.

Hatchett walked over to the fence line where a piece of vine, green and ropy, hung from a corner post.

"Thought you should see this," he said, putting up a hand to shield his eyes from the sun. "I was missing one of the heifers. She must have gotten over the fence in the last few days. I went looking, but . . ." He shrugged. "Then this morning, I heard her up here, bellowing away. Someone had caught her and brought her back. Tied her up to the fence with the vine, I think."

He met Warren's eyes and nodded as though Warren should know what he was saying.

"I'm sorry," Warren said finally. "I don't quite understand."

Hatchett gestured to the vine on the fence. "That was all he had to secure her there. He must have found her wandering in the trees up that way, on Agony Hill."

Warren still looked confused so Hatchett went on. "There's someone been up there in the woods on Agony Hill."

Eighteen

Alice sat on the terrace with her coffee Friday morning, creating an account of the shopping habits of the residents of Bethany Village. What she needed to know was who might have been in and around the store on the day the cartridges disappeared. It had been a Wednesday, about eleven, according to Dorothy.

Rachel Gearing liked to do her shopping that time of day on Wednesdays. Her son got her things from the market in White River Junction once a week, but that was on Saturdays. She bought some groceries at Collers' and Alice often saw her on Wednesdays. Alice put her on the list. Then there was old Mary Harper. She liked to walk down to get the papers, but her knees were very bad and so it often took her until eleven to get up and moving. And there were the Tewksburys, who drove down once or twice a week to buy donuts at the store. Harold Philmore had the insurance business on Main Street. He was a very early riser, in the office by seven or eight, and he often came down to the store at eleven to get his lunch.

She drew a line next to each name. Four names. It was a place to start. She might think of some more as she went too. Inside, she told Mildred she was going out and took her hat from the rack by the side door. It was a nice sunny day and she didn't want to burn.

Rachel Gearing was at home, working in her garden on the other side of the picket fence that separated her house from the sidewalk. Alice waved away her offer of something cool to drink and said, "I can't stay, Rachel. I just wanted to see if you remember seeing anything strange at Collers' Store, back a couple of weeks ago. I'm just trying to sort out a, well . . . a misunderstanding."

Rachel didn't question this. Everyone in town was used to Alice investigating things. "Depends what you mean by *strange,* Alice. Bea had some very nice loaves of wheat bread, better than her usual and I wondered if maybe someone else had done her baking. That was strange. But I don't think that's what you're asking about."

"No—at least, I don't think it is. You didn't see anyone who seemed . . . suspicious then?"

"Well, Clarence was lurking around. But then, he's always doing that." They smiled at each other. Clarence Parto was the town busybody. He lived in a small apartment over the green and was always walking back and forth, seeing what people were up to. He had an excellent memory for faces and names. Alice had known Clarence since they were children and she was used to his funny ways. She had met people in her life, all over the world, who reminded her of Clarence. She suspected there were doctors in New York or Boston who might have a name for how Clarence was different, but she didn't think Clarence would ever be interested in that name.

"Okay, thank you, Rachel. I should talk to Clarence, I suppose."

"Yes, I wish I could have helped you more. Are we ready for tomorrow, do you think?"

"We always seem to manage it," Alice said. "Though there's a lot to do." Rachel was responsible for making the little cakes that were served with fresh raspberries and whipped cream at the raspberry social for twenty-five cents a bowl. She would start baking them this afternoon, Alice knew. Everyone had their part to play in the preparation of the tent, which was the Ladies Aid Society's biggest fundraiser. Alice always helped with the table linens and collected the dishes they would use. She and Mildred had been ironing for days. And tonight, Alice would begin making the flower arrangements that would grace the tables in the tent. When people came to buy their tea cakes with raspberries and cream, they wanted to sit at a table with a beautiful flower arrangement on it. It was part of the experience. Every year, Alice chose a theme or a dominant color for the arrangements and she knew that people in town—and all those coming back to town for their summer visit—waited to see what it would be.

"I'm doing pink arrangements this year, Rachel," Alice said. "My zinnias are lovely and the salmon ones did very well. That's what gave me the idea."

Rachel nodded seriously and went back to her gardening. Alice thought about how some people would likely consider the attention paid to the fundraiser frivolous. Rachel was a trained musician and teacher, very capable. And Alice was . . . well, though she had never held an actual job, Alice knew herself to be extremely competent at a great many things. Some might say they were wasting their time and talents. But the flowers and the cakes did matter, Alice thought. They were a tradition. And the money raised by the Ladies Aid Society did real good in the community. Good that would not be done otherwise.

Alice stopped in at the insurance office and told Freddie Somers that she needed a word with Harold. "You can go right in, Mrs. Bellows," Freddie said. "He's just been down to the store for his lunch and he's having a bit of a rest."

Harold Philmore was in fact fast asleep when Alice opened the door to his office and closed it again. She slammed it a little, and turned away from the desk, so that by the time she turned around and faced him, he was blinking and awake, his vanity saved.

"Oh, hello, Harold, I'm so sorry to bother you. It's just that I'm trying to clear up a bit of a misunderstanding and I thought you might be able to help me. I know you often walk down to Collers' Store around lunchtime and I was wondering if you might have seen something . . . out of the ordinary a couple of weeks ago. Someone who was acting strangely or perhaps someone you didn't recognize. Was there anything like that, Harold?"

"In the store?" he asked, thinking, still blinking.

"Yes, or on the street. Really anything, or more precisely anyone, out of the ordinary."

"Well, now . . . there were some tourists taking pictures the other day. Three young ladies. They had a car with New York plates and I noticed them because the car had a dent in the right rear bumper and I wondered why they hadn't had it fixed. Perhaps the insurance coverage was subpar. So I noticed them."

"I don't think it would be them I'm thinking of," Alice said. "But thank you, Harold."

"You're very welcome, Alice. Anything else I can help you with? Are your policies all up to date?"

"Yes, they are, Harold." He still looked a bit needy, so she smiled and said, "Thanks to you, that is." She hesitated before saying, "Some people don't listen to your good advice, though, do they, Harold?"

He sat up straight. "No, Alice. I am sorry to say that they don't." He raised his eyebrows and shook his head in an exaggerated pantomime of sadness, communicating his agreement with Alice's implication without actually naming the person to whom she referred. "It's a terrible thing, tragedy compounding tragedy, when a person is insufficiently insured or not insured at all."

Alice pursed her lips. "They say Hugh Weber didn't believe in insurance," she said in a very quiet voice. "He thought it was 'money down a rathole,' if you can believe it."

Harold looked shocked for a moment and then he shook his head again. "Alice, you would be surprised at how many people feel the same. And so often, too often, those people are the ones who, when the unthinkable happens, find themselves high and dry. They become believers in the value of insurance then, let me tell you."

Alice had to turn away so that Harold wouldn't see her smile at his seriousness.

"Oh, Alice," he said before she was out the door. "I forgot. There *was* something strange. I'd forgotten it until just this minute. But it wasn't in the store. It was at our place. A few weeks back, just like you said. Florence's little dog, Orlando, he wouldn't stop barking one night. All night, barking and barking. We let him out and he barked at something and I heard something in the bushes. I thought, *Well, perhaps there's a bear about, or a raccoon.* We don't often get them, being in town, but . . ." Harold shrugged. "In the morning, though, I found muddy footprints on the porch. Someone had come right up on the porch! And it wasn't a bear, Alice. It was a man."

"Was anything missing, Harold?" Alice was alert now. "Did you notice anything missing?"

"Well, that was the strange thing. Nothing was missing. So why did he come up on the porch? I'll tell you, Alice, Florence and I puzzled over it. We thought maybe he was thinking about breaking in, but Orlando scared him off. You know what they say, the bark of a dog is worth the best lock any day. It's the psychological factor, you see. I always say that good security is like good insurance. You appreciate it when you—"

Alice cut him off before he settled into his subject. "Yes. I ought to be going, Harold. So much to do today. See you soon. Say hello to Florence for me."

Out on Main Street, Alice spotted the distinctive figure of Clarence Parto, walking slowly past Collers' Store. He was looking through the big plate glass windows, seeing who was in the store. This was normal for Clarence. He liked knowing what was going on. Alice walked right up to him and said, without preamble, "Clarence, I need your help. Do you remember seeing anything unusual here at the store a couple of weeks ago?"

Clarence looked at her suspiciously. "How do you mean *unusual,* Mrs. Bellows?"

"Well, like, someone doing something they don't usually do. I know you keep track of the usual, well . . . the way of things, Clarence. And I know you would notice if anything was out of order."

Clarence glanced back toward the store. "I don't think so, Mrs. Bellows. But that doesn't mean there wasn't anything. You might remember that I had a very bad cold and so I didn't get out to do my usual errands for nearly a week."

"That's right, Clarence. I'd forgotten. I trust you're feeling better now?"

"Oh yes, much better."

"There's nothing worse than a summer cold, is there?" Clarence agreed and they said their goodbyes.

Before she got the car out and went up to see the Tewksburys, Alice decided to take a chance that Mary Harper was home and not too tired. Mary was eighty-five now and though she hadn't said anything, Alice knew that her days were numbered, though due to an actual illness or just an awareness that her body was winding down like a ticking clock, she didn't know. But whenever she saw Mary, Alice made a special point of taking an extra moment to be kind to her and to soak in the presence of a person who had been in Alice's life since she was born. When Mary was a teenager, then Mary Hall, she had been the Mary in the Universalist church's pageants to Alice's angels and animals until, at seventeen, Alice herself played Mary. Mary married Willy Harper the summer after she finished high school and they settled down to raise three girls in the small house just off the green. Alice thought all of those girls must have their own grandchildren by now. And so life went on. When Alice had returned to Bethany from

Washington, DC, to live there full-time after Ernest's death, Mary had welcomed her with a pound cake.

It had been a very good pound cake.

But when Alice approached the pretty white house on School Street, just off the green, she knew that Mary wasn't there. The house had a sleeping feeling, the blinds drawn—Mary never would have kept the blinds drawn at eleven if she were home—and Mary's black-and-white cat, Mr. Frog, was not sitting on the porch watching people walk by. If Mary was home, Mr. Frog was sitting there. Alice had a sudden panicky feeling. Perhaps Mary had not woken up this morning. Perhaps Alice should go in and check on her.

But then she saw Genevra Bell watering her plants next door and she walked over, noticing, because she couldn't help it, that Genevra's cosmos and marigolds were parched. She had not kept up with the watering during the dry days of late July.

"Is Mary out, Genevra?" she called.

Genevra turned the hose toward the ground. "She's staying with Teresa for a few days, up in Burlington," she said. She lowered her eyes to the water overflowing on the ground and said, "She was going to see a doctor up there, I believe, a friend of Teresa's husband." Her face told Alice everything she needed to know.

"I see," Alice said. "You'll tell me if there's anything I can do, won't you, Genevra?"

"Of course. Teresa's bringing her home tomorrow, I believe."

Alice took one last look at Mary's house, wondering to herself if Teresa or one of the other girls would move in once Mary was gone. Probably not. Teresa's husband was a doctor at the hospital in Burlington. The other girls lived in Massachusetts somewhere. Their husbands had good jobs too, and their children had settled with their own children where they were. Alice sighed. The children who had grown up in Bethany seemed to be flowing out of Vermont like the water from Genevra's hose. They came back for holidays and summer vacations and Old Home Day, but there wasn't enough for them to make lives here anymore.

The interstate would change all of that. At least that's what they said. Alice knew there would be benefits to her neighbors, but she also shared some of Hugh Weber's fear about how it would change things. She had seen enough of life—and enough of the world—to know that there would be good and bad coming to Vermont with the new roads. But unlike Hugh Weber, she knew there was no point in trying to stop it. It would come in any case. You had to be ready. That was the thing.

New people would arrive in Bethany, but they were likely to be people attracted to the qualities Hugh Weber claimed to want to protect. So they would be summer people, looking for peace and quiet, a counterpoint to their lives in the city, or they would be back-to-the-landers, looking for a place to live more simply.

Alice knew some of them might be looking for an escape from the problems of the world too. The Canadian border was not far and some of the young men who would likely be called up to service in Vietnam might be among those coming north. The papers were full of vague warnings about increased draft quotas and the lottery. The Falconer boy was an officer, as was Barbara Falconer's fiancé, Tony Lindsey, so they had gone already, Greg Falconer to somewhere in Vietnam already, Tony Lindsey to some sort of training in Georgia. Had any Bethany boys been called up? Alice didn't think so.

Not yet anyway.

The Selective Service had declared certain occupations as exempt and farming would surely be on the list. Manufacturing jobs, teachers, certain civil servants, including police, they would also receive exemptions, unless things got much worse, which Alice, who had seen wars bloom slowly and then gather momentum, feared they would. Increasing the quotas must mean something. What about boys like Richie who worked in shops?

Or no longer worked in shops? She felt a sudden rush of panic, imagining poor Richie in a uniform. He wouldn't last long.

Well, that digression had gotten her into a philosophical mood. Back on the green, she thought about who she wanted to talk to next. She needed to drive up to the Tewksburys' and ask them if they'd seen anyone in the store. And then maybe she'd go to the market in Woodstock and see if they had any fish. The truck often came on a Wednesday.

She told Mildred where she was going, tied a silk scarf neatly around her hair, got in the car, and set off. But as she neared the Gerharts' house on Church Street, she slowed as a familiar-looking sedan pulled out of the driveway and turned right onto the main road. It was Richie, alone in the car. Alice gave him some space, slowing almost to a stop before setting off again with a couple hundred yards between them. When he reached the Woodstock Road, he turned.

Alice, her heart speeding up as she pulled the scarf more tightly around her hair, turned too.

Nineteen

Warren spent Friday morning at the barracks completing paper-work, organizing his desk, and looking through old case files.

He had been thinking about what Fred Fielder had said during Warren's visit to the newspaper office. The editor had asked about an apparent homicide from back in the spring, a burglary and shooting at a house in Bethany. Warren had meant to ask Tommy about it and now he tried to remember the details. The homeowner had been from Washington, DC, Fielder had said. Was it possible there was a con-nection with the fires on Agony Hill? Warren searched through the case files Pinky had given him, but he couldn't find one on the case. He'd ask Pinky when he got back.

The file with Hugh Weber's letters was in his inbox and Warren took it out and read through them again. He was struck, as he had been the first time, at how much the totality of Hugh Weber's corre-spondence read like a suicide note. Combined with the facts of the other farmer's suicide, it seemed so clear what Weber had done.

And yet the autopsy had said it could have been homicide. *Could have been.*

And, there was the other fire, which seemed like too much of a coincidence for Warren's taste.

Tomorrow was Old Home Day and Warren knew that most of the troopers as well as the local police and sheriff's departments would be directing traffic and managing crowds for most of the day. Pinky and the other troopers had been told to go home early today.

But Warren wasn't officially on duty tomorrow and he had the afternoon free. He decided to go back to Agony Hill to look at the site of the fire at the camp and to check again for signs of whoever it was who had tied up the cow that Hatchett had mentioned yesterday.

He passed the Webers' farm, not seeing any signs of them out front, and went on slowly to the end of the road. The site where the camp had stood was now a pile of blackened timbers and ash. The fire investigator had taken some of the debris away and Warren had instructed Pinky to bring anything of interest back to the evidence room at the barracks. But still, he spent nearly an hour looking around the site where the cabin had stood. It would need to be almost completely rebuilt, but he liked the location, nestled onto a hillside and backed by trees and the woods rising behind it, with a lovely view of the hills and rolling pastures to the west. He had the thought that he would like to sit in a rocking chair on a porch here and watch the sunset. The thought was followed by pain: Maria would have liked it too. A place like this might have been a retirement dream for them, once he had finished his career and their children were off living their own lives, a place for them to all gather for holidays . . . But of course that would never happen now.

He gasped, the grief hitting him so suddenly he didn't have time to prepare his body for it. It was almost like a seizure, the way it came and took him and there was nothing he could do but sink to the ground and go limp and let it have its way. He bent his head and let the sobs come.

As the paroxysm subsided, he sat up and heard a bird call from the woods, a high, thin silvery note, clear as a voice. For a long time, perhaps an hour or more, he sat on the ground as the bird sang and others answered. The trees bent with the breeze that had come along the valley from the east.

Warren felt almost cheerful as he wiped his eyes and got back in the car, gazing one more time at the view from the ruined cabin.

¤ ¤ ¤

Back in town, he stopped at Collers' Store for some milk and bread and he was waiting to pay when Roy Longwell came into the store with one of his officers. He nodded to Warren and then went up and handed the woman behind the counter a piece of paper. Warren heard him explain that the police department was suspending all street parking during the parade tomorrow and that the Collers should tell their customers that any cars violating the parking ban would be ticketed.

"Everyone in town will know," he said. "But outsiders might not." Warren wasn't sure but he thought that the police chief glanced his way when he said it. The woman behind the counter—one of the Collers' daughters, Warren thought—made a sarcastic remark about how a ticket might be just the thing for some of these out-of-towners and Chief Longwell laughed and thanked her, taking one of the donuts in the jar on the counter and telling her to put it on his tab. Warren, on impulse, put his purchases down on a nearby shelf and called out to the chief, following him and his deputy out onto the street.

"Chief Longwell," he said. "I know you're busy. I wonder if I could have a minute. I just wanted to ask you about a case."

Longwell didn't say anything, but he inclined his head as if to say, *Go ahead.*

"Mr. Fielder at the newspaper asked me about a shooting, back a few months ago, I guess. A man from Washington, DC, who'd recently bought a vacation cottage in Bethany? You must have responded when it was called in, but I didn't see anything in the case files. Can you tell me about it?"

Longwell pressed his lips together and his eyes followed a group of teenage girls laughing and whispering as they came out of the drug-store. They were wearing brightly colored summer dresses and they made a nice picture against the tents and the Ferris wheel already set up on the green. When he looked back at Warren, his eyes were placid. "Well, I gave my report to Tommy Johnson, so if he didn't give it to you, you'll have to take it up with him," Longwell said.

Hearing the edge in Longwell's delivery, Warren hurried to explain it away. "I'm sure it was just an oversight or maybe my fault in missing it, but can you tell me something about it? Any chance there's a connection with the Hugh Weber case or the other fire?"

Longwell turned to the officer with him. "You remember going out to that house, Phil?"

"I do." The officer nodded.

"It was a strange one, wasn't it, Phil?" Longwell spoke slowly, deliberately, as though he was setting a trap. "No sign of a break-in outside, but someone had turned a few pieces of furniture over inside. The guy, now, he was lying right in the middle of the living room, like he'd been standing there happy as a clam and then someone just up and shot him. I'd guess a .22 pistol was our weapon, but I don't know because Tommy Johnson never sent me the autopsy. I gave him our report, but I don't know what happened to it after that."

"Was there any evidence at the scene? With a break-in, there should have been prints," Warren started to say. "Maybe we can compare to—"

"That was all Tommy," Longwell said shortly. He reached up to wipe a thin layer of perspiration from his forehead. It was hot in the direct sun on the sidewalk. "He's the man for the science. Now, I've got things to do. Be seeing you, Detective Warren."

Twenty

Alice drove carefully, keeping her speed equal to Richie's so that she wouldn't get too close. If she hadn't been planning on going that way she might have felt a bit guilty about following him, but of course she wasn't following him, she was just going about her own business. They just happened to be going the same direction.

Richie drove just a couple of miles over the speed limit most of the way there and Alice found it easy to keep up with him. It was a nice day for driving, the air warm but not too oppressive, the scent of sun on asphalt and growing corn blowing over her face. Richie slowed as they approached Main Street and Alice held back, waiting to see what he'd do. At first she thought he was going to continue right through town and keep heading west on Route 4, but when a car pulled out of a space on Main Street, he quickly—impulsively, Alice thought—turned in and sat there idling. She couldn't very well pull in next to him so she continued on and, quite luckily, found a spot farther down on Main Street. She looked back and saw that Richie was still sitting in the driver's seat of the car. She couldn't see what he was doing without walking along the sidewalk—in which case he'd see her—but something about his slumped posture, the way his head had fallen to the steering wheel, made her think that he was grappling with a huge emotional weight. After a few more seconds of the slumping, the attitude of struggle, he opened the door, got out of the car abruptly, and crossed the street. Alice took her basket from the front seat and got out too, walking along the sidewalk and pretending to gaze at the window displays as she watched Richie's reflection head off in the opposite direction on the other side of the street. He was walking slowly and Alice was sure she detected reluctance in his demeanor. He paused once, then continued walking slowly and—

"Alice Bellows!"

Alice swung around to find Wanda Crannock approaching her on the sidewalk. Arthur, a few steps behind, gave her a barely imperceptible raise of one eyebrow. "Alice, I thought that was you! I was just saying to Arthur that I must write to you and here you are, in the flesh! We've bought a place here in Woodstock, Alice. Isn't it lovely? We'll be up for summers and we'll be able to have lots of visits with you."

They embraced and Alice made all of the appropriate exclamations of surprise and delight. She had always liked Wanda, a soft, gentle creature with candy-floss blond hair that was now almost entirely snowy white, a facility for cooking and domestic things, and a maternal attitude that had drawn everyone in the various expat circles she and Arthur had moved in around the world to her table. Alice and Ernie had enjoyed many meals made by Wanda's hand. She had not relied on servants the way so many of them had, but instead had learned to make local cuisines herself. And she had provided, Alice thought, something essential for Arthur as he went about his secret and dangerous business—normalcy, domesticity, unconditional acceptance and love. Alice had done her best as the wife of an intelligence officer, but it had not come easily to her, not the way it seemed to for Wanda. In fact, especially in the early days, Alice had chafed at her role. Which was how she had begun to work for Arthur some-times, taking on jobs that only a woman could take on. It had been Arthur who had suggested it to Ernie. Ernie hadn't cared. He had been gone so much that Alice thought he didn't care what she did, as long as she didn't complain about their strange life.

"It's so exciting. How is the house coming along?" she asked Wanda, subtly shifting the direction of her body so she could glance back toward Richie. Where was he going?

"Oh, you know. Houses," Wanda said, sighing. "Everything takes twice as long and costs twice as much but we think it will be ready for Priscilla and her boys to come for a visit at the end of the month any-way. We're staying at the inn here while the work is completed and it's lovely to be on vacation. You're in Bethany, aren't you, Alice? I saw the news about the fires and I said to Arthur, 'That's where Alice and Ernie's place is!' You don't know the man who was killed, do you?"

"I knew him a bit," Alice said breezily. "In a place like Bethany, everyone knows everyone, in the end."

"Well, I hope it's not an indication of crime in this area," Wanda said distastefully. "We came here to *get away* from all that."

"I wouldn't worry about it too much, dear," Alice said, catching Arthur's eye and stifling a smile.

"I remember when you solved that mystery that I had in Rabat, about my maid who was stealing. I was so grateful to you."

"Except she wasn't stealing," Alice said meaningfully. "Was she?"

"Of course, that was the mystery, wasn't it? You were so brilliant, Alice, how you figured it out."

Arthur had been mostly silent but now he said, "Wanda, dear, we ought to leave Alice to her shopping. I've got to get back for that phone call, you remember." Something in his voice made Alice look at him as he spoke and she saw him glance quickly toward the street and then lower his head, as though he didn't want to be seen. Was Ar-thur on the job? Suddenly his presence here on her home turf seemed sinister. Alice felt the back of her neck bristle with awareness. Was this a chance encounter? With men like Arthur, few things happened by accident.

That sliver of a thought she'd had in her garden prodded her then. *Was* Arthur here for her? After all, the things she knew about him made her a danger, to him and to others. After Ernie died, Alice thought she had left it all behind by moving back to Vermont and making her life here, but she knew better than anyone that you never really left those things behind.

"Of course," Wanda said, patting her hair back into its neat arrangement. Her blouse was a cheery shade of yellow and it suited her, the little daisies at the neck coordinating with the ones on her purse. She had always liked clothes. Alice had a flash of a memory—Wanda, laughing in a market, wearing a tunic made of bright red cloth that they'd bought from a street vendor.

Alice, on edge now, smiled to hide her discomfort and told Wanda she'd be in touch to plan a dinner. They said their goodbyes and Alice turned around just in time to see Richie pulling out of his parking spot and heading back toward Bethany. Whatever he'd been doing in Woodstock, it hadn't taken him long.

Alice scanned the opposite side of the street. Where had he gone? The shops along the section of Main Street where he must have been headed were, in order, the pharmacy, the jewelers, the general store, and Drake Outfitters, where you could buy boots and . . . hunting gear and ammunition. Could Richie have been taking ammunition from the store and reselling it at Drake's?

Alice crossed the street, waving a thank-you to a farmer in a truck who slowed to let her go. When she opened the door at Drake's, a bell tinkled somewhere in the store and she looked up to find herself in a cluttered shop, filled with red and green wool jackets and tall gum boots and other things for hunters and outdoorsmen. She had only been in a handful of times and the man behind the counter did not appear to recognize her. She smiled at him and browsed the jackets, choosing a red-and-black plaid one that was on sale and steeply discounted. When she brought it to the register, she got out her checkbook and started making out the check, looking back toward the door to say, "I thought I saw my neighbor Richie Gerhart coming out a few minutes ago. Was he just in here? I've been meaning to ask him about his grandmother." She handed the check over and watched as the man wrote out the receipt.

"Wouldn't have been him," the man said. "We've been quiet here this morning. You're my first customer of the day. This time of year, no one's thinking about what they'll wear out in the woods yet."

"I suppose that's to my benefit," Alice said cheerfully. "I got an awfully good deal on this jacket. My nephew will be so pleased." The man, who didn't look as pleased as the imaginary nephew, nodded and handed her the bag.

Driving home, Alice felt deflated, like she had failed Dorothy. Maybe Richie had stolen the ammunition. Maybe he'd brought it to Woodstock and been planning on selling it at Drake's but then lost his nerve. Maybe he'd seen Alice when she was talking to Arthur and Wanda and he had been afraid of being spotted. She parked in her drive and, remembering that Mildred had asked her to buy sugar, walked down to Collers' and handed over a handful of change to a grim-looking Dorothy. When she asked the girl how she was today, Dorothy couldn't even give her an answer in English. She merely grunted and turned away from Alice to fetch a bag to put the sugar and a newspaper in.

It was exceedingly unpleasant, and as Alice left the store, on edge now too after her encounter with Arthur and Wanda and overwhelmed by all she had to do to get the flower arrangements ready for tomorrow, she felt as though a dark cloud had descended upon the town, though the sun was shining. At home, she made herself a strong gin and tonic and sat out in the garden with the newspaper. The headlines were not quite as gloomy as her mood. President Johnson had signed the voting rights bill. Alice felt a small rise in her chest. It was a bright spot, though she knew that it would not go unanswered in some quarters. The last year had shown them that. Why, Alice's dear friend Patsy Remick from Virginia had a son who had been working in Mississippi with the young men who were killed there while registering voters. Was this just the way of the world, progress and resistance in an endlessly repeated cycle? Alice sighed.

There was a large article about the Viet Cong's losses in recent combat in Vietnam, though there was also an article about how US bombing campaigns had failed to cut Viet Cong supply lines and a small item about a crippled US bomber crashing in Nha Trang and killing civilians on the street. Alice knew, from Ernie, that much of what you read in the papers was, if not actually false, exceedingly incomplete. You had to look at the whole picture, rather than any one piece of reporting, and the whole picture was that things were perhaps not as rosy as the defense department would like Americans to believe.

There was a story about the new draft quotas, making the point that though many more men would be called up, many of them would be ineligible for physical reasons, or mental ones. Alice, of course, was not eligible to be drafted, but if she were she didn't think she would find this reassuring.

The local news consisted of the usual, a couple of collisions, the theft of a car from the post office lot, a longer-than-usual social section since it was August and Old Home Day and prime visiting time. Alice learned that the Richard Martins had been in New Brunswick, New Jersey, for the week, visiting with Mrs. Martin's family. Jean Gilman was entertaining friends from California and planned to bring them along to the Old Home Day celebration. She saw that Terry Spaulding's brother, Petey, was back for a visit and planned to attend Old Home Day. Alice had always liked Petey. Unlike Terry, he was a good-hearted man, generous and compassionate. He was very like their mother, while Terry had taken after Rick Spaulding, and while Terry had taken over their father's farm, Petey had become a dentist and lived in Hartford, Connecticut.

There was no report of any thefts at stores like the Collers', which was a disappointment. It meant that it was more likely that the solution to the theft lay closer to home.

Again, Alice felt the presence of a dark cloud over Bethany. It was spoiling what was usually one of her favorite weekends of the year. She would have to do something, she resolved to herself. She would have to do something soon.

Twenty-one

Warren took a shower and stood for a moment in front of his closet. He had winnowed his wardrobe when he'd moved out of the Boston house last year, before he'd gone out west. As a result, he didn't have many clean clothes to choose from. It would have to be the pale-blue polo his mother had sent him for his birthday and a pair of almost-clean khakis. Dressed, he felt normal again. The air had cooled a bit and as his hand hovered over the gin bottle downstairs, he decided on the spur of the moment to have his cocktail, and maybe some dinner too, at the Bethany Inn.

It was a pleasant walk down to the other side of the green and it was only when he saw a well-dressed couple walking ahead of him that he remembered it was Friday night. Well, he'd find out what the nightlife was like in his new hometown.

Doctor Farnham's Tavern was at the back of the inn, a cozy bar and restaurant with a huge stone fireplace decorated with an old pair of skis and fifteen small tables in the square room. It had been empty when Warren had his clam chowder the other night, but now it was almost full, tables of couples and groups of four or six eating and talking. He spotted Barbara Falconer in a group of young men and women. They were laughing and she was telling a story, her friends listening with obvious affection and interest. He found himself wondering if her fiancé was one of the men at the table. When she saw Warren, she smiled and waved and he waved back. He sat at the bar and ordered a gin and tonic.

"You want something to eat?" the bartender asked him. It was not the older man from Warren's first visit. This was a much younger man, with longer sideburns than most of the men in Bethany, and a blue button-down shirt that looked like Brooks Brothers.

"Yeah, what's good? I had the clam chowder the other night and it was fine, but . . ."

The man—boy, really—leaned over the bar and said, "Let me tell you something since you're new. Vermont's not really the place to get seafood."

Warren grinned. "Thanks for the tip. Can I just have a hamburger?"

The bartender gave him a thumbs-up. "Good choice."

Warren sipped his gin, his mind settling down and starting to work again. One thing was clear to him now. There was someone in Bethany who knew about the fires, who had been living in the woods, and had perhaps been involved in both fires or, at the very least, had been a witness to one or both. Someone who had not shown his face. This was interesting and warranted further investigation. They would need to search the woods for Jorah Hatchett's mysterious cow wrangler.

And of course, the more Warren learned about Hugh Weber, the more he wondered about how he'd treated his wife. If he'd been abusive, well . . . Warren had been involved in a few homicides where the killer had been a fed-up wife. In most of those, once he learned the details, he came to feel that he couldn't blame them, even if it was his job to exact justice.

His hamburger came and he ate it with pleasure, finishing every last bite and every bit of the generous portion of french fries. All that walking around had given him an appetite.

"Busy tonight," he said to the bartender. "Is it always like this?"

"Nah." The man, only twenty-one or so, said, "It's Old Home Day tomorrow. They're all back to see their families and old friends." He nodded toward Barbara Falconer's table and Warren understood suddenly what he was looking at: school friends, scattered to other towns and cities and states, home again and catching up with the friend who had stayed. He wondered suddenly whether Barbara Falconer wanted to be living here in her hometown with her parents or if it was something to do with the fiancé.

"So it's a big thing then? I've been seeing posters over all town."

The bartender shrugged. "I guess. I'm not from here, but it was a good time last summer. Lot of people, food, music, and so forth." His face did something complicated. Regret, pleasure, fear, Warren thought he saw.

Warren considered him. "Where are you from then?"

"Chicago." He sighed, looking sheepish. "I'm at Dartmouth right now. Met a girl from Connecticut up at Killington . . . well, she's my wife now. And we . . . well, our little girl was born in October. Her old man has a place not far from here and he bought us a house here in town so I can finish up and graduate and . . . I'm working here just on Fridays and the weekends to make some extra money." Warren saw how it was. A pregnancy, a shotgun wedding, the wealthy father setting the young couple up in Vermont, away from his own business and social life.

"I'm Franklin Warren," he said, reaching across the bar. "I'm the new detective at the state police barracks. Just moved to town."

"Erik Sorensen," the bartender said, wiping his hand on a towel folded neatly on the bar and shaking Warren's hand. "Nice to meet you." He went off to pour drinks for a group that had just come in.

The place had an appealing atmosphere, Warren decided. He was alone, but he didn't feel lonely. He put cash on the bar and was about to go when he thought to ask Erik Sorensen about whether he'd met Victor Weber yet.

"I believe he's staying here at the inn," Warren said. "Tall guy, in a nice suit. Not the most . . . polite character."

"Oh yeah," Erik said, grinning. "He's a real piece of work. He was in for his supper and some drinks, ordering everyone around." He composed his face then, remembering. "I'm sorry he lost his brother, though. That's a bum deal."

Warren realized suddenly that he'd meant to check with David Williamson again about the estate. Had Sylvie Weber or Victor Weber heard anything from New York? He'd try to catch him tomorrow at Old Home Day.

"Did Hugh Weber ever come in?"

"Once in a while. I don't like to speak ill of the dead, but he was an ugly drunk. When he did come in, I usually had to cut him off."

Warren nodded. "That fits with what I've heard. Did he bring his wife? When he was drinking, I mean."

Erik shook his head. "No. I never saw her in here. He liked to sit at the bar and look around and start up conversations with anyone he thought was his intellectual equal. Let's just say he didn't put many people in that category. But if there was someone from the college in here, a professor or something, and Hugh Weber got wind of it, he'd find a way to start talking with them and try to show off how brilliant he was. Once he found out that I'm a Dartmouth student, well then I was all right in his opinion and he decided he'd deign to talk to me." He started to roll his eyes and then remembered that the man was dead and settled for a head shake.

"He ever get into trouble? Starting fights and so forth?"

"Few times. Chief Longwell dragged him out and drove him home a couple times because he was too far gone."

Erik had to go off to help some other patrons and so Warren said good night and got up to go. Barbara Falconer's party was leaving too and as they all went out into the night, she turned to him and said, "How are you, Mr. Warren? Or is it detective or something?"

"How about just Warren?" he said, smiling. "That's what most people call me." She introduced him to the friends, who said hello somewhat impatiently. They'd all had a lot to drink. Her eyes were glittering and her friends were laughing and ribbing each other. "We're going back to my mom and dad's for another drink," she said. "You're welcome to join us."

"Yeah, come along, Officer," one of the young men blurted out. "We promise we won't break any laws."

Warren smiled. "I think I'll skip it, but thanks just the same. I'm saving my energy for this Old Home Day thing tomorrow. I hear it's not to be missed." They all turned to look at the white tent and Ferris wheel already set up on the green. Smaller tents lined the edges and bunting had been installed on the gazebo. Warren had seen a poster advertising a concert and a pie-eating contest after the parade.

Barbara smiled. "Well, I don't know about that. Coming from Boston, I think you might find it a bit boring, but it got this crew to come home anyway. We all went to school together and I haven't seen them since last year."

He thought about reconsidering the drink invitation for a moment, but only a moment.

"Enjoy. I'll see you there." For a moment, he watched them walk off, some sense of protectiveness arising when he saw one of the young men stumble. But he was only happily drunk and he seemed fine to walk along to the Falconers'.

As he made his way home, the windows of the houses along the green offered Warren glimpses of all those lives, parted curtains revealing a couple sitting in one living room, a family at a table in another. As he passed Alice Bellows's house and turned into his own driveway, he saw her in the kitchen window, working on what seemed to be a flower arrangement. Behind her were buckets filled with pink and white blooms. He turned away when she was in mid-gesture so he never knew what she had been about to do.

That was how it was with other human beings. Until you started digging, you only ever saw snapshots of their lives. Even then, you had to remember that there were things that happened out of sight.

You never really knew what happened when you weren't there.

Twenty-two

Saturday dawned hazily, the air stagnant in the house by six A.M. Warren lay in bed for a long time. He wasn't on duty, but he wanted to see what Old Home Day was like and get himself some pie, and he also wanted to use it as an opportunity to check up on his new neighbors and see if he could learn anything about whoever it might be who was plaguing the town.

The thermometer in the kitchen was already at 75 degrees by the time the coffee was ready. Warren drank it outside in his backyard, listening to the brook trickle slowly behind his house. A few birds trilled halfheartedly. Next door, the sounds of a radio and women talking filtered out. He watched Mrs. Bellows's housekeeper going in and out the side door, taking boxes and baskets out to the Rambler.

He was on his way back inside with his empty cup when Mrs. Bellows herself came out, struggling a little with a large box filled with the flower arrangements he'd seen her creating last night.

"Good morning," she called out cheerily. "I'm taking these down to the Ladies Aid tent on the green. Will you be coming to Old Home Day, Mr. Warren?"

He put his cup on the ground and went to help. "Here, let me get that for you." The back of the car was filled with more arrangements in cardboard boxes and he fit the one he took from her in next to them. "I was thinking about it. What exactly happens at Old Home Day?"

She wiped her hands on the apron she wore over her yellow dress. "Well, there's a parade at ten, and then music and lunch and a pie-eating contest and a pet show. The library has an open house and book sale and the churches are open for tours. The Ladies Aid Society puts on a raspberry social—that's what these are for. I highly recommend that you save some room after lunch."

"I'll be sure to," Warren said. "It seems like the perfect way to spend a summer day. Very quaint and, well, Vermontesque." He smiled broadly at her.

Mrs. Bellows's eyes flashed and then settled on him in a way that made him feel he'd disappointed her. "Do you know what the origin of Old Home Day is, Mr. Warren?" He shook his head and she said, sharply, "It was started around the turn of the century, to lure back the sons and daughters who had abandoned their hometowns for better soil, bigger places. Farms and lovely farmhouses lay empty and rotting because their former inhabitants had moved west or went to the cities for work. Towns and villages emptied out, leaving behind all the . . . social problems you might imagine, not enough people to form a thriving society, not enough workers to pay the taxes, not enough . . . well, not enough people, if you see." He didn't see, but she had worked herself up into a state of agitation so he nodded as though he did.

Alice Bellows took a deep breath and said, "So, yes, it has now become a happy occasion for people to return home to visit, but the landscape is still dotted with empty farmhouses and fallow land, and that is not *quaint* by any stretch of the imagination." She smiled then, to show that she was just correcting the record and that there were no hard feelings, he thought, and she allowed, "It *is* a lovely way to spend a summer day, though."

"I'll definitely be there then," he said, chastened. "And I'll make sure to give the Ladies Aid my dessert business. Can I help you with any more of those?"

"No, thank you. Mildred has the last one and then we'll be off." She glanced toward the sky. "I might bring your umbrella, Mr. Warren. It looks like rain."

⋈ ⋈ ⋈

The parade was late in starting, as parades involving children and animals and large, slow-moving vehicles often are, and by the time Warren heard the distant strains of a marching band, it was nearly ten thirty. The green was packed and he found himself pleased that, even though he had only been a Bethany resident for less than a week, he recognized more than a few of the spectators lining the road on either side of the green. There was the lawyer/fire chief, David Williamson, with a middle-aged woman who must be his wife, and an older couple who had to be his parents or in-laws. A young couple held hands next to them—a son or daughter and paramour, back for a visit, he supposed. Warren waved and resolved to speak to Williamson later. A bit farther down the line of spectators were the Falconers. Barbara and one of the young women who'd been at the tavern with her last night were holding small American flags and wearing sunglasses, their hair under blue bandanas, their legs bare under denim skirts.

Across the street, in front of Collers' Store, the woman who he'd seen behind the counter at the store had come out to watch. As the parade approached, Warren saw Roy Longwell keeping the road clear across the way, looking hot and uncomfortable in his uniform.

Warren searched the crowds for Sylvie Weber and her children, but he didn't see them anywhere. Of course they wouldn't be here. It wouldn't be appropriate, so soon after her husband's death. It would be suspicious if she *was* here.

But Warren had the distinct feeling that Sylvie Weber didn't care much about what was appropriate and what was not. Or rather . . . actually, he wasn't sure exactly what he thought about her. She did not seem to hold conventional views and yet, perhaps she didn't want to offer up her children for speculation or judgment. Warren knew something about judgment.

The marchers came into view. First was a marching band made up of musicians of many different ages. Warren smiled at a small girl twirling a baton and a teenage boy playing the trumpet. Then came some kids with dogs on leashes, a few with ponies or calves on leads. One of the ponies was decorated with a cacophony of floral garlands, so many it seemed to be bowing its head in protest. There were men with teams of oxen, walking slowly along the road. Each team deposited at least one pile of fresh manure on to the street and Warren wondered who would have to clean it up. Next were the floats, one for the library—a Little Red Riding Hood theme, complete with a little girl in a red dress and cloak and a boy in a wolf costume. There was a progression of floats that seemed to be for alumni of the high school. Warren recognized one of the men who'd been at the tavern with Barbara Falconer the night before on the Class of '57 float.

There were fire trucks—Terry Spaulding's son and son-in-law Gordo waved from the windows of two of the trucks, the kids with them throwing candy to the spectators—and decorated cars and then at the end of the parade, the veterans: twenty or so men, dressed in uniforms and walking slowly and deliberately along the street of their hometown, a drummer behind them, beating a mournful rhythm. Warren recognized Jorah Hatchett, wearing a navy uniform and marching precisely in step with the other men. The crowd got very silent and many of the people watching put their hands on their hearts or saluted the men. But from somewhere in the crowd, Warren heard a shouted "No more war!" and then an echoing "US out of Vietnam!"

He turned to find the source of the statements but the speaker was somewhere in the crowd. Behind him were the Falconers; Barbara Falconer was pressing her right hand to her heart, and her father, his own hand at his side, watched but did not react. About one hundred yards behind the veterans, a lone man marched. He was tall, gray-bearded, powerfully built, and dressed in ragged fatigues, the loden jacket tattered and frayed. And he was holding an American flag upside down, brandishing it in front of him, an expression of defiance on his face.

A hum of disapproval in the crowd started quietly and then built as he passed. Someone yelled out, "No war!" and then someone else yelled, "Disgraceful!" The man kept walking and the hum stayed just a hum and then he was past them and after a few minutes the parade was over and the crowd filtered back to the green, where a band had started playing in the gazebo. Warren found Pinky helping to direct traffic and said, "Who was that?" knowing what the answer was before Pinky glanced away and said, "That's Jeffrey Sawyer, the one I was telling you about."

"He ever done that before?"

"I don't think so," Pinky said. "But he might have written a letter to the editor, about Vietnam, you know."

Warren nodded. That was interesting. If Hugh Weber had been of a mind with this Jeffrey fellow, and had expressed some passion around US involvement in Southeast Asia, then that ripple of anger he'd sensed in the crowd might have given someone a motive to hurt him. What if some rabidly patriotic townsperson had gone up there to talk to him and there'd been a fight? The assailant, whoever they were, might have set the fire to cover up his crime.

"Thanks, Pinky. I'm off to sample the food."

"Enjoy," Pinky said. "Hey, if you're over that way, would you mind poking your head into the tavern at the inn? They're open all day and sometimes you get some of the guys overdoing it, happy to be home with their friends, you know?"

Warren gave him a wink. "You got it."

Things seemed quiet at the tavern so he decided to have his lunch at a tent sponsored by the high school's student government association. A plate of baked beans, ham, coleslaw, and sweet pickles almost filled him up, but as he passed the Ladies Aid Society's raspberry social booth, he found he had just enough room for a bowl of cake with raspberries and sauce and whipped cream. Alice Bellows was behind the table and he gave her a dollar bill and told her to keep the change. "I trust you'll put it to good use," he said, with a smile.

"Oh, yes. We provide scholarships to our Bethany High School graduates and have a fund to help out families going through difficult times. Thank you, Mr. Warren. Did you enjoy the parade?"

"I did, thank you." Something in her expression made him say, "It was a good introduction to some of the different . . . elements in Bethany."

She took two quarters from the next person in line and handed over a bowl, then turned back to him. "Yes, Mr. Warren. I believe it must have given you a good picture of things."

"Do you know Jeffrey Sawyer well?" he asked. "I understand he's the reason that Hugh Weber came to Bethany in the first place."

Alice Bellows smiled at someone over his shoulder and then frowned as she thought about how to answer. "Not well. He keeps to himself. But I've had a few interesting discussions with him over the years." She saw where he was going, though, and said, "He and Hugh Weber had a falling-out of some kind and, as far as I know, had not been in touch in many years. But you might want to look into the source of the disagreement."

"Right. Thank you, Mrs. Bellows. I'm going to go and eat my

raspberry cake. It looks delicious. And the flowers will make the experience all the more pleasurable." It *was* delicious, the cake light and airy and the raspberries and vivid sauce both tart and sweet, evoking a memory Warren couldn't quite access. What had Sylvie Weber said, about the jam? *When you eat it, you'll be going back in time to today.*

He had it then. The memory. Maria had brought home a box of raspberries from the restaurant one night. He searched for the word and found it in the taste memory. *Lamponi.* They had eaten them all in one sitting, greedily grabbing for them out of the flimsy box, the juice squishing out between their fingers as they laughed and playfully fought over the last handful.

Grief swept over him and he had to bow his head for a moment to get control of himself.

He blinked and found himself again in the tent, surrounded by Alice Bellows's flowers. When he thanked her and placed his totally empty bowl on the table, he thought she had read his mind; the look she gave him was both pitying and sympathetic.

Strains of music—"My Old Kentucky Home," he thought, somewhat bemusedly—came through from outside and he went back out into the humid, close day to see what was happening.

Twenty-three

Sylvie had not been planning to go to Old Home Day. She had made the decision the night before, telling the boys that they had too much work to do and that they would stay at home. They had been disappointed, but had not pushed back, even Louis, who had been talking about Old Home Day in the same way he talked about the Bethany Fair, remembering its delights and speculating about what it would be like when they went this year. Last year, he had ridden a pony and eaten two pieces of cake when Hugh was off talking to someone about selling some of their heifers. Hugh had never been aware of the cake and Louis had never told him, mentioning it to Sylvie only in quiet moments when he knew Hugh could not hear. She had been expecting tears from Louis; he had just nodded and absorbed the news stoically.

But then, after the younger boys were in bed, Scott had come out to find her where she was bringing the washing in and said seriously, "Is it because of . . . because of the fire, that you don't want us to go, I mean?"

She had stopped folding the sheet she'd taken down and turned to look up at him. "Well, yes, I suppose that's why," she said. "I don't want people looking at us, feeling sorry for us. I don't like that."

"I wouldn't like it either," he said. "But maybe it would be . . . maybe it would take the boys' minds off it. It might make it better for them." He looked away and she reached out to touch his shoulder, trying to say with her touch what she couldn't put into words. His face was in profile against the almost-dark sky. She caught a glimpse of her oldest brother suddenly, something about the shape of Scott's forehead.

"Let's see how we all feel tomorrow," she'd said. "It may be raining and then we won't want to go anyway."

But though the skies looked threatening, it didn't rain in the morning and by the time they'd finished chores and she'd made lunch for them, she felt lighter, almost optimistic, and she said, "You know what, let's go down and get some cotton candy! I've been thinking about cotton candy!" and the younger boys had smiled, confused but excited by the turn of events. Scott had looked apprehensive but pleased and said he'd go out and start the truck up. She hadn't driven in a while and as they'd clambered in, Scott next to her and the other boys in the bed, she said, "I've almost forgotten how. It will be good when you can drive us to town, Scott," and he smiled shyly. It wouldn't be long now. He was supposed to start high school in September, but she worried he might feel differently about it now. She'd have to talk to him, even if she'd been avoiding it. He felt so much, saw so much. There was so much unsaid between them, so many things they would have to figure out now. And yet, she didn't want him to have to be old before his time. She had been taking care of babies before she was ten years old in her large family, always too many mouths to feed and not enough to put in them. Her parents had done their best, but she had hoped for something different for Scott. But now . . . Sylvie sighed as the truck bumped onto County Road. In the back, the little boys laughed and hung on to the sides of the truck bed, comfortable on the pile of loose hay that had been in there for weeks now.

The green was still full of people when they parked the truck at four. Scott and Louis ran ahead and Andy held Daniel's hand so he wouldn't get lost. There were more tents than she remembered from last year, people selling crafts and jams and jellies. She should have brought her jam after all. How many jars might have been bought out of sympathy? The boys were already waiting at the cotton candy tent when she got there and she took out a few of the bills Mrs. Bellows had tucked into the basket and bought everyone their own cone of cotton candy—a rare indulgence.

People were staring; she knew they would. But she found she didn't care as much as she had thought. Let them stare.

Barbara Falconer came up to them and the boys stood there shyly, watching her, while she said, "Sylvie, all of you. I'm so very, very sorry for your loss."

"Thank you," Sylvie said. She had always liked Barbara. Barbara had told her a few times how bright the boys were and had made her feel that she was doing a good job with them. It was interesting, Sylvie thought, how when someone told you you were doing a good job, it made you *want* to do a good job. That was how it had been with Barbara. When Barbara took the job at Goodrich Hill School three years ago after she finished at the University of Vermont, she had immediately noticed that Andy was a strong reader, though he needed to work on his math. She had praised Sylvie for giving him so much exposure to books and writing and then said, "You can work with him on his times table, if you want. You've done such a good job with the reading that he'll have them in no time," and Sylvie had found that she *wanted* to work with him and, sure enough, he'd gotten them right away. That was the kind of student Andy was. You only needed to push him a little in the right direction and then he had it immediately. Hugh had been a bit jealous of that sometimes, Sylvie thought, of how quickly Andy understood things, how quickly he could get all the way *inside* an idea or a fact. It was ridiculous, a grown man being jealous of a boy, but nonetheless Sylvie had known it to be true.

Barbara gave Sylvie a reassuring pat on the shoulder. "How are the boys? Is there anything I can do to help? I hope you got the basket we sent to the Uptons."

"Yes, thank you. It was delicious. We're okay, all things considered, though you can help me convince Scott that he should go to high school," she said, checking to make sure he wasn't listening. "I think he might have decided he needs to stay home now, to help me. But I can manage fine. I want him to go."

Barbara smiled. "Of course. Leave it to me. I'll work on him."

And while Sylvie finished her cotton candy and let her mind float just a little as she watched the crowds, Barbara asked the boys about the animals and told them about the puppies and then she said offhandedly to Scott, "Oh, Scott, I meant to tell you. The new woodshop teacher at the high school is wonderful. I told him all about you and about the little table you made for the school last year and he said he is going to look for you on the first day of school. You'll like the new math teacher too. She's very smart. She'll be able to keep up with you."

Barbara chatted with the boys and Sylvie looked around at the crowds. The Ferris wheel and merry-go-round moved at the other end of the green. There was something so pretty and festive about the white tent and the tables and colorful banners hanging by each one. Outside the Ladies Aid tent, there were tables with large pink flower arrangements from Mrs. Bellows's garden. *Blossoms of light? Drops of color?* How to describe the cheerful colors of Old Home Day? Her brain was tired, but she wanted to take a picture of it, to remember later.

The voice from behind her snapped her back. "Mrs. Weber. I'm very sorry for your loss."

It was Jeffrey Sawyer, taller than she remembered, tall enough that she had to tip her head back to see him, a hand shielding her eyes from the sun. He had a long gray beard and he was wearing army clothes, a tattered olive-green jacket with patches and badges on the pockets and shoulders, and olive-green trousers. She was confused by that at first and then she remembered that the veterans usually marched in the parade. Hugh, who had not served because of his terrible eyesight, had always seemed uncomfortable when they marched past.

"Thank you," she said. She didn't know what to say after that. Sylvie often felt that she didn't know what to say to people. They looked at you as though they were expecting something, like there was a script, but no one had given the script to her. It was hard to translate her thoughts into words sometimes. But he just nodded as though he also did not know what to say. A loud popping, like a gunshot, startled them both and when she looked up at his face, she could see he was anxious. But then he said, "One of those old cars that was in the parade."

She nodded and he was turning to go when an angry voice came from behind him.

"What did you mean by that? What did you mean by that display in the parade? That was shameful. Are you a communist or what?"

Gordo Forbush, his face red and angry, pointed at Jeffrey Sawyer. He was drunk, Sylvie knew. She recognized the unfocused look of his gaze, the way he overpronounced the word "communist," like it tasted new in his mouth. She felt her body freeze, her mind go narrow. She knew too well the electric tension in the air between the men. When they were like this, when drink was involved, well, things moved very quickly. She didn't know Gordo well, but she had heard enough stories from Hugh to know he had a reputation for fighting.

"I was just exercising my right to free speech, Mr. Forbush," Jeffrey said. "That's what I fought for over there, after all." He said it breezily and started to turn away, but Gordo wasn't going to let it go. He grabbed Jeffrey by the arm and spun him around.

Jeffrey shrugged him off and then drew himself up and put his hands on Gordo's arms and looked down at him. "I don't want to fight with you," he said. "I want peace with all men."

Where were the boys? Sylvie looked around. If this was going to be a fight, she didn't want them to see it. She reached up to wipe sweat from her forehead. It was very hot standing out here in the sun and she needed some water. The baby kicked, as if protesting the heat, and she put a hand on her belly, feeling a bit dizzy.

A few people had gathered and Sylvie could feel them all holding their breath. Gordo was staring up at Jeffrey, his face crumpled in anger. Jeffrey stared back impassively. After a long moment of tight silence, Gordo swore and stumbled away.

Relief washed over her. She called to the boys and said they would walk around the green and then it was time to head home. She was so tired all of a sudden, exhausted by the week and the grief and the worry and the heat. Above the green, the skies were gray now, but no rain had fallen. The air seemed infused with energy.

It felt now like everyone really was staring at them. She had had nothing to do with the argument between Jeffrey and Gordo Forbush, and yet everyone seemed to think she was a part of it. She felt suddenly that they needed to get home now, *right now,* and she tried to smile at the woman walking toward her, holding a baby. Sylvie couldn't remember her name, but she was married to Erik, who worked at the tavern. Perhaps he was working today. Hugh had told her about Erik, that he was a Dartmouth student and seemed to be "a bit more intelligent than your usual fellow in town." Sylvie had met them a few times in town, had sat in the waiting room at Dr. Falconer's with Erik's pretty wife, hardly more than a girl, who started to raise her hand in greeting.

Suddenly, she saw Hugh's brother approaching. He was coming from the direction of the inn and like Gordo, he was quite drunk already. She could tell from the way he weaved and held his arms at his sides to steady himself.

Sylvie felt everything start to blur. All she cared about was getting the boys away from him. She turned, looking for them, but everything was strange, blurry and indistinct. She thought she heard Louis's voice call out *"Maman?"* But she wasn't sure. She closed her eyes, trying to gather her strength, and suddenly, he was right in front of her.

"Are you enjoying your newfound wealth, Sylvie?" he slurred, looking at her with a mixture of disgust and wanting that made her terrified. She couldn't find a single word in her head, though she thought she might have made a small, strangled sound.

"I needed that money and he promised it to me," he said in a low voice meant only for her. "Did you make him change his will?"

What was he talking about? She stared at him. "I don't know . . . I don't know what . . ."

"I'm his executor, or did you forget that? I called the bank and they told me all about the accounts. You're a rich woman now. Are you happy? *Are you happy?*"

"I don't know what you're talking about," she managed to say. "Anything he had . . it's for his children."

"If they're even his," he spat out, the words tangling on his tongue. "He told me about you, you know. He said he thought you'd be a good *breeder.* Turned out he was right." He was really slurring his words now, speaking slowly and trying to enunciate. "But I wondy . . . wonder about you. He told me he'd never leave anything to you, because you're too stupid to know what to do with money. Simple, he called you! He knock you up? Is that why you married? Because you tricked him into—"

She heard someone say, "Mr. Weber!" and then Victor leaned forward and she could smell the whiskey on his breath and feel his hands digging into her arms as he tried to make her look up at him and she turned her face away and closed her eyes and felt the world start to slip. *The boys, where were the boys?*

"Mr. Weber, step away!" It was Chief Longwell. "Mr. Weber!"

"Are you okay, Mrs. Weber?" someone asked her. Warren, the policeman. She recognized his voice and she opened her eyes and tried to tell him to make sure the boys couldn't hear, but then a wave of nausea rose up. Everything slowed down and she felt as though she were hearing the voices in slow motion.

She heard thunder and felt rain on her face and then everything went dark.

Twenty-four

Warren had noticed Victor Weber for the first time not long after he'd arrived on the green that morning. He had seemed sober then and so when Warren saw him the second time, coming from the direction of the tavern, he had felt a flash of alarm at the way the man weaved past the tents. Warren decided to follow, to keep an eye on him and—if he was honest—to see if he might reveal something in his inebriated state. Warren had the sense that there was something Victor Weber was holding back and he wanted to know more about the man's statement that his brother had promised him something in his will. He'd followed him for a bit and then lost him in the crowds on the green.

The crowds had dissipated somewhat as it got on toward late afternoon. Families who had come for the parade had had enough and the people and groups running the tents were looking nervously at the increasingly gray and hazy skies and starting to pack up their wares.

Warren was watching the pie-eating contest when Fred Fielder greeted him, shaking his hand and saying, "Fred Fielder, Detective Warren. We met the other day at the newspaper office."

"Of course. Hello again, Mr. Fielder. Are you having a good time?"

"Oh, yes, the kids love Old Home Day. And it's nice to see old friends again. How about you? What do you think of our little hamlet?" Something about Fielder's intense expression made Warren think that whatever he said was going to be turned into a splashy headline: "New Cop Finds Bethany Boring." He just murmured something about it being a very nice event.

"Say, I meant to ask you if you're a fisherman, Detective Warren. Are you?"

Warren smiled. "Well, I am, actually. Did some fly-fishing out in Montana last year. Really enjoyed it."

"Ahhhhhh, Montana. I've never been but I can just see it now, sun sparkling on the lazy rivers, fish jumping to the sky . . . Was it like that, Detective Warren?"

"Pretty much."

"Well, you'll have to come fishing with me sometime. I know all the best spots around here."

"I'd like that, Mr. Fielder. I'm pretty busy right now getting up to speed on my new job, but maybe in a little bit."

They looked out across the green, smiling at the crowds and the festive atmosphere. Warren was trying to think of an elegant way to extricate himself when Fielder said nonchalantly, "Heard you're considering that fire at the Webers' murder now, huh? Any sense of who might have done it?"

Warren tried not to smile at the all-too-obvious tactic. "Mmmm, we're looking at some different things. What's your thinking on it, Mr. Fielder?"

Fielder suppressed his own small smile. It would be a battle of wills then. "Oh, I'd say it could have been any one of quite a number of people. You have to think about who benefits, I suppose . . ."

He let it trail off and Warren wondered whether he knew something about the will.

"Mmm," he responded again. "Or who he may have made angry."

Fielder looked up then, his eye caught by someone across the green. "I know someone who's angry, Mr. Warren. I was over at the tavern and he was shouting about being overcharged."

Warren followed his gaze. Victor Weber stalked across the green, searching the crowd, and Warren felt his policeman's instinct go into overdrive. Victor was looking for someone.

"Excuse me, Mr. Fielder," Warren said. "I think I'd better go and check on things." He knew that Fielder would follow and if he was honest, he was a bit relieved to have another man for backup. He scanned the crowd but didn't see Pinky or Chief Longwell anywhere.

Somewhere in the distance, a clap of thunder sounded and a gust of wind whipped at the peaks of the high white tent. That was all the rest of the people on the green needed. Everyone looked skyward and began making preparations to leave.

And then Warren saw Victor approaching a small group of people at one end of the green, drawn like a moth to whatever it was that was happening. It took him a minute to understand what he was seeing.

The tall man in army fatigues who had been holding the upside-down flag was standing very still while Terry Spaulding's son-in-law Gordo shouted something at him, his finger out and pointing. The man seemed to draw himself up to his full height, but kept his body rigid and seemed to absorb the anger being hurled at him. Gordo grabbed him by the arms and Jeffrey Sawyer—Warren recognized him now—said something as he escaped and put his hands on Gordo's arms in turn. The men seemed to be locked in an angry embrace before Gordo turned and walked away.

Warren looked for Victor and found him watching the scene, a look of amusement on his face. He had enjoyed the exchange, enjoyed the drama and the tension. And then, at the exact moment that Warren recognized Sylvie Weber, standing off to the side a bit, holding a cone of cotton candy, he saw Weber see her too and start to approach.

Roy Longwell and one of his officers had noticed the commotion too and Warren watched them jog over, their hands out in front of them, clearing a path.

Warren felt sweat trickle down the back of his shirt as he followed. By the time he reached the group and pushed through the spectators, Sylvie Weber was ashen-faced and Victor Weber was leering drunkenly at her and saying, ". . . told me all about the accounts. You're a rich woman now. Are you happy? *Are you happy?*" She seemed to protest and then he got right in her face, muttering something Warren couldn't hear, and then, "He told me he'd never leave anything to you, because you're too stupid to know what to do with money. Simple, he called you! He knock you up? Is that why you married? Because you tricked him into—"

"Mr. Weber!" Longwell ordered. "Step away! Mr. Weber!"

"Are you okay, Mrs. Weber?" Warren asked her. Where were the children? He frantically scanned the faces in the crowd for those of the Weber boys and then suddenly, the oldest boy, Scott, was coming toward them. The younger boys had realized something was going on and were paused in motion, watching to see what would happen. Scott was big enough that he could take on his uncle, or might think he could, if it came to that. It couldn't come to that.

Longwell used his body to separate Victor Weber from his sister-in-law, positioning himself between them so that the man would have to step back and putting a hand on his holster so that Weber would remember he was armed.

"He *said* I'd be taken care of. The bastard never liked me," Victor was mumbling. Warren looked for the younger boys but couldn't see them. The crowd was moving away and Warren had the strong sense of *something* about to happen. He felt as though he was standing at the edge of the sea and a wave was about to crest and overtake him.

Drops of rain, fat, aggressive, no mere sprinkle, hit his face and a clap of thunder, closer now, boomed above them.

Sylvie Weber's eyes fluttered, then closed.

Warren reached for her. The crowd of people standing around looked toward the sky as a flash of lightning lit up the clouds. Her eyes rolled up in her head and she fell, her body crumpling like a marionette with its strings cut. He only caught her at the end, his hands under her arms arresting her fall.

Longwell got ahold of Weber and muscled him away.

"I didn't do anything," he protested drunkenly. "I didn't touch her."

"Someone find a doctor!" Warren shouted as he got her onto the ground and bent to feel her pulse. It was fast and light in her neck and when he touched her shoulder her eyelids fluttered and she moaned. It was raining in earnest now and he brushed a few big drops from her forehead, carefully stroking her dark hair away. Norm Falconer was there then and he took over, feeling for her pulse. "I want to get her over to the surgery," he said. "So I can examine her." He looked grim, his eyes worried. Warren had the sudden, terrible thought that she'd lost the baby and he felt lightheaded.

"I didn't touch her," Weber slurred. "I just wanted to talk to her about my brother."

"Well, you've earned yourself a trip back to the station with me," Longwell told him. His officer had Weber's hands handcuffed behind his back.

"Are you arresting me?" Weber looked shocked. "You can't arrest me. I didn't do anything."

"We'll see about that," Longwell said. "Right now, we're just getting you over to the station."

Warren thought about what to do and finally told Pinky to go along to the station. "I'll help Dr. Falconer get her inside and then I'll come over." Pinky nodded. Weber seemed subdued now and allowed himself to be led away, still protesting that he hadn't done anything.

"Dr. Falconer, let's get her to the surgery and then I'll take the boys back to my house while you examine Mrs. Weber," Alice Bellows said. She had appeared suddenly and Warren had the sense she'd been watching the scene unfold too. From the bag on her shoulder, she retrieved a large black umbrella, opened it, and held it over Sylvie, who was still on the ground.

Warren nodded and he helped Falconer lift her. Her eyes were open now and Falconer said, "Mrs. Weber, you fainted. We want to get you inside so we're going to take you to my office."

"The boys," she murmured, looking around at them. Her eyes met Warren's and he felt a tug in his chest at the fear he saw there. "The boys are here."

"They're coming with me, Sylvie. They'll be just fine," Mrs. Bellows said. "We seem to have some extra raspberry cakes and I thought they may be able to help with that." The younger boys, looking worried, had assembled now and followed Alice across the green while Falconer and Warren got Sylvie Weber upright and helped her across the street and into the surgery. They got her onto a low couch in the examination room and she murmured her thanks, gripping Warren's hand with her small cold one. "It's going to be fine," he said. "You're safe with Dr. Falconer." She nodded, a hand on her belly. Warren felt lightheaded again. His stomach pitched. Something about the doctor's office, the couch, her hand, it was dredging up a memory of Maria, something he didn't want to face. He shook his head and mumbled that he'd wait outside and he was sitting in the waiting room with his head between his knees when Barbara Falconer came rushing in then. "Is she okay?" Barbara asked. "That awful man, bullying her like that."

"Did you see what happened?" Warren asked her once he'd sat up again. She nodded. His vision still felt slightly off, but he took a deep breath and felt his body relax. Barbara handed him a glass of water, saying, "You look like you could use that."

He looked up at her and found her smiling sympathetically. Her blond hair was tied back and her clothes were soaked through, the bottom of her skirt dripping onto the carpet. "Thank you," he said, smiling back. "There was . . . there was a lot going on there. They got him to the station?"

Barbara nodded and went behind the receptionist's desk to fetch two towels. She handed one to him and used the other to try to absorb some of the rainwater that had soaked into her clothes. "Yes, he was meek as a lamb. I think he's quite drunk. Men like that fold once they're confronted, don't they? He's all cruel bluster, I'd say, but when it comes to it, he's afraid of his own shadow."

Warren tried to dry his hair a bit with the towel, but it was like bailing a boat with a teaspoon. "You'll have to get a change of clothes," Barbara said. "Do you want some of Dad's? I've got to go up and find some dry things."

"No, thank you. I'll just make sure Mrs. Weber's okay and then I'll have to go along to see if they need my help with Victor Weber."

Barbara seemed about to say something and then seemed to think better of it. "Good luck," she said. "It really was quite shocking, the way he went after her. I'll see you soon, I'm sure. I hope that didn't ruin the day for you."

"No, it was a lot of fun up until the fight. I'll put it on my calendar for next year." He winked and she smiled and went through the door to the house.

Rose Falconer came out minutes later and said, "She'll be okay, Mr. Warren. The baby's heartbeat is nice and strong. She just fainted. We're going to let her have a nice rest and then Norm and I can get the boys from Mrs. Bellows's and take them home."

Warren sighed with relief. He thanked the Falconers and said he'd go and check to make sure Victor Weber was behaving himself.

It was now pouring rain, the sky crackling and booming with thunder outside the windows of the doctor's office. He made a mad dash across the green and he was passing the inn when he decided to duck inside and see if anyone had witnessed Victor Weber's drinking. He found it packed in the lobby, families and couples having sought shelter there, waiting for the rain to pass. They had probably thought the rain would end in a few minutes, but now they were stuck and many had moved into the tavern to wait. No one was at the reception desk, so he poked his head into the tavern and found Erik Sorensen behind the bar. Sorensen waved and Warren asked him for a glass of water.

"You heard about the incident with Mr. Weber?" he asked. "Was he in here drinking before it started to rain?"

Sorensen looked sheepish. "I think it might be my fault, Mr. Warren. He came in and asked for a drink and I gave him one. I didn't know it'd hit him so hard."

"I'm betting he'd already had a couple before you served him. I don't think it'll turn out to be your fault. Anyway, he seems like the kind of man who might have caused a ruckus even without the drink, you know?" Warren winked at Erik Sorensen. He felt sorry for the younger man. He looked so worried.

"You can say that again. The first night he came in here he barged ahead of a guy from Boston and almost started a fight. Then after you came in last night, he came down and wanted to buy a whole bottle of whiskey. I told him I couldn't do it but he made such a fuss that the hotel manager said I should just hand it over. That's probably how he got so drunk today."

"I'd say so," Warren said. He was about to go out to wait for the manager when he realized what Erik Sorensen had said. "Hang on, when was the first time he came in here? You said you only worked Fridays and weekends. Does that mean he was here last weekend?"

"Yeah, I guess that's right. It would have been Sunday he checked in." Sorensen looked up, realizing the implications of his words. "The night of the first fire."

⌐ ⌐ ⌐

Warren found Pinky in the reception area at the police station, chatting with the young officer sitting behind the desk. "Where's Weber?" he asked as he came in, shaking himself on the rubber mat next to the door to get the worst of the accumulated moisture off his clothes.

"They've got him in a holding cell," Pinky said, looking up.

"He sober enough for me to talk to him?"

Pinky shrugged. "Yeah, I'd say just about. He's lost a bit of his fight."

He told Pinky about Erik Sorensen's revelation. "I confirmed it with the manager at the inn. He checked in late Sunday afternoon. He was in town when his brother died."

Pinky's eyes widened. He turned to the officer behind the desk. "Hal, can you ask Chief Longwell if we can talk to Mr. Weber?" The man nodded and went into the back of the station. It was Longwell himself who came back. He'd gotten soaked out on the green too and he looked smaller somehow, his uniform trousers clinging to his legs, his thick helmet of dark hair flattened out. "What's this all about, Mr. Warren?" he asked. "That fellow back there hasn't been charged. I haven't decided what I want to do with him yet."

"I know. But I've just found out that he was here in Bethany on the Sunday of the fire that killed his brother. I need him to confirm it so I can start interviewing witnesses. That's all I'll ask him."

Longwell studied Warren for a moment, as though he wasn't sure he was telling the truth, but Warren could see that he was interested now, and he could see that he hadn't known Victor Weber was in town the day of the fire. He seemed to be thinking and finally he said, "All right, come on back. But I want to be there."

Warren nodded. He told Pinky to come too and they followed Longwell through a door and along a dark hallway. The holding cell was really just a room with no windows and a reinforced door and when Longwell opened it with a key from a large, old-style ring, Victor Weber, sitting on a narrow bunk against one wall, immediately started asking what they were going to do with him and why he was still there. They'd given him black coffee; the small room smelled strongly of it. Longwell rolled his eyes at Warren and held the door open so they could all go in.

"Why are you here?" Victor asked Warren. "Tell him to let me go! I did nothing wrong."

"Mr. Weber," Warren said. "I just want to ask you about something. You were here in Bethany the day of the fire. Why didn't you tell me?" But as he said it, Warren realized it was his own fault. He had never asked Victor Weber exactly when he'd arrived. He had told Pinky to check with hotels and inns in the area, but they had gotten distracted by other things.

Victor snorted. "You didn't ask and why is it any of your business? That was between me and my brother."

"Did you see him on Sunday?"

"I don't have to tell you! I want a lawyer."

"Just answer the question, Mr. Weber." Longwell leaned toward him and Victor shrank away.

Warren held his gaze. "I'm investigating a suspicious death, Mr. Weber. You have relevant information. We can charge you and book you in and you can call a lawyer and go through the whole rigamarole, or you can just tell us what happened on Sunday."

Victor sighed and slumped back on the cot. He looked terrible, years older, his face wan, his eyes tinged with yellow. "Look, I drove up from New York to talk to him. I saw him very briefly."

"When?"

"The afternoon of the fire."

"Sunday?"

"Yes. I drove up to talk to him and then later I decided to stay the night at the inn because I'd . . . well, I was too tired to drive all the way back to New York." *Too drunk*, Warren thought.

"What happened?"

"What do you mean?"

"You drove up to the farm . . ." Warren prompted him.

"Yes. I went up there and he came out to see who it was. He didn't even invite me in, just asked what I wanted. My own brother! I hadn't seen him in fifteen years!"

"Why did you think you might be included in his will?"

Weber looked away, embarrassed.

"Mr. Weber? We can do this officially tomorrow or you can tell me right now."

Weber closed his eyes briefly, then said, "I've had some financial problems. My own shares in my father's company were sold and . . . the proceeds lost years ago. I have expenses and I . . . thought I might see if he could be reasoned with. That's why I came up. I was hoping I could convince him to transfer his shares to me, since he seemed to hate the company so much! I didn't realize he'd already sold them. Years ago, he said he didn't want them because he resented our parents so much. He wanted to 'live authentically'! I thought maybe that was still the case. I hadn't seen him for a long time." The air had become hot and sticky with four bodies in the tiny room.

"Tell me what happened."

"I drove up there Sunday afternoon, once I'd arrived. It took some doing to find that . . . *place.* I'll tell you that. I got up there and I pulled in and he came out. He was quite aged, my brother. I was shocked. He didn't seem right, in the head. I told him what I wanted to talk to him about and he . . . told me to go away. He said he'd sold the shares years ago, that he had no need of the money, that he pretended it didn't exist. I think he wanted to see me slavering for it. He tried to tell me he didn't care about all these things. That he had found the secret to a happy life and that was simplicity, living off the land. He tried to lord it over me. But I could see he wasn't happy himself. He told me to go, but before I pulled out, he patted me on the arm and said, 'Don't worry, Vic, you'll be taken care of in my will. I promise you that.' I thought maybe he was going to leave something to me, but he was talking about the book! It was a joke to him!" His shoulders dropped and he sagged on the bed. "Could I have some water, please?"

Longwell opened the door and called out to one of the officers, who brought a glass of water.

"Was that it?" Warren asked him after he'd gulped the glass. "You didn't go back there again that day or night?"

"No," Victor Weber said. "I went back to the inn and, well, I had a few drinks. I thought I might go back and try again the next day but then . . . in the morning I came down for breakfast and they were talking about the fire. I tried to go up there but the fire trucks were blocking the way. I came back and tried to think about what to do. I was shocked. He . . . after all, he was my brother."

"What did you mean when you told Mrs. Weber that you knew about the accounts, that she was a rich woman now?"

"I talked to the bank in New York yesterday. When he sold the shares, he told them to do what they wanted with the money. They put them in stocks and bonds and now the accounts are worth ten times what they were. My father's hard work! And it's all hers!" He slumped farther down on the cot, a pathetic figure now, reeking of gin and black coffee. Warren almost felt sorry for him, until he remembered the nasty bite of his words to his sister-in-law, the way her face had looked when she'd fainted.

"I'll ask you again, Mr. Weber. Why didn't you tell me you were here in town?"

"Well, I'm not stupid, Mr. Warren. I could see by then how it would look. That I'd gone to try to talk to him. I didn't want you to think I'd made him so distraught he burned himself up!"

Warren thought for a few seconds. He did not believe that Victor Weber had told the whole truth. But he believed he had told most of it.

"Thank you, Mr. Weber. Just one more thing. When you went up to your brother's farm, did you see Mrs. Weber or the children?" Warren was wondering why she hadn't said anything about her brother-in-law stopping by. Had she lied to him? He still couldn't get over the feeling that she was holding something back. Roy Longwell looked up at that and Warren could feel him listening intently for the answer.

"Nah. He said they were moving some animals around. He'd come up to the house to get some tools to fix a fence."

Warren nodded. "Thank you."

Weber ran a hand over his head. "What's going to happen to me?"

"That's up to Chief Longwell," Warren said.

Victor's voice got very quiet. "Is she going to be okay?"

He waited a moment longer than necessary before answering. "Yes, Mr. Weber. She and the baby will be fine."

He thought Weber actually breathed a sigh of relief. Warren was turning away when Victor said, "I do have something else to tell you, Mr. Warren, for your investigation. As I was driving away from the farm, I saw someone, a man, with a beard and ragged clothes. He was hiding in the trees close to the farm. He was watching the house."

Twenty-five

In the end, Alice decided to go straight to the source. She had learned that there was a time to be cagey and there was a time to be direct. Her instinct told her that this was a time to be direct.

The day after Old Home Day was a Sunday, clear and sparkling, the thunderstorm and the hours of rain that followed having cleaned everything out so that it felt more like spring than summer. At church, the Reverend Call talked to the congregation about the concept of homecoming. He quoted Robert Frost and he welcomed those who were returning to Bethany for the week. Alice glanced at the Falconers, sitting three across in their second-row pew. Barbara had seemed to be enjoying herself yesterday, until the incident with Victor Weber, that was, but Alice knew that the absences of Greg Falconer and Barbara's fiancé, Tony Lindsey, must be weighing heavily on her and her parents' minds, especially with President Johnson's recent speech about the need for increased troops.

She was pleased to see that the congregation responded warmly to the sermon. The Reverend Call had gone down to Alabama in March and when he returned, he could not stop talking about what he had seen in Selma. There had been whispers that the multiple sermons on the subject were . . . a bit much. Alice had understood why he could not let it go; he had known the ministers beaten there, had known the minister killed by the white mob. She had told him to speak what was on his mind, that she would answer the whispers. She had only had to speak sharply to two members of the congregation, in the end.

When the service was over, she did not linger long, saying a few quick hellos and then returning home to change clothes.

The Gerharts lived along Church Street, in a small section of recently built Cape Cod–style homes, each with a driveway, garage, and small back lawn. The development had been the brainchild of Dick Byrnes and, just as Dick had promised, the small houses had appealed to young families and also to couples who had sold their farms or wanted a smaller house in their old age.

Alice knocked on the door and was pleased when Richie came around the side of the house from the garage, wiping his hands with a rag soaked in turpentine. She looked past him to see a sawhorse set up next to the garage, with a door balanced against it. He was painting.

"Mrs. Bellows?" He looked confused. He knew Alice, of course, from the store, but they were not on social terms and Alice had never been particularly friendly with Richie's parents.

"Richie," she said. "I'm so sorry to bother you. But I need to ask you something. I know that you've had some trouble at the store. And I know that Lizzie's father has accused you of stealing. I don't think you'd do something like that and, well, you know about these fires, don't you?" He nodded morosely. "I'm sure you can feel it too. Something isn't right in Bethany. And we need to get to the bottom of it. If you didn't steal those cartridges, well, then someone else did. I want to find out who it was."

She watched his face as he took in what she was saying. Richie was a quiet soul, but his emotions showed on his face. What Alice saw there was raw hope. He had thought his case was beyond redemption and she had offered him a tiny sliver of possibility that it wasn't. But then he considered another moment and she saw his face fall again.

"I wish I knew who took 'em," he said quietly, the smell of the turpentine rising in the air around him. "It surely wasn't me, Mrs. Bellows! I swear it. But I didn't see anything or anyone and . . ." He trailed off.

"And . . . ?" Alice asked after a minute.

"Well, I had gone into the back, even though Bob told me to stay out behind the counter, keeping an eye on things."

"So someone could have come in while you were in the back," she offered. "Why didn't you tell Bob that?"

He looked down at the ground. "I was embarrassed, Mrs. Bellows."

Alice tried to make her voice gentle, cajoling, as though she were speaking to a small child. "What were you doing, Richie? What were you doing in the back that you didn't want to tell Bob about it?"

He struggled with himself and then he shook his head sadly and said, "I'm too embarrassed to tell you, Mrs. Bellows." Alice tried not to show her surprise. What could it be? Pornography? An affair with someone who had agreed to meet him at the store? Neither seemed quite possible.

"Richie, we all have our little secrets, don't we? I promise I will be very discreet. But this is bigger than you and me, you know. Mr. Weber is dead and that camp belonging to the people from Boston has been burned down and whoever did it might also be the person who took the cartridges."

He struggled some more and then, wordlessly, he reached into his pocket and came out with a small black box. He handed it to Alice and when she saw the words printed on the outside, she understood what she had gotten wrong. It had not been Drake Outfitters that had been the purpose of Richie's trip to Woodstock. It had been Pendergast Jewelers.

"I was gonna give it to Lizzie that night," he said. "I hid it in the office. I was so worried about losing it, though, that I kept going back to check on it and it must have been . . . it must have been one of those times I was checking that they were taken."

Alice breathed out. Thank goodness it wasn't pornography or an affair. "Why didn't you explain to Bob?"

Richie took the box back from her. "I wanted to ask Lizzie first, before I talked to Bob. It seemed like what she'd want me to do. Lizzie . . . she has her own mind, Mrs. Bellows. I like that about her, even if some don't. And if I mentioned it to Bob and she found out later . . ."

Alice saw it. "He might have ruined the surprise and Lizzie might have been mad he knew before she did?"

"That's right. I thought that it would blow over. I thought Lizzie would stick up for me and Bob would realize that I'd . . . that I'd never do something like that. But . . ." Poor Richie looked around at his parents' yard, perplexed by how everything had come apart. "I tried to take the ring back last week but I couldn't do it, Mrs. Bellows. I want to marry Lizzie. I really do. I just . . ."

"Richie," Alice said. "I'm going to help you, but I need you to think very hard. You said you didn't see anyone who might have taken the cartridges, but did you see anyone who you are sure *didn't* take them, if you see what I mean?"

He furrowed his eyebrows. "Someone who didn't take them?"

She would have to spell it out. "Someone who might have been a witness."

"Oh, yes, well, I saw the Tewksburys walk past, but they didn't come in, and then Mr. Williamson came to get his papers, and Barbara Falconer came in and bought some meat for their bitch that's had the puppies. And Mrs. Harper came too. I remember because she didn't look well and I said something to Lizzie about it. That was before Bob discovered the cartridges were missing."

"Thank you, Richie," Alice told him. "I'm going to go and talk to Mrs. Harper. I hope we'll have news soon."

¤ ¤ ¤

Alice found Mary on the porch, sitting with a bowl of green pole beans. She was staring into the distance and absentmindedly snapping the ends of the beans. When she saw Alice, she put the bowl down and motioned her up onto the porch. Alice saw a shadow of pain sweep across her face. The cancer was quite far along then. Alice knew that look and she knew that Mary was likely near the end.

"Hello, Alice," Mary said. "It's funny, I was just thinking about you and now here you are."

Alice took one of Mary's thin hands in hers and squeezed it warmly. "I hear you've been up to Burlington, Mary. I stopped by the other day and Genevra told me. I'm so sorry you're not feeling well."

Mary smiled. "I am too, but it's to be expected, isn't it, things coming to a close at my age. I've been lucky, Alice. In so many ways."

The sun was angled perfectly, shining onto the porch so that it was warm, but not too hot. Mary had a handsome crop of blue and violet morning glories twining along the porch railings and the leaves provided ample shade. It was the perfect time for a good long chat. Alice sat down next to Mary and inquired after her grandchildren. She had remembered correctly that there were now a few great-grandchildren and Mary reeled off their names and ages and accomplishments. Alice always felt slightly uncomfortable at these recitations of the successes of people's offspring. It seemed to her that the reciter's pride was based entirely on the genetic connection they had with the child. She supposed people felt responsible for their children's accomplishments, though in her experience, they rarely claimed their children's failures. Alice didn't understand it, but she knew to make the right sounds and gestures and she could see how much pleasure it gave

Mary to talk about her family. It was her legacy. It was what she would leave behind.

What will I leave behind? Alice thought to herself and then she let that go, because it was not something she wanted to think too much about.

Finally, Mary said, "Were you just passing?" with a raised eyebrow.

"You know me too well," Alice replied. "I wanted to ask you something. I know you often do your shopping around midday. There was a bit of an incident at the store a couple of weeks ago. Something went missing. I suspect that this missing item is the source of the tension in the store, and between Lizzie and her father. You may have picked up on it. Have you seen anything around town that might shed some light on this situation, Mary?"

Snap. Mary dropped a topped and tailed bean into the bowl. Her hands went silent while she thought. "Well," she said finally. "There was the man with the jacket."

Alice waited. She didn't need to prompt Mary. Mary was just old and a bit slow to organize her thoughts. She would get there.

"I saw him for the first time not long after the Fourth of July," she said. "He isn't local. I assumed he was a tourist or a college student out for a drive, but then I saw him again, right around the time you say this incident in the store occurred. He was young, but his clothes were quite, well, shabby and dirty. He had a beard and he had not had a bath. What made me notice him, however, was his jacket. It was hot and he was wearing a jacket. That seemed strange to me. But then I never saw him again so I assumed he was staying in town but had gone back to wherever he came from."

"Mary, the new state police detective, Mr. Warren, is looking for a man who might have set the fires up on Agony Hill. Do you think this could be the same man?"

Mary turned to look at Alice, a shocked expression on her face. "I didn't think of that, because in my mind he had gone, you see. I sort of . . . closed him off. I suppose that could be the man, though where was he all this time?"

Alice considered that. "Mary, do you think you might be able to identify this man, if you saw him again?"

Mary grinned. "Not his face, but I think I could identify his jacket if I saw it. It was an old buffalo plaid hunting jacket, green and black, just like the one Willy wore to deer camp. It made me think of Willy is why I noticed the man, I think. And because it seemed so strange to wear that coat in July. I would recognize that coat."

Alice thanked her and walked slowly back toward the green. That coat was indeed suspicious, she thought to herself. The only reason to wear a jacket like that on a hot day was that you needed a place to hide something.

Something like eight boxes of rifle cartridges, Alice thought.

Twenty-six

Is that Goodrich Hill Road as in . . . you?" Warren asked Pinky as they followed the long dirt track out to Brook's End, Jeffrey Sawyer's place six miles out on a dirt road past Goodrich Hill Road Sunday morning. He had called up Pinky at home and asked if he'd be willing to drive out with him. Pinky had said he'd be happy to, but he had to go to church first. He sounded sheepish when he said that he'd drive his mother home after church and then come meet Warren at the barracks.

"Ah, yeah, there have been Goodrichs here since 1780. One of my uncles lives a mile or so back, in Goodrich Corners."

"Is that a different town?" Warren asked. He had been wondering about this. Some people referred to the location of his new home as Bethany Village and others as Bethany.

"Well, see, the town is called Bethany, right? But the village, where the green is, that's called Bethany Village. Then the other villages in the town are Goodrich Corners, North Bethany, Millersville, and Boston Hollow. You'll get it once you've driven around a bit more."

Warren nodded, trying to fix the names in his mind. "You been out to his place before?" Warren asked, slowing to steer around a huge rut in the road.

"Couple times, I suppose. Not for a while, though. Maybe five years ago. Helped my dad take a cow out there." Pinky hesitated and Warren glanced over at him just in time to see him blush as he said, "He's . . . a bit intimidating."

"How so?"

"Well, you saw him in the parade. He likes to make his point and he doesn't care what anyone else thinks." Warren didn't see how that translated to intimidating, but he knew he'd find out. It was just the two of them. They were armed, but perhaps he should have brought a few more troopers with him.

They turned onto a drive marked with painted signs that said, KEEP OUT! BROOK'S END PROPERTY!

"Ironic, isn't it?" Warren said, smiling. "You have a place where you're trying to get people to come live in peace and so forth and then you tell people to keep out."

"Yeah," Pinky said. "I think they got tired of kids trying to sneak down and get a look at 'em." He blushed crimson again and said, "I remember hearing from some other boys that you could go down there and see women without their blouses on. My brother and I tried it once but they were just slaughtering chickens." He paused. "In their blouses."

Warren laughed.

Up ahead they saw some buildings come into view, a few sheds and barns and then an old farmhouse painted an odd salmon-pink color, the paint peeling alarmingly. A clothesline was draped with a row of dungarees and long underwear, a few dresses and undergarments. There was a small log cabin–like shed off to one side, newer than the other buildings, and a huge pile of what looked like scrap wood and metal. The farm was down in a little hollow. There was no view of the landscape, as there was up on Agony Hill, and Warren found that it made him claustrophobic and anxious. There was something closed-off and, well, terminal about Brook's End.

Pinky parked the car in front of the house and almost immediately, Jeffrey Sawyer came out onto the porch wearing a long apron, stained with something dark and red, and holding a hatchet.

He put the weapon down when he saw Pinky, but didn't come closer, and when Pinky said, "Good morning, Mr. Sawyer," he called out, "What do you want, Trooper Goodrich?"

"We just want to talk," Pinky said. "This is the new detective out of the barracks, Franklin Warren. You might have seen him yesterday at Old Home Day."

Jeffrey Sawyer said nothing. Warren caught movement in one of the windows on the porch. There was someone else in there. His hand went to his holster, just reminding Sawyer that he was armed in case they had plans for an ambush, but Sawyer saw the gesture and called out, "Come on out. You're making this new cop nervous. If he's anything like Chief Longwell, a nervous cop is not a good thing."

The door opened slowly and a small woman, dressed in dungarees a size or two too big for her and a man's shirt, came out onto the porch. Her hair was long and gray and she was wearing a blue bandana over it. She glared at them and stayed quiet.

"Mrs. Sawyer," Pinky said, nodding to her.

"She's not Mrs. Sawyer," Jeffrey said, stroking his gray beard and smirking at them. "Why don't you ask her what her name is?"

Pinky flushed and Warren stepped in to save him further embarrassment. "I'm Detective Warren, Franklin Warren, ma'am. Can I ask your name?"

"Willow," she said after a long moment.

"Willow . . . ?"

"Just Willow," Jeffrey said when she didn't answer.

Pinky, looking confused, said, "But you must have another . . ."

"Labels, labels, labels," she taunted. "It bothers you that you can't put me in a box, doesn't it?"

Pinky started to say something else, but Warren gave a slight shake of his head. "Mr. Sawyer, em, Willow," Warren said. "We're sorry to disturb you, but we just want to ask a few questions about Hugh Weber and your relationship with him. Would it be okay to come up and sit down on the porch to talk?"

A black dog that had been sleeping next to the door rose slowly to its feet and ambled to Jeffrey's side. He scratched its ears and stepped aside to indicate they could come up.

There were a couple of wooden Adirondack-style chairs pulled up to the railing and Warren took one and Pinky the other. Jeffrey remained standing and Willow placed herself in front of the door, as though she thought they'd try to barge through. It made Warren wonder about what might be inside the house, what she was so worried about them finding. "We've been told that Hugh Weber originally came to Bethany because of you, that you knew each other. Is that right?"

Willow made a noise that told them exactly what she thought of Hugh Weber. Jeffrey nodded. "That's right. But I hadn't seen Hugh in years. I'm sorry he's dead. But there was no longer any relationship there."

"How did you hear about the fire?"

Jeffrey considered that. "At the post office, perhaps the next day. As I said, I was sorry to hear the news. He wasn't a good man, or a kind one, but he was a human being. And I love all human beings."

"You bought this farm when?"

"In 1950." Jeffrey looked away and then he said, "Hugh and I were both part of a political group, at Columbia. The group talked about how we could live differently, without fear and war and materialism. There were a few of us there on the G.I. Bill, after fighting for our country. We didn't ever want to kill again or to have to take advantage of others just because they happen to be poor. I wanted to buy a farm and Hugh said he would join me and we would create a new kind of society."

"Was it a communist group?" Warren asked. "Your political group?"

Jeffrey laughed. "Why the incessant need to label things, Mr. Warren?"

"Labels, labels, labels," Willow said again, in the same mocking tone of voice.

Warren kept going. "So, what happened? You came up here and bought the farm? How did you afford it?"

"It was quite cheap, Mr. Warren. We have done all of the improvements you see here. It was practically falling down when I arrived. Hugh did lend me some money and he moved in and we started to farm. But then he decided he would be better off on his own—the capitalist impulse was strong in him, despite what he said—and so he left." It had the feeling of a practiced speech.

"Was that the source of the bad blood between you and Hugh Weber? That you'd borrowed money from him? Did you ever pay him back?"

Jeffrey snorted. "Money! The almighty dollar! Why is our society so obsessed with money? He had the funds to buy the farm and I didn't. Once it was spent, the money was gone! What did he think I could do? I told him he was welcome to continue to live here, to share in all we had, but he didn't like sharing, never did. He talked a big game, but when it came down to it, he was greedy at heart. He moved out and bought his own place. I guess he met poor Sylvie soon after that and, well, I don't know how he convinced her to marry him, but somehow he did. I feel sorry for her, and for those boys."

"Did he continue to ask for the money?" Warren asked. "Was he angry about that?"

This time, it was Willow's turn to snort. "Hugh was always angry about something," she said. "It was hard to know which thing it was."

"Where were you the night of the fire?" Warren asked suddenly, just to see how Jeffrey reacted. He didn't want to repeat Victor Weber's words, since the man wasn't at all sure it had been Jeffrey he'd seen up on Agony Hill.

"Right here. Where else would I be?" Jeffrey said calmly. But he glanced at Willow and Warren had the sense that he was trying to communicate something to her.

"He was here all night," she said, too quickly.

"So you didn't visit Hugh last Sunday?"

Jeffrey screwed up his face in disbelief. "No! That's the last thing I'd do."

Warren pointed to the window of the house, through which he could see some stacks of boxes and newspapers, a couple of chairs around a table. "Anyone else living here?" he asked.

"Not at the moment," Jeffrey said. "We have some dedicated new homesteaders who will be joining us soon, though." Willow sighed. Warren had a sudden vision of her life, welcoming new people with big ideas who would never pull their weight, who would leave when the hard work got boring.

Warren stood up and Pinky did the same. "Well, if you have nothing else to tell me, we'll leave you. You can't think of anyone else who might have wanted to do Hugh Weber harm, can you?"

Willow laughed and Jeffrey looked uncomfortable when he said, "I thought the fire was set by Hugh, Mr. Warren?"

Warren just raised his eyebrows. "I can't comment on that, Mr. Sawyer. But we need to look at all the possibilities."

Jeffrey Sawyer looked out across the little barnyard. "Well, then I feel sorry for you, because there are very few people in town who wouldn't have liked to do him harm, starting with Chief Longwell. If you're looking for a murderer, you've got a big job ahead of you."

⊐ ⊐ ⊐

"What do you think about him?" Warren asked Pinky once they were off the property and back on the main road to town. "I didn't like the way they handled the alibi question."

"I didn't either. There was something about the way that she . . . It was like they'd planned it."

"You're absolutely right," Warren said. "You have a good instinct, Pinky, you know that?" Pinky, delighted, blushed furiously.

Warren asked him, "What do you think about the interstate coming through here? You think it's a good thing?"

Pinky, surprised, turned to look at Warren. "Well," he said finally. "They say it'll be finished up through here in the next couple of years, so whether I think it's a good thing or not, it's coming."

Warren smiled. "That's true. But what do you think? Will it be good for these towns along the border? Will it bring business?"

"I suppose it will. They say White River Junction will get a lot of business out of it, since the two interstates have to meet up there, but my dad says a lot of farms are going under. One of his cousins had a farm that got split in two, the house on one side of the road and the barn on the other. They decided to sell. If you can't get to your barn, you don't have much hope of keeping your farm going, do you?"

"So, good and bad?" Warren asked.

"I suppose. Or . . . just different." Pinky grinned then. "More business for us, right? We didn't used to get so many car accidents, traffic stops, people stealing cars, burglaries. Now we got all that. And more besides."

Warren hesitated before saying, "When I visited the newspaper office to ask Fred Fielder about the letters to the editor, he asked me if there was any news on a shooting out at a cottage owned by a man from Washington, DC, back in May. Did you respond to it?"

Pinky turned quickly away from the window. "Samuel Armstrong?"

They came to the intersection of Goodrich Hill Road and the state highway leading back to town. Warren braked at the stop sign and then turned left. "Yeah, I think so. Did you go out to that one? There wasn't anything in the case file."

"I wasn't working that day. I guess the chief found him and then Lieutenant Johnson went out later that day. He told me there wasn't much to find. The guy was dead, all right, and they could tell he'd been shot, but there wasn't any evidence at all. Lieutenant Johnson said it was like someone had flown in through an open window, shot him, and flown out again. Like he was never there. They got nothing else out of that house. I think Lieutenant Johnson was a little embarrassed by it. He didn't want to talk much about it."

"Huh." Warren saw the barracks up ahead and slowed the Galaxie down to let a squirrel amble across the highway. "I'll have to ask. There must be a good reason the file wasn't in with the others."

Pinky didn't say anything, but when Warren looked over, he'd flushed a deep shade of rose.

Twenty-seven

Sylvie lay on the couch in the living room, watching the sunlight shifting on the lilac bushes outside the window. Scott had brought her a cup of tea and now she heard him admonishing the younger boys to play quietly so they wouldn't disturb her. "Dr. Falconer said she has to rest," he told them.

"Can we go to the swimming hole later?" Louis stage-whispered.

"I don't know," Scott said, his voice an octave lower as he tried for manly authority. "We have to do all the chores. And then we'll see." She couldn't help smiling at him repeating the words she and Hugh had said so many times.

"You don't have to be quiet," she called out to them. "I like hearing your voices. And I'm fine, just tired. How about if I sleep for a bit and then we'll go swimming? It's an easy walk down there and I can rest while you go in the water."

She heard Louis squeal with delight and Daniel came shyly to the door and looked through at her. "You can come in," she told him. He came running, climbing up onto the couch and snuggling into her body. She held on tight, breathing in the smell of his hair until Scott told him to come outside and help them with the cows.

She slept for an hour or more and when she woke up, she felt restored and went to find them outside. It was a lovely day, clear and dry, summer showing off the best of itself before it gave way to fall.

They were in the garden and she called out, "Come on then. Let's go swimming," and they dropped their tools and ran through the field, Daniel disappearing into the tall grass just before the trees. The temperature dropped as they climbed down to the banks of the brook and Andy shivered as he stripped down and waded into the water. She sighed, realizing how late in the summer it was now. This might be their last swim of the year. School would start in a few weeks and she . . . what would she do, alone all day with only Daniel for company? Of course, before long there would be the baby too. She leaned back against the rock and closed her eyes, enjoying the feeling of a thin slice of sunlight coming through the trees until she heard Daniel shout and opened them again to check on him.

He was delighted with a stick he'd found and he showed it to her. Once she'd made all the appropriate sounds of appreciation, Sylvie's eyes drifted to the bank across the water, the exact spot where the man had stood all those weeks ago when she'd looked up to find him watching.

She found that it was hard now to remember exactly how it had happened. Her memory of that day had become fuzzy and indistinct, and yet parts of it were crystal clear, as sharp as the reflected image of the trees in the still water next to her. Her feet had faltered a bit as she climbed the bank and she'd put a hand out to steady herself on a small birch growing among the rocks and jewelweed. The little tree had felt soft and papery beneath her fingers.

She remembered the chill she'd felt when she saw his eyes. They were desperate, flat, and that was when she'd known that something was wrong with him.

And yet she couldn't remember exactly what he'd said once she'd reached him. A bird had called, she thought, and she'd glanced back at the boys to make sure they'd stayed put, and then she'd looked down at the knife.

Daniel shouted again and she came back to herself, putting the memory out of her head.

"I'm cold," Louis shouted. "The water's so cold!" And yet he was grinning from ear to ear. Louis loved extremes of anything.

"Should we go back?" she called to them.

"Not yet," Louis said. "Just a little bit more."

If Hugh had been waiting at home, she would have told them it was time to go. But he wasn't.

A single yellow leaf fell from a tree above her.

"Okay," she called back. "Just a little bit more."

Twenty-eight

On Monday morning, Warren showed up early at the barracks. He poured himself a cup of terrible coffee and then he sat at his desk for nearly thirty minutes, thinking through the remaining threads he had to pull on the Hugh Weber case. He had a message from Chief Longwell, telling him that Victor Weber had been allowed to return to the Bethany Inn, with a caution that he should stay in the area, and also that they had done another search of the woods on Agony Hill, but hadn't found any sign of the arsonist. He put in a call to Tommy, to ask about Samuel Armstrong. When he'd done that, he went out to the dispatch desk and found Pinky chatting with Tricia and one of the other troopers.

"Pinky, where's all the stuff we recovered from the camp in the second fire?" Warren asked him.

"In the evidence room. I can show you. I meant to ask you about whether it should go up to the lab."

"That would be up to the fire marshal. Probably," Warren told him. "Let me take a look first, though."

He got the boxes down and noted approvingly that Pinky had put the items in their own bags or boxes and labeled each with the date and the location where it had been found. The beer cans were in separate bags, each labeled. Warren put a clean sheet on the table next to the shelves and looked through the items one by one. There wasn't much of interest and he suspected that most of the items had belonged to the Frederickses, who owned the cabin, though he'd need to confirm that. But there was one thing that he thought might have belonged to the arsonist.

Outside the camp, the firemen had found a charred cardboard box. Inside were an empty milk bottle, a couple of cans, and a piece of burnt cloth. Warren used a ruler to turn over the cloth.

"Cheesecloth," Pinky said, when Warren called him in and asked him what it could be.

"Ah, thank you. This is a steel can but I can't tell what was in it. The label's gone, burnt away."

Pinky leaned over to look. "Peas, maybe. Corn. But I don't know." Warren nodded and carefully removed the items from the box, then turned the box over. The wet ground must have protected the bottom of the box from the fire because it was remarkably intact. "It looks like it originally held something from a veterinary supply company," he said. "ProVet. Does that ring a bell?"

"Yeah, I think there's a dealer in Rutland," Pinky said.

Warren looked more closely at the side of the box.

"There's part of a label here," he said to Pinky. "Is there a magnifying glass somewhere?"

Pinky disappeared and came back with an old-fashioned one, with a black bone handle and brass around the glass.

They peered at the label through the glass. Typewritten numbers swam into view, part of an order number or shipping code, Warren thought. He read out the numbers to Pinky and then asked Tricia to find the number of the veterinary supply company. Once he had the receptionist on the phone, he told her he was trying to track down an order that was mailed to an address in Bethany, date unknown.

"That's going to take some time," she said. "It was mailed to Bethany, you say?"

Warren hesitated. He wasn't positive it had been mailed to Bethany, but chances were good and it would narrow things down and make the search go faster. "Yes," he said. "Let's start there anyway." The woman said she'd call back once she found something.

"What should we do now, Pinky?" Warren asked him. "No use sitting around here waiting for the phone to ring."

"Well," Pinky said. "I was thinking about that heifer, the one tied to the fence. Maybe there's some other evidence there at Jorah Hatchetts', footprints or . . . We know he was there, so we could maybe find a path and follow it . . ." He blushed, unsure exactly what he was getting at.

"No, that's a good thought. We'll head there now." Warren clapped Pinky on the shoulder. "Good thinking." The praise elicited another round of furious capillary action and Warren went ahead to the cruiser to save Pinky any further awkwardness.

They found Jorah Hatchett in the barnyard, tinkering with a large piece of machinery attached to the back of a tractor. He didn't acknowledge them in any way as they got out of the cruiser and made their way over to him, but he must have been aware of their presence because after Pinky cleared his throat in announcement, Hatchett muttered, "Hold this," and handed a pair of pliers to Pinky. He bent to fiddle with the long chain that connected to the tractor and after a loud clanging, he came up with the end of the chain and nodded to Pinky, taking the pliers back from him. Then he let the chain drop and said, "Well?" It was as though they'd been wasting his time for an hour or more.

"Oh, yes, Mr. Hatchett, we were just wondering if we could ask you about the cow, about the person who might have tied her up," Warren stammered.

"The heifer? On the fence? What about it?"

"You said that you thought someone might be in the woods, up on Agony Hill. We think you may be right. Do you have any idea who it could be?"

"If I knew, I would have said," he muttered.

"And you didn't find any . . . clues?" Hatchett made Warren feel verbose, like he was talking too much. The man shook his head. Warren waited. Nothing more was forthcoming. "Oh, well, is it okay with you if we go up and look around a bit more for evidence?"

"Sure," Hatchett said. "Go ahead."

He had already turned back to the tractor when they heard him say, "You won't find anything, though, after that rain Saturday."

"He's right, you know," Warren told Pinky. "Any footprints on this side of the hill washed down the slope with the rain. But we'll look for anything else. If this man led the animal down the hill, he might have dropped something on his way."

They traced a path up from the place where the heifer had been tied up, looking for broken branches or twigs. Pinky pointed out one spot where a branch might have been recently snapped, but it was hard to know if a human had caused it. After an hour of looking, they walked back to the car, passing Jorah Hatchett, who was still tinkering with the tractor. They thanked him but he didn't look up from his work.

They were nearly back to town when Pinky sat up straight in the passenger seat and said, "Hey. Slow down. I think I saw something back there."

Warren slowed and, checking his mirrors carefully, reversed along the empty road. "Where?" he asked Pinky. It was shadowy on the shoulders, the overhanging trees making long dark shapes on the road.

They'd backed up about three hundred yards when they saw a

flash of red in the grass on the opposite shoulder. Something about the color was unnatural enough that it raised Warren's alarm. "That's it," Pinky said. "I think there's someone down there on the side of the road." Warren pulled over and put his hazards on.

Warren thought about how many times he'd responded to traffic accidents as a young officer, how deaths and injuries often came after the initial event, when motorists got out of the wreck and stood on the shoulder waiting for help, how Good Samaritans could be hit when they pulled over to help.

They jumped out and dashed across the road. Pinky got there first and when Warren arrived, he felt his stomach rise toward his throat and he turned away for a moment so Pinky wouldn't see his distress. It wasn't the blood, exactly, though there was plenty of that, but the way the body was arranged that set off some deep trigger of recognition in his brain and his body. He closed his eyes and breathed deeply.

Then he opened his eyes again and felt his detective brain kick into action.

Victor Weber was lying absolutely still in the thick grass and tangle of weeds at the side of the road, his head back and his arms splayed out, one lying in a pool of stagnant water. His clothes were muddy, the white of his shirt soaked through with bright red blood that was flowing from a large wound on his head.

Warren felt his vision contract and blur. Everything seemed to narrow down to a thin channel in front of him that contained the dead man and then, oddly, Pinky's face. The sky behind him rotated. He tasted metal.

"Are you okay, Detective Warren?" he thought he heard Pinky say from far away.

"Yes, I'm . . ." He was trying to stand still, to make the spinning stop, but it was impossible, and as he fell, all he could see was blood and he wasn't sure if it was Victor Weber's, or Maria's, or his own.

Twenty-nine

Alice had a busy day Monday that included a library trustee meeting as well as lunch with Judith Perkins in Windsor and then a couple of hours with the rest of the Ladies Aid Society, cleaning up from Old Home Day. They had made $252, which was a new record.

It was a lovely day, less hot than it had been. The rain on Saturday had cleared things out and taken the humidity and heat with it. She thought she could detect a single, glittery note of autumn, cool and clear, and she lingered on the green, which was almost back to normal.

She stopped at Collers' for a bag of sugar and walked home slowly, anticipating a still and silent house since Mildred had the day off. But she knew when she reached the side gate that Arthur was waiting for her. This time, he'd balanced a small stick on the post. It was a trick he'd used before in their acquaintance and though anyone else would have assumed it had fallen from a tree or been left there by the wind, something about the angle alerted her immediately. She felt a quick pang of caution and this time, she didn't discount it. Whatever Arthur was up to, he wasn't telling her the whole story. And whether she was actually in danger from him or not, Arthur's presence here in Bethany signified danger for *someone*. Because Alice knew a lot of things about Arthur, she could easily be swept up in that danger if she wasn't careful.

Thinking, she took the sugar to the kitchen, slipped a small paring knife into the pocket of her dress, picked up the Sunday *Times,* the day's *Rutland Herald,* and the weekly edition of the *Bethany Register* and tucked them under her arm, and then walked cautiously through the garden, unable to resist the urge to deadhead a lily as she passed. She went to the little café table at the back of the garden and finished reading the papers while she waited. There was much of interest in the news today. She was almost done when he stepped out of the bushes.

"Hello, Arthur," Alice said. "It's lovely to see you again so soon."

"And you, my dear." He kissed her cheek and they stood there together listening to the sound of the water. He looked utterly innocent, dressed in a seersucker jacket and trousers and a snowy-white shirt. "Well done, by the way, playing along the way you did when we ran into you. And we really do want to have you to the house for dinner."

"Of course, you know acting was always one of my strengths, Arthur. And as for dinner, I'd love that. Please let me know if you need recommendations for carpenters or plumbers or any of that sort of thing."

"Yes," he said. She could hear the impatience in his voice, though. He had something to tell her. She waited.

"I have the information you asked for, about this Warren." He had something interesting. Alice could tell by the way he said it. *Warren.* "As soon as I mentioned his name, my contact at Boston PD knew who I was talking about. It was quite the story. He's from a good family. Father has a furniture company and was a bit of a war hero as well, it sounds like. In any case, this Franklin Warren, well, he bucked his parents' expectations. He got a good degree from Tufts and then he decided to become a policeman. Did all right, became a detective when he was twenty-five. But his parents didn't like it and they liked it even less when he married an Italian girl named Maria Fortunato. Met her when her parents' restaurant in Little Italy was robbed. His parents all but disowned him. They'd only been married a year or so when he came home to find her stabbed to death in a pool of blood on the kitchen floor. At least that's what he said. She was pregnant too. Terrible business. His fellow officers immediately put him under the microscope. He said he'd been out jogging but hadn't seen anyone at the track, and he behaved strangely, they said. Couldn't stop crying. Something about his behavior seemed off to them. He was probably a day or two away from being charged when two things happened. The first was that they found blood that didn't belong to her in the kitchen. Wrong type. It wasn't his type either. And then an alibi came through for him. A couple of boys from the Tufts track team said they'd seen him jogging during the time she'd been killed. He'd done nearly six miles around the track and when he was done, he spent some time stretching. He was there almost two hours, so it covered the time. He couldn't have done it. Or at least was very unlikely to have done it."

"Poor man," Alice said, shaking her head. "He's not a murderer. I can tell you that."

"Anyway, he quit his job. Couldn't stand working with the men who'd accused him. He went out west for a year, no one knows exactly what he was doing. He came back to Boston and somehow or other he got this job up here. Anyway, it seems like he's beyond suspicion at this point, though they've never made an arrest—it's still an open case—but you might like to be careful just the same."

Alice nodded. "Thank you, Arthur. I appreciate that."

"You're welcome. And now, I have a favor to ask of you."

"Oh yes, I thought you might," Alice said, raising her eyebrows.

"Do you know what it's about?" Arthur looked genuinely surprised.

"Yes, Arthur, I think I do. It's about this, I believe." She folded the newspaper to the story she'd just read and held it up. "The story's on page six of the *Rutland Herald*. This writer, Kalachnikov, has settled not far from Bethany. A remote cottage in the woods. He's a Soviet dissident, isn't he, ostensibly on our side, but you, Arthur, are here to keep an eye on him. Just in case." She couldn't resist giving him a triumphant grin. She felt very proud of herself.

Arthur laughed out loud. "I can't put anything over on you, old girl. That's right. It's not so much him we're interested in, you see. Although, you never know. But anyone who might visit him would certainly be of interest to us and with your connections in the state, well, you might see or hear something that could be useful. You'll tell me if you do? Using the old methods."

"I will," Alice said, keeping the promise light. She didn't know yet what she would and wouldn't tell Arthur Crannock. "You know, I have an old friend who lives near him. Cecilia. We were bosom buddies in college. I can make something of the connection, I think. Yes . . ."

"I knew I could count on you." He winked at her. "No contact with subject unless unavoidable. Background only, right? I'll be off, but we'll see you soon. Wanda will call you up about a date for dinner."

"See you soon, Arthur." She waited until he was gone and then she sat down again and reread the article that was actually of interest to her. Not the one about Anatoly Kalachnikov.

She had known about Anatoly Kalachnikov for weeks now. The famous writer, a dissident who had defected after a literary festival, had settled in Vermont back in the winter. This was interesting, but not as interesting to Alice as the fact of Kalachnikov's residence in combination with the very small item at the bottom of page nine of the *Bethany Register*.

State Police Detective Lieutenant Thomas Johnson had no comment in the case of a Washington, DC, man shot to death in his newly pur-

chased home in Bethany in May. Additionally, Franklin Warren, the newly arrived state police detective from Boston posted at the Bethany barracks, refused to give this reporter a comment. The shooting happened in the house on Downers Road May 6, but police appear to have made no headway in the case.

Bethany real estate agent Harry Best reported that Armstrong, a State Department employee, had bought the house in January, and was anxious to assure the Bethany Register *that he does not believe there is rampant crime in Bethany. "No interested parties should be dissuaded from buying a lovely summer property in Bethany," Best said. "This was probably a fluke."*

Alice glanced over at Franklin Warren's house, where the driveway was empty. Surely he was out detecting. Alice would talk to him and hopefully he would find out who had stolen the cartridges so Bob Coller would have to apologize to poor Richie.

As she walked back slowly through the garden, Alice found that her spirits had improved. Arthur thought he'd put one over on her, but he hadn't. She would do what he asked and she would watch and wait and try to figure out what had happened to Samuel Armstrong. Had it been Arthur? Or was Arthur just interested in who it *had* been? She wasn't sure yet.

There was still a dark and heavy mood hanging over the town, but for the first time in a long time, Alice had a real purpose, a life-or-death one. She intuited, if she did not know for sure, that her own fate, and perhaps Arthur's as well, depended on how she handled what came next.

She stopped to take a beetle from the leaf of one of the tall zinnia plants in the side border.

Carefully, making sure she did the job completely, she crushed it between her fingers and flicked the corpse onto the gravel path.

Thirty

Warren didn't pass out. He just sank to the ground and sat there for a moment, trying to get his equilibrium back. When the dizziness had passed, he looked up to find Pinky still staring down at him.

"Detective Warren? Are you okay?" Pinky was asking.

Warren sat up slowly, rubbing his cheek, which must have hit the ground when he fell.

"I'm okay. I'm fine." He stood up slowly and looked down at Victor Weber. The man's face was barely recognizable, covered in blood, and the gaping wound on his forehead told Warren and Pinky its source. "Jesus," Pinky said in a low, horrified voice.

"Go radio it in," Warren told him. Pinky did it quickly and then came back to look at the body. "We need to check to make sure he's dead," Warren said, still shaky and lightheaded. "You know how to feel for a pulse?" He tried to use a didactic tone of voice, to indicate to Pinky that this was a learning opportunity, when in fact, Warren was worried he'd faint for real if he had to lean over the bloodied face that reminded him too much of Maria's.

Maria's eyes had been open, though, and Victor Weber's were closed. But if Pinky didn't know how to check for a pulse, Warren wasn't sure he'd be able to manage it. But Pinky said, "Yeah, I can do it," and started to lean over Victor Weber.

There would be a rhythm to all of this now, the photographs, the autopsy, the interviews with possible suspects. He would of course have to look at Sylvie Weber—could she have asked someone to do this for her? Who?—and anyone else who Victor Weber had interacted with while in Bethany.

Because Warren was quite sure that someone had chased Victor Weber down and bashed his face in.

Warren stood behind Pinky as he leaned over the body and a wave of alcohol-scented air rose up to meet them.

"Whoa," Pinky said. "I guess he'd been at the bottle. Do you think he drank himself to death?"

"Maybe—" Warren started to say when suddenly, the body came to life, Victor Weber's chest convulsing and his hands coming up to defend himself. "Wha?" he slurred drunkenly. And then, just as suddenly as he'd awakened, he was unconscious again, this time snoring loudly and rolling over as though he thought he was in a soft, warm bed rather than bleeding out in a muddy ditch on a desolate rural road.

Warren cursed, adrenaline surging through his body from the shock of Victor Weber's resurrection. He was still fragile from his fainting spell but together he and Pinky managed to elevate the unconscious man's head while they waited for the ambulance to come.

Chief Longwell arrived first, the lights and siren going on the cruiser. Once they got Victor Weber onto a stretcher, he came over, looking at Warren like it was somehow all his fault. "What happened?" he asked accusingly.

"We don't know," Warren told him. "We found him on the side of the road and it looks like he was assaulted or . . . something. He's also drunk as a skunk so I don't think he'll be able to tell us anything for a while."

They searched the shoulder, near where Weber had been found, but no evidence presented itself. The dry sand and gravel at the edge of the road offered up countless tire treads; the spot in question was at a curve in the road and most cars that traveled it braked just before they reached it.

"What was he doing out here?" Warren asked Pinky, once the ambulance was gone and Chief Longwell had gone along with it to try to get a statement from Weber at the hospital. "It's a long walk from the inn."

"You think he was heading up to Agony Hill?" Pinky asked.

"Maybe, but why?" Warren asked. "You think he was going up there to do her harm?"

"It's a possibility . . ." Pinky didn't sound convinced.

Warren studied the younger man for a moment. "Pinky, what was the first thing you thought when we found him? When we thought he was dead?"

Pinky said, "Someone from the tavern. Someone he insulted after he'd been at the bottle, who followed him out."

"Interesting." Warren didn't want to say what he'd thought, that somehow Sylvie Weber had gotten her revenge. It was ridiculous. There was no way she could have done this.

"That what you thought too?" Pinky asked.

"Not exactly. But I was thinking, what if there's someone who saw what he did to Sylvie Weber Saturday and maybe thought he needed a good punch in the face?"

Pinky looked dubious. "I don't know . . . Doesn't seem too likely . . ."

"You may be right. But it's got me thinking about Hugh Weber.

What if Sylvie Weber has a . . . suitor in town. Someone who's . . . I don't know. I just thought about that cow that was tied up. Could someone have been . . . waiting for her up there, waiting to meet her?" The speculation felt uncomfortable to him. She was a widow, a pregnant woman! But Warren did not have a lot of naiveté left about what human beings were capable of.

Pinky looked horrified. "But she was a married woman and she's . . . you know."

"Wouldn't be the first time, Pinky. I think that tomorrow we should do some asking around on that front. And I want to know a bit more about the fire at the camp. Maybe there's a connection to the Webers."

"Okay, but it seems a bit . . . wrong to be asking around about her like that when her husband just died."

Warren saw what he meant. "Well, is there any way you can do it discreetly? Who knows what's going on in this town? Who's the biggest gossip you know?"

Pinky thought for a moment. "Mrs. Gendon. She works for Mrs. Bellows. She knows about everything. And then, I guess there'd be the Collers, on account of having the store, and when it comes down to it, Mrs. Bellows too." He thought for another moment. "Chief Long-well, now, he makes a point of keeping up on all the local gossip. He says it helps him keep the peace, but my mother always said he just likes to know things because it gives him power."

¤ ¤ ¤

Warren found it hard to focus back at the barracks and he was getting ready to head home when Tricia poked her head in and said, "We heard back from that vet supply company in Rutland. They found the label."

Warren stared at her. "That quick?"

"Yes, well, they have a very modern ordering system. She ex-plained it all to me. Even though we only had half the number, it was the right half. You see, the first half of the number is the date when the order came in and the town, in this case forty-three for Bethany, and the second half is the customer number. Each regular customer has their own—"

"You can explain that later, Tricia," Pinky said kindly. "I think Detective Warren wants to know who it was sent to."

"Oh yes, of course. Well, it's a bit strange, I'd say. Because it was the Webers. The box was sent to Hugh Weber, some cattle dewormer, she said. Back in the winter."

Thirty-one

By the time Warren turned onto Agony Hill, it was nearly seven. The Churches' bull was at the other side of the field, barely visible though the evening haze.

The night was warm and fair, the kind of summer evening Maria had always reveled in. She liked to go out for supper on nights like this, because it was too hot to cook and because she loved to walk through the streets of the North End seeing people she knew in their summer clothes, drinking wine at outdoor tables. Sometimes, they would go to her parents' restaurant, where they were greeted like royalty, sometimes not, since her parents didn't have a large patio. Maria, who had only lived in Italy for a few early years of her life, had always said that Italian summer evenings must have imprinted themselves on her brain because she lived all year for balmy nights. Warren remembered holding her hand as they walked, the feel of her hip bumping his, the smell of her lemony face cream.

The cows gathered silently at the edge of the paddock to greet him when he got out of the Galaxie. He looked up at the barn. He was still wondering if someone might have climbed down from it, but looking at it again, he saw it was indeed impossible. The boards on the outside were completely smooth. You couldn't climb down and it was too high to safely jump. You would need a ladder. And of course they had not seen a ladder.

But maybe there was a ladder hidden away somewhere and Sylvie Weber had lied.

The sky was turning pink and orange over the distant hills. When he knocked on the door, no one answered, so he turned the handle and opened it slightly. "Hello? Mrs. Weber?" he called out. Again, no one answered. He pushed the door open a bit more and stepped inside. The house was cool and smelled of burnt butter. He called out again, for cover, and quickly crossed the entry hall to the door leading to the kitchen.

He wanted to understand more about the family before he asked Sylvie Weber about the box from the vet supply company. He had the feeling that she was hiding something and he wanted to get a better sense of her before they talked. The kitchen revealed her as an unenthusiastic housekeeper, he thought. It wasn't squalor, exactly, but there was a pleasant mess in the place, dishes in the sink, but likely only from today, a baking pan on the top of the large cookstove that revealed the source of the burnt butter smell. The stove was warm to his touch.

On the kitchen table, someone had placed a jug of wildflowers, tall colorful stalks of black-eyed Susans and a white flower he didn't know the name of. Something about it was pleasing to him and he had the surprising thought that if he were a painter, he would paint the arrangement.

He was not a painter. Indeed, he'd never done anything creative in his life, but he appreciated those who did. He loved to go to the Museum of Fine Arts and look at the paintings.

Mail littered one end of the table, but he didn't dare touch it. Instead, he turned to the wall above a small table pushed against the far wall of the kitchen. It seemed to be a work table, as it was covered with blank sheets of paper and a small milk bottle that contained a few sharpened pencils. Someone had been writing poems in the same hand as the ones he'd seen taped up around the house.

Flitting tiny flies, someone had written on one sheet. That was it for that page.

His eyes wide, full of the forest's secrets, read another. *The city washes from him in the trees' deluge.* "Deluge" had been crossed out and "*raining freshness*" written instead. It was the next line that made anxiety run through him. *White shirt, rumpled like bedclothes, the black tie a city scar, he emerges as in a birth, damaged, innocent, no longer lost.*

He'd been wearing a white shirt and black tie the day he'd been lost in the woods.

Was this poem about him?

Now, his explorations felt different. He searched the wall above the table for evidence either way, but the papers pinned there were shopping lists, reminders, bills that needed to be paid. Hugh Weber's letters to the editor were pinned there too, the latest one carefully centered on the wall with an air of pride. The poems were scattered as an afterthought.

In the living room, he looked around at the furniture, a mixture of shabby pieces and really good-quality antiques, and then walked through to the dining room, where someone seemed to be organizing papers; there were stacks of them, bank statements and electric bills and typed correspondence, everything lined up neatly on the floor next to a large bureau.

He called their names again, to cover his snooping, and was about to look more closely at the piles when he caught movement outside the large window and saw them out there, Sylvie Weber and the children working in the vegetable garden. Quickly, before they saw him inside, he went back out the front door and around the side of the house to the garden.

It was impressive, a large plot the size of a small house, with different sections for tomatoes, greens, tall stakes with brown vines winding around them. Sylvie Weber was using a hoe to clear weeds from between two rows of what looked like spinach. The boys were spread out across the garden, one picking tomatoes, two crouched on the ground pulling weeds. In the gloaming, it all looked like a French painting, the bruised sky and the dark figures, out of time in their undefinable clothes.

When she looked up and saw him, he saw fear cross her face. She put the hoe down and started walking toward him, a hand up to shield her eyes, though it wasn't bright anymore.

"I'm sorry to bother you, Mrs. Weber," he called out. "I wonder if I could have a quick word." Behind the lines of the fence, her face was washed with golden light. She looked staggeringly beautiful. He felt suddenly self-conscious of his clothes, his shoes, his body. She nodded and he heard her say to the boys, "Finish up in here and then go bring the sheep back into the barn before it's dark. I heard howling last night."

She wiped her hands on her dress, picked up a basket, and looked at him one more time from behind the fence before coming around through the gate and meeting him on the other side. The sun had dropped farther toward the horizon—indeed, it seemed to be gathering speed, hurtling toward the tops of the hills, leaving the sky bloody behind it, the red and purple spreading out across the expanse. They couldn't help themselves; they stood and looked at it until it seemed to be fading and then she wordlessly led him back toward the house.

They had shared it, the beauty of the sunset, which would never be repeated, and he felt tied to her.

It was darker inside now and he waited in the entryway until she switched on a lamp in the living room and led him inside. In the kitchen, she put the basket of vegetables next to the sink and filled two crystal glasses from the spigot in the wide sink. She handed one to him and led the way back to the living room. Then she motioned for him to sit on the sofa and took a seat in the armchair.

When she looked at him expectantly, he stammered out, "Are—are you feeling better? I expected to find you resting."

"I'm fine," she said. "Don't worry, I let the boys do the difficult work. I was just showing them what to do."

He smiled. "I won't tell Dr. Falconer then."

She smiled back. "Thank you. He'd worry but I'm fine, really. It was just the heat Saturday, and the stress of Hugh's brother saying those things. Mr. Hatchett brought us some hay and he said Victor had an accident. Do you know what happened to him?"

"We don't know yet, but he should be okay. I heard from the hospital before I drove up here. He didn't try to contact you, did he? About your husband's accounts?"

"No, but we don't have a phone. Mr. Williamson drove up today to tell me that Hugh had money." She looked away, embarrassed. "That's where the checks came from, Mr. Williamson said. Hugh never told me, but anyway, we won't have to leave the house, which is good news."

"It is good news." He hesitated, not sure how to start, not sure how to address the issue of the box.

Surprising himself, he couldn't keep from asking, "How did . . . how did you and your husband meet?"

He needed to know, not for the investigation, though perhaps it was important to that. But it was just that he was curious.

She frowned and said, "My father had a farm in Derby, near the border. That's where I grew up. My parents came over the border and my father worked on the farm, as a young man. Then the owner died and left it to him. He went back to Hatley and got my mother. She didn't speak any English when she came, or later really. My father was a smart man, though he hadn't had much schooling and there were nine of us." She smiled. "Too many for what the farm could produce. I was seventeen. I'd just had my birthday. I'd left school and was working at a shop in Newport. My father drove me and my sisters in to work each day. One day, a man came in. He was interested in me, in what I did, where I was from. I was reading a book and he noticed and . . ." She looked up. "He told me he liked to read books and write and when I told him I did too, he asked me all kinds of questions. He listened to me talk about the poetry I liked. He was thirty-five years old, but I didn't think about that at all. He was quite smart, had been to college. And he was very interested in my life on the farm and what I knew about animals and crops. He wanted to have a farm, you see. He said he was going to buy one."

She took a sip of her water.

"He came back a few times. We talked. He said he had a lot of books and he could give me some. He was planning on buying a farm in a town called Bethany. I'd never heard of it, but he made it sound nice. We . . . I don't know. We spent time together. He wanted me to come with him, but I said my father wouldn't let me go if I wasn't married. A couple of days later, my father said Hugh had come and asked if he could marry me. My father said yes. I . . . was happy to go to a new place, to live with books." She shrugged, her face blank. "That was it. I had Scott before the year was done."

Warren nodded and sipped his own water.

Finally, he said, "Mrs. Weber, I need to ask you about the man who we think set the fire up at the camp. We think you might know him. We think you gave him something, cans of food maybe. Is that right?"

Sylvie Weber sighed heavily, turning her face so that the light from the lamp put her in profile. Her hands went, automatically, he thought, to a basket next to her chair. There was a piece of knitting, a bright blue length of stitches that he supposed would be a scarf or the sleeve of a sweater. It was some kind of comfort to her, something to do with her hands. She seemed to think better of it, though, and left it alone. Finally, she said, "I didn't tell you about him because I couldn't see how it mattered. He doesn't want to be found, you see, and no one asked me about him so it's not like I was lying."

Warren tried to keep his voice calm. "No, of course not. No one's suggesting that. It's just that we need to know about him, in case he had anything to do with all of this." He spread his hands around at the house, the farm, hoping to encompass all the terrible things that had happened since the first terrible thing, the fire that had taken her husband's life.

"He didn't have anything to do with all of this," she said. "I promise."

"Maybe not, but we need to know about him," he said, a little sternly, as though she were a child. "When did you, well, meet him?"

She turned to him and said, "It was back in the beginning of the summer. We'd been haying. First cut. I'd taken the boys swimming down by the brook. There's a swimming hole there. It's the best place to swim because the water comes right down and it moves so quickly it never warms up." She smiled. "On a really hot day, it's the only way to cool down, you see. And it's all green and . . . wonderful there. I looked up and there was a man standing there, watching us. He told me to come up and talk to him. He had a knife and I thought . . . I thought he was going to hurt me . . . or us, but when I got up there, he said he was sorry, he didn't mean to scare me, it was just that he was hungry. He had been living in the woods and he'd tried eating some plants he found, but they made him sick."

"Did he tell you why he was living in the woods?" Warren asked her.

She smiled. "Yes, the poor boy. He said he had come to Bethany to live with some friends, but it 'hadn't worked out.' From what he said, I think it might have been Jeffrey . . . Mr. Sawyer's farm. He didn't seem to want to talk about it. He asked if I had any food scraps I could give him and he asked me not to tell anyone he was here. He said he'd go away if I could just give him some food. He had found a place to stay."

"When was this?" Warren asked.

"I would say around July first. Just before the fourth anyway."

So he'd possibly been living at the camp for a month before the fire. "What did you say?"

"I told him I'd send one of the boys back with some food. I felt sorry for him, so I filled up a box with some old cans of beans and peas and corn we had. Then I added a big chunk of cheddar cheese and two loaves of bread. Hugh had just baked them and I had to make up a story about one loaf falling in the sink and getting wet. Andy took it down to the brook and gave it to him."

"And you trusted him, you trusted that he wasn't a danger to you or the boys?"

She laughed. "Yes, he was . . . I don't know quite how to describe him. He's just a boy, really. His clothes were . . . I don't know. He was wearing city clothes that were all . . . ruined and a wool hunting jacket that was too big for him. He was sweet, just hungry."

City clothes. He studied her in the low light. One hand was absent-mindedly rubbing her belly and a piece of her dark hair had fallen over a cheek. Was the poem he'd read about this other man then and not about him at all? He felt an absurd flash of jealousy, deep and painful. Warren realized with horror that he found her beautiful, desirable, that he couldn't stop looking at her, at the details of her face, her neck, her hand . . .

He cleared his throat and sat up straighter in his chair. "You use the present tense, Mrs. Weber. Have you seen him since then?"

"Just twice. It was a lot of food, you see, and maybe he's gone." She looked away.

His voice was harsh when he said, "I don't understand. I don't understand why you didn't tell your husband. Was Hugh violent? Did he beat you?" He wanted the surprise of it. He sensed there was something about the relationship she wasn't telling him and he thought he could get a reaction out of her this way.

Her eyes were direct on his. "No, it wasn't like that. You see, when I realized that the boy had been living out at Brook's End, I knew if I told Hugh he'd just start worrying about it, thinking about it too much. Anything about Jeffrey bothered him, got inside his head sort of, if that makes sense. If he even saw him for a few minutes, in town or at the auction up in Fairlee, he'd stew about it for days, drink too much, get furious about little things. So it was better not to mention anything having to do with Brook's End at all."

"Had he seen Sawyer recently? Your husband?"

"No. And that was why I didn't want to tell him about the boy. I thought he'd forgotten, maybe."

"But why didn't you tell me about the boy? Why didn't your sons?" He couldn't keep the fury out of his voice. "I asked you if there had been anyone around, if anything strange had happened!"

The look she gave him almost broke his heart. She was scared of him, her eyes wide and full of fear. "He said he couldn't get called up. He didn't think he'd survive it," she whispered.

He saw it then, the boy, traveling north, away from a letter telling him to report for his physical, or perhaps just the newspaper stories about the increased quotas. Had he been on his way to Canada? Warren had heard of men who did this. No one he knew. His own letter from the Selective Service had come right after he had accepted the job in Vermont and he had been exempted on the basis of his profession. But there must have been no exemption for this boy. Now that they needed more men over there, there would be even fewer exemptions. Somehow, the boy had hooked up with Jeffrey Sawyer and then he'd ended up starving in the woods.

"You won't turn him in and make him fight, will you?"

"That's not my job. I don't care who fights and who doesn't. You don't even know if he's eligible. I only want to know what happened to your husband! If you see this boy again, you have to tell me. We'll bring him in safely." He could feel the frustration rising through his throat. "Mrs. Weber, what do you think happened to your husband?"

"I don't know," she said, in an exhausted way. "I don't know, Mr. Warren." She looked like she was about to cry and he felt, for the first time, her fragility. He knew that pushing her was going to lead to her giving her grief its way, perhaps for the first time.

He knew what it was like to keep grief at bay, the feeling when something finally gave it a channel. He let it go, thanked her, and they both stood. In that dark room, with only the weak light of the one lamp, he could feel her breathing, could see the outline of her body against the white wall when she turned. He was seized by an idea so mad that he put it out of his mind before it could even be articulated, and he was stepping away from her, getting as much distance as he could, when they heard someone yelling, "Ma! Ma!" and the front door slammed.

It was the second-oldest boy, the very handsome one, and he came barreling into the room, saying, "Flora, Ma, Flora's leg is broken. She's lying down in the field."

"One of the ewes," Sylvie Weber said to him before turning back to the boy. "How bad is it, Andy?"

"I don't know. Scott said to come get you."

She looked up at Warren "I'm sorry. I have to . . ."

He spoke before he'd thought it through. "Do you need my help? You shouldn't be exerting yourself."

"No, we'll be fine." He could see her reconsidering, though. "Well, maybe. If we need to carry her up, I don't know if I can . . ." She touched her belly.

"Of course."

"Andy, you get the flashlight from the drawer. Come on, quick." As she stepped into the light, Warren could see the stress on her face. In the hallway, she opened the closet and rummaged, coming out with a rifle that she tucked under her arm. She took what looked like a few cartridges from a box on the top shelf and put them in the pocket of her dress.

Something pinged in his brain. He didn't have time to chase it down, though, because the boy came with the flashlight and she was off and walking quickly through the door.

"You won't need that, will you?" Warren asked as they walked, nodding at the gun. She ignored him.

It took them five minutes of walking in the beam of light for them to hear the other boys shout, "Over here," and she started running toward the sound.

The sheep was on the ground, lying so still that Warren thought she might already be dead, but when Sylvie Weber put a hand on her leg, she jolted. The animal seemed almost in shock, her eyes staring in the beam of the flashlight. "It's broken," Sylvie said, trying gently to stretch it out, which made the ewe jolt again. When Warren looked down at it, he could see it was at a strange angle, the lower part of the leg bent and pointing away from the ewe's body. He felt lightheaded, his stomach gone acid; he wanted to look away but he was embarrassed.

"Should we try to carry it up to the house?" he asked.

"No, there's nothing to be done." Her voice was quiet but commanding.

The boy holding the flashlight gave a sob and she went to him, putting a hand on his head, and then loaded the .22. The oldest boy, Scott, said, "Do you want me to, Ma?" and she quickly shook her head. Warren thought he saw relief on the boy's face and something pass between them. He felt at sea. She was going to kill the sheep, right in front of him, in front of the boys. He wanted to protest, to stop this. "Why don't you let me . . ." he started to say, intending to say that he would take the sheep to a vet, that he would pay for it if she couldn't, but she misunderstood and handed him the gun.

It was heavy in his hands, too heavy. "Are you sure . . . ?" he ventured.

"She's in terrible pain," she said. "It can't be healed. There's nothing to do."

When he lifted it, he couldn't get the balance right. The pool of light from the flashlight bobbed around the ewe's head.

Scott held the animal still. Sylvie Weber knelt, awkwardly, and helped. "It's okay, Flora," she said softly. "It's okay." She pointed to a spot at the back of the animal's skull. "Here," she whispered. "Six inches away." Warren tried to steady the .22. His brain was a hurricane, everything swirled and rushed. He felt dizzy and staggered back, the muzzle bumping against the sheep's back.

And then, for the second time in two days, he saw Maria, the pool of blood beneath her, the way she had stared at the ceiling. Her eyes had been so familiar and yet so unrecognizable. He'd shouted her name over and over, as if he could call her back . . .

The vomit came up so suddenly he barely had time to turn away. "I'm sorry," he said when he'd finished. "I can't." The gun had already fallen away and Sylvie Weber quietly picked it up. Warren's eyes were closed when he heard the shot.

¤ ¤ ¤

Warren and the oldest boy, Scott, dragged the carcass back up the hill and they wrapped it in a tarp. "Lenny will come tomorrow," Sylvie murmured to the boy. He led the other boys back to the house and Warren followed her out of the barn and toward his car. She was quiet. He had to say something, but what could he say? He felt his shame like a too-warm sweater.

"Thank you for your help," she said, starting to turn away, and before he knew what he was doing, he was reaching for her arm, holding her wrist, turning her back toward him. There was just a little light still in the sky and from the house. He could barely see her face. Only her eyes shone out of the gray murk.

"I'm sorry," he said. "About before. I . . . My wife was killed. I found her. I . . . I thought of her and I couldn't."

Her eyes were huge, surprised. She nodded slowly, staring at him, and didn't answer.

"I . . . I'm sorry. I'm sorry you had to do it, with your . . . with, your condition."

The night was crowding around them, the darkness thick and full of hidden things.

"It's okay," she whispered, seemingly spellbound. "I don't mind killing, when it's the kindest thing."

He let her go and turned toward the car and by the time he had backed out of the drive and looked toward the house again, she was already inside, her figure moving in the lighted interior.

Thirty-two

Alice watched through the side windows for the headlights of Franklin Warren's car. When they appeared, a bit after ten, she slipped into boots and stepped out into the side yard. He was almost inside when she called, "Mr. Warren? I wonder if I might have a word."

He turned and in the wan light from the porch bulb, he looked like someone who had been through a war. His shirt was rumpled and dirty, untucked over his trousers. There was blood on it. His face was drawn and tortured.

"My word, you look like you've had a night! Are you all right? Let me make you a drink," she said. He started to protest and then she saw the idea of the drink appealed and he nodded, resigned, and let the screen door slam and followed her into the house. She poured them each a glass of the best Scotch she had and gave him a slice of Mildred's bread and two thick pieces of cheddar. He ate gratefully and drank half the Scotch in a gulp.

"I apologize for the state of myself," he said. "I was up at the

Webers' and a sheep was injured and had to be put down." His eyes clouded. Alice watched him. Whatever had happened up there had traumatized him. She wondered what it could be. Then she remembered what she'd learned about his wife and she knew it must be that. Seeing blood, it must have shaken him.

"How awful."

He ran his fingers through his hair. "I keep thinking about those boys and . . . her. How terrible that they'll have to do these things now."

"I would say Sylvie can handle it," Alice said. "She's quite capable. People don't see it, because it's not the kind of capability that matters to them." She wanted him to understand this thing about Sylvie. She needed him to understand it, so he wouldn't pity her. "Hugh . . ." She waved her hand. "He was . . . superfluous. She'll be fine. Assuming she has some money."

She half hoped he would answer this question for her about the money, about whether there was any, about whether there was enough. But he didn't. Perhaps he didn't know.

"Was there something you wanted to ask me?" Warren said after a few moments of silence.

Alice said, "I won't beat around the bush, Mr. Warren. I believe there is a person, a stranger, who is in our town. I believe this person has stolen items from the store and I believe he may also be the person who set the fire up at the hunting camp on Agony Hill." She recounted the theft at the store, the problems it had caused, and her conversation with Mary Harper.

It wasn't what he was expecting. Alice could tell that right away. He looked up and considered her for a moment. "Could this woman identify the person she saw?"

"She's quite elderly and her memory isn't what it was, but I think she might be able to give you a . . . sense of things. She couldn't be relied on for eyewitness testimony, though, nothing like that. I'm telling you so that you can go and find this man. She said he looked like he hadn't bathed in a while and that his clothes were very dirty. That suggests . . . certain things to you, doesn't it? That perhaps he's been sleeping rough in the woods?"

He nodded. "Thank you," he said. But he didn't go any further with it. That was curious. It was as though he knew already about this man and about what he was doing in Bethany.

She studied him. "You're welcome," she said. "Can I pour you another drink?"

She saw him hesitate and then he nodded. She went over to get the bottle and poured him another three fingers. He drank gratefully and when he looked up there was something so vulnerable about him that she said, without thinking, "I have to confess something to you, Mr. Warren."

"Yes?" His eyes darted up to hers, interested. He seemed fragile suddenly, as though he was in pain and was trying not to let it have its way.

She went on, "A friend of mine is connected to the law enforcement community in Boston. We were talking about one thing or another and he, well, he knows of your . . . situation. He told me about your wife and I want to tell you that I am so very, very sorry."

Again, pain, raw and fresh, crossed his face. He gripped the highball and took a desperate drink. "Thank you," he muttered.

She'd made a mistake but she hurried on. "I'll be frank. He also told me that you were beyond suspicion and that you had been terribly mistreated by your colleagues. I am so sorry for that too and I hope you will not spend a moment worrying that your new neighbors might somehow hear about this tragedy and harbor any thoughts that the events did not, well, did not happen just as you stated. I will make sure of it."

Now, gratitude mingled with the pain. He didn't speak, but he met her eyes and nodded again, holding back emotion. They sat in silence for a few moments, the hall clock ticking, the house, her house, which she knew as well as her own body, settling and creaking around them as the air outside cooled. "Mrs. Bellows," he said after a moment. "I had a friend on the force in Boston, an older man who was an intelligence officer during the war. He was posted in Cairo at one point and he told me a lot of stories about his time there, how things were in those years. It seems to me that your husband must have been more than just an embassy worker. He would have been OSS, I'd say."

She almost laughed. How extraordinary of him to bring it up. She couldn't confirm it, of course, but she smiled pleasantly and said, "Ah, that was the war. Such a confusing time."

Warren didn't press the matter.

Though she already knew from Arthur, she asked about his family and he told her about the furniture company, and about his brother, who was in furniture too and who, despite towing the family line in all the important ways, had failed spectacularly at marriage, having reached the age of thirty-three with two embarrassing divorces already under his belt. Warren implied, without coming right out with it, that he was a womanizer.

They talked institutions. Warren and the womanizing brother had both attended Tufts, as had the father. Alice, who had gone to Boston University, determined that they knew some people in common, Boston being really quite a very small place when it came down to it, and they moved on to how Warren was getting on with Pinky and the rest of the troopers at the barracks.

They chatted while he finished his drink and she fancied that he seemed lighter, more carefree by the time he said he must get to bed. She walked him to the door and remembered about the wool coat when she saw the bag on the bench in the hall. "Mr. Warren," she said. "I find myself in possession of a very nice coat for which I have no use. I think it might fit you perfectly. May I give it to you? For the colder weather?" He tried it on and proclaimed it indeed perfect.

He was already on the other side of the screen when he said, "I noticed that when you told me about the stranger in Bethany, you didn't say that this unknown individual was the person who set the fire at the Webers'. I have to ask you, Mrs. Bellows, do you know anything about what happened up at that farm the night of the fire?"

Well, well. He is indeed as sharp as he seems. Alice couldn't help but smile a little. "Mr. Warren, if I knew what happened up at the Webers', I would of course report that to the police. But you're right that I don't think this . . . *traveler*, shall we call him, is responsible for what happened up at the Webers'. It feels . . . different to me, not of a piece with these other, petty crimes."

Warren nodded, smiled, and said, "Thank you for the drink. I needed it. And for the talk." He hesitated and she had a quick glimpse of a younger, boyish Franklin Warren. "I needed that too."

Thirty-three

Sylvie walked down to the lower pasture at dawn, leaving a note for the boys that she'd be back after checking to make sure there weren't any other injured ewes or lambs. She had slept badly—she always did, as this stage of pregnancy, and finding Flora and putting her down had troubled her mind—and she felt fuzzy and disoriented. The sun was just peeking up above the line of trees and the thought popped into her head that it was like a glowing egg yolk. *Sun. Yolk. The sun of the yolk. The egg is a son and has a son* . . . She laughed. Silly. Ah, well, she'd have to think that one out a bit more.

The lamb, fat and nearly as tall as the grown sheep were now, was lying near the tree line. It had been disemboweled, some of the entrails eaten. Whatever had killed it had likely been feasting on it when the boys came down and saw the wounded ewe, and it must have waited in the trees until they were gone to come back for its meal. She had heard what she thought were coyotes calling at night sometimes, their howls and yips echoing around the valley, multiplying themselves endlessly.

Sylvie stood for a moment, looking at the body, then bent to hoist it by the rear legs. She dragged it to the gate along the fence line, the remaining entrails behind it like a strange tail. With difficulty, she pulled it through the open gate and then closed it again behind her. Dr. Falconer would be furious if he saw her, but she knew that this kind of exertion wouldn't hurt the baby. Being active, moving her body, had always made things easier, something that Hugh at least had understood and not bothered her over. She was able to drag the big lamb, by the front legs this time, a hundred yards into the woods. The coyote—or whatever the creature was—could have it; it had been out in the warm air and it wasn't good for much else now, but she didn't want to draw the beast into the field where the sheep were again; there must be a place in the fence where it could get through. *I'm sorry,* she thought, watching the lamb's still form for a moment, as though it might move.

She was about to walk back to the field when she caught sight of a bright flash from the trees. It was a metal cup, she saw when she walked over to it, and it was not the only strange thing in the woods. Someone had suspended a red canvas tarp in the trees, forming a makeshift tent. Inside was a bedroll, and a small paper bag. Next to the cup, which was sitting on a low stump, was a knife, the knife she'd seen the day he'd surprised them at the swimming hole.

She would have to tell Warren that she had found the boy's camp. Warren was already suspicious of her, because she hadn't told him about the boy before, and she knew she'd have to say something.

Such a strange man, Warren. She had felt a sense of recognition the first time she'd met him, as though she knew him, as though she'd seen him before, though of course that was impossible. He had sad eyes and she'd guessed he'd had some sort of tragedy even before he'd told her about his wife. He . . . unsettled her.

Yes, she didn't like it, but she'd have to tell him.

She took the cup off the stump and placed it upside down on the ground a ways away, a kind of message. Maybe he'd understand it as the warning she intended. She would tell Warren, but the boy might be long gone by then. He would have a chance to flee.

He had been so hungry when he spoke to her the first time, so hungry and weak that he hadn't realized at first that he was holding the knife. When he saw her terrified look, he dropped it and apologized, explaining that he was just wondering if she had any food. That's all he wanted, he said, just something to eat. He wasn't going to hurt her. He'd told her his story, the same one she'd told Detective Warren, and she had promised to send one of the boys out with a box. She'd explained where they would leave it and he'd been so grateful he'd practically cried.

She'd left him another box, a few weeks later, and wondered if he was even in Bethany anymore. But when she went to check the next day, it was gone.

They had been busy the next few weeks and she was startled and surprised when she'd gone to check on the sheep the Sunday of the fire and he had come out of the trees, apologizing for scaring her, but asking if he could have some more food. "I tried to wait as long as I could," he'd said. "But there's nothing left. Even just a coupla cans would tide me over." They had stood in the field, chatting for a few minutes, and then she'd promised to leave a box at the end of the barnyard later. When he disappeared into the woods again, she'd looked up toward the house, feeling suddenly that she was being watched, but only the sheep were there.

At least, that's what she'd thought.

Sylvie sighed. She looked one last time at the ram lamb, remembering suddenly the night he'd been born. Hugh had been tired from three nights in a row of being up with the ewes, so Sylvie had taken the middle of the night barn check. It had been a chilled, crystalline night, early March, a sparkling layer of hoarfrost on the grass as she walked across to the barn under a moody half-moon. Flora was already laboring, a long ropy line of the water sac already visible, and Sylvie had checked the other ewes and then watched until the big single ram lamb was born. He came fast and stood quickly. She'd seen him suckle and she'd cut the cord and been back in bed within the hour. A nice, uncomplicated one, she'd told Hugh the next morning.

Well, he'd been born, he'd lived, he'd died.

She felt oddly sad. After one more look, she started for the house.

Thirty-four

The messages were waiting for him when he arrived at the barracks the next morning. One from David Williamson, asking Warren to stop in at his convenience. One from the hospital, letting Warren know that Victor Weber was stable but not conscious yet. And one from Sylvie Weber. Tricia told him that Sylvie had had one of the boys walk down to the Uptons' to use the phone. *He's camping in the woods,* was the message. *Where the sheep was.* The words had confused Tricia, but Warren knew immediately what they meant and he'd called out to Pinky that their thief and arsonist had been camping in the woods below the Webers' sheep fields.

It was a lovely morning, clear and bright, with a hint of fall on the air. Warren was surprised to find that the two Scotches had somehow been harmlessly absorbed by his body. The late night, too, seemed to have had almost no effect. In fact, he'd felt almost cheerful as he'd come out into the bright early morning. Over the top of Alice Bellows's fence, he had seen the boy who helped her in the garden shinnying up one of the fruit trees, a pair of pruners under one arm. The boy reached up to grab a limb above himself and climbed even higher. Warren had watched him for a moment, amazed at his youthful dexterity, and at the scene, the freshness of the air, the beauty of the gardens. Perhaps he'd start running again. It would be very easy on these back roads. Maybe there was a track at the high school as well. He had a barbell stored in the basement at the house; he could begin lifting weights again, get himself back into fighting shape.

And then, the message from Agony Hill.

Still feeling oddly vigorous, he and Pinky parked on River Road between the two farms so that they could come up behind the Webers' fields. This time Warren dressed for the job, in canvas work pants he'd bought while he was in Montana and a long-sleeved shirt. Pinky was in hunting gear, olive-green pants and green shirt and tall boots that looked made for walking through the woods. Warren decided he would have to get a pair of boots like that.

As they climbed along the hillside above the river, Pinky took two apples out of a pocket and handed one to Warren. "Apples just starting," he said. "These are my favorites." The flesh of the apple cracked in a satisfying way when Warren bit into it. The taste was startlingly sweet and fresh.

"Mmmm," he said appreciatively.

"My grandfather raised our trees from seeds he got from an apple he ate at his friend Harold's house in 1892. The apple was so good he saved the seeds in his pocket."

"That's a good story," Warren told him. "And a good apple." Pinky blushed with pleasure.

By the time they had finished with the apples, they had crested the hill and began walking along the ridge toward the Webers' property. "She said the camp was near their lower sheep field," Warren called up. "I got turned around here the other day, but on the map it looks like a pretty straight shot."

Pinky seemed to know where he was going, so Warren relaxed and followed behind. It was cool and damp in the woods and once he'd settled into the rhythm of his pulse and his legs moving on the trail, he found he could hear birdsong and, far away in the distance, the trickling of water. The air smelled of pine and rich, rotting soil; along the path, shelflike mushrooms grew on crumbling logs.

Twenty minutes of walking brought them alongside a brook and they climbed next to it until they reached the bowl-shaped pool where Warren had gotten turned around the day he'd become lost in the woods. "The field should be just over there," he told Pinky.

"Walk nice and quiet. If you see him, make this hand signal and I'll do the same," Pinky said, holding one hand in the air and folding the fingers down against his palm. "If we can catch him unawares, we can bring him in easy. I imagine he's hungry and tired of sleeping rough."

They started, mindful of their steps on the vaguely delineated path, which was carpeted with dead leaves and small sticks and branches that crunched beneath his feet. Warren watched the way Pinky moved, his knees slightly bent, his steps slow and deliberate, his feet placed carefully, heel first and then a roll onto the rest of his foot. He clearly spent a lot of time walking quietly through the woods and Warren felt a quick pang of awareness of his outsider status. He followed Pinky's lead though and found that by walking in that manner, he could keep his feet from making so much noise.

They hadn't been walking very long when Warren saw Pinky's hand come up. Up ahead, through the foliage, he could just barely make out a flash of red. Warren and Pinky stopped walking. Silently, Pinky took a small pair of binoculars from his pocket and held them up to his face. He turned and mouthed, *He's sitting. I'll go around. Walk slowly.* Warren waited until Pinky had made his way around to the other side of the spot to start walking toward what he now saw was a man, a young one, sitting on the ground next to a red tarp hung from the branches of a tree to make a shelter. Pinky looked up and met Warren's eyes. He raised his hand and called out, "Police. You're under arrest. Please put your hands in the air!"

Warren moved quickly through the trees, holding his gun out in front of him.

The man—boy, really, Warren saw now, Sylvie Weber had been right—stood up and waved his hands in the air. "Don't shoot me," he called out. "Please don't shoot me. I'm not doing anything, just camping out here. I can do that, can't I? A guy can camp in the woods, can't he? It's still a free country!"

"Stay still," Warren shouted. "You're under arrest."

"But I didn't do anything. Come on, man. I didn't do anything. I didn't do anything, I swear it!" The boy, slight, dark-haired, straggly-bearded, wearing a green-and-black plaid wool jacket like the red one Alice Bellows had given to Warren, held his hands up in the air and scrambled to his feet. Warren got out his handcuffs and hand-cuffed the boy's hands behind his back. He smelled rank, of body odor and woodsmoke and urine, and he had the look of someone who was wasting; Warren had seen alcoholics and drug addicts in Boston whose bodies hadn't been nourished in weeks and this man had that look about him, hollow cheeks, eyes too big in his head. He felt slight and weak as Warren put a hand on his shoulder. He wouldn't be a danger.

"Do you have any weapons?" Pinky asked him.

"Yeah, yeah, man, I got a rifle over there." He pointed and Pinky ducked under the tarp and came out with a rifle and a box of car-tridges. "I'm sorry. You can give it back to them. I wouldn'ta taken it if I wasn't starving. I swear it, man."

"We'll take him back to the barracks," Warren said to Pinky.

"I didn't do anything," the boy protested again, looking wholly shocked. "What are you bringing me in for?"

"The theft of those rifle cartridges for one thing," Warren said. "And maybe some other things as well. Like arson."

The boy was shivering, though he was wearing the wool jacket. "Those cartridges, I'll pay for them. My father can pay. I was planning on going back to make it right when I could. I was gonna try to shoot a deer or something. As for the fire at that camp, that was an accident," he said. "I swear to you. That was an accident. Look, I'll tell you anything you want to know," the boy said. His eyes were huge and dark in his gaunt face, but there was a scrappy twinkle in them, the twinkle of someone who had not been defeated by the world yet. "But oh, man, I'm hungry. So first, can I have something to eat?"

⌗ ⌗ ⌗

Pete's Lunch was a low-slung diner halfway between Bethany and Woodstock on Route 4. Pinky said he thought they could chat there without being too obvious and when they drove in at eleven, Warren saw he was right. The parking lot was almost empty. Warren turned to Isaac Rosen, for that was what he said his name was, a fact confirmed by a New York State driver's license, and leveled a serious stare at him. "I'll buy you a burger and take the cuffs off if you tell us everything we want to know," he said. "But you're going to sit on the inside of the booth, with one of us next to you, and if you try to take off or any funny business at all, we'll put you back in cuffs and you won't get to eat your burger. Got that?"

"Yeah, yeah," Isaac Rosen said. "Yeah, yeah, I got that." Once inside, his eyes shone as he watched the couple seated at the table next to them dig into their sandwiches.

Pinky told the waitress that they wanted three burgers and a basket of onion rings. "Bring this gentleman a vanilla milkshake, okay?"

"Actually," Isaac Rosen said. "If it's all the same to you, I'd prefer strawberry."

Pinky and Warren exchanged an exasperated look but Pinky nodded. "Strawberry," he told the waitress.

"Okay," Warren told Isaac Rosen. "Tell us."

Isaac Rosen glanced back toward the kitchen, a wolfish, hungry look on his face. "First of all, I swear I didn't mean to burn that place down," he said. "I swear it. I was just—"

"First, tell us how you ended up in Bethany," Warren said sternly.

Isaac nodded enthusiastically. "Okay, so I'm from New York and I was a sophomore at Amherst, you know where that is?" Warren nodded. "But I'm not much of a student. I was pretty much flunking out. My father, right, he was the one who wanted me to go. I liked the parties all right and the girls that came to 'em, but the classes . . . not so much." He shrugged. "Finally, the dean said that I probably shouldn't bother coming back. Which would have been fine, except for one thing."

"The draft," Warren said. Isaac looked up guiltily. Reading his mind, Warren said, "Look, I'm not the Selective Service. I'm just trying to figure out these suspicious fires. If it's nothing to do with that, I don't care about it."

The boy hesitated and then he said, "I hadn't been called up yet, but I figured it was only a matter of time with the new quotas. I thought about Canada and I was actually trying to get some money together when I met a girl in New York who told me she'd heard about this guy in Vermont. He had a farm where everyone was pitching in to produce food and where I could live peacefully and in harmony with nature. She said the guy was against the war and was willing to take in anyone who didn't want to go, that he'd even hide me if it came to that. She said it was in a town called Bethany."

"Brook's End?" Pinky asked him.

Isaac nodded. "Yeah, I shoulda thought it out more, man, but I was desperate. I hitchhiked up here in February. Told my father I was going back to school and hoped they wouldn't call him."

"So?" Pinky asked.

"So, the first couple days I got a sense of what was going on there. This guy, Jeffrey, he had a wife—not his official wife, but they acted like they were married. Her name is Willow and I liked her a lot. She was funny and she was a good cook. Jeffrey, though, man, he was no fun. He wanted us on a rotation, shoveling out the cow stall and the pig stall and he wanted me to kill chickens and shit like that. Sorry. Things like that. I practically fainted the first time and I told him I wouldn't do it. He said I had to earn my keep somehow, so I started making tables and chairs and things to sell. Then I built them a little log cabin sort of thing, a barn, where they could keep some animals. I like woodworking—I'd done some at Amherst—and I'm pretty good at it. But he was always going on about how I wasn't contributing. And I'm tellin' ya, it was boring there. At night, he wanted us to sit around and listen to like, Beethoven or whatever, and read books about history or farming or something. I've never been much of a reader and I'm not too good at sitting still like that." He shook his head grimly at the memory.

Delia came with the food then and Isaac Rosen fell upon his burger like a wild animal on a carcass, even after they told him he could make himself sick. He tried talking while he ate but they told him to finish his meal. He smiled gratefully and ate almost the entire basket of onion rings. Delia came to take their plates and when Pinky asked Isaac if he wanted some pie, he said, "Oh, man, you mean it? I'd kill for a piece of peach pie." A grin broke out on his face. "Guess I shouldn't say that to a couple of cops, right?" Warren and Pinky tried not to smile and said they'd have pie and coffee too.

"So what happened with Jeffrey and Willow?" Warren asked.

"Ah, right, so I just took off. Well, I took a tarp out of the barn and I took this jacket, it was hanging on a peg in the house, and I took an old backpack I found in the barn and put the tarp and some cans and things in it and I just took off. I felt bad about stealing that stuff, but he sorta owed me, if it came down to it, from building that barn for him. I left early one morning and just started walking. Didn't know what to do, to be honest with you. I didn't have any money left; Jeffrey made me give him everything I had when I arrived. I—and I'm not proud of this. I'm no thief. My father owns a very successful company, for god's sake—but I snuck into that store a few times and I took a few things, some beef jerky and a few cans of soup. Then I started walking around, looking to see if maybe someone had left some food on their porch or something. I thought I might find a place to make a campsite. But I found something even better than that."

"The camp up on Agony Hill," Pinky said.

"Yeah. Door wasn't even locked. I figured I could stay there a bit and figure out what to do. I watched it for a while to be sure no one was going to come back."

"It sounds like your father is a wealthy man," Warren said. "I don't understand why you didn't just go home."

"Well, the problem is, he didn't know where I was. He thought I was at college and then I wrote them a letter and I said I was working at college for the summer. You get me? So I couldn't just go home. He woulda had me at the draft board in about three minutes. I thought I could camp out and figure out what to do and how to tell him I wasn't going back to college. But I got hungry. I thought there'd be more berries in the woods, you know? Anyways, when you're hungry you don't think straight. You ever experienced that?"

Pinky, who seemed to like Isaac Rosen, said that in fact he had.

The pie came. Warren knew it would be good before he slipped his fork into the golden-brown crust, the edges artfully crimped, and bright sliced peaches in their own sugar syrup burst forth onto his fork.

"Oh, that's good," Isaac said. "Wow. I think that's the best peach pie I've ever had."

"Delia is quite the baker," Pinky said. For his part, Warren alternated forkfuls of the tender, crispy pie with swallows of the excellent coffee, strong and hot, a stream from the cream pitcher swirling into the dark liquid. He didn't even try to continue the interrogation until they'd all finished.

"Now," Warren said finally. "What happened up at the camp?"

Isaac looked rapturously happy as he finished the last bite of his pie. "Well, there were some cigarettes and some food up there, a few cans, but I finished those and I didn't have any more food. I tried to stick it out, but shoot, being hungry's no fun. You can't think about anything else. So I thought about stealing some more food from the store, but I felt bad about it, you know. Didn't seem right. And I'd just need more before long. There was a rifle at the camp, though, so I decided I'd steal a box of cartridges. Then I could go up in the woods and shoot a deer. I'd learned a little bit about butchering from Jeffrey. Cows, but still . . ." He shrugged. "I went up and I saw a deer, a big one too, but I shot at it and it ran away. I tried to shoot a squirrel, but man, that's a small target."

"What about Mrs. Weber?" Warren said. "She said she gave you some food."

"Yeah, I felt awful bad about that, about scaring her like that. I had been looking for mushrooms and plants and things in the woods and I think a few of them made me sick. I was starving when I came upon them swimming. I had my knife and I called down to her, realized after she must have thought I was threatening her, so when she came up, I put it on the ground, see, and I said, 'I'm not going to hurt you. I'm just stuck out here and I need some food.' She said okay, she'd send one of her boys back with a box. Oh, it was good. Bread and cheese and some jam she'd made. I ate that with a spoon and it was so good. I tried to save some."

"She left another box a few weeks later?"

Isaac nodded and took a long sip of his coffee. "I guess that brings me to the fire at the camp," he said, guiltily. "I feel awful bad about that too, I'm telling you. I was cooking one of the cans of soup she gave me, Mrs. Weber, that her name? And I fell asleep in the chair there in the camp. Being hungry makes you awfully tired, anyway, and when I woke up, the wall next to the stove was on fire. I don't know what happened. I think maybe a spark came out or something. I tried to put it out, threw water on it and everything, but there wasn't any point in it. The place went up like a woodpile. I'm truly sorry. I am. You can tell the people I'll try to get some money to give 'em. I was watching, hoping they could save it, but I ran away when the fire brigade came, you see, and someone started chasing me." Recognition dawned and he pointed his fork at Warren. "Was that you chasing me? I was watching and then all of a sudden, there you were." Warren confirmed that yes, it had been him in the woods that morning.

"So you had to sleep outside after that?" Pinky asked him.

"Yeah, I still had the tarp, but man, I didn't like that. Never one for camping, see. And there was this cow that followed me up there." He looked up at them with an expression of bewilderment. "She came from one of the farms nearby and I ended up tying her to a fence 'cause she kept making noise. I saw a lot of people while I was walking around in those woods, farmers and so forth. I was so lonely I really wanted to talk to someone, but I couldn't, could I?" He shook his head. "It's not good for a guy, being alone that long."

Something clicked in Warren's brain then. He pushed his coffee cup aside and looked at Isaac. "What about the first fire?" he asked. "The fire at the Webers'? Did you see anything that night?"

Isaac looked up guiltily. "Well," he said. "I was still at the camp then. I came out and talked to Mrs. Weber—that was the same day as the fire—and she said she'd give me more food, so I waited a bit. I went at night so no one would see me."

Warren tried to keep his voice even. This might be it. "What did you see, Isaac?"

"I hung around at the edge of the field and watched. She hadn't left it where she said she would, but I heard 'em talking, fighting like, and, well . . . anyway, she never came out so I went back to the camp. But then the hunger really got to me, so I went back, thinking maybe she was waiting till it was dark. First thing was her old man, the one who died, he came out of the house. He was drunk as a skunk. He could barely stand, staggering around, and he came out and went in the barn. Musta been doing his chores."

The diner was getting busy now and Warren was suddenly conscious of all the ears that might be listening. He didn't want to interrupt the flow of the story, though.

"And then what?" he asked.

"And then nothing. I saw him go in and then I waited a bit, to see if she was gonna come out with some food. I had to hide in the trees, like, so I didn't have a good view but I heard a car start up and I went back down to the camp again. An hour or so later, I could smell the smoke and I could see the flames. I ran up 'cause I thought maybe he got stuck in there, but by the time I got up there, the fire truck was already there. If it hadn't come, I woulda helped, maybe tried to pull him out. I didn't know what to do after that."

Warren studied him. "You said you heard them talking earlier that night. Fighting. What did you hear?" He found that he was afraid of what Isaac was going to say and he held his breath as he waited for the younger man to speak.

"I didn't hear what they were actually saying, but someone was mad, him probably. I heard . . . not words, but he was upset. You know what I mean by that? It was a man's voice and it was too loud, the words too short. He was yelling at someone."

Warren leaned forward, breathlessly waiting. "Did you hear anyone else's voice?"

"Nah . . . whoever he was talking to didn't talk back, at least not loud enough for me to hear."

Delia came and cleared away the rest of their plates and coffee cups. Warren was thinking, trying to put it all together. *Drunk as a skunk. Not loud enough for me to hear.*

"What are you going to do with me?" Isaac Rosen asked. He seemed happier now, his eyes not quite so desperate, his face relaxed and contented. He was a good-looking kid despite his gaunt face and dirty beard, Warren decided, his eyes kind and alert. He reminded Warren of a friend he'd had in his childhood. Ian. He'd been bright, brilliant even, but not one for school. He'd been too nervy, always tapping or moving or standing up and sitting down. Warren wondered suddenly what had happened to Ian.

Warren stood up. "I don't know yet," he said. "But for now we're going to take you down to the county jail." He caught a flash of fear in Isaac's face and added quickly, "You'll be alone in your cell and it's warm and not too bad there."

"Food's actually pretty good," Pinky told him.

"Okay." Isaac stood up too and yawned. "I could use a nap actually. I haven't slept for real in weeks." He turned to go, not looking for permission from Warren or Pinky. Outside, he slid into the back seat as though Warren were his chauffeur.

Thirty-five

Sylvie sat on the couch in the front room and listened to the house. It was still strange to her, being alone. *Sole. Solitary. Sole, I sit.* The boys, even Scott, were fast asleep, exhausted from a day of work. She was tired too, the baby making her hips ache and her brain fuzzy. But she wanted to feel what it was to be alone now. It was yellow and brown, she decided, the silence yellow, the space brown. It hummed around her in waves. It wasn't all bad, but she was aware of Hugh's absence and it felt strange, gaping, too big, white.

The evenings had been pleasant once, before he started drinking so much. They had read to each other or just chatted, about the boys and the farm, making plans and discussing things. He had told her about books she should read, describing the plots and the characters so that she felt she had read them. When he first brought her to Agony Hill and they unpacked all of his books into the bookcases he'd built in what had been the Hicksons' parlor, Sylvie thought that she was luckiest girl in the entire world. To have all of these books, to be allowed to read them whenever she wanted. But there had always seemed to be so much to do. Once Scott came, she was always working and it was only in the evenings that Hugh let her sit and read the books. When she started writing poems, he sometimes asked her to read them aloud, and then he started writing his stories and letters and articles and reading those too, asking for her advice on how to make them better.

They had been happy for a while like that, alone in their little world up on Agony Hill, before things started to change. Before the gin. Before his letters. Before he'd gotten the rejection letters for his "book."

Suddenly, she remembered the day they'd met. He'd come into the drugstore where she worked at the counter, and bought a packet of pills for his bad stomach. It had been a quiet day and she had taken a book from the rack, a Nevil Shute novel about a woman marching across Malaysia, and she was reading it, careful not to break the spine so that she could put it back when Gary came back from his lunch break.

She'd looked up to find a tall man watching her. "Why are you reading like that?" he asked. "Books should be read extravagantly, completely, not timidly, as though you're afraid to *live* right down in them!" He had sounded stern and she'd been a bit afraid of him when she explained that the book wasn't hers so she didn't want to break it.

He smiled then. "Well," he said, handing over some bills, too much for the pills alone. "I've bought it for you, so you can read it however you'd like now. Break it wide open!"

Taking him literally, she'd looked right at him and opened the book as wide as she could. It had made a satisfying sound as the paper opened and the spine broke. He'd laughed and really focused on her then and she knew, because men had started to look at her like that, that he thought she was pretty and that he liked her. She thanked him and sure enough he was back the next day and this time he asked if she might like to go for a walk. She said all right, but it would have to be after she finished working.

When he came to pick her up, he asked about her favorite books and they talked without stopping. She didn't think he was very handsome. He was much older, for one thing, almost thirty-five, and for another he had a strange way of talking, as though he were teaching a class rather than having a conversation. She had liked the way he talked about the world, as though it were his and hers to explore. "When I take you to London," he'd say, or, "You'll love Rome." He told her about how he'd come to Vermont with a man named Jeffrey, who had a farm and wanted to show that it was possible to live freely, without regard for things like marriage or taxes or capital. She gathered that he and this Jeffrey had had a fight, though, over money, and later Hugh had told her about how he lent Jeffrey five thousand dollars and Jeffrey had never paid him back.

When he said he wanted to take her to Bethany with him, where he was going to buy a farm and they could live the way people used to live, off the land, without having to capitulate to modernity, and would she go with him, even if they weren't married, she'd told him she'd be happy to go but that her father wouldn't let her unless she was married. He had sighed and said that well, they might as well get a license, but they could still live freely, without "strictures." Did she understand what he was asking her, he said then, did she understand what it meant to live with someone and be his wife? And then he grabbed at her breasts and pulled her toward him and kissed her. She didn't like it. He had bad breath and the kiss was very wet, but somewhere in there he said he had boxes of books and that they would be theirs now, both of theirs, and that she would have a house to keep as she pleased, and she said yes without really thinking about it.

"Well, Sylvie," she said to herself now. "You made your bed." It was a thing her mother had liked to say, to tell them that everything that happened was their fault. But Sylvie had always hated it. People made mistakes, especially children, and Sylvie had never said those words to her own boys. If something bad happened, the person who was responsible for it would spend enough time blaming himself or herself for the calamity. What they wanted to hear was that they would have company as they sought to solve it. "We'll figure it out together," Sylvie always told the boys when they had amends to make or messes to clean up.

She smiled to herself. She actually did need to make her bed. She'd washed the sheets that day and hung them out in the dry air, then folded them carefully. Bed. It was time to go to bed.

Still smiling, she shut off the lights and climbed the stairs to the bedroom. The air had a slight chill and once she'd put the sheets back on and undressed, she got beneath the quilt and found she missed Hugh's warmth. Shivering, she put a hand on her belly, felt the baby move and shift beneath her skin. They would keep each other warm, this baby and Sylvie. Was it a girl, like Hugh thought? December. She'd know in December.

"I'll see you soon," she whispered, closing her eyes, burrowing under the covers, and smelling the warm smell of the laundered sheets. The baby kicked faintly once, then twice, as if in answer.

Thirty-six

This time, the road out to Brook's End didn't seem so long. It was the next morning and Warren, freshly showered and full of his own strong coffee, Pinky next to him in the passenger seat, recognized a few of the landmarks, the first turn, the tree with a NO TRESPASSING sign on it. The old black dog came out to bark at the car, then slunk away when Warren and Pinky got out and started walking up to the porch. They knocked and it was a few minutes before Sawyer, dressed only in a bathrobe, tufts of gray hair protruding at the neck and mingling with his long beard, came out onto the porch, the door slamming hard behind him. His eyes were puffy and Warren thought they'd woken him up.

"What's the meaning of this? You can't just come onto my property anytime you want!"

"I'd like to talk to you, Mr. Sawyer. It won't take long. I need your help."

Sawyer smiled. "You need *my* help? That's something, isn't it? What makes you think I want to help *you*?"

Warren put his hands out. "Mr. Sawyer, I'm new here in town. I'm trying to do my job and make a good impression. A man, your friend, is dead. I need to find out how he died and all I'm asking is that you answer a few questions for me."

Sawyer didn't say anything, but his body language shifted and he inclined his head, telling Warren to ask his questions.

"We asked you if you knew anything about the fires and you never mentioned that you'd had a man living with you until recently and that the man left suddenly one night without an explanation. Why didn't you say anything about him? Didn't it occur to you that he might be relevant to our investigation?"

"Who are you talking about?" Sawyer asked, looking—to Warren's mind anyway—genuinely surprised and confused. "What do you mean?"

"Isaac Rosen," Warren said.

"Isaac? He's back in New York by now, isn't he?" The dog came up on the porch, sidling up to Sawyer to have its ears scratched.

Pinky took his green trooper's hat off and said, "No, Mr. Sawyer. He's been living in the woods on Agony Hill and it was Isaac Rosen who accidentally set the fire at the camp."

Sawyer was genuinely confused. "What . . . Isaac? But he disappeared one night and I just assumed he'd gone back to New York."

Warren leaned against the porch railing, trying to show he was relaxed and that he wasn't going anywhere. "We just need to confirm some details of his story."

Jeffrey rolled his eyes. "What was his story? I wouldn't believe much of it if I was you. Isaac was full of talk but ultimately unable to commit to the routine here. He misrepresented his interest in our way of life."

"So, he arrived sometime in February, is that right?"

"I don't remember the exact time, but yes, around then," Jeffrey said. The old dog yipped and Jeffrey reached down to caress its ears. "I think he thought it would be one big party and he was quite surprised about the level of work it actually takes to sustain ourselves here at Brook's End." The screen door banged open and Willow, also wearing a robe, came out onto the porch, trailed by another old dog, this one black with a white snout.

"What's going on, Jeffrey?" she asked. Then she saw Warren and Pinky. "Oh, it's you again."

"These officers are just asking about Isaac."

Willow rolled her eyes. "He went back to his rich daddy, didn't he?"

"Isaac set the fire at that camp up on Agony Hill," Jeffrey said quietly.

Willow's face froze. "He killed Hugh? Why did he do that?"

"No," Warren said. "The other fire. The fire at that camp."

Willow just looked confused.

Warren tried to wrest back control of the interview. "Is Isaac the first man you've had here who didn't want to go to war?"

"No comment," Sawyer said, holding his chin up and looking out toward the trees.

"Mr. Sawyer, I don't care who you have living here, but you and Hugh Weber didn't like each other and it's possible someone who was staying here picked up on that dislike and decided to go after him. Anyone stay here who might have decided to settle your score for you?"

Oddly, Jeffrey looked offended at that. "Of course not. We wouldn't have anyone staying here like that. And besides . . . well, like I said, we wouldn't. This is a place of peace, Mr. Warren."

Warren looked around, taking in the details now. The homestead was neater than it had appeared at first. The large vegetable garden was well-weeded and the porch furniture, though old and shabby, seemed to have been recently mended; a new leg carved of pale wood made a fourth with older ones on a chair, their paint peeling. In the distance, he noticed a section of paler wood on the side of a barn, the new pieces fitted in seamlessly with the old. In a few years, no one would even notice the repair. And then there was the brand-new shed.

Isaac Rosen, Warren realized.

"You should have told us about him," Pinky said sternly. "We're carrying out an investigation here."

"That's no business of mine," Sawyer said. "That's your problem. Now, if there's nothing else . . ." He started to turn away. Warren was seized with anger at the man's smugness, at his contempt for Warren and Pinky and their errand.

"I'm not finished with you," he said. "I want to know where you were the night of the fire at Webers', the night Hugh Weber died. You said you were here, but I don't think you were."

Sawyer looked panicked, which told Warren he'd gotten it right.

He started to say something, then hesitated. Willow, who had been watching the exchange, swore under her breath and went into the house. Jeffrey watched her go.

"Where were you, Mr. Sawyer?"

"I don't have to tell you," Jeffrey said. "I know my rights! We still have some freedoms in this country, though they're slipping away." He crossed his arms in front of his chest.

The door slammed open again. "That's where he was," Willow said, handing Warren a piece of pale yellow paper printed with a large headline and words beneath. "At a meeting at the college." Warren read the words on the paper: "Why U.S. Involvement in Vietnam is Immoral and How to Resist."

Willow frowned. "You go ask the students who were there, they'll tell you he was there until late."

"Is this true, Mr. Sawyer?" Warren asked him. "Is that where you were?"

"I refuse to answer that question. You'll use my answer to create a file so you can track me. I know Chief Longwell already has one. I know what he's up to. Longwell's a fascist. Have you discovered that yet, Mr. Warren?"

"I just need to know if you were at the college, Mr. Sawyer."

"No comment!" Warren met Willow's eyes and she nodded.

Warren sighed. "Mr. Sawyer, I don't know anything about any file and I don't care about your politics and I don't want to track you. Is there anything you can tell me about Hugh Weber that might help in our investigation? Some people are saying he killed himself, like that farmer last year, Forrest Germond. You knew Weber well, at one time anyway. You think he had it in him to do that?"

Jeffrey looked out toward the vegetable garden. "His ego was too big," he said finally. "When I heard he'd set that fire, I thought it must have been an accident. Hugh Weber thought he was a gift to the world. No way he'd take that gift away."

Warren nodded and stood up. Pinky followed suit. "Thank you," Warren said. "Did Isaac do that repair over there on the barn? And that barn there?"

Jeffrey Sawyer nodded. "He was a good carpenter," he said. "Wasn't good at much else, but he had a way with wood."

¤ ¤ ¤

"I believe him," Warren said in the car. "Or her, I suppose. I want you to see if you can find any of the students who were at the meeting, though they may not want to talk. I bet he was there just like she said though. And they confirmed Isaac Rosen's story. So where does that leave us?"

Pinky looked out the window. "Well, we had two unsolved fires and now we just have one."

Warren laughed. "You're right, Pinky. We're right back where we started. And now that we know there wasn't an arsonist loose on Agony Hill, it probably makes it more likely that Hugh Weber did set that fire."

"But . . ." Pinky prompted him. Warren knew he hadn't sounded very sure.

"But . . . there's that skull fracture. And there's Victor Weber getting attacked by someone. And there's Isaac Rosen hearing Hugh Weber yelling angrily the night he died. Or," he corrected himself, realizing what he'd said, "*someone* yelling angrily."

"Someone might have visited him," Pinky said.

"That's right." Warren braked at the stop sign at the end of Goodrich Hill and turned onto the state highway. "You heard anything around town, Pinky, about Sylvie Weber or anything else?"

"Not really," Pinky said, as Warren pulled in at the barracks. "But I'll go see my aunt Patty tomorrow and ask if she's heard any gossip."

They made some follow-up calls and worked on paperwork until it was time for lunch. By the time they'd checked on Isaac Rosen, eaten roast turkey sandwiches at Pete's—no peach pie today, but the coconut cream was pretty good—and driven back to the barracks, it was midafternoon.

Tommy Johnson was inside when they got back, his feet up on a desk, talking to someone on the phone and taking notes on a pad. He waved when he saw Warren and after a few utterances of "Thanks, yup, I'll tell him. That's right," he hung up the phone and waved them over. "So you found the arsonist," he said cheerily. "Good work! You think he's got anything to do with Hugh Weber?"

"He doesn't have anything to do with that," Warren said, explaining about Isaac Rosen and their visit out to Brook's End. "But he says he heard a man yelling like he was mad about something, not long before the fire. Hey, any word on Victor Weber's condition?"

Tommy rolled his eyes. "He's up and talking and asking for a drink. Says he remembers going for a walk from the inn and that's it. The next thing he remembers is waking up at the hospital. Between the booze and the knock on the head, I'd say he's lost at least twenty-four hours."

Warren felt his spirits sink. Whoever had attacked Victor Weber had been saved by the man's lapse of memory.

Pinky headed out for road duty and Warren sat at his desk, thinking about warm summer nights and barns and Isaac Rosen, camping in the woods. The windows were open next to his desk and the cool air came through, washing pleasantly over his face. He thought about head wounds and bullet wounds and break-ins, and he thought about his father's old friend Tommy Johnson, who at this very moment was laughing about something with Tricia at the dispatch desk.

He went over and stood there awkwardly for a moment, listening to Tricia tell a story about something she'd once heard on a party line while calling her sister. Warren still needed to get his phone installed. It had been so busy he'd forgotten all about it.

"Hey, Tommy," he said quietly, when there was a break in their conversation. "I thought I'd go out and get some fresh air. You want to come with me?"

Tommy's eyes snapped up, suddenly wary, and he seemed to try to read Warren for a moment before he smiled and said, "Sure thing. It's nice out today, isn't it?"

They went out the front door and by silent agreement, walked around to the parking lot, checking to make sure none of the troopers were out there before they stepped into the shade of a big willow tree at the edge of the small patch of lawn behind the barracks.

"What is it, Frankie?" Tommy asked. "Everything okay?"

Warren reached out to touch a trailing willow branch. It was starting to turn color, yellow from the bright green it had been only a few days before. "Samuel Armstrong," he said finally.

Tommy's body stiffened but he didn't say anything for a long moment. Finally, looking down at the ground, where a line of ants was disappearing into an anthill, he said, "Yeah?"

"Fred Fielder asked me about it, caught me out actually. I just said, 'No comment,' but then when I looked, there was nothing in the case files. Nothing. I haven't been here long, but I've been here long enough to know that a thing like that, a burglary and an execution-style shooting in the middle of the night on a quiet country road, well, that warrants a case file."

"It's not ours anymore, Frankie," Tommy said after a long moment. "That's why there's no case file. Because it went to someplace else. Someplace I can't tell you."

"But it's in our jurisdiction and if it has anything to do with Hugh Weber, then I need to see the reports. I'm stuck on this, Tommy. Someone shot that man and got away with it and someone may have killed Hugh Weber. I'm hamstrung if I can't connect the dots here! I'm new, I want to do my job. You know how that feels, Tommy. I want to see justice done. That's the job, it's why I came up here!"

He was angrier at Tommy than he'd known and his voice had risen as he was talking. When he was done, Tommy's eyes widened and Warren thought about how his elfin face must have been part of what made him a good investigator. You just couldn't believe he was holding out on you. He looked too innocent.

Now, Tommy's eyes were apologetic as he said, "It doesn't have anything to do with Hugh Weber, so don't worry about that. You can take my word for it, I've been doing this a long time." Tommy, deeply uncomfortable, started to walk back to the barracks but Warren reached out and touched his arm.

"Who took it from you, Tommy? The guy was a State Department employee. Is that why? Who told you to bury that file?"

Tommy turned and gave Warren a sympathetic look. "Better if you don't know, Frankie," he said. "Now, I've got to get on the road."

☒ ☒ ☒

The Bethany white pages listed Roy Longwell's address as 126 Church Street, just down the street from the police station. It was a medium-sized white Cape Cod–style house, new and neatly kept, and after he had parked the Galaxie down the street, Warren walked up the stone path and knocked on the front door. It was starting to get dark. The windows along the front of the house were open and through the screens, Warren could hear the Red Sox game on the radio.

The woman who answered the door was thin, gray-haired, austere-looking, not at all the wife he would have imagined for burly Roy Longwell. She stared at Warren and waited for him to speak, rather than offering a greeting. A smell of roasting meat wafted deliciously from the inside of the house.

"I'm sorry to bother you, Mrs. Longwell, but I was wondering if I could talk to the chief," Warren said, his voice squeaking a little. He was nervous, guilty about going behind Tommy's back. "I'm Franklin Warren, with the state police."

She must have been used to dinner-hour visitors because she called back over her shoulder, "Roy!" without acknowledging Warren or inviting him in.

Longwell came out quickly, muttering, "Follow me," and leading Warren around the side of the house to a small backyard almost completely taken up by a large vegetable garden. Longwell, dressed in tan khaki workpants and a flannel shirt, unspooled a length of hose from the side of the house and bent to turn the spigot beneath it. When, after a few seconds, a stream of water came from the end of the hose, he directed it to a row of tall, prolific tomato plants at one end of the garden and said, "What can I do for you, Detective Warren?"

A cricket chirped from the bushes and Warren watched as the water soaked the soil underneath the plants. "I wanted to ask you about that shooting," he said. "The guy from Washington."

Longwell didn't look at him. "I told you I don't have anything about that. You should ask your friend Tommy Johnson."

"Well, I wasn't able to get what I wanted there, Chief Longwell. I'm trying to make a go of my new job and I want to find out what happened up at the Webers' the night of that fire. I want to see justice done. It seems odd to me that there is an unsolved burglary and shooting not far from where Hugh Weber died and I want to know about it. I thought you were being deliberately unhelpful before, but I think I may have missed your meaning. You said you didn't find anything. That there was nothing to find. You meant there really was nothing, didn't you?"

Longwell moved the stream of water to the next plant before he said, "Cleanest crime scene I ever saw. The guy was dead on the ground and there was some blood on the floor, but there was nothing else. No prints, no mud, no dust, no hair."

"Someone cleaned the scene," Warren said.

Longwell nodded. "You ever heard of a burglary where the burglars cleaned house after they were done?"

"No, Chief Longwell, I haven't."

"Well, there you go. Tommy Johnson came down the next day, he looked around. At first, it seemed like a normal investigation. But then Tommy's tune changed. He clammed up something good. I don't know what he found because he didn't tell me, but I'll tell you something, no one wanted to talk about it after that."

"Thank you," Warren said. He wasn't sure what he'd learned, but it seemed important to know it. "This Hugh Weber thing, what do you think is going on here, Chief Longwell? Someone attacked Victor Weber, almost killed him. Do you think the community is in danger?"

The cricket chirped again, joined by another one, and finally a third.

A tiny, smug smile touched Roy Longwell's lips. "I'd say no. If you hadn't stopped by tonight, you would have received a call from me, Detective Warren, just as soon as I'd finished my supper. I just heard from one of my guys that a young woman from Rutland called the station this evening. She was feeling guilty because she was in Bethany the other day and she was driving perhaps a bit too fast along Route 5. She wasn't paying attention, warm day, the sun was in her eyes, you know how it goes, and she hit something. Thought it was a woodchuck or a cat, something like that, and she kept going. But then she saw an item in the newspaper, about a man found injured on the side of the road. She's been stewing about it, feeling guilty, and finally she decided she ought to call us up and turn herself in."

"Victor Weber." Warren said. "He wasn't attacked. He was hit by a car."

"That's right. The car knocked him against a tree on the side of the road and his head caught on a branch. Who knows where he was going, but he'd drunk himself into a stupor and probably stepped out in front of the car. I doubt charges will be filed."

He moved on to the final tomato plant, directing the water to the roots and watching the soil darken, a satisfied expression on his face.

"So that's it," Warren said. "I'm right back where I started with Hugh Weber and a fire that may have been suicide or may not have been."

"That's right," Longwell said. And then he looked up at Warren and said, "It's tough, isn't it, Detective, the ones you can't solve? The ones where questions remain, even after you've done your best. Worst part of the job, isn't it? I expect you know that all too well."

He was talking about Maria's murder. Warren was sure of it. He didn't know what to say, so he just stammered out a thank-you and said he had to be getting home.

Longwell nodded and went to the side of the house where he replaced the hose and turned off the spigot. They walked around to the front and Longwell said something that Warren didn't catch.

"Excuse me?"

"Nothing, Detective Warren. Have a nice evening."

Thirty-seven

Alice had been watching through the living room window and when she saw Warren's car pull into the drive next door, she slipped on a light cardigan, took a small basket from the kitchen hook, and slipped out into the night. This was what she'd come to, stalking her new neighbor, pretending that she'd just come out to check something in the garden.

Everything was in a state of change. A light breeze rippled through the flower beds and over the surface of her ponds. The light from the house illuminated a single yellow leaf helicoptering through the air and falling at her feet. Fall was coming. She hurried to the gate and went though it in a businesslike way, as though she were on a vital mission. She looked up and tried to put on a surprised look when she saw him, his face in half-shadow, his shoulders low and dejected.

"Hello, Mr. Warren," she said. "I was just coming out to check on some fungus I saw on this apple tree." She gestured toward the tree at the side of the garden. Its branches overhung the garden fence.

"I have some news for you," he said seriously, but with a little bit of a twinkle that made her think maybe he knew she'd been waiting for him to pull up.

"Oh?"

"We've solved your mystery of the missing rifle cartridges."

"Really?"

"Yes, there is a man who's been, well, sleeping rough on Agony Hill and he's admitted to stealing the cartridges from the store, along with some food items, and to accidentally setting the fire at the cabin up there, the one that belongs to the people from Boston. I'm not sure how we'll be handling him, but he'll have to make restitution. He's not a bad sort really, New Yorker, came up to live at that place, Brook's End, got himself into a fix. He fought with Jeffrey Sawyer, and took off into the woods." Alice watched him while he talked. When he said the word *woods*, his eye twitched, as though he had a traumatic association.

"What will happen to him?" Alice asked.

"Oh, we'll let him go tomorrow. If he can find a way to make it right with the Collers and the owners of the cabin, then I don't think he'll be charged." He sighed.

Alice smiled. "I think, Mr. Warren," she said carefully, "that you have made an excellent choice. If he makes restitution, that is. Justice so often depends upon . . . proportionality, doesn't it? Law enforcement is most effective and, um, authoritative, when citizens believe that the punishment fits the crime. I've seen it many times."

"Yes," he said, frowning a little. "Well, I knew you were worried about the young man at the store, so I wanted to be sure to let you know." He tucked the paper bag he carried under one arm and kept moving.

"Would you like something to eat, Mr. Warren? I don't have much for my supper, only some cold salmon and cucumber salad, but I'd be very happy to share with you. You look exhausted."

He studied her for a moment, as though he were considering. "Do you know?" he said. "I am exhausted, but I actually feel like cooking. It's a hobby of mine. Do you mind if I shift your invitation around and invite *you* to join *me*? I'm not a bad cook and I find it, well, rejuvenating."

She smiled at him. It was a sincere invitation. "I'd be delighted," she said.

"Good. Let me just wash and get things started and then perhaps you could come over in thirty minutes or so?"

She said that would be lovely and went to change, getting out a bottle of Montepulciano that she had been given by an old friend from the intelligence services, a friend who had access to excellent Italian wines.

By the time she knocked on his back door at eight o'clock, there was a delightful smell of tomatoes and garlic and herbs emanating from the kitchen. *Italy,* she thought. *He's conjured Italy for me.*

"Detective Warren," she said. "You do surprise. A policeman and an obviously skilled chef, all in one. Imagine that!"

He laughed. "Well, you haven't tasted it yet." But he inclined his head and said, "My late wife, Maria, her family was from Sicily and her mother is perhaps the most gifted cook I have ever come across. Maria didn't like to cook very much—no way she could measure up, you see—but she taught me the basics and I found I quite enjoyed it. It's a . . . an approach, I think, more than a specific technique. Good ingredients, of course." He winked. "And please just call me Warren. Everyone does."

Alice allowed him to open the wine and took a glass from him. "My husband and I spent a year living in Rome, after the war, of course. We ate so many wonderful meals." They talked about Rome while he cooked. He had visited there, it turned out, with his parents when he was sixteen. When he mentioned his parents, there was a reticence, a resistance that she assumed was related to their disapproval of his marriage. But perhaps it was something else, his choice of career, his unwillingness to join the family business. There were so many reasons that people became estranged from their families. Alice had seen most of them.

The breeze picked up, swirling through the windows of the kitchen, and the wine did its work. Alice found that it was pleasant chatting with her neighbor about travel and about the past. They talked about Rome and Paris and she felt relief seep into her bones. It could be proven now that Richie was not a thief after all. Mr. Coller would have to apologize and if Richie and Lizzie were going to be married, well, it wasn't a bad way to start off a marriage, was it? With one's father-in-law feeling guilty and beholden? Bob would have to give Richie a raise. When Lizzie and Richie had decided things, well, Bob would have to give them his blessing now. Yes, Warren would go down and talk to the Collers first thing tomorrow morning and everything would be put to rights. She was sure of it.

Warren took four pieces of chicken from the refrigerator and seared the skin until it had been rendered into goldenness. Shallots went into the pan, and some wine and fresh herbs, and he fussed over it and then he tipped them out onto simple white plates he took from the cupboard and smothered them in the tomato sauce, adding a chiffonade of basil at the end. They ate at the kitchen table, chatting companionably. The chicken, as she'd known it would be, was excellent. He made strong coffee when they were done, with no discussion of whether it would ruin anyone's sleep.

"This Brook's End," he asked her as they drank their coffee. "What do you know of them?"

"Oh, Jeffrey Sawyer," she said. "Well, he's an interesting case. He came up about fifteen years ago and bought that farm. Got it very cheap. I believe Hugh Weber provided the funds. People weren't sure at first what he meant to do with it. He wanted to farm, you see. He had an idea about communal living, everyone contributing to the greater good. Like Hugh, he'd read Helen and Scott Nearing's book.

He thought he'd invented something new, but of course there isn't anything new about it."

"No love lost between him and Hugh Weber," Warren said. Alice thought it was more studied than he meant it to sound. He wanted to see if she had any information about the feud between the two men.

"No, you'd expect it, wouldn't you? Two very similar personalities," she said carefully. "They might as well have been brothers, though Hugh had a cruel streak that I don't think Sawyer has."

He looked up in surprise.

"I expect you'll be closing the Weber case now," she said casually. "Won't it be a relief?"

Those brown eyes snapped to hers. "What makes you think that?"

"Well, this fellow, the New Yorker, he's changed things, hasn't he?"

"I'm not sure what you mean, Mrs. Bellows. This man—his name is Isaac Rosen—there's nothing to suggest that he killed Hugh Weber."

"Of course not," Alice said, trying not to say too much, but trying to say enough. "But perhaps . . . well, I sensed you had come to some sort of conclusion."

He looked genuinely shocked. Perhaps she'd misjudged things. "I don't know what you mean," he said. "We're still investigating."

"Yes." She took a long sip of her coffee. "Mr. Warren, the other night you guessed that my husband had an . . . official role in Cairo during the war, a role beyond that of . . . well, of what we told people he was doing there. You were, of course, correct. My husband was an intelligence officer. I knew some of what he did, but of course there was much of it that was beyond my understanding."

He nodded and she went on. "I haven't told many people, but my husband was surely murdered, in the course of his work. There was a different story of course, heart failure while on a business trip. You understand? That was what they told me, but I knew."

Warren's eyes widened. "When was this?" he asked after a moment. "I'm so sorry."

She was not surprised when twenty minutes later she saw the lights go out in the house next door. Warren's headlights swept across the fence and the car reversed and headed off in the direction of Agony Hill.

She waved away the sympathy. "It was ten years ago now, ur circumstances that were . . . murky. He was in Berlin. I will per never know the truth. I don't know exactly why I'm telling you except to tell you that it is possible to live quite well and quite ha with, well, I suppose with ambiguity, is what I am trying to tell I miss my husband but knowing exactly how he died and who him would be . . . an unproductive obsession. Do you see?"

He did not see, she thought. But he said, "Yes, Mrs. Bellow so very sorry."

"I'm past that part of it," she said, annoyed. He wasn't gett meaning of her words at all. "That's not what I meant."

He studied her for a moment. "I understand," he said. " ask you something. This man, Samuel Armstrong, who was l an apparent burglary in May. Did you know him? Had you ε him?"

Alice made a conscious effort to keep her face compos Mr. Warren. I never met him. He had only just bought the hc see, when he was killed."

"That's what's so strange to me. If he didn't know any had no connections, then why was he here?"

She stood, leaving her coffee cup on the table. "I'm afr help you there, Mr. Warren. Now, it's been a lovely evening be going."

He still seemed confused, but he smiled and inclined l thanks for the compliment. "Good night," she said, and h wanting to leave him with his thoughts, and made her v the quiet house. She was not often lonely, but somethin encounter had left her a bit bereft. She went into her s and sat in her chair, thinking, and then put on the radio on her current needlepoint, finishing the lower-right qu stitches describing the paths of a geometric garden. Th labyrinth at the center and she let herself travel its paths

Thirty-eight

Warren drove the six miles up to Agony Hill quickly. There was a bright moon high in the sky now and at the turnoff, he could just make out the bull, a hulking form on the ground under the tree. He didn't stand but he did turn his huge head as the Galaxie sped by, as though he knew it was Warren and he knew what he was going to do.

He could feel the red wine still sparkling its way through his system. He wasn't over the limit, but he wasn't exactly sober either. Things seemed narrowed to a thin, lit corridor in front of him on the road. Was it the wine that had delivered sudden clarity to him when he had looked across the drive to Mrs. Bellows's garden after he said good night to her? Or was it the conversation?

Turn around, Warren, he said to himself. *You can do it tomorrow.*

He kept driving.

The farmhouse was dark and as he idled for a moment in the drive, to give her time to come down, he went over it all in his head, how it must have happened.

Then he shut off the car, took a flashlight from the glove box, and, passing the truck parked in the driveway, the bed still filled with hay, Warren walked over to the damaged barn, the darkened timbers like the shell of a bombed cathedral. Stepping inside, he shone the light up on the walls, raising the beam of the flashlight to the high window, too high for any man to climb. *By God, they're lucky they didn't lose it all.* Who had said that? Tommy? It seemed so long ago now he'd come up to Agony Hill for the first time.

The air smelled faintly of woodsmoke, he realized. Someone, somewhere had built a fire in their woodstove or fireplace. Or perhaps someone had been burning brush. The hint of woodsmoke made him think of fall. It was coming. In a few weeks it would be September. He thought then of Forrest Germond. He had known the machines were coming, had known that everything was ending, just the way that Warren sensed the fall coming. He had been in the grip of something bigger than himself, a madness, or perhaps a sort of mad clarity. Warren understood it now. And he understood what had happened to Hugh Weber, what Hugh Weber must have done.

The fire was the part that had flummoxed him, but now he saw it, now he saw what had happened.

She opened the door immediately when he knocked. There was one light on in the hallway, but the house was otherwise dark and she was in deep shadow as she stood there waiting for him to say something.

"Mrs. Weber, I'm sorry to bother you so late at night," he said. "But I need to speak with you. May I come in?" She didn't answer, just held the door open and then led the way to the kitchen. She was wearing a man's flannel robe, blue-and-green tartan, wrapped around her body and tied at the waist, over the slight swelling of her belly. She sat down in the rocking chair by the big cookstove, as though there was a fire there, and looked at him expectantly. Not knowing what else to do, he sat at the kitchen table, feeling like a small boy being forced to eat his dinner. Her hair was loose and it lay across one cheek like a fan.

"I think we've made some progress in the investigation into your husband's death," he told her. "I think I know what happened the night of the fire. But I wondered if there's something you might want to tell me."

He had learned over the course of his career that you got better results in interrogations if you didn't back people into corners.

But she didn't say anything, just stretched her feet out toward the stove, again as though there were a fire. It must be habit, he thought, seeking comfort from the big, warm life-giving apparatus. Her feet were bare, her skin almost glowing in the dark kitchen. Her toes were very uniform, the nails neat ovals, pale pink like the inside of a sea-shell.

She didn't offer anything, so he went ahead.

"One of the first things someone said to me was that you were lucky you didn't lose the whole barn. You were, of course. It was filled with hay. It should have been gone by the time the firemen arrived. But I talked to Mr. Williamson and he said that he was amazed at how quickly they were able to respond to the fire. They were able to save most of it. He talked about how Scott must have driven like a bat out of hell to get to the phone."

She didn't say a word so he went on. "It seemed to us at first that your husband must have killed himself after setting the barn on fire, because the bolt was shot across the door on the inside and because the fire had been set from the cot where he lay. There did not seem to be a way that any person could have induced your husband to lie down on the bed, killed him there, and then set the fire and closed the bolt and exited the barn. The only window was high above the ground and attempting to jump from it seemed like certain death."

The cat entered the room and jumped up into her lap. She stayed silent.

"But then I saw a boy climbing an apple tree and I realized that a man couldn't do it, but perhaps a boy could. I saw how someone young and strong could have set the fire and put the bolt across the door, then climbed up and out of the barn. There was still the issue of how this person got down, though."

They both looked up as a board creaked somewhere in the house. Warren waited but nothing happened and so he went on. "You have a farm truck. I saw it the morning after the fire and when I checked just now, there is still a deep bed of hay in it. Someone could jump onto that bed of hay from the upper window quite safely, I think." He imagined Isaac Rosen, lurking in the trees. *I heard a car start up . . .* Not a car, but a truck.

The footsteps in the hall came fast and urgent. The boy was there before Warren could even stand up. He loomed in the doorway and Warren had a sudden memory of the power of his body when he was this boy's age. Fourteen. He'd had the body of a man at fourteen, his muscles suddenly developed, his height giving him an advantage he couldn't get used to. This boy was six feet tall, like his father had been, his muscles rippling under his T-shirt.

"I did it," he said. "You can take me now. She didn't know anything about it. Leave her alone."

Thirty-nine

Sylvie watched Scott standing there, his face the face of a man, yes, but also the face of the baby she'd nursed, the boy she'd laughed with, the suddenly tall boy who still cried when he was hurt or when it thundered. Her Scott. Her boy.

It was because he was only a little older than Scott that she'd felt so inclined to help Isaac, she'd realized. He was just a boy too and when he'd told her how hungry he was and why he'd been living in the woods, she'd felt an urge to take care of him, despite how mad she knew Hugh would be if he found she was giving away good food.

And how jealous he would be if he knew she was talking to a strange man.

Hugh must have seen them talking. It was the only thing she could think of when he'd started screaming at her that Sunday evening, the evening of the fire. It had started with him asking what was for supper and when she said she had made tomato pie, he had raged that she must have given away all the meat in the freezer because it was shameful that she'd feed him tomato pie when he knew there was meat.

Other people had meat for supper, other people had proper Sunday dinners. Other people had better farms and better land and better wives. He had dissolved in a fit of jealousy without a precise target.

His jealousy had seemed to consume him lately, his obsession with the fortunes of other people so all-encompassing that he couldn't think of anything else.

And then he'd found the box of food she'd been putting together. He'd found the package of bacon she'd included.

"Did it go to the man I saw you *consorting* with?" he'd asked and when she'd turned to him, bewildered, not sure what he meant, she saw something there she hadn't seen in a while, a deep pain and humiliation that entered his eyes when he spoke about his family, or about Jeffrey Sawyer.

He was very drunk, she realized. And that was dangerous too.

"Was it the man from Dartmouth, the poet?" he taunted her. "Is that who you were talking to? Is that who you give food to, who you visit in the woods?"

"Hugh, please." The boys were right outside. She didn't want them to hear.

"He liked your poems, did he?" he asked. "I bet he liked you too. Is that why he came up to visit you? To see your *poems*?"

"Hugh, please," she'd whispered. "The boys."

And she must have put a hand on her belly then because his eyes lit up and he said, "Ah, is that the way it is? Is it even mine or is the baby his? Is that why you've given him the food?"

She didn't say anything. There was no arguing with him when he was like this.

The memory was all confused now, touched by what had happened after, but she knew that he had gone over to the window and pulled from it one of her poems, tearing the paper where it was taped to the window. "Is this it? Is this the one he liked?" he screamed at her. "I don't know why! It's nonsense! Stupid, illiterate nonsense. It's not really poetry, it's nothing but words! It doesn't even sound like poetry." He started ripping it up and that was what moved her to action.

"Stop that," she told him, reaching for the torn paper. "Stop it, Hugh. Why don't you go out to your office and I'll bring you some dinner."

But he'd ignored her, and taken another one from the window, holding it above his head.

"Please, Hugh," she'd called out. "Please don't."

And that was when she'd looked up to find Scott watching them, standing there in the low light from the kitchen lamp, just the way he was standing there now, listening to her and Warren.

Forty

Warren looked up at the boy. He was terrified, and determined. They both looked to Sylvie Weber then and she sighed and said, just to the boy, in a quiet, intimate voice. "Scott, *ma cherie. Scott. Nous ne savons pas si nous pouvons lui faire confiance.*" Her French was fluent, slightly nasal, and he remembered her saying she'd grown up against the Quebec border.

Warren, almost without thinking, said, *"Non, Madame. Tu peux me faire confiance."*

She turned, surprised, and then said in English, "Scott, sit down across from Mr. Warren."

The boy started to protest, but then, with a quick severe glance from her and a *"Si vous plait,"* he sat down and slumped sulkily in the chair.

"How did you get out of the barn?" he asked the boy.

But it was Sylvie Weber who answered. She sighed, a hand on her belly. "It was just like you said. Scott locked the door and climbed up the wall inside to the window and I pulled the truck up there so he could jump down. Then we went inside the house and waited until we could see the flames and smell it and he took the truck down to the Uptons' to have them call the fire department. Then we waited." She finally sat up a bit in the chair and looked at Warren.

"Who set the fire?"

She looked up, then at Scott. "Me," she said. "That was me. I poured some gasoline on the cot and dropped a match."

"Was that before you locked the doors?"

"I went out. Then Scott locked the doors and climbed out."

"Mrs. Weber, I don't think you would have sent your child into a building where you had just set a fire."

She shrugged. There was something Gallic about the shrug. She didn't care what he thought. *The nerve of her,* he thought to himself. *The absolute nerve!*

"How did he die?" he asked her. "Was it you?"

Now she looked away. *"Oui,"* she said stiffly, the French word nearly mocking him. "It was my fault. I did it."

The boy started to say something, but she went on. "I took him in there and set the fire."

"Why did Scott go in?"

She spoke quickly. "To lock the door."

"Was he already dead? How did you get him in there? He was a large man, tall and heavy."

"I'm strong," she said, looking away.

"I don't think it's possible."

"Well, it was."

Warren had to stop himself from shouting. "Why did you kill him, Mrs. Weber? Had you thought about it ahead of time?"

She shook her head. Now she looked him in the eyes. "It just . . . it just happened. It was an accident."

"Was he beating you?"

She shrugged, didn't say anything for a long moment, and then she nodded.

"Ma," Scott said. "Stop." He turned to Warren. "I did it. But I didn't mean to." He sobbed then, a quick, gaspy breath, and Warren saw, out of the corner of his eye, Sylvie Weber start to get up and then force herself to sit down again.

The boy sat there and cried, the tears running down his face. Warren waited but when neither of them spoke, he said, "Tell me what happened. You'll feel better after you do."

The boy gestured toward the windows and Warren thought he might see someone out there until Scott said, "Her poems. He was ripping them down and throwing them away. She told him to stop and he just kept doing it. He kept yelling that they were silly. That she shouldn't write them. But she loved them and she was crying and . . . I tried to stop him and he fell. It was an accident."

The house was silent. Warren looked up at the windows. Now he could see it, a thin piece of paper, which must have been taped to the window and then ripped off, leaving behind only the seam of white and cellophane tape against the glass. It had been there all along. It was only the darkness beyond that made it visible now.

Warren looked to Sylvie Weber. "Is this true?" He felt awareness dawn, as though his mind had a window and it had opened to the sunlight. It was the feeling of a case coming into focus, the essential thing, the thing he'd been waiting for, lumbering into view.

The boy was crying now, reliving it all. He was collapsed against the wall and Sylvie Weber stood and went to him, taking him in her arms, smoothing his hair, whispering to him in French. Warren let her comfort him. It took twenty minutes or so, but finally he wiped his eyes and then she said, "I'm going to make us something to eat. It's better to talk with something in your stomach, I think." The tension had gone from the room. The boy seemed better, lighter, and when Sylvie said to him, "Go get some bacon from the freezer," he went out through the woodshed door. Warren thought for a moment about following him, to make sure he didn't flee. If the boy took off, Warren would lose his job. He was certain of it. But he didn't care. He stayed seated.

The energy in the room had shifted. "He didn't mean it," Sylvie Weber said quietly. "I swear to you. It was just an accident."

Warren nodded. He watched as she got a fire lit in the cookstove and settled a large cast-iron pan on top of it. She took a can of something from a high shelf, sardines, he saw, when she turned it toward the light.

Warren saw her eyes dart to the door. The boy would be back any second. He didn't have much time.

"Mrs. Weber, you said before that your husband didn't abuse you. That he didn't hit you. Were you lying to me?"

She shook her head. "He never hit me," she said. "His father hit him and his brother. He vowed that he'd never do that. He didn't, even when he drank. But he . . . It was just that he was jealous. He wanted to be a writer, you see, but no one wanted to publish his pieces. And then Mrs. Bellows showed one of my poems to a man at the college." She smiled shyly. "He liked it. She came and told us . . . both. After that Hugh was . . . angry. Jealous. That day, I taped up a new poem. I like to see them in the window."

The door opened. Scott was back then with a small package. She hacked off a few slices of bacon with her knife and dropped them in the pan. Then she put a few more logs into the top of the stove, making an adjustment that seemed to make the bacon suddenly sizzle.

"Your mother was telling me that your father was jealous. Of her writing," Warren said to Scott. The boy nodded solemnly. He was a tall, good-looking kid, Warren thought, really looking at him now. Not extravagantly so like his brother, but he would be a handsome man. He looked like her, but Warren could see the dead man's genes there too, the brow and thick hair that were very much like Victor Weber's.

Scott nodded again. "It woke me up," he said. "I heard him yelling and thought I would go and . . . well, check on her."

Warren thought of Isaac Rosen, who had also heard Hugh Weber yelling.

"What was he yelling about?" Warren asked.

He and Scott both looked at Sylvie. "Well, it's . . ." Sylvie's voice caught. "The boy in the woods, I told you about him."

"Isaac?"

"Yes, well, I'd offered to put out another box of food. I was getting it together and Hugh came in. He asked me what I was doing. I tried to hide the bread and cheese but he knew something was going on; I think he'd seen me talking to Isaac. He started talking about my poems." Sylvie poked at the bacon in the pan. "He had been drinking," she said. "And he started ripping up my poems. He did that sometimes. He had been trying to write some himself out in the barn and he couldn't . . . the words wouldn't come, and he . . . he came in and took mine. He tore them up. Usually I just let him, but I was angry that night because there was one I really liked. It was about the water and . . . the baby. The man at the college asked if I had any more and I thought I could send that one, but Hugh . . . I tried to stop him. I told him the man might send it to a magazine and we might get some money for it. But that made him so angry. He didn't like when I mentioned money. That was when Scott came in. Hugh was trying to get the poem out of my hand."

"I told him to stop," Scott said. "He held it up high, above his head. I jumped to try to get it, and he turned away and he . . . tripped on that chair." He pointed to one of the chairs tucked in around the table.

Sylvie finished. "Hugh fell . . . fell back into the corner of the stove." She pointed. "Right there. He hit his head. At first he seemed a bit stunned. He wasn't bleeding or anything, though, and then he seemed fine. I thought he was fine. He shouted at Scott and at me again. He was holding his head like it hurt a little, but . . . like I said, there wasn't any blood, and he stormed outside to the barn. He was spending more and more time out there anyway and so we didn't go after him. It started getting dark. We had our supper and he didn't come back. I waited—it was better to wait and let him calm down usually—and then after I sent the three younger boys up to bed, I took a plate out to him. Scott said he wanted to go with me. In case." She glanced at her son.

"The lights were on. He was lying on the cot. At first I thought he'd fallen asleep, but then I realized his eyes were open. He still had his hand up to his head. He was dead."

The kitchen was absolutely silent.

"He had bleeding on the brain," Warren said quietly. "From the fall into the stove. If it killed him that quickly, there was likely nothing that could have saved him."

Sylvie looked at her son. "See," she said gently. "That's what I told you."

The boy shook his head. "I was fighting with him. He wouldn't have fallen if it wasn't for me."

"You were protecting me," she said.

Warren turned back to her. "What did you do?"

"I thought about calling the police. I did think about it. But I knew what people would think and I didn't want . . . I didn't want it to follow Scott around his whole life. He would have been known as the boy who . . . He did nothing wrong. He's such a good boy." She looked back at her son and put a hand over her mouth, sobbing suddenly. "*Such* a good boy. But people look down on us. They would have held it against him, his whole life! I couldn't let that happen."

"What did you do?" Warren asked, more gently this time.

She took a long, shuddering breath, bending over the pan for a moment and then getting control of herself again. "I came back to the house and I was thinking, about that man who didn't want them to take his property for the interstate. Hugh was furious about them taking that land. I thought, well, maybe people would believe he'd done the same thing. So I gave Scott the matches and told him to dump gasoline, bolt the door, set the fire, and then climb up and out the window. I knew he could do it because he was always climbing up there, just for fun. All the boys did." She smiled and then her face fell again as she went on. "I said I'd come around and pull the truck up for him to jump into, so it looked like Hugh locked himself in and set the fire himself. We did it like you said. I got out and he drove the truck right down to Uptons' to use the telephone." She looked up guiltily. "Before it really even got started. That's why they got there so quickly."

He watched while she fished the solid pieces of the bacon out of the pan, then cut five thick slices off the loaf of bread on a cutting board on the counter. She carefully lowered the slices of bread into the hot fat, leaving them there until they had crisped up and were golden. She put one slice on a plate for each of them while the remaining two slices cooked, then sprinkled them with salt and put a few sardines and crumbled bacon on each one. Warren lifted his to his mouth and took a huge bite. It was perfect, salty and crispy and smoky. When he was done eating, he watched as she made the other two. He had another slice, as did the boy, and then they sat there for a long time, in companionable silence, until they heard an owl call outside the screened window.

Finally, Warren turned to the boy. "Scott, you must never tell anyone what happened," he said, standing up. Suddenly, he felt quite strongly that he needed to get off Agony Hill as soon as possible. He went around to where the boy sat and he said, "Scott, stand up and look at me."

Scott did as he was told.

"You did nothing wrong. You were protecting your mother and you didn't want this to happen. You won't be able to talk about this and it's going to bother you, but you have to know that you did nothing wrong. You are a good person, a good boy. Do you understand?" Scott nodded.

Warren turned to Sylvie, thinking out loud. "Do not say anything. Ever. You would both be in terrible trouble. I would be in terrible trouble." Her eyes were wide and as she nodded, he felt a small flopping inside his chest, a realization, and he understood what it was and he understood what he had to do. "It happened just like you said. He went out to the barn and then you smelled the smoke and Scott drove the truck down. Do you understand?"

"Yes," she whispered.

Warren fixed his gaze on her, made his voice formal and stern. "Mrs. Weber," he said loudly, as though someone were listening. "I wanted to let you know that we have determined that your husband did in fact die by suicide. My investigation around Bethany revealed that he was quite unbalanced about the interstate and he seems to have taken his anger out on himself. He set the fire and a falling timber hit his head, causing the fracture. The case will be closed."

He nodded at her and he was already out the door when she called to him and he saw that she had followed him out into the night. He turned back, his senses alive and raw.

"Thank you," she said. She was close enough that he could smell her breath. He could have taken her in his arms then. On the porch, without the boy knowing. She was lovely, warm and soft and full of thoughts and ideas he suddenly wanted to know about. What books were her favorites? What was the rest of the poem she had written about him? *Had* it been about him? And what was the poem her husband had tried to destroy? He wanted to read it! He wanted to know!

But of course he couldn't. He'd realized two things at the exact same moment: that he was half in love with her and that he could never tell her. Ever.

It was ridiculous! She was a widow of a week! Even if she returned his feelings, or said she did, he could never tell her because he would never be sure if her affections were real or if she was humoring him because he held her life and the life of her son in his hands. He was a danger to her. She was a danger to him. If anyone ever found out, they would all be in trouble for covering it up. He must kill all thoughts of her, kill all thoughts of *it*, the thing that had appeared in front of him, real and lovely, as he sat in her kitchen.

He gave her one last look and went to get into his car and then he drove down off Agony Hill in the darkness, his car alone in the land-scape as he made his way back to town.

Forty-one

October 1965

Alice waited while Lizzie wrapped the cheese for her and then said, "Thank you, Lizzie, I so appreciate that. Now, what do you have that I might take with me on a visit? I'm driving over to Reading today, to have tea with my friend Cecilia Norris."

"There are some nice pound cakes that Dorothy made this morning," Lizzie said. She looked happy, Alice thought, though with Lizzie it was difficult to tell. It wasn't like she'd smile at you. But she was wearing her hair in a new, more attractive style, curled a bit and down around her face, and her blouse was a shade of pink that gave her a bit of life. The ring sparkled on her finger and when Alice's eyes dropped to it, Lizzie blushed a bit. Richie was stocking the shelves at the back of the store, not far from where his supposed transgression had taken place, and Alice called out to him and waved hello. He looked up and nodded and gave a small wave.

Alice had the funny thought that if Lizzie and Richie had children, they would surely be the most grim-looking children who ever existed, but of course things didn't always work out that way, did they?

The children were just as liable to be jolly, happy little children who laughed and made too much noise.

The news of the engagement had made its way around town in the days after the investigation into the fires up on Agony Hill was closed, one declared accidental and the other suicide. Bob Coller had apparently apologized to Richie and all was forgiven. It was now apparent that Dorothy was indeed to have a child and Alice felt a strange sense of hopefulness. Babies, coming into the world. Dorothy's and Sylvie Weber's too. New people.

She had visited Sylvie the day after Franklin Warren had closed the investigation, declaring that Hugh Weber had died by suicide. Sylvie had looked nervous at first and Alice's suspicions about the whole thing were confirmed by the terrified way she watched the oldest boy out the window. But when Alice had remarked that now that everything had been settled, they could get back to coping with their enormous loss and look ahead to their new life, and added that her boys were such *good boys,* all four of them, and that Alice knew they would help Sylvie any way they could, Sylvie seemed to relax. She had even given Alice another poem to take to the old friend of Ernie's who taught poetry at the college.

Alice took the cake and the cheese and put them on the front seat of the car, next to the chrysanthemums she'd cut that morning. She'd called Cecilia and lied about coming over to see someone else in town and of course Cecilia had asked Alice to tea. It would be the perfect opportunity to find out what Cecilia knew about this Soviet writer. Alice would get some background information about who he socialized with in town, if he ever had visitors. And then on subsequent visits she could see how he was settling in. She might even be able to pass by his house, get a glimpse of the man.

And then she would try to find out about this Samuel Armstrong, to see if there was a connection. She knew that it might be dangerous, getting too close to the truth about what had happened to the man and whether it had anything to do with the writer. If there were some agent or double agent, posted here in Vermont, keeping an eye on Kalachnikov, well, then he might know who Alice was, who Ernie had been. She would have to be very careful on this first visit. Yes, it could be very dangerous indeed, but then doing nothing was dangerous too. It was not an accident that Arthur Crannock was here in Vermont. Alice knew that with absolute certainty. Whatever Arthur had planned for Alice, she needed to be prepared. And the only way to be prepared was to put the pieces together, to understand the field of play.

Alice tied her scarf around her hair, tucked the amulet Arthur had given her into her skirt pocket, and started the car. She did love the back roads she'd take over to Reading. The leaves hadn't quite started turning in earnest, but fall was in the air.

It was a beautiful day for a drive.

Forty-two

Warren had arranged the hike with Pinky the day before. "I've been thinking about climbing the mountain," he said. "Because it's there, I suppose, and before it gets too cold. You've done it, haven't you? Would you like to come along, be my guide?"

"Sure," Pinky said. "It's a great hike. Nice views from up there. The best trail up is the one from Horaceville. Should I pick you up in the morning?"

"No, I'll meet you there," Warren had said. "I have an errand to do first."

He didn't offer any more information and Pinky didn't ask.

Warren called his parents at eight. His father picked up and Warren heard in his voice a layer of exhaustion that he knew was either related to the business or to Bradford, Warren's brother. When he asked his father how he was, though, Allen Warren said, "Very well, thanks, son. Your mother too." They made small talk about the weather and his parents' social life for a bit and then Warren's father said, "I had a letter from Tommy the other day. He said you've done good work so far." There was a small bit of pride to be found in the words, which made Warren unreasonably happy and then angry too, remembering the times that he had ached for an ounce of it.

"Well, it's been busy," Warren said. It had, lots of car thefts and burglaries to investigate, though no violent crimes since he'd closed the Weber case. He hadn't seen much of Tommy, who seemed content to let Warren handle things now he'd closed the Weber case in a way that had made life easier and simpler for Tommy and had not required filing charges or coordinating with the state's attorney.

"We thought maybe we'd come up for a visit," his father said, a bit haltingly. "We could stay at the inn there and you could take us to see the fall color." Warren said that would be nice and his father agreed they would talk again to settle on a date.

He performed his errand and met Pinky at the trailhead at ten, a bit of sun in the day already, though as they went, it grew cooler and cooler, as though they were leaping ahead in seasons as they climbed. After about an hour, they reached a jutting rock that Pinky said was called the Leviathan, and they climbed out onto it and looked down at the land below. From here, Agony Hill was a low hump in the foreground. In the distance was the river, and the long dark scar of the interstate construction. The leaves were a ripple of color down the sides of the mountain, yellow, red, and orange.

Looking down at the new road pushing north, Warren thought he saw what had been in that old farmer's mind when he set fire to his farm. It did seem wrong somehow, the marks made upon the landscape, like claw marks or the trail of a surgeon's knife. He hadn't been able to bear it, Warren thought. It had been too much. He himself had felt that way in the year after Maria's death. Once, hiking in the Montana wilderness, trying to forget, he had come upon a high cliff and had stood at the edge for nearly an hour, trying to force himself to jump. In the end, he had wanted to keep walking, he found. You either wanted to keep walking or you didn't.

Warren pointed to a patchwork of green and a small, golden dot in the center of it. "There's that bull," he said. "It's too far away, but I wonder if he's looking at the mountain, if he's looking at us."

Pinky studied the dot for a moment and then he said, "I imagine so. He's always looking at the mountain."

"What do you think he's thinking about?" Warren asked him.

Pinky looked thoughtful and then he said, "Maybe he's wondering what's on the other side."

Warren laughed, which confused Pinky, who blushed a bright shade of crimson. "I think you're right, Pinky. I think that's what a bull *would* think about a mountain." The air was thinner now and Warren could smell balsam.

They kept climbing until they reached the top.

Forty-three

Sylvie finished hanging the laundry out and then walked down to the lower fields to check on the sheep. There hadn't been any more coyote attacks, but she knew that they were out there and that, as the nights got colder, they would be hungry. But all was well now, the flock grazing peacefully on the still-green grass. It wouldn't be green for much longer, though. Soon, they'd be eating hay in the barnyard and she felt the familiar panic of wondering whether they had enough put away. With what Mr. Hatchett had brought them, though, there should be enough now to get them through the winter. Besides, she could buy some if she had to. As it turned out, there was quite a lot of money in the accounts Hugh had set up in New York. Mr. Williamson had helped her take five thousand dollars out and put it into the local bank. She had gotten word from a lawyer in New York that Victor Weber, who was ill, was no longer able to carry out his duty as executor, so Mr. Williamson would take over.

Sylvie had wondered many times about why Hugh had never told her about the money, about why they had scrimped and saved and gone without when he could have taken out money to make things a little easier. She had even talked to Mrs. Bellows about it. "I think, you know, that it was about control for him," Mrs. Bellows had said. "He had more control over all of you, he could make you live the way he wanted to live."

Sylvie had thought about that a lot and sometimes she thought Mrs. Bellows was right. But other times she wasn't sure. Hugh had found satisfaction in the work, she thought, and maybe he thought that if the work wasn't necessary, they wouldn't find it as meaningful. In any case, she wanted to be careful with the money; there were things she needed to do to fix the house once they'd finished the barn and Scott said they would need a new tractor before next summer, but for the moment, she could afford to buy a bit of hay if she needed to.

Isaac Rosen was going to do a lot of the work of repairing the barn from the fire. He was staying in town, he'd told her, renting one of the rooms over Collers' Store in exchange for building some new shelving, and part of the arrangement with him not getting charged for the fire was that he rebuild the camp for the Fredrickses and do some repair work on Sylvie's barn. Franklin Warren had arranged it all and the boy had already started, pulling down the timbers that were beyond saving and putting up new boards. He said he'd have it buttoned up by winter. Mr. Hatchett had given him a load of wood to do the repairs with, wood that he said he didn't need anymore, though it looked to Sylvie like it had come straight from the lumber mill.

It wasn't until she knew that they could stay in the house that she was able to feel with a sense of finality that she would never sleep up against Hugh's warm body again, that he would never kiss the top of her head as he passed her chair, that she would never again laugh at something he said. She had sobbed then, remembering the day they had come back to the house after the wedding. Nude together for the first time, Hugh had taken her hand and led her to the magical swimming hole by the brook, where he had told her she was beautiful and that they would be very happy, and they had bathed in the cool water in the darkness, and she had loved him. At least then she had loved him.

They had buried what was left of him on a warm day in September, the Reverend Call saying a few words for her and the boys. She had ordered a stone with his name and dates and the words, "Writer, Farmer, Husband, and Father." He would have liked that, "Writer" coming first. Sylvie had not visited the gravesite, but she thought that they might when some time had passed, when the boys had started to forget him.

She heard a small bark before she was back to the house. Assuming someone had stopped by, she came around to see who it was. She didn't want a strange dog worrying the cows. There wasn't a car parked out front, but her boys were all standing there, in a huddle, their heads bent toward each other.

"Look, look!" Daniel shouted.

Scott turned and she saw suddenly that he was holding something in his arms, a small yellow bundle that was wriggling and licking his face.

"It a puppy, Mama, it a puppy!" Daniel told her.

"My goodness, what's this?" She looked down the road.

"Mr. Warren brought him," Scott said. "He said he's for me, he's meant to be mine, though they can help take care of him. He's one of Dr. Falconer's puppies. He's a real nice pup, Ma, purebred. Mr. Warren said I could take him hunting and name him and everything." He met her eyes and she tried to think what to do.

"Ma, he said if you say no, he'll take him back, but he said he's away too much, and Bounder, that's what I'm going to name him, Bounder, he needs walks and to be out on a farm, like out here. He needs me to take care of him. He's mine for always. That's what Mr. Warren said, Ma."

She smiled. He was clever, Warren. She didn't like owing him any more than she did, but she couldn't say no now.

"Isn't he a good dog, Ma?" Andy asked, his face shining.

She reached out and let the puppy sniff her hand. He was round and golden, like a fat little grain of wheat. *Plump grains, waving furiously . . .* She looked out over the fields. *Spun sun. Golden gauzy . . .*

"Bounder," she said, touching Scott's shoulder, telling him it was okay. "I like it. It's a good name, Scott." She leaned down and whispered to the puppy. "Welcome, Bounder."

Acknowledgments

Writing a book set in the past, even the relatively recent past, presented a host of challenges and opportunities. I loved doing the research for this book and I am incredibly grateful to the Vermont Digital Newspaper Project, the Vermont State Archives & Records Administration, the Vermont Department of Libraries, and the Vermont Historical Society for making archives of Vermont newspapers available to researchers.

Librarians at my local library, the Hartland Public Library, were so helpful in finding necessary texts for me.

I am indebted to the many people who shared with me stories of this period in Vermont and New England history. My father, Dave Taylor, my uncle Steve Taylor (whose scholarship on the coming of the interstates and farming in the Upper Valley was inspirational in numerous ways), and my aunt Helen Taylor Davidson were all so helpful and I send them huge thanks and lots of love. My amazing husband, Matt Dunne, shared many stories and answered many questions and I am grateful to him for that—and for all the other ways he aided in the writing of this novel.

Abe Dunne provided me with a lot of research help. Thank you, Abe!

I'm grateful to Phil Hobbie, Martin Philip, Chuck Wooster, and Emily Howe and John O'Brien for help with some sheep details!

Thanks also to my neighbor David Singer for answering my questions.

A big thank-you to Vermont Department of Public Safety Commissioner Jennifer Morrison and to Lieutenant Colonel James Whitcomb for helping me find people to talk to within the Vermont State Police. Captain JP Sinclair (Ret.) kindly answered many questions for me. I am especially grateful to former auxiliary trooper and Vermont State Police historian Brian Lindner, who provided me with so much information about the early days of the Vermont State Police and the Bureau of Criminal Investigations. I so appreciate his scholarship and passion for history. All historical inaccuracies or alterations to proper procedure for the purposes of plot are mine and mine alone!

Big, huge thanks go to my agent, Esmond Harmsworth, and the whole team at Aevitas Creative Management and to everyone at Minotaur Books—you all take such good care of my books! Thank you to my editor, Kelley Ragland, and to Madeline Houpt, Sarah Melnyk, Allison Ziegler, and David Rotstein. You are the best.

I feel so lucky in my author friends. Thank you for cheering, commiserating, and writing amazing books!

As always, I am overwhelmed by the love and support of my family and friends during deadline crunches, launch days, writing retreats, brainstorming sessions, and anxious waiting. Thank you to Sue, David, Tom, Otis, and Edie Taylor, Vicki Kuskowski, and, of course, to Matt, Judson, Abe, and Cora Dunne. I love you so much.

About the Author

Sarah Stewart Taylor is the author of the Sweeney St. George series, set in New England, the Maggie D'arcy mysteries, set in Ireland and on Long Island, and *Agony Hill,* the first in a new series set in rural Vermont in the 1960s. Taylor has been nominated for an Agatha Award and for the Dashiell Hammett Prize, and her mysteries have appeared on numerous Best of the Year lists. A former journalist and teacher, she writes and lives with her family on a farm in Vermont where they raise sheep and grow blueberries. You can visit her online at SarahStewartTaylor.com.